Grantville Gazette II

Sequels to *1632*
Edited and Created by

ERIC FLINT

GRANVILLE GAZETTE II

This is a work of fiction. All the characters and events portrayed in this book are fictional, and any resemblance to real people or incidents is purely coincidental.

A Baen Books Original

Baen Publishing Enterprises
P.O. Box 1403
Riverdale, NY 10471
www.baen.com

ISBN-10: 1-4165-2051-1
ISBN-13: 978-0-4165-2051-1

Cover art by Tom Kidd

First printing, March 2006

Library of Congress Cataloging-in-Publication Data:

Flint, Eric
    Grantville gazette / compiled by Eric Flint.
        p. cm.
    "Volume 2."
    First volume of this work appeared in an electronic format.
    ISBN 1-4165-2051-1
    1. Seventeenth century--Fiction. 2. Alternative histories (Fiction), American.
3. Fantasy fiction, American. 4. Science fiction, American. I. Flint, Eric.

    PS648.F3G73 2006
    813'.54--dc22

                                                        2005035503

Distributed by Simon & Schuster
1230 Avenue of the Americas
New York, NY 10020

Printed in the United States of America

Contents

Preface

Eric Flint

As you can perhaps deduce from the simple existence of a paper edition of the second volume of the electronic magazine the *Grantville Gazette,* the first issue—which we did as an experiment, to see if there would be enough interest in such an oddball publication—proved to be successful.

Quite successful, in fact, better than either I or my publisher, Jim Baen, had expected. The magazine's been doing well, also. Five volumes of the *Gazette* have been published thus far, with more issues in the works.

Now that I know the *Gazette* will be an ongoing project, at least in electronic format, I've got more leeway in terms of the kind of stories I can include in the magazine. A number of the fiction pieces being written in the 1632 setting are either long or are intended as parts of ongoing stories. There are two examples in this issue: Danita Ewing's "An Invisible War" and Enrico Toro's "Euterpe, episode 1."

In terms of its length, "An Invisible War" is technically a short novel. In the electronic edition, it was serialized over two issues of the magazine, the second half appearing in Volume 3. Since that wouldn't be suitable for a paper edition, I included the entire novel in this volume.

Enrico Toro's story is somewhat different. Neither he nor I know what the final length of this story will be. Not to mention that in later volumes of the magazine, his story begins to intertwine with a series written by David Carrico. "Euterpe" is written in the form of episodes, each told in epistolary form by the narrator. I wanted to include it because (along with Gorg Huff's story, "God's Gifts") Toro's piece approaches the 1632 framework entirely from the angle of how seventeenth-century people react to the events produced by the Ring of Fire.

Most of the stories that appeared in either the first volume of the *Gazette* or the anthology *Ring of Fire* approached the situation either entirely or primarily from the standpoint of American up-timers. What I especially liked about the stories by Toro and Huff is that up-timers are never the viewpoint characters. In the case of "Euterpe," Toro is using an actual historical figure and trying to imagine how a young musician of the time would react to the sudden influx of music writ-ten over the next several centuries. In the case of Huff's story, the character is a fictional Lutheran pastor trying to grapple with the theo-logical implications of the Ring of Fire.

Given that there are a few thousand up-timers in the 1632 setting and tens of millions of down-timers, it seemed about time to me that we started getting more of their view of things into the series.

Although not quite to the same degree, Chris Weber's short novella "The Company Men" also approaches the setting primarily from the standpoint of seventeenth-century figures. In the case of his story, which is an adventure story, that of two mercenary soldiers of the time. And in John Zeek's murder mystery "Bottom Feeders," we get a nice mix of viewpoints.

There's a nice mix of stories in this issue, I think, in more ways than one. They range from military stories like Mike Spehar's "Collat-eral Damage" through stories involving the struggle to establish modern medical care (Ewing's "An Invisible War"), and everything in between. The same is true for the factual articles, where you'll get a treatise on seventeenth-century swordplay as well as a discussion of the practical challenges posed by geology and mining in the context of the technical resources available to the characters in the series.

There are a number of questions readers have asked me concern-ing where the 1632 series is going, the status of various novels in the series—especially *1634: The Baltic War,* which is the direct sequel to *1633*—and how and where the *Gazette* fits into that. Since answering those questions takes a fair amount of space, I'll deal with them in the Afterword at the end of the book. I think prefaces are best kept short and sweet.

FICTION

STEPS IN THE DANCE

Eric Flint

"Stop whining, Harry," said Anne Jefferson. "If I can do it, you can do it."

"No way am I posing half-nekkid," growled her male companion. He gripped the rifle with both hands, as if ready to deal with any threatening horde.

Any horde.

Mongols.

Huns.

Famous artists.

"Ha! The truth about Macho Man, exposed to the world at last! A coward. A craven." Anne swiveled her head to give him her best sneer, even if it was mostly wasted in the twilight. The lamps which were starting to be lit in front of the taverns on the street in Amsterdam didn't yet add much to the illumination.

"I'm *not* a coward," Harry Lefferts insisted stubbornly. "And I'm not cravin' anything at the moment except relief from pushy women."

He tried a lusty grin, directed at Anne. Alas, it was a pale version of her sneer.

"Not relief from all women, o' course. Just pushy ones. If you were to change your ways . . ."

"I'd call that a nice try, except it's so feeble." She tried to stride forward, but the combination of the absurd sorta-wedding dress she was wearing, the cobblestoned street, and her seventeenth century Dutch version of high heels caused her to stumble.

Fortunately, Adam Olearius was there to catch her arm and keep her standing, if not exactly steady. He'd been walking alongside her ever since they'd left the USE embassy, as he listened to the repartee between Anne and Harry.

Smiling, as he did so. By now, several weeks after Harry's arrival in Amsterdam, Adam had long since recognized that Harry was not a rival, despite the young American's seemingly irrepressible flirting. In fact, he'd rather come to like the man, even if he was a little scary at times.

Scary this time, too, in a way. Adam had been keeping an eye out for the possibility that Anne might stumble, which Harry had not. Adam had a very personal interest in the young woman, and was more familiar than either of his companions with the hazards of negotiating the streets of the era. The cobble-stones as such hadn't caused Anne to stumble. Rather, her shoe had skidded in the material covering one of the stones. There were unfortunate consequences to using horses for transport in cities.

Partly, too, because Adam Olearius was a more solicitous man by nature than Harry Lefferts was or ever would be. And finally—being honest—because he was not pre-occupied with the prospect of shortly becoming the model for one of the half-dozen most famous artists of the time. Of *all* times, actually, judging from the American history books Adam had read.

So, he'd been half-expecting the stumble, and was there almost instantly. But Harry was only a split-second behind him. Somehow, he managed to shift his grip on the rifle and his footing in order to seize Anne's other elbow, with such speed and grace that Adam was not really able to follow the motions.

In the three short years since the Ring of Fire, Harry Lefferts had become a rather notorious figure in certain European circles. For several reasons, one of which was his skill as a duelist. Seeing the way he moved, Adam had no trouble understanding the reason.

Yes, frightening, in its way, especially given the man's incredibly sanguine temperament. Fortunately for the world, Harry was also—

as a rule—quite a good-natured fellow. He was not actually given to picking fights, Adam had concluded, after observing him for several weeks. He was simply very, very, very good at ending them—and instantly ready to do so if someone else was foolish enough to begin the affair.

That notoriety, of course, did not fit well with Harry's official role as a combination "secret" agent and what the Americans called a "commando." Anne Jefferson had teased him about it.

The other two women in the USE embassy in Amsterdam had not. Rebecca Abrabanel had subjected him to a long, solemn lecture on the subject. Gretchen Richter had subjected him to a short and blistering excoriation.

Blistering, indeed. Adam happened to have been there himself, to hear it. The expression one of the up-timers had used afterward struck him as most appropriate. *She really peeled the paint off the walls, didn't she?*

Had she been a man, her tirade might have led to a challenge.

Although . . . perhaps not. Adam was pretty sure that Gretchen Richter was one of the few people in the world who intimidated Harry Lefferts. If not as proficient as he was with weapons, she was every bit as ready to employ them—and with attitudes as sanguine as his, and then some.

There was more to it, though. Adam knew, at least in its general outlines, how Harry had first met the woman, very shortly after the Ring of Fire.

"Shithouse Gretchen," was the way Harry sometimes referred to her, when she'd done something to get on his nerves. But he never said it in front of her—and there was always more than a trace of grudging respect even when he did. In the end, for all his often-debonair manners and the way he was idolized by a number of young European gentry and noblemen, Harry Lefferts was a hillbilly and a former coal miner. Getting one's hand dirty, and being willing to do so, was something he deeply respected.

Oddly enough, Harry's thoughts seemed to have been running parallel to Adam's. After Anne's footing was steady again, Harry released her elbow and went back to his grumbling.

"And why me, anyway? Shithouse Gretchen's *built* like a damn brick shithouse. And *she's* willing to pose."

"Don't be vulgar, Harry," scolded Anne.

"Who's being vulgar? The truth is what it is. Those tits of hers would intimidate a Playboy bunny—and it's not as if she's kept them under wraps. Not hardly. Not after she posed for *Rubens*."

He barked a laugh that was half-sarcasm, and half genuine humor. "Ha! You watch, Anne! Give it a century or two and that damn painting will be hanging in the Louvre. Or the—what's it called?—that famous museum in Spain. The Pardo, I think. Lines of tourists a mile long all shuffling past to stare at the world's most famous tits."

Olearius suspected he was right. He'd seen the painting himself, on the two previous occasions when he'd visited the mansion where the Spanish had set up their headquarters for the siege of Amsterdam. The enemy commander, the cardinal-infante Don Fernando, had it prominently displayed in his salon.

A bit odd, that was, given that the painting romanticized Don Fernando's stubborn Dutch opponents. Ruben's whimsical version of the future painting by Eugène Delacroix which would have been called *Liberty Leading the People* depicted a bare-breasted Gretchen Richter holding a flag on the ramparts of Spanish-besieged Amsterdam.

Had the Spanish commander of that siege been a different sort of man, Olearius would have assumed nothing more was involved than any man's interest in such a remarkable female form. But . . .

No, that wasn't it. To be sure, for all his slender, red-headed boyish appearance, Don Fernando was a very vigorous man—and not one upon whom his official title as a cardinal weighed any too heavily. But he was no bumpkin, either, easily distracted by mere lust. Olearius was quite an experienced diplomat, and he'd already come to the conclusion than Don Fernando was as shrewd as any prince in the long and successful history of the Habsburg dynasty. If Don Fernando had chosen to have that painting prominently displayed in his headquarters, there was a political reason for it.

More likely, several reasons. Don Fernando could be surprisingly subtle for such a young man.

"Shit," Anne muttered. Olearius glanced over and saw that she'd finally spotted the cause of her mishap. They'd reached a well-illuminated corner and the contents smeared across the sole of her shoe and partway up the sides were now easily visible and quite evident.

"Yeah, sure is," said Harry cheerfully. "Look on the bright side, though. It's just horse-shit. Someday I'll tell you about the time Gurd and me had to wade through—naw, it's too disgusting."

He started to reach for the handkerchief he had in his pocket, but

Adam had already drawn out his own and offered it to Anne.

"Thanks," she said, smiling at him warmly. But the smile vanished as soon as she spotted the men starting to spill out of the tavern on the corner. "Oh, damn, here they come. Stand in front of me, guys. Appearances Must Be Maintained."

Adam and Harry moved to block her from the sight of the night watchmen emerging from the tavern. Adam, with a solemn demeanor. Harry . . . not.

"Stop grinning, Harry," Anne hissed, as she stooped down to clean off her shoe.

"Can't help it," he insisted. "Besides, don't get paranoid. I'm not grinning at you, I'm grinning at the flag that guy is carrying."

Olearius had noticed it himself. Anne glanced up from her labor.

"Why is a Dutch soldier carrying a U.S. flag?" she wondered.

"It's a real one, too," Harry said. "Old one, I guess I oughta say. Not the NUS flag. Fifty stars."

He seemed genuinely aggrieved. "Damn. They musta got it from Grantville. Some bums will sell anything."

"They might have made it themselves," Adam pointed out. "Holland is a textile center, after all, and Amsterdam has plenty of seamstresses."

The mystery was solved, as soon as the night watch came up. One of them extended the flag to Harry. "You will need this," he explained, in heavily accented English.

"Why?" Harry asked, as he took the flag. He used the Dutch word. One of Harry's many talents was a proficiency with languages, and his Dutch had gone from non-existent to semi-passable in just a few short weeks.

Semi-passable, at least, for practical purposes like ordering beer and getting directions. There was not much chance he'd be able to argue pre-predestination with Dutch theologians, even assuming Harry had any desire to. A proposition about as unlikely as a wolverine becoming an opera enthusiast, in Adam's estimation.

The night watch soldier shrugged. "Word came from the Spanish to send one with you. The artist requires it, apparently."

That still left the mystery of where the flag came from. But the night watchman answered that also. Smiling, he added: "We took the one from the tavern wall. Make sure you bring it back. The owner had it made himself and he likes to keep it up. He thinks it's a good luck charm."

"Well, sure," replied Harry.

*   *   *

Getting through the walls of Amsterdam was easy, of course, with the night watch leading the way to the gate. Getting through the Spanish siege lines beyond to the cardinal-infante's headquarters . . .

Proved to be not much more difficult. Spanish officers were waiting to guide them through the maze of trenches and earthworks, all Castilian hidalgo courtesy. They were respectful toward Adam, even more respectful if openly curious toward Harry, and, of course, almost effusively gallant toward Anne.

There was no fear, here, that she might stumble on treacherous footing. The Spanish had even laid planks through the trenches, solely on her behalf. Even if she had stumbled, the press of officers around her would have prevented any undignified fall.

"Bunch of leches, you ask me," Harry muttered at one point to Adam. "You better keep your eye on them."

Olearius shook his head. "Even granted that the Castilian reputation is well-deserved, that's really not what's involved here. You forget, Harry. Anne is the one who gave them the chloramphenicol. The formula, at least. Someday, that might very well save their lives, and those of their families."

That brought a scowl to Harry's face. "I still think Mike was crazy to give it to them."

Adam couldn't resist. "Surely you won't vote for Quentin Underwood in the next election? He shares your opinion, I'm told."

The scowl deepened considerably. "Not a cold chance in hell. I don't care what fancy positions the bum occupies in the here and now. Far's I'm concerned, he's still the stinkin' manager of the stinkin' mine I used to work in. Sooner vote for the Devil."

He spread the scowl around. "Or one of these damn hidalgos, come down to it. Betcha *they* never heard of 'forced overtime.' Still . . . Mike was crazy," he concluded stubbornly.

There was a time when Adam Olearius might have agreed with him. But his experiences as a diplomat from the duchy of Holstein during the siege of Amsterdam had led him to develop a great respect for the acumen of Mike Stearns and his Sephardic wife. However much Stearns' surreptitious delivery of the formulas for antibiotics to the Spanish might violate the usual notions of strategy, Olearius had decided that the tactic was a splendid illustration of one of those uptime saws he'd become fond of: *crazy like a fox.*

Lesser statesmen simply thought to defeat their enemies. Stearns was seeking to shatter them into splinters, and turn half the splinters into his allies. Or, at least, sideline them into neutrality.

He might very well succeed, too, Adam thought. How else to explain this night's peculiar expedition except as one more step in an intricate diplomatic dance? A four-way dance, at that—Stearns, his wife, the Prince of Orange, and Don Fernando—and one being invented on the spot.

Five-way dance, really, since the cardinal-infante had to maintain his own sure-footed steps when it came to the reaction of the King of Spain and his notorious chief adviser, the Count-Duke of Olivares.

They arrived, finally. By now, the night had settled in, and all that illuminated the Spanish headquarters were sconces and lamps. A multitude of them—with what seemed like mirrors on every wall to enhance the lighting.

Amazingly, on the pristine flooring of the entrance salon, Anne stumbled again. But the cardinal-infante himself was there to catch her.

As gallant as any of his officers, he set her back upright with nothing more than a cheerful laugh. As if the younger brother of the Spanish king took assisting common women for granted.

He probably didn't look at it that way, however, Adam reflected. Whatever the Americans themselves might think, or say, or write—or even, astonishingly, practice at least most of the time—the aristocracy of Europe had generally come to the conclusion that they qualified as nobility.

Why not? In the end, if you stripped away all the trappings and the mythologies, the nobility of Europe owed its present exalted position to the crude fact that its ancestors had been the toughest men of their time. That, or the richest, or both. Today, three years after the Ring of Fire, only a handful of lunatic counts and the emperor of the Turks—who was known as Murad the Mad—tried to deny that the up-timers were both mighty and wealthy.

Hearing a little stir behind him, Adam turned and saw that four Spanish officers were clustered around Harry. They were frowning at him, and he was responding with a scowl of his own.

Harry had quite a formidable scowl, too. Fortunately, he was not stupid.

"I was *told* to bring the rifle," he said, almost snarling the words. In perfectly fluent Spanish, not to Olearius' surprise, albeit with an accent that had more in it of Italy than Castille. He'd originally picked up the language in the course of his journeys with Mazarini, Adam guessed.

"It's not loaded, you—" Fortunately, again, Harry left off the rest. He simply, with a quick and smooth motion that made his proficiency with the weapon obvious, drew the bolt and exposed the empty chamber.

The Spanish officers clustered around him still more closely. Now, however, with professional interest in the exotic up-time rifle, rather than suspicion. They began peppering Harry with technical questions, which he answered readily.

Much more readily than Olearius would have expected, in fact. He suspected that was another subtle step in the dance.

"This is the same sort of rifle that shot Wallenstein at the Alte Veste?" asked one of the Spaniards.

"Pretty much," Harry replied. "The caliber's slightly different. This is what we call a '30-06.'"

The four officers eyed him closely. "Could you make such a shot?"

Harry hesitated, for just a split second, before answering. Male pride at work, probably. Then, chuckling, he shook his head.

"No, I couldn't. I'm a very good shot, but Julie Sims—Mackay, now—is just plain out of my league."

"So it is true? It *was* a woman who fired that shot?"

"Sure was." Harry held up the rifle a moment, as if studying it. "With this, and me shooting it . . . I figure I could hit a target up to five hundred yards. Maybe six."

The cardinal-infante had come over himself to follow the conversation. Olearius saw him frown for a moment, as he made the necessary mathematical translations into Spanish distances.

The frown was replaced by a look of keen interest. "*That* far? Our siege lines are within that range. Some of them, well within. Yet you have never shot any of my soldiers."

Harry gave him a look that Adam found it difficult to interpret. Complicated, it seemed to be. There was something in there of menace, something of calculation, something of cold amusement, and . . .

Yes, exasperation.

So. *Another* step in the dance—and, as with so many, one that the dancer found too fancy for his taste.

Luckily for Europe, Olearius mused, Mike Stearns and not Harry Lefferts was the choreographer here.

The cardinal-infante tossed his head a little. "Tomorrow morning, we will see."

Don Fernando called over his shoulder to the servants against the far wall. "Up in my chamber. There is a old hunting hat in the wardrobe. The one with the red stripe, not the blue one. Bring it down here."

One of the servants sped on his way. All graciousness, now, the cardinal-infante bowed slightly and waved his hand toward a wide door on the side of the salon. "Please, come. Rubens is waiting."

The sitting was the usual tedious business. The night watch was kept waiting, while Rubensconcentrated on the portrait of Anne and Harry Lefferts. More precisely, the portrait of Anne, a slim and attractive figure in a white gown, gazing serenely at the flag draped over her lap. All that would ever be seen of Harry was a grim and menacing figure standing guard with a rifle beside her and off to the side, but one whose face was mostly concealed by a "Caterpillar" cap.

Harry had insisted on the cap, as a condition. *Gotta keep my anonomaly as a secret agent.*

Rebecca Abrabanel had burst into outright laughter, hearing that. Even Gretchen Richter had smiled.

"Okay, so I know I'm not pronouncing it right," Harry grumbled. "It's still true."

"It is not that!" Rebecca held a hand over her mouth to restrain any further laughter. "It is just . . ."

"Ridiculous," Gretchen finished for her. "Preposterous comes to mind, also."

Her smile was gone. She didn't quite glare at Harry. Not quite.

"Ridiculous," she repeated, almost hissing the word. "After the public duels you've fought—not to mention the bastards you've probably left scattered across half of Europe. Secret agent, ha!"

She began taking toddling little steps across the main salon of the USE embassy, waving her hands like a small child. "You will see! 'Mr. Secret Agent,' soon pursued by a horde of infants. 'Papa!' 'Papa!'"

That started Rebecca laughing again. Even Harry had smiled.

"Still," he insisted, after she was done. "It's the principle of the thing."

*   *   *

But perhaps it was just as well, Olearius concluded by the end of the evening. Rubens had managed to sketch enough of the portrait for the Holstein diplomat to get a sense of the thing.

Yes. Anne, in that white gown—the purpose for which was now clear—would be the center of it. Anne, with her pretty young face, and serene expression. Holding the flag the way a young expectant mother might hold a quilt she was making for her coming child. With that dark, grim, faceless, frightening figure in the background—all painted in dark colors, except for a gleaming flash from the rifle barrel—to serve the more observant eye as a reminder.

Yes, splendid. All the more so in that Olearius was quite certain that the cardinal-infante had commissioned the painting. Unlike *The Trojan Horsewoman*, this was not a project that Rubens had dreamed up himself and then foisted onto a reluctant patron.

A reminder—but to whom? The Spanish soldiers? The cardinal-infante himself?

Both?

Or, perhaps, someday he would send it to his older brother. As a way to ameliorate the anger that was already coming from Madrid; or, at least, provide himself with an excuse.

"Done, for tonight," Rubenspronounced. As courteous as ever—the great painter was an accomplished diplomat in his own right—he smiled at Anne and Harry. "Tomorrow evening, the same time?"

"Of course," said Anne cheerfully.

"Sure," muttered Harry. Finally, seeing that the damn artist had set aside his brushes, he removed the cap.

Don Fernando had left the studio, soon after ushering them into it. Patron of the arts or not, watching a sitting was a boring business. In any event, as commander of the Spanish army that had overrun most of the Netherlands, there were always pressing demands on his time.

But he was there, punctiliously, to see them off.

"Tomorrow morning," he said to Harry. He lifted his hand, holding a battered old hat. "I will have this placed somewhere visible on the siege lines."

"Sure," muttered Harry.

*   *   *

The first shot came just a few minutes after daybreak.

"He missed," said one of the cardinal-infante's officers, with great satisfaction.

"Wait," cautioned Miguel de Manrique. Unlike the officer who had spoken, the cardinal-infante's chief lieutenant had experience with the Americans. He'd been in command of the Spanish troops at the Wartburg.

Don Fernando gave him a questioning eye.

Manrique waved his hand. "The weapons are not magical, Your Highness. At this range, even the wind matters. Remember—all accounts we've gotten are agreed—the Sims woman missed her first shot at Wallenstein also. So let us wait."

Perhaps two seconds later, the hat went sailing off the wall it had been perched upon. A moment thereafter, they heard the sound of a distant gunshot.

An aide ran to retrieve the hat. When it was brought back to the cardinal-infante, he saw that a bullet hole had been added to the crown.

"Yes," he said. "A splendid painting. I shall have it hung in the main salon."

A few nights later, when the sittings were finally done, Don Fernando had a few last words with Harry.

"That peculiar request you made, two nights ago."

Harry inclined his head, smiling.

"I investigated. It is indeed true that you killed no one coming into the city."

The smile vanished. "Had orders," Harry growled. "Stupid as they might be."

"Yes." The cardinal-infante was smiling, now. "I suspected as much. Very well. When the time comes, send me word and I will see you—and your men—safely through our lines. To wherever else you might go—and do note that I neither ask nor make any conditions. Except a promise that you are not going to Spain."

"Nowhere near Spain. Ah, Your Highness. My word on it."

"That's done, then." Turning to Anne and Olearus, the cardinal-infante smiled still wider. "You look splendid in that gown, Mademoiselle Jefferson. May I hope to see you in it again, someday?"

The long hours of sitting seemed to have fixed serenity upon the young woman's face. She simply inclined her head toward Olearius and said, "Ask him."

"Ah . . ." said Adam.

Diplomacy was called for, here. An intricate dance, with steps of its own.

"I certainly hope so," he said.

Anne nodded, as serenely as ever. "Apparently, yes, then."

"Jesus," grumbled Harry. "Can't anybody around here do *anything* straight-up?"

As one person, a nurse from America and a diplomat from Holstein and a prince from Spain gave Harry Lefferts an identical look.

What a barbarian.

Collateral Damage

Mike Spehar

"A single event can awaken within us a stranger totally unknown to us. To live is to be slowly born."
—Antoine de Saint Exupery

"Just perfect," Jesse muttered in disgust.

"What was that, *Herr Oberst*?"

Jesse jammed his hands into the pockets of his flying jacket and looked at his copilot, Lieutenant Emil Castner, who was leaning against the wing, studying his map. The lieutenant had moved there to get away from the crowd of mechanics swarming around the nose of their aircraft. Jesse had likewise moved away, after earning a glare from Chief Matowski for repeatedly butting in on his work.

"Nothing, Emil," Jesse said. "Nothing at all."

The young German nodded uncertainly and turned back to his map. Approving of his copilot taking the chance to get better prepared

19

for the flight, Jesse rubbed his neck and moved slightly toward the mechanics, then thought better of it. He always hated it when a supposedly ready aircraft broke down before takeoff. Standing around, waiting for the wrenchbenders to work their magic, never failed to grate on his nerves and this time was no exception. He strolled away and, for about the tenth time, patted the left sleeve pocket of his flight suit, where, in another world and another time, he had carried his cigarettes.

Damn, he thought. *You'd think I'd have gotten past that habit. What's it been—two years, since I've last had a smoke?*

Sometimes, such as when he was flying or waiting to fly, he could almost forget the circumstances that had brought him here. The cataclysmic Ring of Fire that had mysteriously transported the West Virginia town of Grantville into seventeenth-century Germany had created a psychological crisis for all of the Americans caught in the event. Their subsequent battles against the threats of hunger, disease, and hostile neighbors had quickly pulled the Americans together, though it had been a hard struggle. And still was.

The United States of Europe and their allies were still engaged in a desperate struggle against formidable enemies. Only the fall before, through the machinations of Cardinal Richelieu, the countries of Spain, England, and Denmark had joined the French in the so-called "Ostend Alliance," with the intent of capturing the Baltic, crushing the independent Netherlands, and, eventually, eliminating the growing power of the USE. Luckily, the Alliance's initial attacks had been thwarted at Luebeck and Wismar, in no small measure through the impact of American technology, hastily adapted for war. Now, in the early spring of 1634, the struggle continued on land and sea.

The Battle of Wismar had been particularly hard on one Colonel Jesse Wood, retired USAF tanker pilot and, by appointment of Prime Minister Stearns, chief of staff of the USE Air Force. For it was at Wismar that he had first taken his unprepared air force to war and had learned the price of combat. In the course of the action, Jesse had watched his protégé, Hans, turn the tide of battle by diving his aircraft into a Danish warship. Though helpless to prevent it, Jesse still blamed himself for Hans' death. Over the months since, his grief and guilt had gradually turned to a cold rage against their enemies and Jesse wanted nothing more than to get back into the war.

*   *   *

"Hey! Colonel Wood!"

Jesse mentally shook himself and looked back toward the aircraft. Harvey Matowski was waving a greasy rag at him, while his assistants replaced the engine cowling. Resisting an impulse to run, Jesse deliberately strolled back to the aircraft. Emil had already climbed back into the rear cockpit and was strapping in.

Walking up to Matowski, Jesse asked, "So okay, Harvey, what was it?"

"Just dirty plugs, sir. Maybe some water in the line, too. Can't tell till we crank her up. You still want to go?"

"Yes, of course, Chief. The war isn't waiting on us, you know."

"Yeah, I know, sir, but . . ."

"Spit it out, Chief," Jesse said grumpily. "Is the aircraft ready to fly or isn't it? They're waiting for us in Hessen."

"Well, yessir, it is." Harvey paused to spit. "But you know as well as I do how touchy that supercharger has been. I don't much like the idea of it cutting out on takeoff with this load you've got."

Jesse looked at his chief mechanic and considered his words. Glancing up at the clear blue sky, he noted that the day had already started to warm a bit. Still no clouds.

An unseasonably nice day, Jesse thought. *Be a shame to waste it. And we better do this before Stearns changes his mind. Still . . . Damn it!*

"Okay, Chief. Call those munitions troops back here. We'll take off all but the two inboard rockets. That way we'll still be able to take off, even if the blower quits. The real payload's underneath, anyway. Does that suit you?"

Matowski nodded and walked off. Jesse gave the cowling fasteners a couple of thumps and did another quick walk around. Everything on the exterior was as it should be, though it never hurt to check a second time. He paused a moment to admire the aircraft's paint job. He had to admit, the Gustav was a damned fine looking machine, the best that American technology and German craftsmanship could build. Compared to the Belle, it was big and low slung. The sun glinted through the now open sliding canopies. The wings and fuselage were painted blue-gray overall, so new that there were few blemishes anywhere. White star wing flashes gleamed, as did a large red numeral "1" on each side of the vertical stabilizer. His eyes drifted to the nose art and he unconsciously grinned. One of the young pilots had read about the American Volunteer Group and his excitement had fired the imagination of the aircraft riggers. The result was a leering shark's mouth painted on the nose and cowlings, complete with predator eyes.

If nothing else, maybe we can scare 'em to death, Jesse thought.

Twenty minutes later, the rockets had been removed. Jesse and Emil had run their checklists and the engine was purring as if nothing had ever been wrong with it. Tower confirmed there was no traffic inbound. Jesse pushed the throttle forward and flicked the supercharger switch with his little finger. Hearing the whine of the fan, feeling the engine surge, he noted the time and released brakes.

His mission was to put the fear of God into Grantville's primary enemy.

His target: Paris.

Takeoff was uneventful and Jesse felt the familiar rush that comes from leaving the earth behind. The anxiety and uncertainty that waiting always generated in him quickly faded as he began a cruise climb on a heading just south of due west. The small southerly wind, so unusual at this time of year, required only the slightest of drift correction. Switching off the supercharger, he set climb power, trimmed the aircraft, waggled the rudder pedals, and spoke over the intercom.

"Copilot's aircraft. Take her to eight thousand on this heading, Emil. Set altimeter at 29.92"

From the rear cockpit, "I have the aircraft, Herr Oberst. 29.92."

After Emil shook the stick, Jesse clicked twice and removed his hand. He wrote the takeoff time on his kneeboard and picked up his map, already folded for the route of flight. A carefully drawn line cut across Germany, over the mostly empty green of the Thuringenwald, past Fulda, towards a small village north of Frankfurt am Main and Weisbaden, to a temporary field where they were scheduled to refuel.

Ambach, Omberg, Ombach, he suddenly realized he'd forgotten the name of the place that hadn't warranted a name on his map. *Doesn't matter. I've been there before and I can find it, no sweat. An hour or so on this heading should get us there. About forty minutes late.*

Jesse stretched his back and shook his arms, trying to get comfortable. He'd been flying too much, he knew, and it was taking a toll on his body. He now had two pilots he could count on to instruct the others in the replacement Belle, but the workload had risen again when Hal Smith and his team had rolled out the first Gustav. Hal had poured every bit of his knowledge and talent into the sleek plane, assisted mightily by their experience with the *Las Vegas Belle* and her twins. The Gustav's improvements were enough to gladden Jesse's heart, considering he intended to send pilots to war in it. Sturdier and much faster than the Belle, the Gustav also boasted numerous improvements visible only in the cockpit, including G-meters, rotating compass repeaters directly in front of the pilots, a heater/deicer, and a speed brake. Most importantly, it could carry a really usable war payload on the multiple hard points under the wings and fuselage. Such as they carried now.

But the very high quality of the Gustav had urged Jesse to fly even more, so eager was he to get it into the fight. An abbreviated flight test program had shown the Gustav to be a nimble flyer, yet with a solid, steady feel. That encouraged Jesse to begin immediately experimenting with dive-bombing techniques on a hastily acquired field outside of Weimar, using sand-filled practice bombs. He packed as much training into each flight as he could, taking a different copilot on each sortie until they were all comfortable with the aircraft and could extend and retract the heavy speed brake with little trouble, though most were sweating when it came time to land.

Still, he had driven none of them harder than he drove himself and the effort had begun to tell. The repetitive four or five Gs experienced in each dive gradually wore at him, straining his back and arms terrifically. Kathy had taken to meeting him at the end of each day he flew, so frightened had she become about his health. But, despite the scolding of his wife, Jesse refused to stop. Only after she had appealed to Dr. Nichols, who pulled duty as senior flight surgeon, had Jesse relented and taken two days off. But only two. Then he'd gone back to a full schedule of flying, trying to will his young charges into the proficiency he knew they would need all too soon.

The Gustav was approaching the temporary field when Jesse realized all was not well. Fearing what a bad landing would do to their load, he had decided to do the honors. The two pilots had already performed the Before Land Checklist and, as a precaution, Jesse had planned a low flyby before landing. He was immensely glad he did.

He had feared their delay would result in his ground crew deciding they weren't coming today, as had happened before. He could see now he needn't have worried. Crossing the field boundary, he was shocked at the sight of at least three hundred people scattered across the landing zone. Apparently the locals were in on their little secret. Some were on horseback, but most were afoot, and many of them seemed to be picnicking with their children. On his airfield.

"God damn it!" Jesse yelled.

Emil wisely said nothing as Jesse flew the length of the field and pulled up left into a modified downwind. Jesse had pulled his canopy back and locked it open for landing. He now wasted his time frantically waving the crowd below off the field, only to see most of them gaily wave in return. He turned final and performed another flyby, much to the delight of the crowd, they being unable to hear his curses. Only the line of Swedish cavalry now chivying people off the field prevented Jesse from further profanity. By the time he pulled up to a normal downwind, he had regained his composure and even a bit of humor.

"You know, Emil," he chuckled. "I always did like being in an air show. Remind me to smile when we get to Paris." He looked into his mirror and caught the usually stolid German smothering a guffaw.

"*Jawohl, Herr Adler, mein* hero!" Emil said with a mock salute.

Jesse returned the salute in the mirror. "Okay, *meine Schatzie*, let's see if we can now land without hitting a cow or a goat."

The landing was uneventful and Jesse taxied over to the small shed where his two ground crewmen had spent the past four days. The crowd, still cheering madly, was surging behind the line of now-dismounted troopers. Jesse smiled and waved, until Sergeant Sauer climbed up to help him unstrap.

"Good morning, Sergeant," Jesse said through a frozen grin. "Let me guess—your relatives have arrived?"

"No, mein . . . No, sir!" the NCO said. "Henni there." He pointed to a young airman now scuttling towards the shed after setting the chocks. "He went into the village last night and had too much to drink. The *dummkopf* told everyone at the *stammtisch* he is the pilot, waiting for his *flugzeuge*. This morning, I see this." The sergeant waved his arm helplessly at the assembled multitude. "Most have never seen an aircraft before. They want to see him fly." His expression was so woebegone that Jesse's false smile slowly thawed into the real thing.

"Well, at least the French don't know we're coming," he said slowly. "Tell me, Sergeant, do we still have the fuel or did Henni use it for a bonfire last night? You know, just to impress the girls?"

"Oh, no, sir. I mean, yes, sir! We have the fuel ready for you."

"Well, *zehr gut*, Sergeant. Very good, indeed," Jesse raised his hand. "Now, how about helping me out of here?"

Thirty minutes later, they were ready to depart. Jesse had reluctantly found himself explaining to disappointed townsfolk that Airman

Henni only flew on special occasions, which their current mission surely wasn't. His little chore in diplomacy wasn't helped by grinning Swedes, who knew better. He wound up promising that Henni, who was most assuredly one of their finest pilots, would give a flying demonstration tomorrow, after their return. Jesse didn't know who was more upset at the prospect—Henni, who saw the hole he was in getting deeper and deeper, or Emil, who was genuinely outraged at the airman's effrontery.

An additional fifteen minutes later, they were once again at eight thousand feet, headed slightly more south of west, into unknown territory. Into France.

The flight to Paris would be a long one, almost at the limit of the Gustav's range. However, through long practice Jesse was quite accustomed to dead reckoning and the challenges of navigating by map, clock, and compass. With Emil on the controls, cruising through a still cloudless sky, he had little to do but contemplate his mission, mulling their plan of attack over in his mind. The steady droning of the engine lulled him into a moody state of mind and he felt no desire for conversation.

I wish Hans was here, Jesse thought. Since Hans' death he'd tried to not get any closer to his young charges than necessary and sometimes he worried that he lacked a real feeling for their abilities. His criticisms had become harsher and light moments such as he and Emil had shared only an hour ago were increasingly rare. *I may have to send 'em to die, but I won't, I can't, have my guts ripped out again.*

His choice of Lieutenant Castner for this flight was, in a way, typical of his new temperament. Emil was nothing like Hans Richter, who had taken a joyous pleasure in flying. Where Hans had done things with flair, Emil was methodical, almost mechanical. And where Hans had liked to talk, Castner rarely spoke, except when directly addressed. As a result, the normally garrulous Jesse knew next to nothing about the lieutenant, except that he did his job reliably.

And that should be enough, Jesse thought sternly. *He's a weapon of war, as much as this aircraft. And no more. The last thing I want on this mission is someone questioning my decisions.*

Jesse recalled the last conversation he'd had with Prime Minister Mike Stearns about the mission. Stearns had voiced his reservations, though he didn't go so far as to actually forbid the flight.

"Are you completely sure about this, Jesse?" Stearns had asked.

"From what you've told me it's an awfully long way, in a new aircraft. And I'm still not convinced we'll get the results we want, even if you succeed. Far too much can go wrong."

Jesse had stifled his annoyance, an increasingly frequent emotion he felt when dealing with Stearns. Ever since Wismar, he'd become more and more irritated at any expression of caution, no matter the source. He knew the prime minister had more sources of information than he had. He knew Stearns had other considerations, other than striking the enemy whenever and wherever, no matter how deadly they knew that enemy was. Jesse knew those things, intellectually, but didn't—couldn't—agree with them emotionally. Not since Wismar. So his answer had been much less guarded than he might have wished.

"Sir! Mr. Pres—ah, I mean Prime Minister, if I could load three Gustavs with these new incendiaries, I swear, with only two days of good weather, we could burn most of Paris to the ground. Okay, so I can't do that—yet. So the good people of Paris get a pass, while the people of Amsterdam starve and die of plague, while armies chop each other to pieces, and our own people die needlessly!" Jesse caught himself. "Prime Minister, I've got one ready aircraft and I can make a good start. At the very least, removing Richelieu . . ."

"Jess, Jess," Stearns had interrupted. "I said you can go, even if I have reservations. As far as Richelieu goes, you know my doubts. Come *on*, Jesse." Stearns had spoken softly and reached over to grip Colonel Wood's shoulder for emphasis. "You can go with the limited objectives we've agreed upon. Understood?"

"Yes, sir," Jesse had replied stiffly, fighting an urge to shake the hand off his shoulder, to reject the familiarity. It was another thing that had begun bothering him recently. He had not been close to Mike Stearns before the Ring of Fire and really hadn't grown all that much closer since. He couldn't help it, he'd always disliked the sense of being manipulated he felt around politicians and he knew Stearns had become a politician of the first order. He couldn't tell if Stearns' friendship was sincere and that bothered him more than anything else. Since Wismar, he'd felt closed off, with no one to share his most private doubts and fears. Stearns' old crony, General Frank Jackson, was no help and Admiral Simpson, who was at least a military professional, was out of touch. Not even Kathy . . . he'd choked off that line of thought and fallen back on a lifetime of military correctness. "I will inform you when the weather is right for the mission. If I may be excused, Prime Minister" He'd left at Stearns' nod.

*   *   *

"Fuck it!" Jesse shook himself back to the present.

"What was that, sir?" Emil asked from behind him.

I must have yelled that.

"Nothing, Emil. Nothing."

Jesse spent the next several minutes checking their progress, grateful for the relatively simple task. Nevertheless, another part of his mind had kept processing his previous line of thought. First, they'd hit the attention-getting targets and then go for the main prize. They had good intelligence and a known location for Richelieu. There would be no opposition, of course, not even ground fire. Fifteen minutes over the city and they'd be headed home. In his gut, Jesse knew it would work. A sudden burst of fury came unbidden to him. *Richelieu, I'm coming to get you, you son of a bitch!*

Jesse had been on the controls for only about fifteen minutes when he first noticed it. Ahead of them, stretching out of sight from side to side was a small weather front. There was no reason for it to be there, but there it was, just the same. It wasn't much to be concerned about, if one was on the ground. Some bending, some slight fold of conflicting wind currents, had created a weak low-pressure system, against which warm air from the south had pushed. Strictly a local phenomenon, it would not have been noticed in either London or Amsterdam, or anywhere else within reporting distance of Grantville. An hour earlier, or perhaps two hours later and it would have been of no consequence to them. But it and they were here now, and it stood between them and Paris. Between them and Richelieu.

Jesse tapped his index finger on the throttle, thinking it over. The line of cumulus clouds ahead was just below them, just beginning to build. During his lifetime, he'd cruised over such ripples a thousand times, barely noticing them. But that had been back when he was flying jets, or turboprops, and had looked down from Olympian heights in pressurized comfort. Today, he was flying in a Gustav, a relatively primitive aircraft, flying with a jury-rigged automobile engine, carrying a heavy load. He knew from the tests that the aircraft could go much higher than their present altitude of eight thousand feet. He also knew that there was no telling how high those puffies out there would reach before he was past them. They might grow into behemoths topping twenty thousand feet or they might not grow any farther than ten thousand feet or so. The weather line wasn't even continuous; the cells were still separate, though that would change as they grew. Still, the smart thing to do, the prudent thing, would be to turn around and wait for tomorrow. Just turn around and go have a beer and a schnitzel with Sergeant Sauer and Henni.

Instead, Jesse pushed the throttle up and began to climb. Tomorrow might see the onset of normal weather patterns, with winds from the north and west and no chance to get to Paris. Behind him was— behind him. Ahead of him was Richelieu.

"Pilot, copilot," Emil sought his attention.

Jesse knew Emil was asking to be filled in, as was completely correct.

Keep him thinking about how, instead of why, Jesse thought.

"Emil, we're going to climb over that weather ahead of us," Jesse said in a matter-of-fact voice and switching to his instructor mode. "Can you tell me the difference between our best-rate-of-climb and our best-angle-of-climb?"

As his copilot recited the technical answer, Jesse trimmed up the aircraft at the best-climb-rate airspeed and watched the line of blossoming clouds now only a few miles ahead. It was too early to tell how fast the clouds were growing, but he could see the tops bulging, expanding, reaching higher and wider. Somewhere under those clouds, a heat source was pushing them up.

Jesse shook his head in disgust.

He aimed at a gap between two baby storms, just beginning to grow and merge. The altimeter passed ten thousand feet and he switched on the supercharger and retrimmed. They were still climbing steadily. As Emil finished his answer, Jesse asked another question.

"Okay, Emil, now tell me about hypoxia. At what altitude do we need to worry about it? Do you know your personal symptoms?" Jesse knew they had some thousands of feet to go before oxygen deprivation would be a problem, but it made sense to prepare.

Emil responded, "Yes, sir. Hypoxia is possible at altitudes above ten thousand feet and the effects depend upon the length of exposure to the thinner air. My personal symptoms include tingling fingertips, blurring of vision, flushed skin, and a burning sensation on my face. Other possible symptoms include . . ."

Letting Emil drone on, Jesse looked left and right, trying to gauge the danger. Portions of the weather line, separate, stronger cells, were already topping their altitude on either side, swelling rapidly. The two storms directly ahead were growing faster now, though still lower than the rest. And getting closer. The aircraft's altitude was now passing thirteen thousand feet, but their rate of climb was slowing. Jesse raised the nose further and trimmed up to best angle-of-climb. Emil was silent now. No doubt he was staring outside. If he had any sense, Jesse thought, he'd be praying.

They were over the edge of the merging clouds, now, climbing up the front of a white mountain of vapor and passing 14,200 feet, hanging on the prop. Jesse's eyes flicked to the engine- and oil-temp gauges and he grimaced at the readings. If the engine quit now, Jesse and Emil were dead.

Climbing slower now, and the clouds ahead were just above them. They were above their tested service ceiling, but that didn't matter. They must be getting some push from the updraft. Silently, Jesse willed the plane to keep climbing.

Jesse idly noted that his breathing was too rapid. He'd been hyperventilating, but couldn't stop it. They were starting to bounce around, affected by the upper reaches of the storms closing around them. Emil was saying something, but Jesse couldn't understand the words because his ears were ringing. He rubbed his numb face and felt dizzy. Wisps of cloud were passing over them, topping them and he noticed the airspeed was dangerously close to stall, but he suddenly couldn't remember what that meant.

"Hans would know," he mused softly to himself. "Wish old Hans was here."

Jesse, lower the nose.

"What?" Jesse asked muzzily. "Hans? Is that you?"

Yes, Jesse, it's me, Hans. Lower the nose, Jesse.

"Hans!" Jesse yelled happily. "God, it's good to hear you, son! Where are you?"

I'm here, Jesse. I'm here. Now, lower the nose, Jesse.

"But the clouds, Hans . . ."

Don't worry about the clouds, Jesse. You're between the cells. Lower the nose now, Jesse. Not too much. Maybe five degrees. Do it, Jesse.

"Okay, Hans," Jesse said dreamily. He released a bit of back pressure. "How's that?"

That's good, Jesse. That's good. Now keep it there.

Jesse vaguely noticed that the aircraft was surrounded, completely immersed in cloud. The blue sky above had disappeared. Daylight faded into gray dimness. The bouncing and jostling got worse, but Jesse couldn't bring himself to care.

"Where ya been, Hans?" he asked. "I've missed you a lot."

I know, Jesse. Watch your ball. Wings level, now.

"Gotcha, Hans," Jesse said. "Jus' like ol' times, huh?"

Yes, just like old times, Jesse.

With surprising quickness, the aircraft burst from cloud into brilliant sunshine. Jesse squinted and turned his head away from the light.

You've got to descend now, Jesse.

"Yeah," Jesse replied and lowered the nose.

Pull off some power, Jesse.

"Okay, Hans. Where you been? I've missed you. Sharon will be so happy. . . ."

I know, Jesse. I've been around. How are you feeling?

"Pretty good, Hans," Jesse smiled. "Back hurts some, but otherwise, just fine. Damn, it's good to talk to you, again."

Same here, Jesse. But I have to go now. Do you understand?

"Oh, sure, Hans. Sure," Jesse said. He shook his head and took a deep, contented breath. Awareness burst into his head and he heard Emil over the intercom.

". . . was magnificent, *Herr Oberst*!" Emil said excitedly. "I confess, I was a bit concerned for a few minutes. The other pilots told me about it—how calm you are when things become really difficult. But to hear you continue instructing while flying through those storms, as if we were merely practicing landings! Simply wonderful, sir!"

Jesse responded carefully. "Yes. Thank you, Emil." Slowly taking stock of their situation, he saw a large, distinct smudge in the distance. Smoke from a city rose high into the otherwise pristine sky and flattened into the typical anvil shape where it hit a temperature inversion. It was Paris.

Jesse waggled the rudders. "Take over for a minute, Emil. Level off at eight thousand."

Emil shook the stick in eager response. "Copilot's aircraft."

Jesse lowered his head and rubbed both palms against his wet eyes. *Goo-bye, Hans*, he thought.

Within minutes, they were approaching the outskirts of Paris. Although it was a huge city for the period, Jesse nonetheless thought of it as shrunken from the city he had visited several times, many years ago up-time. Luckily, the route of the Seine hadn't changed and they followed it toward the city center.

Jesse heard Emil say something over the intercom, but couldn't understand him. Pinching his nostrils between his thumb and finger, he blew hard, in the classic valsalva move. Both ears popped, thunderously, and he could hear again.

"Say again, copilot?" he asked.

"Are you all right, sir?" Emil asked. "Do you want the controls?"

"Yes, yes, give me the aircraft," Jesse said, though he still felt a bit disoriented, a little woozy.

Emil pumped the rudder pedals and Jesse shook the stick. The air was a bit hazy from smoke, and Jesse had difficulty finding landmarks. He decided to descend to three thousand for a better look. From there, they could easily see faces, whole crowds of them, turned upward, many pointing, drawn by the sound of their engine and shiny wings. Jesse almost slid his canopy back to wave and thought better of it. He did waggle the wings, a bit, in the age old signal, "Hello," before remembering their purpose there.

Well, I always did enjoy being in an air show, he thought. *Time to get to work.*

The river turned to the northwest and he followed it, finally recognizing the big, sweeping hook in the city center. Suddenly, he had his orientation, spotting the huge edifice of Notre Dame on its island, with the royal palace, the Louvre, just beyond it. He circled again, much lower this time, looking for the Sorbonne and its supposedly distinctive church dome, but couldn't find it. There seemed to be a hundred church domes in the city.

A thought struck him. "Shit, is it the Left Bank from upstream or downstream?"

"Sir?"

Jesse realized he'd been squeezing the stick and the intercom button in a death grip and loosened his hand. "Nothing, copilot. Stand by for Pre-Attack Checklist."

Jesse figured it must be from upstream, but still couldn't find the Sorbonne. He did, however, spot a juicier target: the Bastille, only recently put in use as a prison by Cardinal Richelieu.

Screw the Sorbonne, that's our first target, he thought. Now that he had placed it, the prison's eighty-foot walls and moat stood out like a thumb. Best of all, a large street led straight from the Bastille to the Louvre. And Richelieu's palace was just across the street from the royal palace. He began to climb.

Cardinal Richelieu heard the shouting through the large windows of his private study. The windows faced the Louvre and overlooked a spacious garden where, a moment earlier, two dozen ladies and their escorts had been playing some silly game. It was their shouts that brought the clergyman to the large balcony above the garden, where he was shortly joined by one of his secretaries. Richelieu's eyes were turned skyward.

"Your Eminence . . ." the monsignor began.

"Yes, I see it, Henri," the cardinal replied. "Rather pretty, isn't it?"

"Uh, yes, I suppose, Your Eminence, but what . . . ?" Henri's voice trailed off.

Richelieu snorted impatiently. "I would have thought it was obvious, Henri. The Americans have come to visit."

He watched as the machine circled and then flew off to the east. It seemed to be climbing and Richelieu idly wondered what sort of weapons would be dropped. Some form of Greek fire or explosives, he assumed. His spies told him the Americans had both. Noting the numeral "1" on the tail, Richelieu likewise assumed the machine was being flown by Colonel Wood. *"Der Adler."* He was suddenly glad that the king and queen were at one of their country estates.

Turning to the monsignor, Richelieu inquired politely, "Henri, would you be so kind as to bring me a glass of wine?"

"Pre-Attack Checklist complete," Emil reported.

"Roger," Jesse replied. They'd drop on the Bastille and climb straight ahead for an attack on the Louvre. The wind didn't matter much with this bomb load. He pulled the nose up, slowing the aircraft, and gave the order.

"Speed brake out!"

Emil flipped the catch and cranked the deployed wheel furiously. Jesse felt the large metal device extend and Emil confirmed what he knew.

"Speed brake out!"

Stooping like an eagle, the Gustav dove. As they passed forty-five degrees of dive, the siren on the left gear flipped open and, as the airflow hit it, began an unearthly howl, dopplering higher as their speed increased. At something over sixty degrees of dive, Jesse caught his target and stabilized the aircraft. Through his sight, Jesse noticed something hard up against the front of the Bastille. Small wooden structures, people, horses, and cattle, many tendrils of smoke. Suddenly, it came to him.

"Christ, it's a market!" he said aloud. He saw the people beginning to scatter, probably due to primordial fear inspired by the siren. Horses bolted everywhere, running through the press, knocking over stalls and people. It was too late to change their target, since their fuel situation was getting fairly critical. He did what he could and tucked further under, centering the castle in his sight. The thought passed through his head. *Collateral damage.*

"Bomb away!" he ordered and Emil obeyed immediately.

"Bomb's away!"

Jesse began his recovery, pulling hard. The siren stopped its wail and, judging the moment, Jesse grunted, "Retract speed-brake!"

Emil released the lock and, aided by the airflow, quickly cranked the device closed and latched it in place. "Speed-brake retracted and locked."

Climbing straight ahead at full power, Jesse tried to look over his shoulder at the target, only to stop when his neck complained, giving a sharp warning pain. He stopped trying to look behind him, though he imagined he'd heard the screams of people as they roared past. He zoom climbed, already thinking of their second target.

Richelieu had clearly heard the siren and then spotted the attacker. Trees and buildings obscured his vision, but he thought he could see smoke rising from the direction of the Bastille.

Odd choice of target, he thought. *Why kill common criminals?*

Craning his head, he spotted the flyer high above, a glint of sunlight off the wings, and took a sip of wine. *Where now, Colonel?*

The siren began its hideous scream again and the cardinal calmly watched the machine dive. The silly women below began screaming in counterpoint and Richelieu wished they'd go away. He finally noted the direction of the descent and the thought came again. *It's fortunate that the king and queen are not at home. They might have been affrighted. These Americans have poor intelligence; they should pay their spies more.*

Henri was plucking at his arm. "Your Eminence, please come inside!"

"Shoo!" the cardinal said. "I must see this. We should be perfectly safe here." He looked at the Louvre and saw no one outside. "Unlike those poor devils over there, I should think. If they are wise, they are already in the cellars."

He followed the . . . *Aircraft, that's the word* . . . and saw it release something, while still at a great height. The aircraft immediately ceased its wail and he followed the thing it had dropped, eager to see the result. Halfway to its target, the object burst apart and Richelieu suddenly knew the type of munitions the Americans had chosen.

Diabolical, he thought. *I wouldn't have credited them with such subtlety.*

With desperation giving him strength, Monsignor Henri grabbed the cardinal and pulled him back into the study, away from the windows. Placing his own body between his master and danger, Father Henri ignored his superior's protestations.

"Maybe it's just as well," Jesse mused. In the long seconds he had spent staring at the Louvre through his sight, it had become clear to him that nobody was home. There was no crowd of guards, no carriages, nothing to suggest a busy court, but the Louvre had looked much as he remembered it, or thought he remembered it.

He continued their climb out and turned to the south. His neck hurt like blazes, likewise, his back. He didn't bother looking back at the target. As he climbed, he looked to his left and saw the graced curves of Notre Dame's flying buttresses. He remembered walking past them long ago with a young woman with whom he had been much in love. Suddenly, he was very tired. He wanted to go home, but he had two bombs, two rockets, and a most unambiguous target left. He'd snuck a peek after bomb release and was certain he'd caught a glimpse of a man in red on a balcony of his last intended target. Richelieu, at least, was home.

"Emil, we'll drop both of the remaining bombs on this pass," he said quietly. "Forget the Left Bank, wherever it is. We haven't enough fuel to screw around."

"Understood, sir," Emil said and suddenly added, "It's a beautiful city, isn't it, sir?"

Unaccountably, a vision of ruined Magdeburg flashed through Jesse's mind. Leveling off, he looked down at the roofs and streets of Paris.

"Yes, it is, Emil," he replied. He performed a turn back north, judged the moment and slowed, once again.

"Speed brake out!"

*   *   *

Cardinal Richelieu had endured enough foolishness.

"Henri, remove your hands and step aside," he commanded. "We are in God's hands, are we not?"

His secretary lowered his head and moved aside and the cardinal stepped back outside onto the balcony just in time to hear the siren begin its scream. He peered into the sky and shivered a bit, despite himself. The aircraft was pointed directly at him. At last, the silly people in his garden realized the immediate danger and began to scatter, though Richelieu barely noticed. He kept his eyes on the aircraft.

He realized the aircraft was still diving, long past the point of its other dives. *Colonel Wood wants to be certain, this time.*

The sound of the siren became impossibly loud and he wondered if his attackers meant to strike him with the machine itself. He knew he should run. Instead, he gripped the balustrade, murmured a prayer, and waited. He caught two objects falling free and the aircraft shifted aspect, flashing low over him with a roar. Richelieu flinched as, with a tremendous crash, the objects struck the ground before him and burst, showering the garden with paper. The cardinal exhaled slowly and noticed his hands were shaking. He'd seen paper scatter from the bomb over the royal palace and assumed those intended for him held the same, though he'd had his doubts at the end. He didn't know yet what was printed on them, but he could guess. Given the unexpected ingenuity the Americans were displaying in this raid, he suspected the leaflets contained excerpts from French revolutionary proclamations of the future. He idly wondered what sort of complications would arise from their message. In the meantime, it appeared God intended for him to remain alive, in service to his country.

Hearing aircraft sounds again grow louder, he looked up and saw the machine pass directly over him toward the Seine. It dipped a little and two flaming rockets soared off the wings and exploded in the river, making Richelieu blink. The aircraft climbed and headed eastward.

Yes, I got your message, Prime Minister Stearns, he thought with admiration. *Very neatly done.*

Despite his weariness and aching back, Jesse felt just fine. It was as if a weight had fallen from his shoulders with his ordnance. In the dive, he had fixated on the motionless red figure in his aiming sight and, for a split second, had considered following Hans' example. His finger had tickled the rocket firing switches and he'd suddenly jerked his hand away. Instead, in the end his delayed drop had failed to deliver the leaflets as intended and he'd wasted the rockets in the river.

Stearns was right, he thought. *I'm not God or an avenging angel. I'm only a man, commanding other men. A victim of collateral damage. Which reminds me . . .* He clicked the intercom.

"So, Emil, you and Henni are going flying tomorrow. Why don't you tell me what kind of flight profile you have in mind."

He began a cruise climb into the afternoon sun and listened with a smile as the young man spoke with growing enthusiasm.

Euterpe, Episode 1

Enrico M. Toro

Editor's note: Giacomo Carissimi and Girolamo Zenti are historical characters. They each gave important contributions to classic music. The first is considered the most important composer of the Roman baroque movement, an innovator of the era; the second was a well-traveled harpsichord maker, renowned for the invention of the bentside spinet. Some of his instruments are still used and copied today.

In 1631 they are both in their prime and at the beginning of bright and important careers.

Then the Ring of Fire came. Its effects slowly but inexorably spread all over Europe, changing the lives of millions of people. This story, the first of several episodes, tells the beginnings of their new lives.

Maestro Giacomo Carissimi to Father Thomas Fitzherbert SJ of the Illustrissimus Collegium Anglicanum in Rome

June 1633,
Very Reverend Father Fitzherbert,

How are you?

I only now have time to write you this letter before leaving tomorrow morning headed for the Holy Roman Empire first and then to Thuringia, in Germany. My final destination is the town of Grantville where I am going to learn and study.

I hope this letter will find you once back from Amalfi as I hope your residence in the *costiera* gave you some relief from the sickness that affects your lungs. You know I have always preferred to sharpen my quills to write music and not words, but I feel the need to share with you all the events that brought me to leave Rome.

I'm writing you in English to show you how the months you spent trying to hammer this language into my hard head have not gone wasted.

This letter and the ones that will follow are maybe another way to make my English fluent, especially if you will feel free to correct any mistakes you will find in my prose with your usual and blessed Jesuitical iron discipline.

I have been told that many inhabitants of Grantville are Germans and, *grazie alla Divina Provvidenza*, the four years I spent as master of chapel at the Collegium Germanicum made my German more than passable and I can always use some French and some Latin. If I am lucky some of them will speak Italian, too!

Anyway, with the prices of parchment these times, I better stop rambling and go to the point. Sometimes it seems there isn't enough paper in the whole world to write all the thoughts and feelings, the joy and the turmoil, that are nowadays in my mind.

It's strange to think how a single evening can change a man's approach to life and how an encounter made a man who felt uncomfortable leaving the Aurelian's walls (you know how much I hated my position in Assisi) travel hundreds of miles to reach a far, almost mythical town. But if there is a man who can make a lazy, contemplative man leave all behind for adventure this is Messer Giulio Mazarini.

I had never met the man before. I only knew him for his fame of being one of the finest diplomats in Europe, a man with a golden tongue and of sharp wits. I have been told that he had just arrived from a mission in Germany. So I wasn't at all surprised once I came to know he would have lectured the students of our seminary in the latest developments in the Holy Roman Empire.

After all, the Collegium Germanicum, where I have the honor to teach sacred music and to direct the choir, has been created to prepare the German clergy to better deal with the dangers of the Reformation.

I wasn't surprised when he attended a concert we gave in his honor in Saint Apollinare, as I wasn't surprised when he visited me in my studio after the cantate and motets were over. Paying compliments to the author is customary and polite behavior, after all. But it was what he brought with him that shocked me.

He handed me a parchment of paper and let me unroll it. While my hands and eyes were busy opening it, he asked: "Many say you are the brightest musician here in Rome, maestro. Can you tell me what is this?"

I stared at it for a while before answering. "It's part of a music composition, it seems. But the writing, it is slightly different; some of the symbols are more complex than the ones I use, more structured, more evoluted. The printing quality is awesome. Where did you get this, if I may ask?"

"Grantville. You did hear about it, didn't you?" Mazarini walked closer to the fireplace where I keep some comfortable armchairs.

"Of course I did. Everybody is talking about it. Yet I think most of what I heard are rumors, like the one that says they are a bunch of demons or warlocks riding monsters who spit flames." Then I added, shaking my head, "Are they really from the future?"

"Yes, they are, and the music you hold is from a piece called the Goldberg Variations, a series of sonatas composed by an artist who will live more than fifty years from now. I think his name is Bach."

I was completely amazed by his words. I confess that I don't know what was shaking more, my hands or my voice.

"Can I borrow it? I want to copy it and try to play it."

"Unfortunately, I am not sure you will be able to do it. The American lady who gave it to me described it as a transcription for pianoforte. It will need another adaptation to be played on an harpsichord or an organ."

"A pianoforte? What is that?"

"A musical instrument from the future I listened to while in the American town. It looks like an harpsichord or a spinet but it sounds quite different: richer, more full, less metallic. They told me it will be invented by an Italian at the beginning of the next century. But that's not the only amazing mechanical thing these people have. You should hear their music recordings, too; it's like . . . Well it's hard to explain. The sound of a whole orchestra coming out loudly from a box. They call it a 'CD player.' It can play music and sounds over and over again."

"What?"

"I'm not sure how it works, but it's as if you play something on the organ and somebody captures this sound and writes it down on a machine like printing does with words. Then, then to listen again what you played, they only have to use again the machine."

"It's hard to believe. A machine that captures sounds?"

"Hard to believe, but nonetheless perfectly real. One of them told me they had been a good help in beating the Spanish army last year."

"A music that defeats an army! Sounds like some kind of joke. That's something I'd like to hear!"

I think he realized how much he had succeeded in capturing my interest and offered to stay longer to talk about that strange place if I had more of my questions. I couldn't quiet my curiosity, so I went to one of the drawers and took a bottle of that smooth muscat from Montefiascone called "*Est Est Est*" you know I love so much. I poured the wine into two pewter cups I keep at hand and lighted a series of candles to have more light in the room.

At the moment I didn't realize it, but we must have been talking for hours. He got my complete attention and I learned many more things about that remote place, all uncanny and extraordinary.

I learned how the people of Grantville allied themselves with the Swedish and the German Protestant princedoms. I learned of their skill in manufacturing things, of their religious tolerance, of their fantastic knowledge of many new subjects in matter of science and medicine and, at the end, Mazarini, suddenly reluctant, told me a few things of their strange and almost utopian ideas about the government of a state.

Only when the night was beginning to turn into a new morning did our meeting come to an end. Mazarini, smiling, made his offer.

"It would be a fine thing if one of our most talented young musicians traveled there to learn more about music, and maybe get familiar with these up-timers, as they call themselves. There is a lot to gain from an unofficial exchange of knowledge."

Some way I knew it was coming, but I wasn't the more prepared for it.

"But, Messer Mazarini, I have my job here and I'm not accustomed to travel for such a long distance."

"I know, I know, but think about how much your natural talent can gain from such an experience. You don't have to make any decision now, of course. Nevertheless, should you agree with me, contact me at the Basilica of San Giovanni and maybe I will be able to help you with your travel."

He is pretty important now but I feel like that man will make an even better career! He knew how to cast the hook, how to make the bait irresistible, and in what exact moment I did bite. A master in human behavior.

Indeed I don't know if it was my curiosity or my love for music, but I suddenly realized that if music from the future, strange new musical instrument and music in boxes existed, I had to see it in person no matter how much I had to travel.

The weeks that followed have been full of frantic activity and preparations for this trip. I live a simple life and I earn well, but my savings were not enough to sustain myself for a long time. So the first thing was to find funds.

The Company of Jesus didn't help with them. They still had not adopted a position about Grantville and told me to wait. If I wanted to go, they would let me do it without losing my job, since it is not uncommon for teachers to take a long sabbatical for study. But the only thing they could have helped with was granting me hospitality in their houses along the way. This was quite satisfying, I must honestly say. Considering the extension of the network of their houses, such an offer looks like a very relevant asset for a traveler.

Besides that, the rector of the Collegium Germanicum invited me to travel for part of the road with a delegation of Jesuits directed to Wien. It would have been safer for me, he said. But, he added, once I left them I would be on my own.

When I was not busy preparing for my trip I passed my time studying the music sheets Messer Mazarini brought me. Some of the symbols were different, but the pentagram, the notes, the clefs, and most of the rest were the same.

The more I studied the music, the more I realized how rich and amazingly moving it was. All my compositions seemed simple, elementary in comparison.

The piece of music I had in my hands was a canon whose voices were not only written at the distance of only half note (one of the most difficult forms of canon) but also they moved as if they were the freely conceived voices of a trio sonata.

And if this was something written not so far away in the future, I was wondering, what about the music written in the later centuries?

My resolve to visit this town in Germany grew day by day.

Unfortunately my financial problems were unchanged, even with Mazarini's help.

I applied to Cardinal Scipione Borghese for a donation of two hundred *scudi*, enough to live well for three years, I thought. The cardinal had always been very liberal with money when arts are involved. But it seems that any patron I could find wasn't very much at ease with the idea of financing trips to such a place of mystery. A place whose soldiers had repeatedly whipped Catholic armies.

Besides, it appears that sponsoring something that sounds like cultural contamination is not appreciated in today's Rome, when a Protestant country is involved. Obtaining a loan from a bank was altogether impossible without some aristocrat or some church institution backing my request.

So, at the end, I got many suggestions, but funds none.

One of the suggestions I decided to follow was to have a partner in this enterprise. Somebody with more financial means. Both Mazarini and my Dutch friend Pieter, the painter know as Il Bamboccio, pointed out that maybe an instrument maker would be interested in studying musical instruments of the future. He could be talked into to reproducing and selling them. Pieter told me that one of his patrons had just bought a new spinet from Girolamo Zenti, who now resides in Rome.

Girolamo Zenti is to instrument making what Caravaggio was to painting: a genius, but with an unruly and crazy life. Despite his being a gambler and womanizer, his harpsichords and spinets are among the best produced. And he is just twenty-six years old.

When I was shopping for a new spinet for the oratory I'd been told that the waiting time to have a Zenti is more than two years. I had not met the artisan previously, but I knew one of his apprentices who had come to Sant Apollinare to fix the pedal of the old harpsichord. So I knew where his shop was: Rione Monti, built in part over the old Suburra of the ancient Romans. With so many brothels and inns nearby, it was the perfect place for an unrepentant sinner like Girolamo.

Curiously his shop is just between the two churches of Santa Maria dei Monti and San Salvatore, where is taking place another of the endless restoration and building works that are filling the town today. Even if since the jubilee the situation has improved, I believe Romans are doomed forever to share their living space and their roads with scaffolds, bricks, and debris.

The first impression one gets when entering the Zenti enterprises is one of business. The shop occupies a whole building. I had to cross a small, sunny courtyard, full of cats and stacks of timbers protected by tarps, to reach the working rooms at ground level.

A man was idly waiting at the front door. His long hair collected in a net and the large knife and sling at his belt showed without chance of mistake he was one of the many bravos who haunt the city today. Hired muscle, probably there to protect Maestro Zenti from unwanted visitors.

He let me into a big room where three people were working to the frames of some instruments. The place was filled with sawdust and the noise of people sanding wood. Shelves were filled with tools and pieces of timber seasoning. I could recognize cypress, walnut, linden, and maybe sorb. Sitting by a desk under a dusty window an artisan was skillfully working on a piece of ivory, carving it, while another was shaping a rosette. There was a rich smell of lakes and varnish.

"Maestro Zenti is in the next room," the bravo told me in a very grim tone of voice, perfectly tuned by many years of threatening people. "He is giving the last touches to one of his creations."

I hurried where told to go and I finally saw Girolamo.

I can understand why women lose their heads for him. He is tall, with broad shoulders, and a slim and muscular body that seems more fit to a warrior than an artisan. He has long, finely cut ash-blond hair, well enhanced by a perfectly cured goatee. He was wearing work clothes, just breeches, a shirt, and a leather apron, but he seemed unusual in that simple outfit.

"Good morning, Maestro Zenti," I began, with a small bow and my best smile on my face. "My name is Giacomo Carissimi, maestro of music and master of chapel of Sant'Apollinare. *Servo vostro.*"

He was sideways tuning a spinet, a magnificent one, I may add. Black, very linear, with an ivory and oak keyboard. And, dear Father, I am sure it was not for a church or an oratory, as the painting on the lid was . . . well, let's say that libertine is an understatement, with all those satyrs and maidens busy in sinful activities.

Blushing, I asked him if it was one of his new bentside spinets.

"Yes it is, Maestro Carissimi," he answered, obviously proud of his work. "As you can see, the strings and spine run transversely to the player and are not parallel to the key levers. The strings are plucked much closer to their center points than on a normal spinet or harpsichord. This helps in producing a strong and sustained tone. But the sound remains less brilliant than the normal spinet no matter how many variations I'm trying to do."

He stood up, lightly touching the spinet with his hand as if to caress it and bowed slightly.

"I'm sorry if I didn't greet you as I should, Maestro. When working, I tend to be too much engrossed in what I do. I'm a great admirer of your work and very honored to meet you."

"The admiration is mutual. I wish there were more artisans of your skill in this world. Now I know why many people deeply appreciate your creations and speak so highly of your work. But, if I'm not wrong this instrument has just one choir of strings at eight-foot pitch. Five octaves compass?"

"Yes, you are right. You have a good eye. Do you want to play it? I'm just finished tuning it."

"It would be my pleasure, but I came here to talk to you."

"I'm sure you can do it while playing. Please! I'd love to have the opinion of such a renowned master as yourself."

"Oh, you are too generous with my fame. I'm not Monteverdi or Stefano Landi!"

"And yet you played many times in front of His Sanctity and other important people."

"If everything goes well, not in the next future," I said wryly.

"What do you mean? Are you leaving Rome?"

"Yes, I am planning to take a sabbatical to make a long trip to Germany."

"You make me curious. Why should someone like you, with such a position, risk his life to go to that unfortunate land plagued with war and famine?"

I began to play the first notes of what I transcripted of that future rich music, and I tried to explain my reasons. I told him about my conversation with Mazarini and my intentions to study the works of the great composers of the future.

Only then I told him about the pianoforte and how he could be the first in learning how to build one in this century and how I would have appreciated to have him accompany me in this trip. He looked astonished and in some way saddened.

"My dear Maestro Carissimi, I would love to visit with you this place of wonder of yours and I'm really honored by your desire to have me as a road companion. But not now. My business is going so well that I don't dare to leave it, no matter how much I may trust my helpers. I've been wandering the last ten years. Now I want to settle in one place and do my job as best as I can. Maybe in the future, yes; maybe some years from now. But please don't despair. If you want, when you come back you may bring some drawings of the pianoforte with you and I will be more than glad to study them with you. Or, better, you may write me, if you wish, and I will see what can I do from here."

He must have understood my sorrow because he walked closer and put an hand on my shoulder. "I wish you the best of luck, for traveling such a long distance won't be easy. Try to never travel alone, especially in Germany. You would be an easy prey for brigands, deserters, and God only knows what else! But if it is meant to be, you will find what you are looking for."

I didn't have any further arguments to use so, after the usual courtesies I left Zenti's shop. Before leaving I told him to send me a message at Saint Apollinare should he change his mind. While walking back home, my mood was sorrowful because I felt that, despite his terrible fame, Messer Zenti could have been a good travel companion. I felt an immediate liking for the man, no matter how different from mine his lifestyle was.

Nevertheless, my sadness never turned to despair. On the contrary, my resolve to go grew even more, if possible. I don't know if I became so stubborn in my youth during the endless hours I spent studying music in Rome and in Tivoli.

Some way I know that Euterpe, the muse of music, is waiting for me and I can't ignore her call. I need to go.

It appeared that I was left only with my prayers. So I did what I could do and prayed to Saint Christopher and the newly appointed Saint Francis Xavier as I never prayed before. Only later did I discover that my requests had been listened to and that Saint Christopher had some fun in doing it.

Two weeks had passed by since my meeting with Zenti. I was rehearsing the next Sunday concert in the church's oratory with the whole group of singers and musicians when I saw walking down the hall, using a tall cane for a terrible gout limp, the best dressed master of chapel of the whole Eternal City.

I must admit that, despite his pompousness and haughtiness, Stefano Landi is a great composer of the *Stile Moderno*. His second opera, *Il Sant'Alessio*, is an ingenious and inventive masterpiece. The opening, the poignant harmonies and the fantastic settings made it an amazing success last year. And one needs to possess some titanical leverage to have Bernini designing the sets!

I stopped the music and I moved to meet the old composer. When the favorite artist of the Barberini family comes for a visit one usually stops and listens.

"Ah, Carissimi, *eccovi qua*. Please find me a comfortable place where I can rest my tired legs. And—please!—let the music start again. I'm sure your musicians can play something without your help. We have to talk." After a moment of silence and a look around, he added, "In private."

I did as he asked, and I walked with him to the near *sagrestia*, the music of a cantata behind us. A little anxiously, I asked him what brought him there.

"You know, we have a common friend in the diplomatic corp. I met Mazarini two years ago when I was preparing *Il Sant'Alessio*. As you probably know, he has personally taken part in the staging of the opera. What you probably don't know is that once he was back from Germany, he asked me to go visit these Americans."

He must have seen the surprise on my face. "Oh, don't worry, I turned his suggestion down. I'm too old and sick to make such a long and dangerous travel. I'm rich and renowned and I want to enjoy here, as long as I can, the fruits of my work. But while turning down the offer I advanced your name. It was you or Luigi Rossi, so you should be grateful."

"Thank you, Maestro." I confess I felt a little stupid.

"Please don't interrupt me—and relax. I'm tired and I want to go home. Make it easy for me. The fact is that it seems you are unable to find the funds necessary, while I can do that easily. There are some very highly born gentlemen that we may call F. and A. who would be very interested in lavishing some money if they could remain anonymous. And I can serve as intermediary."

"That would be wonderful. But I wouldn't know how to repay you for your great generosity."

"Oh, that would be easy! You see, I'm getting old and I don't have much left to live. So I think I can afford a little vanity and know what will be of my fame in the future. I want to know what posterity will think of me. I want to know how and when I'm going to die and I want to know what I will compose in the next years. And, oh yes!" He touched quickly his forehead with the palm of his hand, as if he had forgotten something. "If you can find these compositions and spare me the fatigue to write them it would be even better! Probably our gentlemen patrons would like that you look around, observe things, and report once you will be back in Rome."

"But, Maestro, I don't think I can be like a spy. It's really not one of my talents."

"Oh, no, not a spy, it's obvious that you can't do that. Too naïve. I just ask you to be careful in what you see around you. As I think you will be anyway. Besides, better doing it fully aware and reporting it willingly, than being interrogated in a less pleasant way upon your return, don't you think?"

I must have then gulped visibly because he started a silent laugh and that was almost scarier.

"This is why you can't be a spy. You must just observe things you could see anyway, learn what you can about their customs and habits and remember it. Nothing forbidden or secret. Those who sent me don't want you hanged, but they are curious to know more about the daily life of that place. So do you accept?"

Of course I did; what else could I do? After all, as the Pasquino's satiric poem says: *quod non fecerunt barbari, fecerunt Barberini.*

So, Father, as this letter proves, despite all difficulties tomorrow I will leave for Grantville, Thuringia, with sufficient funds to stay there for years.

Am I nervous? Terribly. Excited? More than ever. Scared? Yes I am. I have three centuries of music in front of me. I will see the works of people who right now exist only in the great mind of the Creator and all this unknown makes me feel frail, uncertain. But at the same time inebriated, slightly intoxicated by all the possible developments I can bring to the art of music.

There is not a day when I don't wonder if I cannot deal with it.

What I have seen is just a fragment of their music and already it seems so much more complex than what I have learned for all my life. Will I be able to understand it? How would a minstrel have reacted, coming into Rome for the first jubilee in the year 1300, if he had to listen to Palestrina's music or to my humble compositions? Would he be able to understand it?

These people seem to have brought a new world into our old Europe. Will I learn from them or will I look just like a savage to them? Just like one of those Indians traveling around the courts of half of Europe without really knowing what is happening. I have in front of me a great opportunity, but a great danger, too. Dealing with all these future compositions may enrich me, but it may also destroy me. What is the sense in creating new music, in experimenting with new compositions if people greater than I have already written this music? I feel we are witnessing great changes. I want to try to ride them, but I cannot avoid fearing being trampled by them.

I am finally ready to leave. I have letters of introduction to the Americans by Mazarini and some letters of credit by my Florentine bankers. In case of misfortune, the rest of my money is hidden in secure places. I will travel light, bringing with me just a chest of clothes and my old faithful traveling spinet.

I will be with the Jesuit delegation, so hopefully safe, up to Austria. Then I will be alone and may the Holy Ghost be with me!

My plan is to follow the Via Claudia Augusta to Donauworth. From there it will be less than two hundred miles to Grantville. I hope the war will leave me alone. Upon your return, you can answer my letter by addressing it to the Jesuitkirche in Wien. They will provide a way to forward it to Thuringia.

All my best wishes and prayers for your recovery. May Mother Mary smile upon you.

Your servant and student
Giacomo Carissimi

The Company Men

Christopher James Weber

1

"I do not *like* dank dark forests, you arrogant English ass." Liam Donovan cursed as he ducked low on his horse to avoid being hit by a low branch.

"I suppose you would be happier strolling down some gentle, sloping, Irish hill, heather in the air and all that?" Thomas North ducked the same branch. The two had been riding in the German forest for the better part of an hour and were beginning to look much the worse for wear.

"Just so," the bulky red-haired Irishman agreed appreciatively. "A civilized geography, that."

"No cover for miles in any direction, conducting secret business for all to see, and practically begging for some government busybody to interrupt with soldiers. No wonder your people lost every war."

"July, 1921," Donovan said coldly.

"Yes . . . Well, plenty of time to worry about that one later," the tall pale Englishman replied in a huff.

*　　　*　　　*

"I do not care for this, Tom," Donovan said. They had finally arrived at the designated meeting point, a quiet bank of the river Saale just south of Jena and hopefully out of sight of prying eyes.

"I do not care for it either. Lynch is *your* friend, I remind you."

"What exactly is that supposed to mean?" Donovan asked.

"The last time we had less than legal dealings with one of your close personal friends from back in Eire, we had half the Imperial army chasing us with the other half wagering on our method of execution."

"What was the good money on?"

"Shot while trying to escape."

Donovan smiled. "Ah. I love the classics."

"Here he comes," said North, when he sighted the small boat by its lamp. "Just like an Irishman to be late."

"He's from Kerry; it's to be expected. Sean Lynch! You demon-spawned son of a whore! Over here!"

"Liam Donovan, you great building-sized bastard. And the right bastard North! Milordship." Lynch bowed with a generous wave as the boat eased gently onto the shore.

"Men have been killed for speaking less," said North dryly.

"Many men in my home have been killed for *much* less," replied Lynch, shrugging. "Oddly enough, by men who spoke very much like you. But that is a separate issue. Let's to business."

The wiry Lynch disembarked and once on solid ground pulled the boat until it was securely ashore. He then reached into the boat to remove a canvas sheet from several boxes.

"Explain to me again how you acquired these goods, Lynch?" North asked suspiciously.

"The usual way—I stole them. And don't give me that sour look, North. I know you're not above such things."

"True. I'll still need a better explanation that that."

"Ha!" Lynch puffed out his chest in annoyance. "But of course he does! He's an Englishman. He steals by native right; others must just-ify themselves. Well, North, these goods were once the proud property of one of the wizard Americans. A 'survivalist,' as they call them, by the name of Newman. Sadly, the good survivalist did not live up to his name. My associates encountered him while he was trying to make a supply run to Jena for food. He even spoke German fluently, but, alas, his boots were a giveaway. A dead giveaway, you might put it."

"Why do all Irishmen insist upon bad puns?"

"We are a literary people, North, for which you should be grateful. The Irish saved civilization, you know. The Americans even have a book about it in their town library."

Irishman himself or not, Donovan was as suspicious as his partner. "I had thought all the survivalists were brought in. Certainly a ruckus would have erupted with this Newman's disappearance?"

"I doubt it," Lynch replied, rubbing his heavy beard. "This one had been in hiding a *long* while. His lair was a thing of beauty. When we looted it we found a number of items that I would be more than happy to sell to my good, close, friends. Have you the money?"

"Aye." Donovan patted the purse at his side, which emitted a distinctly metallic sound.

"Let me see it then."

"Of course." North nodded gracefully. "After we see the guns and ammo."

"All we have seen so far is a few crates," added Donovan, with a very false grin.

"O boyo. I can feel the trust in the forest." Lynch removed the top of the first crate to reveal dozens of cardboard boxes and tossed one of them to North. North opened up the small box and pulled out a nicely ordered collection of up-time bullets in the .308 caliber. Satisfied, he sealed the box and tossed it back to Lynch, who quickly reinserted the cartridge box in its crate.

"The rifles?" North asked with a little more trust.

"Let me at least *see* the money. There are two of you, after all, and only one of poor me." In the lamplight, Lynch's face bore a passing resemblance to that of a pleading beggar. It was all North could do not to laugh out loud.

Donovan waited for the signal from his partner. When North nodded, he removed his purse and loosened the leather strap until the pouch revealed numerous gold coins.

"The equivalent of two thousand dollars gold, don't mind the coinage," said North with a wry grin.

"I usually try not to. Ten rifles, all in good working order. Examine one yourself." Lynch opened the second crate and removed a single rifle from the company of its fellows and handed it over.

While North was not as expert on up-time weaponry as he was in seventeenth-century sword and pistol, he knew enough to verify it as an example of the quite ferocious and lethal weapons the Americans had brought back in time with them. He loaded the second bullet taken from the cartridge box with a smooth, fluid motion and aimed it toward the opposite river bank. A squeeze of the trigger yielded a single loud shot, with a corresponding splash of mud and water.

"Now that you have alerted every man within ten miles, may we hurry about this?" His face sour, Lynch took the rifle away and resealed the crate.

"The third box? Your description back in the Thuringen Gardens was rather vague."

"Ah, but this is the interesting one, laddie. This Newman fellow he had his own little alchemist operation. Making something called nitroglycerin. Fantastic stuff! But be careful and I suggest you don't test this one out, it is . . ."

"Rather temperamental, yes. I have read about nitroglycerin."

"Then you will forgive me if I don't pry this one open and ask that you wait to do so until I have rowed myself downstream. I believe we have established trust, aye? I have to think about my children."

"You don't have any children, Sean." Donovan handed over the pouch of gold.

"I might someday." Lynch winked as he took the gold and hefted its contents for the most cursory of examinations before placing it in his clothing.

"The nitro is in twenty glass jars, with as much padding as I could insert. Remember to take it slow and easy, lads. If you hear the glass rattling, I suggest you start praying for your one day of heaven, before the devil finds you dead." Lynch stepped back in his boat and removed the lamp from its stand, leaning down so that he could get a closer look at what he was moving. Just then a rifle shot rang out in the not-too-great distance.

North, instincts screaming "trap," immediately pulled out saber and pistol and turned to Lynch. But Lynch was searching just as furiously for the source of the noise and making no threatening moves. The Englishman told his partner to remain watching Lynch and then moved off into the forest. Stalking quietly through the woods, North searched for several minutes and listened carefully for any approaching interlopers. When none were immediately forthcoming he returned to the waiting boat, with Donovan's pistol drawn in Lynch's direction. Paranoia was a survival trait both admired and respected in the other.

"Bit of a busy secluded forest we have here, lads, do we not?" said Lynch nervously.

"Some hunter or kinder playing at being a soldier," said North curtly, not wishing to remain any longer. "Let us finish this."

"Then come and help me, lads. The crates are heavy and I don't have the leverage inside the boat."

Donovan holstered his weapons and walked to the rim of the beached boat, grabbed one side of the box he knew contained the bullets, and helped heave it out, handing it to a waiting North. The second crate of rifles was handled in like manner and North carried it stoically over to the waiting packhorses. Then, with careful and meticulous effort, the three of them lifted the crate of nitro out of the boat. Waiting until the other was ready, the two mercenaries slowly carried the crate away from the boat and gently settled it onto the soft ground.

"A little help pushing off would be appreciated," said Lynch, as he sat down and manned his small boat's oars.

The two complied, heaving the boat off the mud and into the river with a placid ripple. Lynch began paddling away and then gave an enthusiastic wave. "A pleasure doing business with you!"

North watched the pucklike man float downstream and then turned to the three crates, and one crate in particular.

"You realize that we are both completely daft."

"Utterly and totally," Donovan agreed. "How are we going to get that devil's brew back to our camp?"

"One excruciatingly cautious step at a time. Come on then."

The two lifted the crate carefully onto the packhorse. While Donovan held it secure, North went to retrieve the ropes necessary for lashing.

"Keep it steady," said North.

"I am."

"No, you're *not*. It almost slipped!" snapped North.

"Well, if you would hurry up. . . ."

"I am not the one who has to have two hours just to wake up in the morning."

"Not all of us are sons of Satan with iron constitutions."

"You can not blame me for who my parents were."

"Oh, yes, I can."

"Piss off."

"Go fornicate a sheep, you—watch out!" Donovan screamed. The nitroglycerin crate slipped out of the lashings and fell to the ground.

Thud.

Crash.

Thud?

No boom?

"Liam . . . why are we not blown into little pieces scattered across half the continent of Europe?"

"Two possible explanations for that, old friend. Either we *were* blown into little pieces and scattered across half of Europe and this is hell, which we are destined to share together—which would most certainly fit my preconception of that place. Or the second explanation . . ."

Donovan leaned down to examine one of the shattered glass jars emitting a distinctive noninflammable odor. "The second possibility is that we are very much alive and you are *never* going to let me forget about this one."

North leaned down next to his partner and picked up one of the intact glass jars. No, it most certainly wasn't nitroglycerin.

"*Newman's Own, Fra Diavlo: Hot and spicy,*" the Englishman read, before tossing the glass jar hard across some nearby rocks. He quickly rushed over to the two other crates, ripping open the covers. Inside the first was sand and rocks, which North was sure was the same weight as a crate full of ammunition. The second crate yielded something slightly different. Rocks and sand.

"But . . . but we saw the rifles. You fired one of them!" Donovan said angrily.

"Did we see the entirety of those crates, Liam? No, we saw what he wanted us to see . . . in the dark. He must have switched them while we were distracted by that rifle shot. One of his accomplices . . . Signaled by the lamp being lowered . . . In our hurry to get out of here we simply grabbed the boxes he indicated and didn't think to look any further. I *thought* it was too good to be true. Lynch had one rifle and box of ammo and that's all we needed to see. There was never any survivalist, no weapons cache, never was any nitro, just a crate full of glass bottles meant to keep our minds on the consequences if we dropped it."

"Probably for the best then . . . if it had been nitro we would be . . . That damned Kerryman! I am going to kill him slow, going to rip his balls off with my bare hands!"

"No doubt."

"How can you be so sodding calm about this?"

"I was just admiring the irony of the situation," said North, shaking his head.

"What irony?"

"We got conned."

"Aye. So?"

"*We* got *conned* . . . by Paul Newman's own."

"Aye?" Donovan nodded, still waiting for elaboration.

North sighed, rolling his eyes. "You cultural barbarian. We are making a trip to the video library when we get back. Bog Irishman probably wasn't even aware of the reference when he planned this. But one has to appreciate the skill and intelligence it required to pull it off."

Donovan glowered, first at North, and then in the direction Lynch had disappeared in.

"Oh, we're still going to kill him," said North, merrily nodding his head. "Slowly, painfully, and any other way we can think up. Still, the *irony!*"

2

"Are you kidding?" Mike Stearns' eyes scanned the members of his cabinet sitting around the table before coming back to his secretary of state.

"I'm afraid not, Mike," replied Ed Piazza. "In hindsight we shouldn't be so surprised. This would be right about the time we should have expected them. Time enough for the news to get there and them to get here. The world's a big damn place here in the seventeenth century."

"The Mughals," Stearns mused. "The freaking Mughal Empire."

"We don't know that for sure, it's just one guy and a wild story," cautioned Piazza.

"I don't believe that and neither do you, and even if . . ." Stearns shook his head. "We can't take the risk. If this guy *is* an official representative of the Mughal Empire, the opportunity is too great—potentially, at least—for us to ignore."

"Ignore, okay," agreed Frank Jackson, "but what can we *do*? Mike, Innsbruck is hundreds of miles away deep into Hapsburg territory. For us to do it would require a massive military undertaking, and we don't have the forces. Nor is Gustavus Adolphus going to give us anybody, not with war breaking out with the League of Ostend."

"And if our little rescue mission comes a cropper, we will have a whole heap of trouble with the southern principalities," commented Piazza. "We're just starting to be on speaking terms with some of them. Our army traipsing through will kill that pretty effectively."

"We have to do *something*," said Quentin Underwood. "The merest possibility of establishing favorable trade relations with them is something we have to pursue. Christ! Forget France. Except for maybe the Ottoman Turks and the Chinese, the Mughal Empire is the greatest power in the world right now."

"So we have to do something, but we can't do what he asks," said Stearns. "Not directly, anyway."

Harry Lefferts cleared his throat. He was not normally a part of cabinet meetings but Mike had asked him to sit in, since he'd had a feeling Harry's expertise might be called for. "I know a guy. Well, two guys."

That afternoon North and his partner sat in the converted office to discuss the week's business. The farmhouse that served as the Albernian Mercenary Company's corporate headquarters was not an illustrious affair. It was, however, located near enough to Grantville that the town's amenities were always at hand. But also far enough away for several hundred armed men to drill without upsetting the neighbors' delicate sensibilities too much. The former owners originally had no inclination to sell. But there are very few of life's problems that couldn't be solved with an influx of cash, which the two expatriates had sufficient in supply.

The houses and barns were only enough to keep a few extended families, really a miniature village. Since acquiring the property, the company had been building outlying barracks to house the men. But a shortage of bricks had halted construction three quarters of the way to completion and it was a good thing much of the company was away on assignment. As it was, some would probably have to make do with tents when the heavy snows began.

"What do you have to report?" asked North.

"The merchant caravan from Prague came back safe and sound, despite the recent unpleasantness. It appears 'state of war' is a rather flexible viewpoint for them. Two minor fights with Bohemian highwaymen, but nothing Hastings couldn't handle." Donovan glanced at the barely legible account Hastings had turned in. "There was a spot of trouble collecting our pay but Hastings handled that manner in his usual subtle way."

"I told you hiring him was the right decision. There is no reason for you to dislike him so much."

"The man is a drunk. After he collected the gold, his men had to carry him back to the farm from the Thuringen gardens. *Five* of his men."

"So he is a drunk. As opposed to which other of our sergeants, I might ask? Besides, he does his best fighting when he is drunk. You should know that."

"Don't remind me," said Donovan, rubbing his chin and wincing at the memory.

"You know how to handle Hastings," said North quietly as he worked out the kink in his neck.

"Of course. I fine him two weeks pay, as usual. He is now seven weeks behind in his pay . . . as usual. At this rate he will be in servitude to us for his entire lifetime and never collect a coin aside from what he can pilfer from our contracts."

"Huh," North grunted. "Don't let the Americans hear, they are rather touchy about slavery."

"Speaking of which, I finished talking with the gunsmith and we can take possession of seventy-five more flintlocks along with forty thousand rounds of ammunition. We still have a sufficient supply of gunpowder and our own mill should be running in a few weeks. Schroeder says he can begin production by November."

"You are still not happy about *that,* are you, Liam?"

"It seems to me a frivolous expense."

"I cower in fear of the Irish hordes and their double-entry book-keeping." North sat up from his desk and tossed the valuable up-time composition notebook into his partner's lap.

"I was being serious, Tom," said Donovan, carefully returning the company's ledger books to the desk.

"So was I." North shuddered appropriately at the memory. "We have been through this time and again. The cost is great but I deemed it necessary. We are in the middle of a war. And we need an independent supply. If we don't have a bottleneck on saltpeter, probably we will end up selling it to the government at three times profit."

"What is more likely is that once production is up and running, Stearns will seize the mill as a 'vital military asset,' under their law of eminent domain. And we will be out the huge expense."

"You, sir, are a pessimist. By that time we will have secured all the up-time weapons we need. And we won't need raw gunpowder any longer."

"At which time you will ask me to build a cartridge factory."

"Liam, you are not exactly the paragon of capitalism yourself."

"I do not know what you mean."

"You recruited another fifteen men today," North responded coldly.

"So I did. And?"

"Are any of them between the age of fifteen and fifty?" With a booming economy, and those not involved in a trade enlisting in the regular army, their private mercenary company did not exactly have first choice on who it hired.

"Some," Donovan stalled, suddenly very interested in the cleanliness of his fingernails.

"And I see they had about forty camp followers between them."

"The lasses can be cooks and washerwomen," said Donovan stoutly. "The lads will help in the fields. We need them, Tom. The farm was supposed to be a secondary income but it is turning out to be quite a secondary expense."

"My shirts are washed so often the stitching is coming loose. Oh, I know, they can sew it back up again too. My meals are served promptly. Six times a day. And I can even take a ride in my own fields with Ariner a whole ten feet before tripping over some brat."

"Winter is coming," said Donovan, halting his friend's rant cold.

"We haven't the space," complained North.

"We will. We have plenty of timber about. The newcomers will build their own barracks. It won't be a proper residence but it will do. It is probably what we should have done from the beginning, instead of trying for brick."

"Most of them will desert come spring."

"Probably, but we will still have the buildings they constructed when they leave, and think of the good this charity will do your soul. Which is badly in need of it, let me tell you. I believe the up-timers call it good karma."

"Karma? Where the hell did that come from?"

"India, I believe."

"North and Donovan have been together several years now," said Harry Lefferts. "They met originally in Amsterdam, when the Dutch sent out the call for any mercenaries in defense of their independence from Spain."

Piazza grunted. "That would have been after the truce between

1609 and 1621 broke down, I assume? They must be old-timers."

"No, they're both in their late twenties. Once the truce was over and Spain attacked again—just another part of the mess we call the 'Thirty Years War'—the Dutch needed as many mercenaries as they could get. As young as they were, both were intelligent and rose pretty quickly within their mercenary company. And somewhere in the course of it, they got to be good friends."

"An Englishman and an Irishman?" asked Quentin skeptically.

Harry shrugged. "For being from different countries, fighting a war to defend yet another, they had a lot in common. Liam had been tossed out of the College of the Holy and Undivided Trinity of Queen Elizabeth near Dublin when it was found out his family was Catholic. The authorities were so pissed off by his false application that he had to get out of Ireland altogether. He landed on the Continent with an extensive knowledge of languages, the classics, and histories, but with barely a penny to his name."

"And North?" asked Mike.

"North left England for less, ah, austere reasons. He's nobility of a sort, being the third son and seventh child of the minor baron of Kirtling. The first son inherited the title and lands. The second son was expected to enter either the army or navy, to defend the glory of England. The third son, if a lord was so fortunate, was usually sent off to the clergy."

Something in Harry's expression caused a little chuckle to ripple around the cabinet room. Harry smiled. "Yeah, that's about right. The Anglican Church doesn't expect chastity. They allow clergy to marry, after all. But they still weren't willing to elevate somebody like Tom North to the holy orders. I guess he had quite a reputation. If he'd been the son of a duke or a more powerful lord, special arrangements might have been made, but . . . he wasn't. And while he was a bit better funded than Donovan, I guess his father made it clear to him not to return home for a good long time. So, Thomas North was alone in a foreign land before finding Liam."

Harry shifted in his seat, trying to marshal his words. "Normally, you'd think, an Irish Catholic intellectual and an English Anglican nobleman would not have much to do with each other. But after discovering each other in a Dutch gaming parlor they found out they did share one fundamental characteristic that surpassed all borders and religions. They like money, and plenty of it, and between the two of them they're pretty good at figuring out how to get it. Since then, their noble quest took them here and there, to whoever was the best paymaster at the time. Eventually they wound up in the Clancy mercenary company loosely connected with Tilly's army back when it was rampaging across Germany. By then, Thomas had risen to command one of the detachments of fifty men used to scout about the flanks of the army." Harry cleared his throat. "This fortunate assignment enabled them to make their unofficial transfer an easy business."

The President of the United States rolled his eyes to the ceiling. "Don't tell me."

"Yup," said Harry, now grinning. "After they heard reports of the newcomer Americans and our effectiveness in the field—not to mention the usual fabulous tales of our wealth—the two of them packed their bags, decamped in the middle of the night, and set out for the, ah, promised land."

Still staring at the ceiling, Mike closed his eyes. "Promised land," he murmured. "Out of idle curiosity, when did we decide to pave the streets of Grantville with gold? And how come I haven't noticed any special abundance of milk and honey around here lately?"

Judging that the question was rhetorical, Harry pressed on. "So, the two of them headed directly toward what most in their situation were taking their distance from. Look, Mike, whatever else, these two guys aren't stupid."

Mike opened his eyes again, still keeping them on the ceiling. "No, apparently not. And, of course, once they got here they wouldn't have had any trouble getting work. In fact, if they're as literate and multilingual as it sounds, they probably did pretty well."

"They loved the place," said Harry. "Believe it or not, what really charmed them the most was our libraries. They both love to read. And, in North's case, I think he loves movies even more."

Quentin Underwood grunted. "They still sound like scoundrels to me."

Harry made a little wiggling gesture with his hands. "Yes and no. I sure wouldn't nominate either of them for the Mr. Morality contest, but they're really not that bad, Quentin. Sure as hell not compared to most longtime mercenary soldiers. The Croat raid last year even instilled in them a mild sort of patriotism, I guess you could call it. Mind you, I think they were mostly determined to keep the libraries intact."

Again, he shifted in his seat. "After the attack, they also decided to go back to the mercenary business. That was because—"

Mike brought his eyes down from the ceiling. "Yeah, I understand. After the Croat raid we relaxed our earlier restrictions on letting mercenary companies operate in our area, as long as they had our seal of approval. Did they ever consider just joining the regular army?"

Harry glanced over at Jackson. "Mike, joining the army was never really an option. And it's just as well, frankly. Either one of them, much less both together, would have sent even Frank into orbit."

"They have a good reputation, professionally speaking," said General Jackson. "I agree with Harry that I wouldn't have wanted to touch them in the regular army. But we've used them for a few courier runs and, mostly, for providing protection for supply trains when our own people were stretched too thin. They always did the job, no complaints or problems, and at reasonable rates. I also hear they do guard duty on local properties and run protection for a few merchant caravans in and out of CPE territory as well. They haven't lost a single one far as I know, and we have a few less highwaymen and bandits to deal with thanks to them." He grimaced slightly. "Of course, they're one step removed from bandits themselves, but all experience shows them to be loyal—as long as they get paid."

"All right," said Stearns, massaging his head. "Harry, do you think they can hack it?"

"Well, Mike, they've been fighting wars since they were in their teens and have more practical experience than everyone in this room combined. In their own way, they're pretty good." He hesitated a moment. "Maybe a bit rambunctious."

"Damn good cardplayers, if nothing else," said Frank.

Mike looked him, surprised. "When did you start playing cards?"

Jackson shrugged. "I don't. But Henry Dreeson says they're damn good. He's played cards with them several times at the Gardens."

"Where?" asked Underwood, coming alert. "In the main rooms or—"

Jackson grinned. "Quentin, when does Henry *ever* play cards in the front rooms?"

There was a moment of silence. To everyone's surprise, once Grantville eventually bowed to reality after the Ring of Fire and the enormous influx of immigrants and lifted its up-time restrictions on gambling, the town's elderly mayor had been revealed as a card shark. He'd become something of a legend in the area's gambling circles. If North and Donovan were able to keep up with him in the back rooms of the Gardens devoted to serious card playing . . .

Stearns came to a decision. "All right, Harry, bring 'em in. If I remember right, Donovan handles most of the business side of things, so I'll talk to him about the contract. In the meantime, I want you to take our guest out to their place and see if he approves. And I want you to personally oversee as much as you can."

Harry nodded, got up, and left. "Now," said Mike, "let's move on to the next item on the agenda."

The cabinet meeting eventually broke up. Mike stayed at his chair, frowning a little.

"Becky's situation bothering you again, Mike?" asked Ed Piazza, when they were alone in the room. He knew Stearns was worried about his wife, trapped in the siege of Amsterdam.

Mike shrugged. "Yeah, sure, it always does these days. At the moment, though, that's not what I'm fretting about. It's what Harry said, at the end there."

"What? His recommendation of North and Donovan?"

"Not that so much. I agree they're probably the best fit we have for this peculiar problem, much as I hate to admit it. But it's how he described them at the end. 'Maybe a bit rambunctious.'"

Piazza smiled ruefully. "Coming from Harry, that's a little rich."

"Still that's not what's eating at me. It's that he *hesitated* before he said it."

Piazza's smile went away. "Oh, Christ."

The Friday night game was perennially held at nine P.M. every Friday in a backroom of the Thuringen Gardens. The game could very well go on all weekend, with small fortunes being won and lost. Of course the same players wouldn't necessarily keep at it all weekend. Busting out or cashing out, they would quickly be replaced by another eager sheep waiting to be fleeced.

"One card," said North as he discarded onto the felt. "And I still say he was and will be a lunatic."

"Two cards," said Donovan when the deal came to him. "He is one of the finest Irish writers that ever lived or will live."

The other players received their cards, sharing knowing looks with their fellows on what was to commence, almost as much a tradition as the game itself.

"James Augustine Aloysius Joyce," said North, annunciating the first syllables like he was giving orders on the battlefield. "The only reason you like him is because you share a name."

"That is not true."

"At age twenty-four he renounced his Roman Catholicism and left Ireland forever. Yet 'history' considers him a champion of those two groups. Bet twenty dollars."

"Call," said Henry Sims, tossing a few chips into the center. "I have to agree with Mr. North here. I had to read *Ulysses* in college, a terrible experience."

"See? Our shire's senior dentist and a man of learning agrees."

"Call," said Donovan, biting his tongue.

"And his punctuation was atrocious," continued North. "Raise twenty."

"Fold," said Sims.

"Fold," said Henry Dreeson.

"He was an artist," said Donovan.

North sniffed. "He was a lazy little git who could not be bothered to learn the English language, raise fifteen."

"I know what you are trying to do." Donovan tossed more chips into the center. "Call."

"Do you now?"

"You are trying to anger me, to involve emotion in the game, to get me to bet heavily so that you can 'clean me out.'"

"When I read *Finnegan's Wake*, I wanted to put a bullet in my brain and have one of my own. 'Finn, again! Take. Bussoftlhee, mememormee! Till thousendsthee. Lps. The keys to. Given! A way a lone a last a loved a long the'—with no period at the end of the novel, I might add."

"He was making a point."

"No, the point is, he did *not* make a point. Raise twenty."

"That is a fine way to end a masterpiece, and if you did not have the intellect of a flea you would understand. Call. It will not work this time because I know you're bluffing."

"Am I now?" asked North condescendingly.

"Yes." Donovan smirked. "You are shuffling your cards back and forth. It is your tell. Call and raise twenty. We have reached the table limit, I believe."

"I leave aside that you have just proved how amateur a player you are by telling me that. There is one thing that you forgot, old friend." North pushed most of his remaining chips into the center. "I knew you recognized that tell three hands back. The one I lost for a whole five dollars. I used it this time to draw you in. The rant on James Joyce just came from the heart. Full house, ladies over threes."

"Damn!" Donovan threw his three jacks down on the table in disgust.

North laughed as he reached out to scoop up his winnings.

"Ahem!" A female voice intruded. North turned to Veronica Dreeson, who had constantly, and without saying a word, kept in the game, pushing forward chips to the end. North had disregarded her as a nonentity since she was very new to the game.

"I am not sure about four fives," said Veronica sweetly, "but ace is high card, yes?"

"Well . . ." North sat back in his chair and took out a cigar. "That's embarrassing."

"You won, honey, you can pick up the chips now," said the mayor of Grantville to his wife.

The German matron grabbed the chips just a shade too quickly for her naiveté to be anything but an act.

"Ha!" exclaimed Donovan. "The great and powerful Thomas North of Kirtling. Fleeced by a tough old German biddy!"

"Quiet," growled North, as he counted up his few remaining chips, a pile significantly shorter than when he walked in this night.

"Nobleman, warrior and son of warriors, captain of mercenaries, captain of industry. What do you have to say now?" sneered Donovan.

"Saint Patrick was an Englishman," replied North.

"Oh, burn in hell, heretic scum!" screamed Donovan in disgust at the disgustingly true statement. He jumped up from his chair and slapped the cigar out of North's mouth.

"Kiss my arse, papist dog! Those are fifty florins a box!"

North threw the first punch. Within seconds, he and Donovan were on the floor doing their best to knock each other senseless. Good friends though they were, poker was as cantankerous a subject between them as literature.

"Should we, um . . . try to halt the counter-reformation?" asked Dr. Nichols, as he stepped uncertainly into the room and around the combatants to buy in for the game.

"Probably," mused Henry Dreeson. "I'm sure it's listed in my civic duties as mayor somewhere. On the other hand . . . Watch the elbow, Liam!"

Smack!

"That one looked like it hurt a bit," said Henry Dreeson, wincing and turning to his wife. "Dear, maybe you shouldn't be here. Ruffians."

"Why not? Is good fight," replied Veronica. "Twenty dollars on heretic scum."

"Done," said Nichols. "Liam's got fifty pounds on him."

Thud!

Smack!

"You suck!" shouted North.

"It occurs to me that we should ask them to take it outside," said Dreeson. "No need to deprive the rest of the town of this show." Like most of the up-timers in the new booming Grantville, the town's mayor had developed a blasé attitude toward tavern brawls as long as weapons weren't used.

"Very civic-minded of you," commented Sims approvingly.

At this point Donovan got far enough disentangled to give his partner a good right hook. North was dazed from the blow, and Donovan, not really intending to do serious damage in what was basically a nice bar fight between friends, let him clear his head. North was going about it in a funny way, though. He was moving his tongue around inside his mouth and making all sorts of strange faces. Donovan was about to ask what was going on when North spit out a small object in the general direction of the card table. It landed next to Henry G. Sims, D.D.S.

"Is that my incisor?" North asked the dentist curiously.

"Um." Sims gave the object in question a quick, expert examination. "Yes, it is, Tom."

"Do you . . ." North turned ominously toward Donovan. ". . . have any idea what I had to go through to have that put in the last time? At the very least you should know what it cost!"

"Now, please, Tom, it was just a bit of sport. No need to get angry. Keep your temper."

"My temper . . ." North belted Donovan with a powerful uppercut, knocking the man unconscious to the floor. ". . . is kept right where it belongs."

"That's the one good thing about being dentists and doctors in a boomtown," said Nichols, as he handed over his lost twenty dollars.

"It's a growth industry," Sims agreed.

Driving took on an entirely different meaning when it was a horse that had to be driven instead of an automobile. A horse in many cases is smarter than a man and it required little steering to find its way back to the stable. The difficulty arose however when the passenger kept falling off the horse, seatbelts being impractical additions. North, not one to let his good mood be dampened, picked up his friend, dragged him back on top of his horse, remounted his own and began leading them both back to the farm.

"Soldier, oh soldier!" North began his song.

> A-coming from the plain
> He courted a lady for honor and for fame
> Her beauty shone so bright
> That it never could be told
> She always loved the soldier
> Because he was so bold.
> Fa la la la, fa la la la
>
> Soldier, oh soldier,
> It's I would be your bride,
> But I fear of my father
> Some danger might betide.
> Then he pulled out sword and pistol
> And hung them by his side
> Swore he would be married,
> No matter what betide.
> Fa la la la, fa la la la
>
> Then he took her to the parson,
> And, of course, home again
> There they met her father
> And seven armed men.
> Let us fly, said the lady,
> I fear we shall be slain
> Take my hand, said the soldier,
> And never fear again.
> Fa la la la, fa la la la

Then he pulled out sword and pistol,
And caused them to rattle,
The lady held the horse
While the soldier fought in battle.
Hold your hand, said the old man,
Do not be so bold.
You shall have my daughter
And a thousand pounds of gold.
Fa la la la, fa la la la

Fight on! said the lady,
The portion is too small!
Hold your hand, said the old man,
And you shall have it all.
Then he took them right straight home
And he called them son and dear
Not because he loved them,
But only through fear.
Fa la la la, fa la la la la!"

The "Bold Soldier" had carried North to his corporate headquarters and the sound of his approach drew little attention. It being Friday night in Grantville, one or both of the proprietors of the Albernian Mercenary Company usually arrived half in the bag. North gave his horse to the night groom. Then he walked over to unceremoniously push his colleague off his horse before giving the reins of Donovan's mare to the groom as well.

Still tonguing the gap in his only recently repaired teeth, North had no inclination to drag Donovan into his bed and was quite content to let him sleep in the stable. He was halfway to the house, passing the scattered campfires of his men, when he noticed an unusual sight in the doorway.

North considered himself a man of the world. He had traveled extensively, and seen many things and many peoples. Never before, though, had he laid eyes on the manner of man in front of him. Even in the poorly lit evening it was apparent he wasn't European. Nor was he dark enough to be a Numidian.

His apparel was also extremely foreign. It was in stark contrast to the heavy northern European clothes. It provided scant protection from the chills of autumn, though the man didn't seem to mind.

Judging from the stern look on his face and the easy manner in which he rested his hand on his sword, North doubted the man would mind taking on all the armies of hell and all the angels of heaven besides. Immediately North placed the stranger in his carefully selected group of people he had no intention of aggravating. Despite his occasional brawling, he was really quite conservative when mortal peril was evident.

That peril was even more evident by the presence of Captain Harry Lefferts. Not so much the man himself. North knew him well enough not to be afraid of the good captain on general principles, like a number of other down-timers were. What *did* worry him was the presence of a very wicked grin on Harry's face.

"I am Salim," said the stranger in exotically accented English, when North approached. "Personal servant and *sowar* to the Subadar, Baram Khan, ambassador-at-large from Shah Jahan."

"But of course you are," said North, taking in the long title along with the exotic guest.

"I would speak with Donovan. This one told he is one I arrange mercenary contacts with. Men here told us he would come soon."

"Mr. Donovan is . . . unavailable at the moment. My name is Captain Thomas North. I am his partner and I lead the company's operations. Please—step into my office." North waved graciously toward the door.

3

It began long ago and far away. But the story was not really that strange to North for its beginning. A little under two years ago the town of Grantville flashed upon the world stage, literally. It took months for this news to filter to the major population centers of Europe, but filter it did. And soon enough, representatives, diplomats, scientists, theologians, and—especially—adventurers of every kind came rushing to the future town of Americans. But while Europe might have considered itself the center of the world, it was not the world. Indeed no empire in Europe could claim the title of greatest, not even Spain or France.

It was the Muslim Mughal Empire of northern India that probably held that title, although the Ottoman Turks and Ming Chinese might have disputed the point. At times the Mughal emperor in Agra had more cavalrymen under arms than the entire population of some European principalities. India's culture was illustrious and ancient. The Mughal military was a mighty force, possessing gunpowder in most cases much before Europeans. Indeed, at times, most of Europe's supply of saltpeter needed to be imported from Mughal territory.

There was great wealth there, also, in specie and jewelry—but much more importantly, there was trade. The Greeks, the Romans, the Arabs, they all came. India had always known traders from the west, and paid them little mind. And then the Portuguese arrived in 1498, and this time it was different. India now became a much more integral part of the world economy and entire regions depended upon the export and import of goods to Europe for their survival. For a hundred years the Portuguese held a monopoly on Indian trade and fabulous wealth flooded into the coffers of Lisbon. Soon enough, though, the other powers of Europe were not content to let Portugal enjoy her monopoly. The Dutch and English, among others, began sending trading missions to treat with Mughal ports.

To maintain their trading monopoly, the Portuguese fought the other Europeans wherever encountered. And, in typical Portuguese fashion, attacked Mughal shipping and installations as well, in a blundering attempt to force the Mughals to expel the other European trading companies. The Mughal emperors were understandably displeased with the Portuguese arrogance, and they flung open their ports to their enemy's enemies. Soon enough, the Portuguese were outcompeted by the shifty northern European merchants and facing *unfriendly* Mughals in India, Portuguese trade subsequently dwindled to a pittance.

This by no means precluded further infighting between the English and Dutch merchants, coreligionists though they may have been. Whole fleets were lost to "privateers" or even flagged vessels in combat with each other. Trade was money and money was power, a commodity that all wished to hold a monopoly on. And they tried any and all means to curry favor with the Mughal rulers.

One of those means was to tell tales of the astounding new occurrence in central Germany and to provide a thumbnail sketch of its wonders.

Shah Jahan was no fool. Already wary of the European interlopers' maritime superiority, he was not content to allow them unilateral access to sciences from the future. And especially not to allow them to feed his people that information on *their* terms, and to *their* benefit. So, eight months earlier, he had dispatched one of his myriad relations on an expedition west in order to establish contact with Grantville on his own terms. Salim had been posted to the expedition as he had had dealings with the English factory at Surat and was one of the few Mughals who spoke their language. Under the guise of the hajj, Baram Khan and his throng of servants had ventured to Mecca. But instead of returning home, he had gone forward to Cairo. A Venetian galley had then been hired to carry them across the Mediterranean to the European mainland.

All through the expedition, the emperor's gold and reputation had smoothed the way. Hiring local interpreters, guides, and transportation was easy. Gold was always a universal language and there were local potentates aplenty willing to show the emperor's representative hospitality.

Shortly after entering the Alps, however, the hospitality had turned excessive. In an isolated manor near the city of Innsbruck, every attempt to leave the hospitality of their Austrian hosts had been shuffled aside. There was always another social event they insisted Baram Khan needed to attend. Then the horses went lame, the provisions sour.

Soon enough, Baram Khan attempted to force the issue and found that he was under virtual house arrest. The eighty men in the expedition made too large a force to slip away during the night—but one man might, and Salim was chosen. A veteran of several wars in the Deccan, he knew how to take care of himself.

His German was nonexistent, and his English practically useless in that region. After a week of effort all he had accomplished was to send a message to a Mughal agent in Cairo informing him of the situation, which had a slim chance of actually arriving and slimmer still of traveling all the way to the emperor. His only option was to continue on with his master's assignment as best as possible, and bring whatever he could back home. He attached himself to a merchant's caravan and after many days of travel arrived in Grantville.

His arrival in Grantville was a surprising situation, to say the least. He was welcomed, of course, but his problem was not something that could be solved with a flick of up-time technology like others could. No . . . this was something that required old fashioned down-time skullduggery, which had led him to the Albernian Mercenary Company.

*   *   *

"So. Let me sum up the situation, if I may," said North, sipping some imported Ottoman coffee in his office. "You want me to take my company, an extremely small one by the measure of our day, across more than two hundred miles of war-torn Europe. Some of it torn up by a side who doesn't like my side very much, nor apparently yours either. To rescue an Indiaman from forces unknown. You do not know how many soldiers the enemy has, what type of incarceration your master is held by—indeed, you do not even know if he is held at all by this point. He might well be rotting in a grave. And if this rescue *is* done, I have no more assurance that I will be paid my quite substantial payment, aside from the word of a servant."

"Yes," Salim replied blandly.

"That's not strictly true," Lefferts interjected. "In the interests of diplomacy, Mike has agreed to underwrite this expedition at cost. So anything you get out of the Mughals at the end, Tom, will be pure gravy. He wants to talk to you guys about it in the morning."

"Well, that's a little bit better. Still . . . basically, the mission is: storm the castle; save the king."

"He is not king," said Salim. "But the rest, yes."

"Riiight . . ." North hesitated for a moment while he contemplated. He contemplated only long enough to appraise the cash value of the expensive adornments the Mughal wore like so many glass beads.

"I like this one," he said cheerfully, thumping his hand on the desk. "We are going to have *so* much fun."

"Ten thousand—all in advance," said North the next morning, in Stearns' office. Ed Piazza and Frank Jackson were present in the room also.

"Did you expect me to say, 'Ten thousand! We can almost buy our own ship for that!' " The President grinned, fully understanding the reference.

"Well, I had to try. Fine then, make me an offer I can't refuse."

"Spend whatever you need on whatever you need—within reason—to provision yourselves. Supply receipts to the department of state along with appropriate wage slips. It should be recouped if this is successful. Salim told me the Mughal expedition was more than adequately financed. As far as profit goes, you can present a separate bill to the ambassador once he is safely in Grantville."

"More paperwork." North shook his head, sighing.

Stearns chuckled. "I didn't peg you as the corporate . . . executive type. More of a hands-on kind of guy."

"Which reminds me, I shall require guns. Up-time ones, and as much ammunition as you can spare. We, ah, have had a bit of trouble acquiring enough on our own. This bold endeavor has a much better chance of success if we have a few force multipliers."

Stearns turned to Jackson. "Frank?"

"Do your guys know how to *use* them?" asked General Jackson.

"I said we had difficulty obtaining *enough*, not any. I have seen to it that enough of my men are fully cross-trained on all the ones we have acquired. And many served in your army at one time."

"I can probably scrounge up enough for a platoon. Presupposing, of course, that we get them back."

"Of course you will!" replied North indignantly. "Do I look like a scoundrel?"

"Yes."

"Yes."

"Yes."

"Tom, have I mentioned today that you seem to be dafter than usual," said Donovan, as the two made preparations later that day.

"Once or twice a minute since you woke up this morning."

"I—"

"Time enough for ranting later, old friend," North interrupted. "Now we need to be about preparations, we need to leave as soon as possible. Winter is coming, as you constantly remind me. How many men do we have for assignment, leaving aside those new 'recruits'?"

"We still have most of the fool Von Fellenburg's finest," Liam replied, not happy at the thought.

When the two had established their mercenary company, they had ample funds but that alone was not enough to draw enough men to their flag. They had something of a name in the mercenary community, and a few came to the service of the Albernian Mercenary Company. But the bulk of the initial forces were from the fool Von Fellenburg's Finest, a rather pretentious nickname the two had given a Swiss mercenary company whose captain was killed several weeks after the two began recruitment. Whether his death was due to malice or a "training accident" had yet to be proven conclusively. He had not been an officer who was well liked by his men. Regardless of that, though, the stout Swiss mercenaries had reorganized themselves and required a new one, likeable or not. But they were soldiers all, not officers, and were quite willing to let others make key decisions for them so long as the pay came on time. So North had folded about seventy of them into the company, much to Donovan's derision at the inclusion of so many Calvinists.

"We *have* fully cross trained them on the new weapons haven't we?" asked North trying vainly to find the appropriate file in his cabinet.

"Yes," said Donovan, handing it over.

"Fine, then." North grabbed it. "We will take the first five squads. If fifty men cannot handle this, the entire company couldn't. Do we have enough horses?"

"Barely. They are rather scarce lately."

"Well, it's the war, you know. Ammunition?"

"Powder and two-hundred shot for each musket. The special ammunition is what presents difficulty."

"We'll take all they gave us. We'll need all the firepower we can acquire. But you are right, it doesn't seem to be enough. What about alternative supplies?"

"I am working on that, the usual channels along with all the usual unusual ones. But it doesn't look good, certainly not before we leave."

"Well it can't be helped . . . or can it? Ha! Look what is coming our way." North pointed out the office window into the courtyard.

"Mother Mary, not him again," said Donovan in disgust as he turned to see out the window.

"Him" was the duo's watcher, the "military liaison" who had been saddled upon them when their operations began, as the necessary prerequisite of operating in the CPE. Private armed forces were something the government was concerned about. Lieutenant Lawrence Quinn, veteran of the West Virginia National Guard, was a nice enough human being when he wasn't on the job. But judging from his face, he was not here on a social call.

The American curtly nodded to them both as he came in the door. "Hello, North, Donovan."

"Lieutenant Larry! Just the man we have been waiting to see." North got up to shake the American's hand furiously before directing him to a comfortable leather chair across the desk from him.

"Another two solders have reported their up-time weapons and ammunition stolen," said Quinn, cutting right to business.

"Those German brutes will sell their soul for another mug of beer."

North shook his head sadly. "It's *terrible.*"

"You wouldn't happen to know anything about those black-market guns, would you, Tom? General Jackson mentioned to me today that you had acquired some."

"Not a thing, sorry to say. But it's fortunate that you came here. It turns out we need a significant supply of .308 caliber bullets."

"Would those bullets be for the rifles I see that pair of troopers are practicing with over there?" said the American, with a wave toward the firing range. "Oddly enough, the same make of rifles reported stolen."

"Of course not!"

"Do we look like black marketers to you?" asked Donovan, scowling.

"I won't tell you what you look like to me, officers and gentlemen and all that." Quinn got up from his chair. "Don't go anywhere."

"Where would we go? We love it here!" protested North, as he watched the lieutenant leave the room. "You filed off the serial numbers I hope?" North asked quietly, leaning close to Donovan.

"I cannot recall. My memory has been rather spotty today . . . for some reason."

"That's a pity."

The bulk of the company's gunpowder weaponry were newly manufactured flintlock muskets, which was already a significant jump ahead of any other contemporary weaponry the mercenaries might face. But North and Donovan had also engaged, through a variety of means, to acquire some up-time weaponry.

Quinn shouldn't have been on their case quite so much, since the sum total of up-time weaponry the pair had pilfered wouldn't have filled a Grantville native's gun cabinet. But ever since losing half a month's pay to North one Friday night, the lieutenant had been not too figuratively grinding his teeth at the two.

Keeping in character after several minutes' inspection, the American returned with an unpleasant look on his face. "You know, I can probably dig up the original up-timer owners to identify the stolen merchandise," Quinn announced.

"And what if you could? We did not know we were dealing in *stolen* goods. We purchased them from a reputable dealer. What was his name, Liam?"

"Um . . . Hans."

"A reputable dealer named Umhans. Sadly, I believe he has since left for Magdeburg."

"If you run quickly you can catch him," Donovan offered.

"I'm not going anywhere," said Quinn firmly. "I see you're loading up the wagons. It looks to be a big deployment."

"We are going to Innsbruck, rescue mission."

"Hapsburg territory, behind enemy lines," Quinn elaborated.

"Which is why we need those bullets so badly, my friend," said North. "You are our military liaison, so *liaise.*"

"The Mughal thing? Every reputable mercenary company in the area would have turned that contract down. I'm not at all surprised you took it. Oh, hell, I'll see if I can dig up a case here or there."

"Bless you, lad," said Donovan.

Quinn shrugged. "I have to go with you on this one. Lefferts and later Jackson both had me under the grill most of the morning. Ordered me to liaise a little more personally. You two could get into all sorts of messes without supervision. And we do not need an international incident right now."

North leaned back and eyed his partner. "Does not his concern for us lowly down-timers give you a warm feeling in the chest, Liam?"

"Deep down in the cockles, Tom," Donovan agreed. "We should be leaving in two days, so make whatever preparations you need."

"I'll be here," said the American, and then he exited the building once more.

"I do believe that boy thinks this is going to be pleasant," said Donovan.

"He scolded and scowled too much," North agreed. "He *wanted* to come along. Shocking, really. An officer and gentlemen by act of Congress abusing his own position just so that he can go out and have some fun."

"The youth today," said Donovan, shaking his head at a man who couldn't have been two years younger than him.

"Well. Weapons, ammunition, food and water, tents and horses, and myriad other munitions."

"All we need now is a plan."

"Don't worry, I have a plan."

"Oh, a plan has he?" asked Donovan, rolling his eyes.

"Oh, it's a good plan. But first, I need money, so hand over the key."

Donovan gave over the key to the gun safe the Irishman had acquired to act as the company's vault. Once he had it open, North sifted through the dollars, guilders, pounds, livres, and florins, but hesitated over a package on the second shelf.

"Feminine hygiene product? What the bloody hell is this doing in there?"

"It's a currency," said Donovan defensively. "Worth more than its weight in gold. And what do you need the money for, anyway?"

"Well, when we get there we will need to improvise. But I imagine we will need a distraction, and or a large hole put in a large wall. So I am going out to obtain some explosives."

"We are not talking about a few guns, Tom. You can not just steal explosives."

North took a handful of gold coins, weighed them in his hands, thought better of it, and added a few more. "Of course not. That's why I need the money." North grinned as he shut the safe's door.

"You have a very nasty look on your face, Liam."

"I don't like this one, Tom, for all the risks." Donovan shook his head. "Why are we doing this?"

"Money."

"We have money."

"Lots of money," North clarified.

Donovan sighed loudly. "Sometimes I wonder about Englishmen."

"Ha! Liam, do you know why Englishmen exclaim 'Mother of God' during moments of particular awe?"

"I assume it's out of respect for the virgin."

"Ridiculous. Are we wretched papists? No, no. The *Madre de Deus* was a Portuguese carrack captured off the Azores one fine summer day in 1592, by a six-ship squadron under the command of Sir John Burrough. When she was brought into Dartmouth harbor she was three times the size of anything an Englishman had ever known. Sixteen hundred tons. In her belly were wonders beyond description but I will try to enumerate them for you. Gold, silver, pearls, amber, jewelry, diamonds, tapestries, bolts of calico, four hundred and twenty-five tons of pepper, forty-five tons of cloves, thirty-five tons of cinnamon, cochineal, mace, nutmeg, benjamin, ebony. Every merchant, thief, jeweler, fisherman, and man jack within fifty miles ran for Dartmouth harbor to help out in the looting. The queen of course wanted her share and many of those adventurous looters lost their heads for their impertinence. One hundred and fifty thousand pounds was eventually garnered for the crown but the entire ship was conservatively estimated to be worth one million pounds. Near enough the sum of the exchequer for 1592. One ship . . . and it equaled all the treasury could spend in that year.

"*Very* shortly thereafter, English merchants began expeditions to the source of this wealth. India, and the spice islands further afield. And in 1600 Elizabeth chartered the East India Company, and every year those bastards lucky enough to have bought stock get richer off trade beyond even our wildest dreams. Regardless of whether we get paid or not after this, I believe having a favor owed by the Mughal emperor's representative is a very valuable thing."

"One million pounds," Donovan said in awe.

"One ship."

"I suddenly feel much better about this, Tom."

"I thought you might."

After an hour's ride, the two entered a small farm on the other side of Grantville. It was nowhere as extensive as their own, merely an isolated ramshackle residence away from the city. But the purpose of that isolation was remarkably similar. The owner didn't want to upset the delicate sensibilities of the neighbors. Because the former postal worker was now in the business of making bombs.

While the place seemed busy enough, with many minions scurrying about, a man in authority was not readily apparent. North dismounted from his horse and took out a cigar for the wait. Tobacco had been readily available to Englishmen since Raleigh; most, however, smoked it in pipes or used it as snuff. During his sojourn on the Continent, North had acquired a taste for rolled cigars in the Spanish fashion.

"That," said an American voice, "is a *very* bad idea."

North turned around to see a tall and girthy silver-haired American with a stolid, unpleasant look on his face.

"So said King James, my dear Garland Alcom. But he is dead and I am not. So I will enjoy my good cigar."

"I meant that's a bad idea because we're dealing with items that get temperamental around flame. So put that out, you stupid limey. Before you blow us to the moon."

"Those things will kill you, you know," said Donovan with a smirk.

A bit hastily, North extinguished his vice. "This dynamite of yours. We require some."

"And we'll need someone to help us," Donovan added.

"What are *you* doing for the next few months?" asked North.

"I'm busy. And you have to pay for the dynamite."

"Well, of course we will pay you. We are not thieves, after all." North tossed a substantial bag of gold into Alcom's hands.

"Lately," muttered Donovan under his voice, remembering the source of the gold. "That still leaves the other matter."

"I've got a few Germans I trust."

"No up-timers?" North asked with some alarm.

"It's the war, you know." Alcom led the two toward the shack.

"I don't have near enough to mass produce," said Alcom, "but I get enough to put out a steady supply for a few people I trust. Which begs the question: how did you find out?"

"For a people that enjoy *usquebaugh* so much there are some of you who cannot handle alcohol well. How many sticks have you?" asked Donovan.

"All told, about four cases of twenty, carefully wrapped and settled in sawdust."

"And the explosives expert?" North asked.

"I wouldn't call any of these guys *experts*. But they know how to transport it, and how to insert a blasting cap."

"Very well then, let's see them," said North.

Only five men were assembled for inspection, and like most private industries in and around a Grantville at war, were made up of the very young and very old. Two boys in their apprenticeships, two gnarled old men, and a lone strongman in his midthirties. At first, North was going to choose him automatically as the man most fit, but then he took a long look at the fair-haired man. While he was a fine specimen of strength, North had to wonder for what reason he was not grabbed up by the army or some other group. And what was most telling was the lack of any sort of mark or wound on him. A man that had never made mistakes or fought in battle does not have anything to learn from. In the end North turned to a gray-haired Teutonic fellow in his midfifties standing with his hands behind his back.

"Do you speak English?"

"*Ja,*" the man replied.

"Why do you work with dynamite?"

"To feed *mein kinder.*"

"You can feed them just as well doing something considerably safer. Why do you *really* work with dynamite?"

"God create world, someday God destroy world. I help. Very devout."

North smiled crookedly. "How many fingers do you have?"

"Nine." The German held up his hands to prove it.

"Oh, I like him," said North, turning to his partner.

"What ever happened to the idea of buying American?" asked Donovan derisively. "Quality craftsmanship and all that?"

"Don't be prejudiced, Liam."

"Fine." Donovan sighed, giving in to the inevitable. "I like him too."

4

The contingent of the Albernian Mercenary Company left soon enough for Innsbruck with little fanfare and less notice. The company made good way until reaching the Alps, but then it was a slog before they were able to reach the outlying regions of Innsbruck. Slipping the company through hostile territory was not unduly difficult. It was an age before nation-states and protected borders with major internal policing. The only thing that could have threatened them was a significant concentration of troops, and such armies were blundering affairs that were easy to avoid.

Unfortunately, that did not mean they could be avoided entirely. Fifty horsemen with only four wagons drew attention. The number of troops could mean one of two things. First, that it was a small but extremely valuable merchant shipment. Or, second, that it was the supply train of a military expedition. Either likelihood meant that scouts were dispatched to ascertain the group's identity and purpose before their long journey was over. No significant force could really be assembled quickly enough to stop them, but North was not at all surprised to wake up one morning to his picket's cry of alarm.

Out of his pallet in a flash, North armed himself with saber and 9mm pistol. He checked his weapon, grabbed his eyeglass, and then made way for a good vantage point. Donovan, Quinn, and Salim soon joined him and they all looked at the assembled host.

The situation was not *too* desperate. Only about a hundred men were evident, which meant two hundred probably opposed them. No artillery; and while some of the infantry carried matchlocks, most were pikemen. Probably some local lord's swift and reckless response.

"Riders approaching," said Donovan, as he looked through his own binoculars. "Looks like a parley . . . God save Ireland! Look at the flag."

Most fighting forces in Europe had a flag to rally behind and follow into battle, even most mercenary companies. The Albernian Company's own was, like its founders, a mix, showing the English Saint George's flag and the Irish flag of Saint Patrick with a certain colorful Latin phrase that was just as well left untranslated. The approaching force had its own standard, and it was one well known to North.

"Steiner," North muttered. "Why did God have to send us Steiner? What did we ever do to God?"

Quinn chimed in. "Who is this Steiner guy?"

"One of the better mercenary commanders Europe has produced lately." North's answer was totally drained of humor.

"Friend of yours?" asked Quinn.

"Once," North replied. "No longer."

With a minimum of preparation, North mounted Ariner and, along with Donovan, Quinn, and John Hastings, sergeant of the company, he rode out to meet his foe. It was possible Steiner did not know the nature of their mission and North thought it best Salim should be left behind on the off chance his presence could be kept a secret. When they reached an approximate midpoint, North dismounted and took out a slender green bag from his saddle. From it, he removed an up-time item that had caught his fancy some months before. It was a green cloth folding chair, lightweight and easily transportable. It was meant for hunting, camping, or some up-timer activity called "tailgating." North sat down on the device—called, ironically enough, a "captain's chair"—and rested his arms on the armrests while leaning back with all the majesty he could muster. Despite the loss of his valuable up-time sunglasses earlier in the year, North was the epitome of cool.

When Steiner arrived, North gave him a small nod, like any proper sprig of the nobility holding court. "Captain Steiner, so good to see you again. How have you been?"

"Captain North," Steiner nodded. Even with the advantage of the imperious height of his horse, he was not quite achieving the same effect of magnificent indifference North was accomplishing. "I have been doing very well, thank you. Better than you, from the looks of things. How many men have you in your company, North? Fifty?"

"At present? That sounds about right."

"Impressive enough . . . for a patrol. I have four hundred here."

"You have *two* hundred here, only some of which are equipped with firearms. And no artillery."

"That will be here shortly."

"*That* is a matter of opinion, one which I do not hold."

"You will not reach Innsbruck or the Mughal," said Steiner casually, showing North that he knew of the other's destination and purpose. "My employers will not allow that."

"And who are your employers?"

Steiner shrugged. "Men with money, who else?"

North was silent, taking a moment to measure his opponents from up close. As always, Steiner had chosen good men for his lieutenants. All were obviously veterans, from the manner they held themselves. They outnumbered him four to one and had the advantage of being on their home territory. They were close to supply and shelter, while North's own wagons were already more than half empty. There was one advantage North held, though. He got up from his captain's chair, folded it, and returned it to its bag, tightening the drawstrings shut. When he reached his horse he retrieved a similar bag with *captain's chair* written on it and turned to Steiner.

"You know where I have spent my last few years, Steiner?" asked North.

"Among witches and wizards, I have heard."

"That's right," said North. "They are witches and wizards, indeed, and they have wonders beyond your dreams. This is one of them, a silly little thing that they didn't even make themselves, but some poor peasant in Cathay did. But you see the quality, the workmanship— here, feel how light it is. Think of its uses on campaign. If they put so much effort into something as silly as this, think of what they have done to their weapons? We here do not have all their secrets, nor even a tenth measure. But we have enough to destroy your force ten times over. You were my friend once and I owe you for your tutelage. So take this gift from me, Steiner, and please do not come across this field."

"I will thank you for the gift." Steiner leaned down from his horse and took the thing, then handed it to one of his lieutenants. "Along with everything else from your dead bodies."

"Not even going to ask me to retreat the field?" North's tone seemed genuinely aggrieved. "You are just going to slaughter me?"

"Yes."

"Why? We have no women, and we travel light. No loot worth talking about."

"This parley is over!" said Steiner harshly. He turned his horse around and trotted back to his own forces.

"Well, that went well," said Quinn sarcastically. Then, seeing Donovan extract a bundle from his saddlebags, he squinted. "Where the hell did you get that?!"

"Around," said North, as he lit one of his cigars. "Tell me, Lieutenant Larry, does your watch still work?"

"Yes," replied the American, uncertainly looking at his wrist.

"Good." North leaned over with his lit cigar. "Would you be so kind as to start your stopwatch, then? Right . . . about . . . now." A slight fizzling noise began.

"I think we had best be going before Steiner begins his advance," said Donovan.

"I agree. That's a good plan."

"This has to be the most stupid, idiotic, harebrained plan I have ever heard," said Quinn scathingly. "It will never work! How can you know when he is going to send men across that field?"

"Hair brained?" North shook his head. " 'Okay,' I have 'picked up' a 'whole bunch' of slang, aphorisms, and American English vernaculars. But someday, someone is going to have to explain to me what hairy brains have to do with anything."

"It's from one of Shakespeare's plays," Quinn replied sullenly.

"Really?" North's eyes widened.

"Yes. *Henry VI*, I think."

"Well. That's embarrassing."

"We do not have to know exactly when Steiner will come," Donovan explained. "But we do have a fairly good idea. He has certain . . . eccentricities, when it comes to battle. All that is necessary is that the device goes off before his men cross the field and not after. And I believe we can accomplish that."

"Hastings!" bellowed North in his command voice.

"Yes, boss," Hastings replied.

"Ready the quaker gun."

"Yes, boss."

"You have . . ." North grabbed Quinn's arm to examine the time. "Two minutes and thirteen seconds. Assuming that Alcom's product is as reliable as he claims, which it almost certainly is not."

The Albernian Mercenary Company was primarily a horse-drawn affair. It didn't have capacity or, truth be told, ability for artillery. What the company did have in significant supply was sneakiness. Dragged along in one of the wagons was a section of scrap plastic pipe painted black. Hastings went about attaching the pipe to two wheels and a chassis, so that the pipe would look from a distance like a very respectable artillery piece. It was then placed in front of the company in direct line of sight of the enemy forces. In the barrel of the pipe was a witch's brew of gunpowder and inflammable materials that would produce a quite spectacular bang and a cloud of smoke. The pipe was elevated and the "gunner" made ready to fire.

Steiner's troops began their advance. It appeared the mercenary commander hadn't embellished all that much after all. A full two hundred infantrymen emerged from the timberline and were marching toward the Albernian camp with a hundred horsemen ready to chase down any of the Albernian forces that tried to run. The Albernians were dragoons; they rode horses into combat and fought while dismounted. They would stand little chance trying to escape proper cavalrymen on the wrong side of two-to-one odds.

If this didn't work . . .

"Five seconds!" shouted Quinn as he read the stopwatch on his wrist.

"Fire!" shouted Hastings. The cannon spewed forth an impressive noise and an even more impressive cloud of what appeared to be gunsmoke. Now all that was necessary was to wait for the timed fuse to ignite the dynamite, and the approaching forces would assume they were under heavy fire.

"Two seconds plus," said Quinn, looking at his watch with a mild smirk. "Four seconds plus . . . six seconds. I told you this wouldn't work."

"What the hell was that dumb German bastard's name anyway?" North asked his partner.

"I cannot remember but I am going to go over there and—"

BOOOOM!!!

"—give that splendid German fellow a mild lecture on punctuality," finished Donovan.

The explosion was impressive enough. But it detonated almost forty yards before the approaching force, doing very LITTLE, if any, damage to the enemy.

"What the hell did that accomplish except convince them our targeting is lousy?" demanded Quinn.

"Scare them a bit," said North simply. He watched the lines continue forward. "Hastings! Reload."

"Reload what? We only laid one charge when we were out there," said Quinn.

"*Timeo danaos et dona ferentis,*" North replied, keeping his eyes on the enemy.

"What?"

"Bloody ignorant Americans. Ask the Irishman. He is always glad to show off his education."

" 'I am wary of Greeks, even bearing gifts,' " Donovan supplied the translation.

"I don't understand," said Quinn.

"So much is obvious." North took out a watch of his own.

"Why did you ask for my watch if you already had one?"

"Because this one . . . was already counting down," said North, carefully examining the display. "I certainly hope Alcom's timers are better than his timed fuses."

"It had better be," said Donovan. "We only had the one."

North looking up from his watch. "Now should do, Hastings."

"Fire!"

The second explosion was a bit more timely and substantial. It appeared that the enemy lieutenant who had received his superior's gift for safekeeping would be conversing with his superiors in the afterlife. Laced with scrap ball bearings, the explosion ripped a hole in the enemy formation, killing and wounding dozens in a very close approximation of a claymore mine. It showered detritus of various forms high into the air. A fairly sizable chunk flew so far as to land a few paces away from North and his officers.

"Was that part of a horse?" Quinn asked in mild shock.

"Mother Mary, I hope not!" replied Donovan.

"Snipers engage! Musketeers! FOOORM RANKS!" shouted North. "Prepare for volley fire! Riflemen, independent fire at will. Cavalry, mount up and prepare to engage. Sergeant Hastings, take command of the detachment. Stand ready, men! He's only a Prussian!"

It was all over within ten minutes.

*   *   *

To Steiner's credit, they kept coming, which was at the root of their destruction. The twin explosions had indeed been frightening but no soldier under *his* command would shy away from the fight. And while courage was hanging by a thread, it did remain. Courage might have impressed an opposing swordsman, pikeman, or even arquebusier. But a .308 bullet fired from a distance was supremely indifferent to it. The Albernian troops with ten modern rifles picked off approaching troops one at a time. And while attrition was slow, it was adding up. By the time the enemy line approached anywhere near effective firing range, they had also been within range of the opposing line of Albernian musket men. Then they came within range of the fifteen of them who were armed with up-time pump-action shotguns, loaded with slugs. The shotgun volleys ripped into the enemy like a scythe reaping wheat, with a rate of fire far beyond anything possible with seventeenth-century weaponry. Steiner's surviving mercenaries managed only two coherent volleys before retreating the field in a mad rush trying to escape.

At that point twenty horsemen under Hastings armed with up-time handguns charged after the enemy and harried the force for well over a mile. Those armed with edged weapons were easy enough to avoid and those with firearms hadn't the time to reload—while the Albernians had multiple rounds in their weapons, with reload a second's effort.

"Well . . ." said North, after most of the fighting was over. "That was fun."

"No, that was expensive," grumbled Donovan. "We have probably just expended almost a third of the entire company's supply of up-time-compatible ammunition. We won't recover a lot of the brass on this battlefield to reload. And while we have scattered this force, we have probably not killed or wounded more than a fourth of them—with God knows how many more still out there."

"Liam, lighten up," said North. "You should think instead of the fine loot we'll obtain from Steiner's camp."

"Fucking Steiner!" exclaimed Donovan in outrage. "He used to be better than this."

"I doubt he had anything to do with it, Liam. You know how a routed army can be. Besides, this looks to have been the work of only one man, anyway." North cast a cold eye on a nearby corpse. The man's head was lying several feet away.

"Every mercenary with a horse fled the field when the outcome was apparent," said Hastings, looking at the same corpse. "The remaining foot soldiers scattered to the four winds. But not before this bastard . . ."

"Well, what can one expect?" said North. "This area is the provinces, for all intents and purposes, with knowledge of other regions slow to filter in. New discoveries are years old when arrived. Local potentates and princes of the church tell their people that Grantville and its denizens are servants of Satan and practitioners of the dark arts. Mercenaries are a normally phlegmatic group of men and not prone to hysteria. But they do have the occasional fanatic or maniac in their midst. And such a man, seeing the blows just delivered, would assume it was the devil's work."

Most of the camp followers were gone, taken away by Steiner's men as they retreated. Not all. Those that could not be taken away—or those whose man lay dead on the field—had been left behind. But one particularly pious mercenary had not been content to allow that. He'd apparently gone about ending women's lives so that they would not be tainted by the minions of Satan. North had found him severing a woman's head with a saber, screaming in one of the European languages he didn't speak. Not that he'd spent much time trying to translate, of course. North had removed the man's head a lot more efficiently than he'd been removing the woman's.

"Tom," Donovan interrupted. "We have a survivor, found in the woods. She, um . . . couldn't get far."

It was immediately obvious why. The Spanish-looking girl, once the dirt was removed, would be quite a beauty. This possibly explained her current predicament. While far from her due date, the girl was obviously pregnant.

"And what the hell are we going to do with her!" said North abrasively, to which the girl visibly flinched. Likely she didn't understand English at all. But the tone could not have eased her disposition.

"We are miles away from any village, none of which are likely to take her in or treat her well. We must take her with us," said Donovan resolutely.

"Brilliant! You bastard of a Celt! They know we are coming! We are now in hostile territory, have yet to achieve our goal, and when and if we do get the Mughal back we are going to be chased all the way back to the CPE on the wrong side of astronomical odds. And you want to weigh us down with a pregnant whore? Who is just as likely to get shot or worse as reach Grantville safely?"

"Yes, I do."

"I've already done my good deed of the day," said North, with a nod toward a steadily cooling body.

"Winter is coming."

"Oh, sod off! You're not Sancho and I'm not from La Mancha. We're mercenaries, damn you! We work for money not glory and song, you . . . you . . ." He ran out of steam.

North sighed, shaking his head. "Fine. She's small, at least. We can fit her in the back of the wagon with the rest of the dynamite." He stalked away in the direction of Ariner. "And if the stuff is as unstable as I suspect it is, let it be on your head."

"Bless you," said Donovan, smiling.

5

Turning around and abandoning the contract was never even discussed, despite the change in situation. Leaving aside the huge expenses already incurred, North had given his word and that still had some value.

Within two days the company had reached its destination and met with another surprise.

"Salim," said North crossly. "Is that well-dressed Indiaman riding in the valley by any chance the one we have been slogging through the mountains and fighting for in order to rescue from incarceration and almost certain death?"

"Yes," the Mughal replied.

"Perfect. Just perfect."

"ROOAAAR!"

"That's a *big* cat." North backpedaled away.

"Apologies, but Baram Khan does not travel anywhere without him," Salim explained. "Is a white Bengal. Very rare. Very tame, I assure you."

"Tame before or *after* he has lunch?" Quinn asked, making sure to keep his distance.

"Usually both," said Salim.

"Just tell me what has been going on during your absence," said North.

"My master wishes to speak to me alone."

"Tell him we have come a long way and I do not think it unreasonable to be part of this conversation."

"My master is . . . displeased with decision to bring you here. He wishes to speak to me alone," repeated Salim calmly.

"*Displeased . . .*" snarled North. "I lost five brave men coming here!" He sighed, reaching into his pocket for the watch. "One hour. I'll be waiting.

"Hastings scouted out the residence our Mughal was posted to," said Donovan, as he sat down next to North. "The townspeople tell us there used to be many more but there are about ten guards that we can see now. Their purpose seems more keeping the townspeople out than the Indiamen in. Hastings also managed to secure another sixty horses. You do not want to know how. But that will still not be enough to saddle every member of the Mughal expedition. Assuming we will be leaving with them at all. I left Salim and he was being bellowed at quite fiercely."

North puffed on his cigar. "Walkie-talkies are wonderful, are they not? Tell me, old friend, what is that word the Americans have for this sort of situation? I seem to have forgotten."

"Clusterfuck," Donovan supplied.

Salim approached the two. Following behind him was Baram Khan, the man for whom all this was for. "Captain North?"

"Yes?"

"My master wishes to know if this is truth." Salim handed a book to the Englishman.

It was an up-time volume, something titled *India Britannica* by a certain Geoffrey Moorhouse. It was remarkably informative. A picture of the Indian Mutiny, with sepoys being fired out of cannons for the insolence of demanding independence. Another of redcoated British lines, pristine, stalwart, crushing the motley native ones. One of a pasty-faced European couple being waited upon literally hand and foot by several dark-skinned natives. Pictures worth a hundred thousand words. The once great Indian Mughal Empire reduced to that.

"This does not have to be the truth," said North, directing his comments at Baram Khan. "It happened long ago and far way, in another universe. In this one, with proper planning, it never will."

North waited for the translation.

"You are of these people, yes?" Salim asked for his master.

"Who gave this book to you?" North replied, trying to avoid the question.

"*You* are of these people. Yes?"

"That book is not the whole truth," said North resolutely.

"It written by British learner at Oxford school."

"How could your master have read this book? Who provided the translation?"

"Grantville is city of Americans, yes, Americans vassals of British, yes? Heirs of men who did this." Salim took the book back with a sudden movement.

"Salim, I need you to translate for me. Please do the best you can," said North, frigidly extinguishing his cigar, an act he only performed during moments of great concentration.

"It is true that in a possible future my people invaded and conquered your people. As it is true your own people did the same to the Hindus under Babur and Akbar and continue now under Shah Jahan. Such is the way of things in times past, and likely for a good long while yet. I make no excuses for my people, as I am sure you make none for your own.

"I am not a servant of my king; I am a servant of myself. I work for money, that is all you are to me. Politics and ideology have nothing to do with it. I came here to secure your release. Now you must ask yourself, why? Why am I necessary? Why were you kept against your will? Why were you given this book? The translation? Is that translation valid? Why, after reading this book, were you released and allowed the run of the grounds? People act out of their own self-interests. In whose interest is your manufactured animosity toward Grantville? And is that hatred in your own best interests, and in that of your emperor's? From what I understand he sent you across half the known world to discover the truth. He ordered you to learn from that truth, and to bring back that truth to him. I suggest you do so, Subadar Baram Khan. My officers and I will await your answer here."

Baram Khan and Salim departed, along with the servants. North patted his chest and was supremely irritated to discover that his last cigar had been disposed of in order to hold a solemn conversation.

"All right, change of plans," said North jerkily, missing his habit. "We only promised to retrieve Baram Khan and return him to

Grantville. We said nothing about what condition he is in when he arrives. So. Here's my new plan: we shoot the Mughal, feed him to the cat, bring the cat back to Grantville and have him stuffed for display in the office as a reminder to us never to take on any more rescue missions." North finished with a questioning look and outstretched hands. "How is this a bad plan?"

"Well . . ." Donovan contemplated for a moment. "We *could* develop the reputation of feeding our clients to tigers."

North rubbed his chin. "A cogent point. But that's a long-term issue, Liam. We are thinking about the immediate problems right now. Do you remember—"

North was interrupted by Hastings' galloping approach.

"Must you arrive so audaciously every time, John?" asked North in a snit. "Would it be so much to ask for you to calmly ride in and give good news instead of shouting that the world is about to end?"

"Yes, boss. Cavalry from the south!" shouted Hastings.

"Steiner?"

"His flag, along with another I do not recognize."

"How many, and how soon?" North started walking toward his own horse.

"Some hundreds. An hour, no more."

"Get over to where the Indiamen are being billeted. Roust out every man. Tell them to leave everything behind but their lives."

"They have ten guards."

"Take twenty men."

"Yes, boss."

"Enough!" shouted North, losing his temper. "Do you hear that sound, Baram Khan? That distant rumble is the sound of a thousand angry men coming here because of you. My company cannot remain here any longer. You must do what you must. Which would you rather have? A journey to Grantville following your emperor's orders, or to continue your long stay here, living on another man's whim?"

"We will come," Salim said for his master, after a hurried consultation.

"God be praised. Or Allah, if you prefer. Hastings! Get them moving!"

"We have hundreds of miles to safety. They'll chase us down," said Quinn.

"We need a choke point, something to delay them," added Donovan.

North was studying the map. "There is a bridge here on the Inn, with no other bridge for many miles upstream or down. We'll lead the pursuit there, and then blow the bridge. They will have to spend hours backtracking, and by that time we will be well into the mountains. We bloody their nose at every pass, valley, ford, rock, and boulder. The plan is not as elegant as I would like, but it will do."

"Our supply of ammunition is a finite one," pointed out Donovan.

"It will last long enough for us to get within range of one of the CPE's military detachments. You have the radio frequencies, I assume?"

"Yes," Quinn replied, studying the map himself. "But these local maps aren't always accurate. What if the bridge isn't there? Or there's another one nearby?"

"What did you say?" North asked with a smile.

"Suppose the bridge isn't *there*, Captain Courageous?"

"No! Do not get him started on that," Donovan pleaded.

"Oh . . . oh, why you have to hit me with them negative waves so early in the morning?" demanded North, in a fairly good impersonation of a New Jersey accent.

"It's midafternoon," Quinn replied, confused.

"Always with them negative waves, Moriarty! Always with them negative waves! Why can't you say something hopeful and righteous for a change? Huh? Why can't you dig how beautiful it is outside? Think positive thoughts. *Think* that bridge will be there and it'll be there. It's a muda butafull bridge, and it's *gonna* be there."

"Someone please explain to me what's going on," said Quinn nervously.

"Video rentals," explained Donovan. "May they burn in hell forever."

"Woof woof woof!" North barked playfully.

"With a Sherman tank?" said Quinn.

"And country music," added Donovan. "He now always quotes from his films when he is nervous. But this one is particularly bad. He has a cousin named Sutherland and is convinced the man is one of his distant relatives."

It was a sad thing, but North was fighting in one of the most beautiful areas he had ever seen. England claimed a few "mountains" but they were nothing like the Alps about him. It seemed grossly unfair that very shortly mortal men would stain God's perfect green earth with their blood.

The company had reached the bridge in time, thanks to the benefits of a head start and a total disregard for farmers' lands. Johan Brecht, the German explosives expert, had gone ahead and laid the charge. Alas, he'd used up all their explosives in doing so. Meanwhile, securing the Mughals' release had been remarkably easy. The men stationed at the makeshift "prison" had not been not ready for a heavily armed and determined force of mercenaries to come bursting through the doors. The Mughal expedition had been given horses where possible. Baggage was left behind where practical. But that still left a number on foot—and an army's march was determined by its slowest members.

"There is something odd about this scene," said North, as he looked at the column. "John Ford would have had a fit, if only because he couldn't film in Monument Valley. A wagon train of *Indian* Indians, heading north, led by a North, to a boomtown of central German Americans."

"God is prone to whimsy, as you have often said," commented Donovan.

"Funny you should mention that, since he has played another joke on us. Johan tells me that after he has laid out all the bundles in the necessary places he only has enough wire left for a short fuse."

"How short?" Donovan asked suspiciously.

"Very short. Someone has to stay to light it. There should be enough time to get away from the blast."

"Should . . ." mused Donovan. "I've always distrusted that word."

"Should," North reiterated firmly.

"This is not a movie, Tom, and you are not some Austrian muscleman. You have a business to run. Give the job to one of the minions; that is what they are for."

"I thought you were the one who placed a higher value on human life?"

Donovan shrugged. "None of them are my friends. Besides, they're mostly Calvinists. Predestination, you know."

"Who do we have that I can trust to do this?"

"Hastings."

"Hastings is a drunk."

"He does his best fighting when he's drunk."

"Yes, well. We ran out of liquor a hundred miles back, and he has a family back home. He has to feed them, fix seven sets of teeth.

Speaking of which, you still have your own appointment with Dr. Sims, don't you?"

"Yes, took me months, and I had to reschedule around this trip. Why are you ask—"

Slam!

North gave his friend a powerful blow to the head and knocked the Irishman to the ground. It was not enough to render him unconscious, but Liam was not able to resist North pushing him into the back of the wagon with the Spanish girl they had rescued earlier. North removed Donovan's pistol and ammunition and then closed the latch.

"Take the cost of the repairs out of my share of petty cash—and take care of that girl!" North bellowed, as he ordered the teamster forward and saw his friend driven away.

"Quinn, I want you to take command of the column till Liam is up and about. Drive them fast and hard. Do not stop till the horses are ready to die. I will give you as much time as I can. If the ambassador gives you much more trouble—shoot him."

"Shoot him?" Quinn asked disbelievingly.

"Diplomatically, of course. Trust Hastings, he knows what he's doing. John, I will need a squad."

"First squad!" Hastings bellowed.

"First squad has too many old married fathers," North interrupted, with a sigh.

"Third squad! Exchange weapons, fall out, and form on the bridge!"

"North . . ." Quinn said shaken.

"You had your adventure, lad. Something to tell your grandchildren about, assuming you can find a girl to propagate with. Now get out of here, you American whelp. Brecht! Are the explosives ready?"

"Yes, Captain. Excellent, good very work, sir. Fifteen seconds, big boom." The German chuckled and headed for the demolitions wagon.

The bridge was two hundred feet across the fast-moving Inn. Autumn in the Alps was not a temperate climate. If the approaching troops attempted to ford the river around the destroyed bridge, most would die of hypothermia before reaching the other side. Assuming the bridge would be destroyed, of course. While the sticks of dynamite certainly seemed impressive enough, North was not at all enthusiastic about his chances. The bridge was made of solid and sturdy stone and the "explosives expert" did not have great experience in the field. But every once in a while all men were capable of great things, if the reigning deities gave them their extra special attention. . . .

"I swear to God, and any others that might be listening, that if I live through this I will never, ever, make fun of Germans again," said North solemnly.

What little cover could be quickly manufactured on the bridge was, and third squad took position behind it. Already the forward scouts of the pursuing army could be seen. A few rifle shots downed a few scouts and the rest scattered. But they were harbingers of a much larger force and would return. North was checking his weaponry and experienced a moment of panic when he thought he did not have an item to light the fuse. He quickly found his Zippo in a pocket, though. Manufactured in Bradford, Pennsylvania, it was one of the few up-time devices that was easily supplied and virtually immortal.

North saw the last of the column heading away, but Salim approached the bridge. "My master wishes to know what is happening," the Indiaman said.

"I suspect he could not care a whit. But since you seem interested, I will tell *you*. You and your master will ride safely away. Then, a very large group of very angry men are going to come galloping down upon me. And I will stop them with ten men of my own."

Salim did not seem to doubt North's determination, nor that of his men. Already the ten riflemen were securely behind cover, removing ammunition from their bags and setting the bullets up for easy reload. Salim had fought in many wars and battles and he certainly knew what the new weapons were capable of. But he also knew what many hundreds of soldiers were capable of.

"Are all men from your island so mad?"

"It's the rain," North explained tersely.

"Captain, they come!" one of the mercenaries yelled nervously when he saw troops appearing, a fact North was already well aware of.

"Fire on targets of opportunity, conserve ammunition. When I signal, teams of two will retreat off the bridge to safety while others cover them until all are off. Remember your numbers. Take cover, and watch your arses!" North took his own advice and sheltered behind one of the commandeered wagons that had been emptied and left behind for this purpose. The wood wouldn't stop a modern rifle or a local cannon, but against matchlocks it should suffice.

"Shouldn't you be going?" said North, when he noticed Salim wasn't moving.

The Mughal pulled out an up-time pistol—North could only assume it was recovered from a dead Albernian—and unsheathed his substantial sword.

"I thought I was mad," said North with a sardonic grin.

"Someday, I will tell you of monsoon."

"Who the hell does he think he is, John Wayne?" Quinn asked angrily. "Why couldn't we just blow the bridge and book it?"

"Time," Donovan mumbled through a bruised jaw.

"What?"

"Bridge blown, they go around. But if we wait, they attack bridge, lose men. Blow bridge with them on it, many die. Maybe Steiner, with luck. Might stop them. We need time for the column to escape."

"So he's going to wait till the last possible moment, constantly under fire, and set the fuse when they're crossing? He'll be lucky to survive."

"Yes."

"Tell me something, my new friend," said North as he fired off another double shot with his 9mm.

"What would you like to hear?" The Mughal took careful aim with his own weapon and fired one of his scarce bullets.

"I should be uttering some epic epitaph at this moment, being the hero of this piece and all that. But the only thing I can think of is 'long live the king.' Normally good enough but . . . well, if the truth be known the current one is a useless little prat. Have any alternative?"

"Allahu Akbar," the Mughal supplied.

"Catchy. What does it mean?"

"God is great."

"If He gets us out of this, He most certainly is." North ducked for cover when he saw the enemy infantry formation on the south bank preparing for another volley. Their fire was ineffectual, most not even reaching North's position. But they were getting closer.

"Well, at least there are no windmills about," said North, glumly leaning against the wagon.

"There is one over there." Salim pointed to a structure in the distance.

"That was a rhetorical statement." North squinted to see that it was, indeed, a windmill. "But—ha!—it figures."

After several more minutes of battle, the riflemen of third squad had taken a significant toll on the approaching troops. The effective firing range for the American hunting rifles was far greater than the muskets they faced. But the rate of fire was now dwindling off, along with the supply of ammunition, and the opposing mercenaries were gradually gaining ground. It was time to think about getting out.

"Begin retreat to the horse holder!" North ordered. "Two by two! First pair, move!"

Return fire briefly intensified as Albernian mercenaries ran away from the center of the bridge to the shore. They then took position and reciprocated for their fellows until there was just North and Salim located next to the fuse. With several dozen horsemen about ready to charge against them.

"Should we not detonate now?" Salim asked, expending one of the last bullets in his automatic.

"Not yet," said North, as he took out the last cigar he had found in his saddlebag and lit it. He could see the troops massing on the other side with the minute figure of Captain Steiner in the distance. North didn't have to imagine the look on his adversaries' face; he knew it well from past experiences.

"You must," said Salim, uneasily taking another glance from cover to review the increasingly deteriorating situation.

North shook his head in disagreement. "I would not be able to live with myself if he couldn't see the smirk on my face."

"You are a madman."

"That is a separate issue. This is a matter of honor."

"We are being shot at."

"You worry too much. Most of them are matchlocks, they couldn't hit an elephant at this dist—ahh!!"

North clutched his leg in pain. It was just a flesh wound through the meat of the thigh, and, fortunately, the bullet had passed through and wasn't left lodged inside of him. Still, North wouldn't be running anywhere soon. He leaned over the wagon and saw soldiers rushing onto the bridge. He fired off again and again until his automatic was empty in an effort to dissuade them.

"Get going!" North ordered Salim.

"Can you walk?"

"No," said North, after an attempt to support his weight on his leg.

"Can you swim?"

"More or less."

"Swim with current, let it carry you away. Cold water will help stop the blood flow." Salim took North's fallen cigar and lit the fifteen-second fuse. "Disgusting habit. Go with God, Thomas North."

Salim grabbed the Englishman and heaved him over the side of the bridge, following right after him.

6

Fifty-five days after departing, the contingent of the Albernian Mercenary Company returned home, after a successful mission, and twenty-eight percent casualties. Winter was upon them and the cold northern European climate was not a welcome one for the visitors from India, a fact that was made known by Baram Khan to the company on a number of occasions.

"If he had kept at that any longer, you might have had a discipline problem," said Lawrence Quinn from atop his horse.

"If he had kept at it any longer I might have allowed one," grunted Liam Donovan. "Salim?"

"Yes, Captain?"

"Your master has still not changed his mind?"

"I am sorry, Captain, no."

"Very well, then, there is still the matter of our fee. Ten thousand pounds, or its equivalent in some reasonably hard currency. I understand he likely does not have that now. So a note for that amount or the equivalent in rupees to be drawn upon in Surat will be acceptable. We can sell the note to the East India Company."

Salim took a moment to converse with his superior. The senior Mughal listened with an impassive look and then was startled, probably when the figure was mentioned.

"My master says, 'I had no idea it be that much. I won't pay it.'"

"Somehow that is what I thought he would say. Boys! Help the Subadar find his purse."

"This is a terrible affront to the dignity of my master, and an unforgivable insult," said Salim, as he calmly watched everything of value be stripped from his master's body and those of his more affluent-looking followers—of whom Salim was not a member. "I should also perhaps tell you that he keeps many gemstones hidden in his turban."

"Thank you," nodded Donovan.

"Quite welcome. If we do not see each other again, I would like to say, I am sorry about your friend. I waited as long as I could."

"I know, just . . . Just do not believe everything in that book."

"What I believe does not matter."

"Was your stay here productive, Ambassador?" Ed Piazza asked Baram Kahn.

His question was translated by Salim but no reply was forthcoming.

"Your accommodations? I must apologize. We usually don't host dignitaries of your stature."

Again, silence.

"And I must apologize for that mercenary company, but what can one expect from hired thugs? We did not at the time have the troops to send to your aid. But I can extend to you now the services of one of our Marine cavalry platoons for your further travels. The Continent is currently—"

"That will not be necessary," Salim interrupted. "Arrangements for travel have already been made."

"Yes," said Piazza dryly. "I have no doubt they have been."

"We will of course return to Grantville on our homeward journey. My master expects that with foreknowledge you will have sufficient facilities available for his use upon our return."

"And *then* we discuss the other issues: treaties, trade agreements, establishment of formal diplomatic relations."

"Such issues will be discussed at a later date," Salim agreed solemnly.

"Yes, I'm sure they will." Piazza nodded stiffly. "Good day to you then, Ambassador, Salim, and we eagerly await your return."

"You were right, Liam, he's been gotten to," said Piazza over a drink in the Thuringen Gardens later that evening after the Mughal expedition had left. "Of course, you didn't help matters with your bill collection."

Donovan grinned. "We pride ourselves on our subtlety."

"The only consolation I get is that any repercussions are years . . . maybe decades, down the line. It won't help the enemy in the here and now."

"There was no changing his mind?"

"Would you? His reaction is perfectly understandable, given what was done to his nation. On another issue: General Jackson has been on my case; the weapons he loaned you were . . . ?"

"Lost in the chaos of battle."

"Of course," Piazza said, thereby giving his official stamp of approval on that version of events. Something told him he might have call to send for the men of the Albernian company in the future.

"There must be something that can be done," muttered Donovan.

"What? An 'accident' on the road?"

"It would solve the problem."

"We don't play that game. Word would get out; it always does." Piazza downed his beer. "I'm sorry about Tom, Liam. His death wasn't worth it."

"They never are," replied the Irishman, ignoring his own drink. "He knew the risks."

"If the outcome had been better we could have arranged a citation. He was technically working on government contract. But as it is . . ."

"Keep your medals. You may run out before this damn war is done."

The corporate headquarters of the Albernian Mercenary Company was beginning to look worthy of its name. Snows were on the ground, a chill was in the air, but all of the buildings were now completed. The company even had a Christmas display, a salvaged string of multicolored lights nailed around the front of the main building. After some initial misfortunes, the power lines had been extended to the farm from the Grantville power plant.

A lone man walked into the settlement from the Grantville road. He was bedraggled and unkempt, bearded and while possessing a small limp he still had a bit of a swagger about him. He approached a collection of Germans busy emptying the business ends of several bottles of local beer. The men did not give the stranger a serious glance. With the winter months upon them all manner of men were trying to get recruited into a business that would house and feed them, let alone provide a nice chunk of financial security.

"*Wie heist du?*" the stranger asked one of the heavy drinkers.

"Hans," the German replied, his attention focused elsewhere.

"Hans . . . ?"

"Hans Grünwald."

"*Danke.* You'll fit right in here, Hans." The stranger clapped the German on the back before entering the building without asking permission to do so.

*   *   *

"I'm sorry, sir. He just barged in here asking where his humidor was. Then called me a haiku-writing motherfu—"

"That is all right, Mr. Geller, I know this person. Why don't you get some sleep?" Donovan ushered the recently acquired servant out the door. Entering the inner sanctum, he spied a disheveled man fumbling about the office, searching, hair tousled, beard overgrown, and with a wild look in his eyes that would have frightened lesser men. "You're a son of a bitch. You know that, Tom."

"My cigars, my movies, and my books, damn you." Thomas North sat down in the house's study with a bottle of alcohol and a glass and set his feet on the desk. Donovan would have to have the chair cleaned, as North's mud-covered clothes were clearly leaving behind stains.

"You expended your entire supply on campaign and did not purchase any more from the Spaniard. The tapes are in a box in storage. And the books I plain and simply stole. The cost of doing business. I would not have done it except I had a report a few weeks back that you were in town for a few hours and then disappeared again. And without even leaving a note! It irritated me."

"I had business." North took a heavy drink, and then coughed. "Jesus! What *is* this?"

"Arrack, and he turned water into wine. The Indiamen did that with dates, though I would not call it a miracle. It was, um, part of our fee. They did not seem to want to leave much behind like we had asked them to."

"I have been drinking for a very long time. I was weaned on wine. In my entire life, that has to be the absolute worst drink I have ever imbibed."

"More?" Donovan asked, ready with the bottle.

"Yes, please," replied North, holding up the glass and leaning back in his chair.

"I really did miss you," said Donovan as he poured. "Since that day on the Inn it felt like a part of me was torn away."

North snorted. "You can stop prancing about the issue, Liam! I kept your precious magnum safe. Spent every bullet in it on my way out, but the pistol is in my kit in the corner." North pointed with his glass.

"Oh, thank heavens," said Donovan, very visibly relieved. "I would never be able to replace it."

"How many men did we lose?"

"Fourteen."

"Some of them left families, I assume. Did we take care of them like we planned?"

"More than we planned. I established the Thomas North Memorial Scholarship Fund, which someday might even be used. But since you were so damn discourteous as to show up alive I am changing the name to the J.A.A. Joyce Foundation for the Arts. I better not get any argument."

"Wouldn't dream of it." North drank again from his Venetian glass.

Donovan pulled a chair from the opposite side of the desk to sit next to his friend facing the window. The two had a view of some of the holiday revelry outside.

"So where did you go?"

"You know where," said North, looking away and putting his boots on the desk.

"How was the city?"

"Same as always."

"And the apothecary, what exactly did you pick up from him before you left again?"

"Heard about that, did you?"

"He was initially reluctant to talk, but I bartered away some of your trinkets."

"Powder of diamonds, if you must know."

"White arsenic." Donovan cocked his head appraisingly. "That is a very painful death."

"Yes it was."

"Did he deserve that?"

North shrugged. " 'Deserve' is irrelevant. It was business."

"Was it?"

"Yes, did you not find it odd? How a book so carefully crafted to engineer Mughal animosity to the English-speaking peoples would find its way to Baram Khan?"

"I did, actually. The entire trip home."

"It was not part of some citizen's private library, nor was it part of some nation's stockpile of stolen up-time books. It was from the Grantville public library. When I flipped open the cover I saw the checkout date. One week before Salim arrived. I assure you, my disheveled appearance has less to do with the road and more to do with the severe scolding I received from the librarian when I returned that overdue book."

"Someone is running an operation right in Grantville, then,"

Donovan mused. "The cardinal?"

"Not personally; he's not a superman. As much as we like to blame him for everything, he could not have done this. But that does not mean it wasn't one of his agents here."

"Someone with enough initiative and flexibility to get that book and get it translated."

"Not even most of it translated, the pictures would have been enough. The Union Jack flying on flagstaffs and mastheads from the Indus to the Ganges."

"Mother of God. *Trade*. That is what this has all been about."

North nodded, taking another heavy drink from the arrack. "We stole it from the Portuguese, who stole it from the Arabs. And the French tried to steal it from us back in the other world. This time they mean to succeed. The Mughal expedition had to make its way to Grantville through Ottoman territory. The French are the only power in Europe that has any real dealings with the Turks; the resident French agent must have heard. And the Ottomans would have been worried, don't doubt it for a minute. The Mughals have recently been more powerful, with the fabulous wealth their region produces. A Mughal empire with a few new technologies and tricks . . . and advance warning of what's to come. Particularly with mad Aurangzeb coming to the throne in a few years.

"The French heard, or *a* Frenchman heard, at any rate. And he halted Baram Khan enough so that the proper propaganda could be produced. The French are not in India at all right now, you know. Not yet. Their company has not been chartered, Dupleix has not even been born. Imagine it with me, Liam. You are Mughal, from a noble family, from an illustrious and powerful nation. And some slimy frog comes up to you. 'Listen, my friend,' " said North in a bad French accent. " 'Look at what these bad Englishman will do, hey. I will not lie to you, have my people ever lied to you? No. But have theirs? Think about what I have said, we mean you no harm, you are not a prisoner, come and go as you please.'

"It was an effective little operation, I have to admit. Soon enough, John Company would not be allowed to trade anymore. Only *French* ships and factories. No India trade of textiles, no East India trade of spices, no China trade of silk and tea."

"Unless a tainted Baram Khan was prevented from returning home," concluded Donovan, understanding what his friend had done.

"Indeed. It is remarkable, really—they put all their eggs in one basket. There really was no true second in command. Salim eventually convinced the man who took over to return home with what they had and come what may. I don't know what the results will be, but at least we have some time."

"Salim convinced him? I would think he would be displeased with your treatment of his master."

"Not as much as you might think. Some bad blood between them, apparently, and he particularly did not mind after I delivered a few choice books to him on Indochina. Heaven help me when that she-daemon at the library finds out."

"Vietnam?"

"The early years, with the French. No need to confuse the issue with that later idiot American enterprise. I then sent a rather long missive off to one of my uncles in London who is on the board of the company. Informing him of the situation and giving my advice. With any luck his response will reach India before any possible French response. Things might be different this time. Quiet trade, that's really all we should be after. From all the books I have ever read, military occupation of India was never a paying prospect.

"I wish I had not had to. I tried, but the Mughal made up his mind before even arriving in Grantville and the few days he spent here only let him find what he wanted to find. The men who did this were very, very good. He just couldn't get it through his head that he was being manipulated. A fault not uncommon to the Mughal ruling class, I imagine."

Donovan cleared his throat. "Yes, well, that might have been partly my fault. There was a sort of, ah, problem with our bill. He was possibly . . . annoyed at us."

"Hastings handled the manner in his usual subtle way, I suppose?"

"Poisoning a man for international trade?" said Donovan, shaking his head. "It does not seem right."

"We did a guy in Antwerp for twenty guilders. When we catch that bastard Lynch, we'll do him for free. This one died for hundreds of millions and the future of Britain."

"Your country," said Donovan harshly.

"Yes. My country, as often as I try to ignore it." North looked at the arrack in his hands. "This bottle seems to have died a much honored, though deserved death. Do you have something with more alcohol content?"

"Moonshine," said Donovan, lifting up another bottle from the shelf. "I have no idea why they call it that, except if you drink it in the morning you won't wake up till the light of the moon. A letter came for you while you were away."

"From my lord father?" North asked, taking the bottle.

"Yes."

"He sent me one before we left also."

"He wants you to return home, I imagine."

"Things are happening in England, things are changing, and men of my skill and temperament are needed. It's probably for the best."

"You really believe that?"

"Yes, I do." North stared off into space. "These Americans are all going to get themselves killed anyway. How much cash do we have in the coffers?"

"Most of our wealth is invested," said Donovan mildly. "Steel, bricks, glass, even sewing-machine companies. Most of the rest is in the bank."

"Sterling?"

"Seven thousand pounds."

"I'll take six thousand of it. You keep the rest, Liam, along with the company. You can even change the name if you like."

"Have a nice life, then, Tom."

"I thought, for a moment, that you might come with me. But—"

North was interrupted by the opening of the study door. Then entered a Spanish beauty substantially less pregnant than the last time North had seen her. He turned to Donovan with a raised eyebrow.

"Meals are now served promptly *seven* times a day. Join me for one last."

North looked for a moment like he would refuse, but it had been a very long time in between filling hot meals, and once the smell hit him he could not refuse. He reached for the tray.

"What is her name, by the way? I don't usually ask, but I am trying to change, near death experience and all that."

"She never told us her real name. Too ashamed I suppose, probably some don's daughter. I started calling her Dulcinea and she usually answers to it now."

"You must be joking." North lifted the first mouthful to his lips.

"Sadly, no. What is also sad is that I did not know your intentions, so I could not lace the food with a sedative."

"What are you talki—oh, shit."

Slam!

*   *   *

What . . .

Who . . .

Fucking Irish.

North woke up, facedown on a cold concrete slab. With an effort, not helped by a minor hangover, he sat up to examine his surroundings. Though North had always somehow managed to avoid this place, he had little doubt that he was secure behind the bars of the Grantville city jail.

"Wakey wakey," said an American-accented voice.

And goddamn all arrogant Americans, which includes the whole bloody lot!

"You are enjoying every minute of this, aren't you?" said North, when his vision cleared enough to see who it was.

"You betcha," replied Dan Frost with a sardonic grin. "Ever since that time."

"I have told you again and again, Chief Frost, I have no idea how that manure got on your squad-car seat. But you should never have tried cutting off the drinks anyway. Closing time, ha! What an absurd notion!"

North massaged his throbbing head, then raised his voice. "Illegal search and seizure, unlawful incarceration! I demand my constitutional rights!"

"That is funny on too many levels to describe right now. But all your rights have been respected, Englishman. You have been arrested and sentenced to six months imprisonment for drunk-and-disorderly conduct."

"Shouldn't I have been conscious for my trial? And what about legal representation?"

"Yes, well. It's the war, you know. We all have to tighten our belts and cut corners on frivolities. And there really was no question about your generally drunk-and-disorderly habits."

"Generally drunk and dis . . . *which* was I specifically charged, tried, and sentenced for?"

"A fight that resulted over a card table one Friday night. With one Liam Donovan."

"He started it," North said, like a petulant child.

"But you threw the first punch."

"Did not!"

"Mr. Donovan is a very prominent local businessman, and he filled out all the proper forms for a complaint. We also have witnesses. Would you call our very own mayor a liar? Shame on you." Frost was unable to contain his amusement. "He and his lovely, mild-mannered wife were very upset at you."

"She won the bet! And since when has D and D been a six-month crime?"

"Normally it's not, but you engaged in a flight from prosecution. We can't have that."

"Oh, kiss my arse. Liam probably filled out the complaint an hour ago. I want to speak to the mayor; I want to speak to the President!"

"Both of them are too busy. Besides, I value their health too much to risk them dying of laughter. Certain folks around here—several thousand, I imagine—have been waiting ages for this to happen to you. There is someone here, though, who will speak to you."

"Liam Aloysius Donovan!" shouted North, wringing the bars of his cage when his friend came into view along with John Hastings. "This wasn't funny in Rotterdam and it's not funny now! Get me out of here!"

"I am afraid I can't do that," said Donovan, after taking a moment to ascertain that the bars were sturdy enough to hold North's temper.

"Do you have any idea what I am going to do to you when I get out of here? And I *will* get out of here. Just like I escaped from Rotterdam, Preston, and half the stockades in Germany!"

"I have a fairly good idea. I still remember . . . parts of Rotterdam."

"Why?"

Donovan frowned. "That's a silly question. It was payday and the merchants from the West Indies had just arrived with a shipment of rum."

"I mean why put me in here?"

"I believe the term is called 'reeducation,' although in your case it is probably misapplied. I am not certain there is enough education in your background to be reed. But I left some reading material under your bunk, anyway."

North took the time to lean over and extract the books from their place and examine the titles. "*The Isles: A History. The Oxford Illustrated History of Britain. The English Civil War and Restoration.*" Scowling, he tossed the books onto the bunk. "I've read them all and a dozen more like."

"Then read them again. You will have plenty of time. We are

building something here, Tom. Leaving aside that we are one of the fastest growing new companies of a new nation, this *country* is something worthy of loyalty. Not one populated by ignorant half-naked savages too busy warring on each other to prevent another people of ignorant *clothed* savages from invading them."

"My home needs me. My father has sent for me."

"Fuck you, Lord North. Your father sent for you because you have money and skills at war. Two things you were considerably lacking when you left home. I am not content for you to destroy what we have worked for and go back to being the unknown and unwanted third son of an insignificant country baron."

"Don't you get it, you dumb bog Irish idiot? I want out! I am tired of this. I killed a man, not in battle but in a fucking garden! He was an arrogant git who probably deserved death, yes, but one who was just trying to serve his country. And for what, for money! I was raised to be better than that. Chivalry, charity, good queen Bess. For England, Saint George, and Harry! Reading *Le morte* bloody *d'Arthur*!"

"Damn strange stage in your life for a crisis of conscience."

"I was dying. Never quite went . . . all the way to dead, but I was very much dying in that river. It made me examine things, and I did not like what I saw."

"For what it is worth," said Donovan, stepping closer to the bars, "I think you're a good man. An Irishman almost, plenty of Norman Anglos who were changed under the right tutelage, you are no different. Behind all the bluster and bravado is a good man. In this whole, long, stinking war you were always one of the best of us. Never raped a woman. Never took more than the peasants could bear when you needed it, and paid when you had it. Yes, you killed a man, you have killed many men. So have I. That one, though, was a tool of the French and would have made them much more powerful than they already are. On the whole they are not a bad people; you and I have known quite a few good ones. Not even a bad government, certainly nothing like what this land would know in a few hundred years. But they have made themselves the enemy of this little principality we have made our home in. And in a Europe populated by nations motivated by greed, land lust, and rational self-interest, these people are trying for something better. And are worthy of defense."

"Lord God! An Irishman named Quixote." North held his head in his hands.

"It is not an impossible dream," said Donovan sympathetically.

"I am going to get out of here. In a damn sight short of six months!" screamed North, regaining his resolve.

"Oh, of that I have little doubt." Donovan smiled. "We have a new contract and I expect to be away for several weeks. Hopefully, by that time your temper will have improved. I have made a suitable arrangement with your jailer, and he will allow one of our secretaries to bring you all the papers you will need to manage the business while I'm away. The secretary will probably be Dulcinea, though I do not think I have to worry about her virtue." Donovan dinged the iron bars with his knuckle. "This cell should present enough difficulty even for you."

"Papers?"

"Forms, books, payroll, resource allocations, and cost-benefit analyses. It occurs to me that we have been going about this the wrong way. In your movies it's always the Irishman that is the reckless, feckless, happy-go-lucky fellow. And the prim and proper Englishman that keeps him in check. *I* want to go out and have some fun for a change."

"I will need to write to my father; he will be expecting it."

"I took the liberty of doing it for you. I fancy my forgery of your signature is well-nigh perfect, as much practice as I've had." Donovan extracted a handwritten piece of paper. "Ha hum . . . To, Dudley North, third Baron North, Commissioner of the Admiralty, Ely Manor, Kirtling . . . Dear father . . . Fuck off . . . Signed, Captain Thomas Xenophon North of the Hibernian Mercenary Company. Wayne Manor, Grantville."

"Of the *Hibernian* Mercenary Company?" North demanded icily.

"You said I could change the name." Donovan folded the note and put it back in his pocket.

"He will never believe I sent that."

"Is it not how you responded to him the last time he wrote you?"

"No!" said North hotly. "I was *eloquent*. You poxy bastard."

"I'm sure."

"De Valera was an American, and probably a Frenchman before that!"

"A hollow and transparent attempt to anger me. Read the books; think about what I have said. Talk to a few of the Americans on a subject other than cinema or high-stakes poker. Try politics for once, though a word of advice . . . not while drinking. And Edmund Burke was an Irishman."

"Sod off!"

"And so was the duke of Wellington. See you in a few weeks." Donovan bowed to his partner and left him to his incarceration.

"Hastings!" North pleaded, before the other man could leave as well. "You are an Englishman. Do not leave me here, man! Please, I beg of you."

"I am sorry; I cannot."

"Hastings! I am your captain and I order you to have me released!"

"Sorry, boss." Hastings pointed with a thumb over his shoulder in the direction of the door. "He is the one who hands out the gold now."

"What gold? You are months behind in your pay!"

"Not anymore. I have been promoted. I am Lieutenant Hastings now. Good-bye, boss."

"Hastings . . . Hastings!"

North was left alone. He spent a brief moment examining his cell and was impressed. It was not the shoddy affair he had been interned in before, but a professional and near escapeproof prison. All bluster to the contrary, he would be here a while.

Bowing to the inevitable, North reached under the cot and inventoried his options.

Not bad, really. The histories, of course. Several novels, Adams Smith's *Wealth of Nations*, a discourse on international relations, and a green ledger book that apparently held the Albernian company's fourth quarter books. Even a supply of cigars had been included.

"Damn you, Liam Donovan, to the seventh concentric ring of hell!" North screamed to all and any who could hear him. "I *hate* paperwork."

Then, sighing happily, he lit his first cigar in months.

Chief Frost's growling voice rolled down the corridor. "No smoking in the jail."

Just One of Those Days

Leonard Hollar

The day had begun badly for Matti. First, as his cavalry troop broke camp, one of the ties that was supposed to hold his bedroll on his saddle broke; and then the spare broke, too! So, by the time he finally got his gear stowed he had to join the rear of the column instead of being at the front in his usual place as a scout. And now, as they were charging up the hill to attack the Croats by that odd-looking building, after working hard to get back to his rightful place near the head of the column, his horse had stepped in a hole, broken its leg, and thrown Matti head over heels to the ground. But that didn't seem to be the worst; Matti had just finished putting his horse out of its misery when a bush had risen out of the ground and aimed an arrow at him. An arrow nocked to one of the strangest bows Matti had ever seen. An arrow three of whose companions were protruding from the backs of three dead Croats not far away.

For the first time in his adult life, Matti Antinpoika, of Captain Gars' troop of cavalry, felt like crying.

"A bush," Matti said to himself, "can't aim an arrow at anyone, so this must really be a person . . . I hope." By this time the bush was making an unmistakable motion for Matti to raise his hands. Not being a fool, hands and arms went as high into the air as he could reach.

Behind him Matti heard his brothers in arms make first contact with the Croats with their cries of, "*Gott mit uns! Haakaa päälle!*" In front of him he saw that the arrow was no longer aimed at him.

It was the noise that roused Curtis Maggard from a sound sleep. The whuffing, grunting sound of a hog at the slops trough. Except Curtis and his mother had neither trough nor hog. Curtis lay there for a moment, then, as realization of what he was hearing penetrated, he flew out of his bed with a shout. "*Mutti, in unserem Garten war ein Wildschwein!*" Curtis got the front door of the house open just in time to see a curly tail disappearing into the woods on the other side of their garden as dawn was breaking over the hilltop.

"Damn and blast! Three months getting that garden up to Mom's standards, and now it's all gone in one night." As he surveyed the damage, Curtis marveled at the amount of damage one boar could do. He also decided there would be a substitute to the menu in the Maggard home for a while. Pork for veggies!

As Curtis put on what he thought of as his tree suit, he considered the irony of life that had returned his mother and himself to the land of their birth. Even if it was almost four hundred years early. He also thought about how much better his mother's state of mind had become now that there were so many people to whom she could talk since, for whatever reason, she had never been able to comprehend the English language and very few people in Grantville could converse with her in German. The Ring of Fire had wrought a great change in Hilda Maggard's life.

Finished with both his rumination and his dressing, Curtis picked up his bow as he headed out the door a few minutes later. The bow, in the Mongol style, was one that he had handcrafted as his masterpiece only two years ago. Quiet, with a draw of well over one hundred pounds, this bow, or its earlier, less well-made kin, had kept the Maggard family in food for the nearly five years since the disappearance of Henry Maggard, Curtis' father.

As Curtis entered the woods in pursuit of the hog, his other talent soon became apparent. He made no sound that would be out of place in the forest. In the woods, Curtis Maggard was a wraith. His stealth in the woods gave Curtis a certain reputation in Grantville and its environs. He always got his deer, or pig, or anything else he hunted.

He also had never been caught getting his deer, pig, or whatever, despite having never gone through the formality of licensure or worrying about a potential meal being in season or not.

Ninety minutes after he began tracking the big boar, Curtis came upon the bodies of three men and a woman. The woman had been decapitated. After a quick look around, and determining that a large number of horses had gone by at about the same time as people had been killed, Curtis took off in a long-legged lope toward the nearest phone. At the high school.

It was only a few minutes before the realization came that the mysterious riders and Curtis had the same destination. With knowledge came action, and action was a change of path. After following game trails that paralleled the track of the horsemen, Curtis slipped over the top of the ridge above the high school just as the shooting began. He watched with grim satisfaction as he heard five rapid shots and saw five saddles suddenly empty. *Hah,* he thought to himself, *Julie must be down there. Let's see if I can't help out just a bit.*

In his camouflage clothing it took little time for Curtis to approach to within a hundred yards of the milling riders in the school parking lot. Three times he nocked an arrow and drew his bow, and three times a horsemen fell. He had just nocked his fourth arrow when he heard more horses coming from behind him. It took only the blink of an eye for Curtis to blend in with the bushes around a deadfall and disappear from sight.

Just as he froze in place, the second group of horsemen galloped past his hiding place. Taking his chance, he let go the arrow he had ready and grabbed another from his quiver. This he hurriedly prepared to fire.

It was then that Curtis realized he had missed his fourth target as he watched the horse that had lunged in the way of his arrow spill its rider and drop to the ground. There also came the realization that he now had an opportunity to take a prisoner. With his bow partially drawn and aimed at the man on the ground Curtis made a small up-and-down motion. That was all it took; the cavalryman's hands and arms went straight up to the sky.

As Curtis approached his prisoner he heard the new arrivals begin yelling, "*Gott mit uns! Haakaa päälle!*" and saw them begin to assault the rear of the people attacking the school. Trusting in the old saying that the enemy of his enemy was his friend, Curtis lowered his bow and asked, "Do you speak English?" At the look of confusion on the prisoner's face Curtis tried a different question. "*Sprechen Sie Deutsch?*"

Matti stood there with his hands in the air, awaiting his fate. Expecting momentarily to feel the pain of an arrow piercing his heart, he was surprised when the bowman released the tension on the string and let the point drift from being aimed at his chest. The bush spoke: "*Gobbledy gook?*" His confusion must have transmitted itself to his captor for the next words were, "Do you speak German?"

"Yes! Yes, I do!" said a very relieved soldier. "Are you from Grantville?"

"Right now, I'll ask the questions, if you please," replied the bush. "Who are you people and who are those people who attacked the school?"

Keeping in mind the status of his commander, Matti was careful in his reply. "I am Matti Antinpoika, and we are a troop of Gustav Adolphus' *Västgöta* under the command of Captain Gars. Those other people are Croats. We picked up their trail two days ago and followed as rapidly as we could. Captain Gars did not—"

The bush interrupted. "So, then, you really are the good guys."

"Why, yes, I suppose we are."

"Good, that means you won't stab me in the back while I take care of a little business." With that, the bush turned its back—yes, it was indeed a man, that was now obvious—went to his knees and began heaving the contents of his stomach. After progressing to dry heaves he stood back up, turned around, and found Matti holding a flask out to him.

"Here, my young friend, drink some of this."

Finally rinsing the taste of bile from his mouth, the man told Matti, "Thanks. I've hunted for the pot for years, but I never dreamt I would ever have to kill a man, much less three. It kind of got to me."

"Well, my young friend, you have nothing . . . By the way, just what is your name? I can't go around just calling you my 'young friend' now, can I?"

"Curtis Maggard, at your service and most pleased to meet you. I just hope you don't mind if I call you Matti, because I don't think I can get my tongue around that last name of yours.

"I have another question for you, if I may," Curtis continued. "Why is it that when everyone else in that bunch of yours seemed to be coming down the hill in an orderly manner, you were off to this side galloping like a bat out of hell?"

"Because I was trying to catch up. Today has not been one of the best in my life." Matti's hangdog expression as he replied caused Curtis to stifle a laugh. "I was assigned as one of the group to stay near Captain Gars because our good captain gets sometimes too enthusiastic in what he does. Unfortunately, I had some problems with my equipment and, of course, since neither the Croats, nor Captain Gars waited for me, I was left to trail along behind. When we topped the hill up there and I saw that we had caught the Croats I tried my very best to catch up so I could carry out my duty to my captain. But then my horse stumbled and a bush, you, took me prisoner. All in all, not such a good day. Now, will you come and help me get my gear from my horse? Perhaps I can catch up one of those left by a less fortunate Croat, hah!"

As the two men approached the horse to retreive Matti's gear, they both saw that the horse had not stumbled in a hole after all. For there, protruding from where it had shattered the cannon bone in the horse's right front leg, was the fourth arrow Curtis had loosed.

Matti began to first giggle and then laugh hysterically.

As the laughter began to subside, Matti turned to Curtis, pointed, and said, "You! You did this. Why did you shoot my horse? Did some devil put you up to this to finish the work he began this morning?"

As he stood there, not knowing whether to join in the laughter or run like hell, Curtis's thoughts went back to his actions during the fight and the charge of the *Västgöta*. As the scene unfolded in his mind, realization dawned as to what had really occurred here.

"Matti, which one was Captain Gars?"

"What? What does that have to do with my horse?"

"Please, Matti, humor me. Was he the real big guy with no helmet on?"

Matti, at this point, became completely serious when he answered, "Why, yes. He has a bullet in his neck or back and can't wear a helmet. And you ask this why?"

"Why? Because that's who I aimed that arrow at, Matti! You did your duty. You saved Captain Gars' life."

The next words out of Curtis' mouth were even louder. "MEDIC, MEDIC!!!!"

For the first time in his life, Matti Antinpoika had fainted.

GOD'S GIFTS

Gorg Huff

In the pages below I will try to relate my slow and torturous route to what I pray is a better understanding of God's will. My name is Steffan Schultheiss. I am not, and never have been, a particularly handsome nor, save from the pulpit, an imposing man. There, God's grace fills me, and all modesty aside, I speak with power and conviction. I am the senior pastor of the St. Nicholas' Church in Badenburg. This is primarily because of the political astuteness and connections of my wife, Margreth. She is the youngest daughter of a former mayor of Badenburg, and was raised to the politics of her situation.

I was born the son of a shoemaker in the year of our Lord 1574. I did well in school, and was given scholarships that led me to Jena, where I did very well in rhetoric and theology. From Jena I returned to Badenburg and became the most junior of pastors. Then Margreth picked me. For which kindness I thank God regularly. Over the ensuing years she has taught me much of the workings of politics in Badenburg. In the year 1625 I was given the post of senior pastor of the largest congregation in Badenburg.

Badenburg is a Lutheran town. St. Nicholas was the more conservative of the two main congregations, each of which had some smaller churches as part of our congregations. St. John's was only

117

slightly smaller in size and, I felt, somewhat loose in its interpretation of the Bible and Martin Luther's teachings.

When the Ring of Fire happened, I was at my desk writing yet another sermon on patience and praying for God's help. The last several years I had had a lot of practice preaching patience and praying for God's help. The war hurt Badenburg in a number of direct and indirect ways. The most recent and severe problem had been the extortion of a group of mercenaries, which the council had been convinced, at the point of a knife, to hire to protect the town.

God's gifts, to me, had always been the little things: the flowers, a baby born safe and healthy. The big things discussed in the Bible—parting the Red Sea, destroying towns that displeased the Lord—were all, I knew, in the distant past. Christ was more subtle, feeding the masses with a few loaves and fishes, turning water into wine. After Christ there was no more need for any big miracles. I rather preferred the smaller gentler miracles, anyway. After all, I had no desire at all to have my hometown added to a list that included such places as Sodom, Gomorrah, and Babel. Besides, I had been taught that all that was needed to understand the will of God was written down in the Bible. Still, I prayed, a bit of help in keeping my home town alive would not go amiss.

So I worked on Sunday's sermon, and prayed for God's aid. When the miracle happened, I didn't see it. When Margreth told me about it, I, like doubting Thomas, didn't believe. I had to see the miracle, and more, before I believed.

As Margreth told it to me, she had been in the market and faced toward the east gate. As she looked down Market Street, she saw a dome of light a bit to the south and well beyond the city wall. She only saw about the upper third of it, and buildings in the way blocked part of that. From what she said the phenomena was a perfect hemisphere miles across. She told me of wondering if Rudolstadt was still there. After the dome of light there came thunder as it follows lightning, but this was not lightning.

Enough people had witnessed the event, whatever it was, that she judged shopping was no longer so important and rushed home to inform me so that I would be prepared to deal with the fear it would cause.

It was a noble thought, and I rewarded it with ill-concealed scorn. It was a distant storm or an optical illusion. Irritated and grumpy with the interruption of my work, I accompanied my good wife to the east wall. I should have listened with more care and less scorn. Crowds were gathering along our route. Questions about the nature of the event were asked of me. I had no answers.

I was ushered up into the gate tower from which I could see some distance. Rudolstadt was still there—I could see the higher buildings. A bit to the south, I could see the results of the event of which Margreth had spoken. One of the mercenaries pointed out the changes. The land had been altered. I knew it wasn't a miracle, for God was sending no more prophets or miracles. Paul had said so in his letters. People would think of it as a miracle, though. How else was one to think of it?

I urged caution in dealing with the event. I continued to urge caution over the following weeks and months, slowly changing the specifics of my comments and sermons as we learned more of what had happened.

I first met Americans in the council house. They were disappointing in that they were simply people, not angels or demons. They told a story that was unbelievable, yet mostly believed. They said they were from the future—nearly four centuries in the future—from a place called West Virginia, in the Americas.

I began to really believe what they had told me about their origins. Everything was too consistent for a fabrication. I visited the Ring of Fire several times over the weeks following its appearance. There was a Catholic church next door to a Protestant church. There were lots of churches, each independent of the others. The books matched the story. All the evidence fit together, each piece supporting every other.

God had chosen to take a hand in the sort of hard material way that He hadn't since Old Testament times. However, the Protestant doctrine of *sola scriptura* said that didn't happen anymore. One of the strongest tenets of the Reformation had been thrown out, not by the overweening Church of Rome, but by God Himself.

I prayed for understanding but it eluded me. The people there were not saints and angels, nor were they demons and devils. Not all the people there were good Christians. The good were not necessarily the Christian, and the Christian not necessarily the good. I was treated well by people who professed Christian beliefs, and badly by others professing the same. I had met kind and caring people who professed to not believe in God at all, and others who were rude in their arrogant certainty that there was no God, even when faced with the clear evidence of the Ring of Fire. There was no pattern I could get a grip on.

I continued to urge caution on my congregation in dealing with the Americans. Still, the Ring of Fire drew me like a moth to a flame.

God had done something special here. I could look at the cliffs God had made and feel His presence. There was a peace and confidence that I had felt before, but never so strongly as I felt it here. This could not be explained away. Whatever it meant, this was a miracle no one could deny. The Ring of Fire and the land within it was holy ground beyond all doubt.

I found it distressing that the up-timers failed to see it. They had from the day they arrived felt free to change things, to modify God's work.

I saw much of the Battle of Badenburg from the city walls. Badenburg would not challenge the new United States in any major way. The one-sidedness of the battle made that clear. The up-timers could, if they would, force us to their will. Why they hadn't done so was less clear. That they hadn't was reason to hope.

I met Pastor "Call me Bart" Campbell at his church in Grantville. He spoke no understandable German and my English at the time wasn't much better. He was one of the friendlier religious leaders from within the Ring of Fire that I had met. Over the following months we had several conversations, each gaining an improved understanding of the other's speech. In time we became friends. It was months later I discovered the heresies, actually read the poem. It had been on his wall all along, but I had not the knowledge to understand.

It was by Leigh Hunt and told the story of the personal salvation of an Arab named Abou Ben Adhen. Not a member of the community of Christ, Abou was still loved by God because he loved his fellow men. This flew in the face of all Christian teaching. For it is only through the grace of God that any of us gain heaven. None of us is so free of sin that he gains heaven by right. And that grace must be accepted and acknowledged.

Yet there it was—not part of the Bible, not learned discourse gained through study of the Bible—contradicting the Bible, in fact. It seemed a betrayal of Christ, and of Pastor Campbell's calling as a minister of the Lord. I remonstrated with him over it. And this is what he said in reply:

"Christ came into the world to let people into heaven, not as a way of locking them out. I know Christ died for our sins, but let me ask you something. Is the apostle Thomas in hell because he didn't believe in the resurrection before he saw it with his own eyes? If he's not, do you really think the Good Lord will condemn to eternal damnation a good man because he was born, lived his life, and died never having heard the name Jesus Christ? Thomas heard. He was there at the Sermon on the Mount, and at the crucifixion, saw Jesus when he returned, and still didn't believe till he had actually put his hands into the wounds."

He was in error. The gospel according to Mark makes it clear that those who do not believe are damned. For a while after that, it seemed, for whatever reason, God had placed heretics in our midst: even those who professed belief denied God's Word. The same Bible said that there would be no more miracles, and yet here was Grantville, delivered in the Ring of Fire.

While not wholly good, the material consequences of the Ring of Fire for Badenburg seemed mostly beneficial. At first there had been a loss of business by the local merchants, but that had changed as they had become more comfortable dealing with the Americans. The up-timers were rich, and as a rule generous in their wealth. The most common complaint I had heard lately was that the poor were unwilling to work for the wages they had found adequate before the Ring of Fire. Grantville paid better.

The winter was easier to survive than expected. American tractors, and other devices, were helping with the harvest. American soldiers patrolled the roads. American workmen and equipment improved those same roads, making the transport of goods faster, safer, and cheaper. Grantville was certainly a material boon to Badenburg, and increasingly to the surrounding area.

Spiritually, that was more of a problem. American freedom of religion seemed to cause no problems in Grantville, save for the basic one that many of the people of Grantville were—or so it seemed to me at the time—damned by their lack of faith. If you know someone is to be damned by their lack of faith in the Lord and yet do nothing to save them, are you not complicit in their damnation? And wouldn't they lead others into damnation by the example of their worldly wealth and knowledge?

I became a timid Paul, faced with Christians whom he could not persecute. I examined the various religious practices in Grantville in hopes of finding fault; errors that I could point out to my congregation, to defend them against the creeping corruption of up-timer ideas. I found many such, and pointed them out with diligence, and at some cost. Political factors suggested a more moderate approach. Margreth pointed this out to me on several occasions, but I would not be swayed.

My revelation came, not on the road to Damascus, but in Grantville High School. Nor was it a light from heaven, but a simple comment. Two of the teachers were discussing the Ring of Fire, as they had no doubt done many times before. One said to the other, "Albert, stop telling God what to do." This struck me as odd because neither of them was named Albert.

Upon investigation, I learned I had stumbled across an old joke. Apparently a Jew named Albert Einstein was considered one of the greatest natural philosophers in history. In discourse with another natural philosopher, he had made the statement "God does not play dice with the universe." To which his fellow philosopher, a man named Niels Bohr, had made the famous reply, "Albert, stop telling God what to do." It all seemed horribly disrespectful to the Good Lord. I was not impressed with their humor.

That night I dreamed of heaven; of thousands of voices raised not in praise of the Lord, but in remonstration. God does this. God does not do that. God condemns this one. God saves that one. I say unto you: if an angel of the Lord should contradict me, do not believe him. God will make no more miracles, send no more prophets. God does not play dice with the universe. No one will be accepted into heaven who has not accepted Jesus Christ. God only loves a few chosen people and all others are condemned. Then the Lord God was looking into my eyes, and into my soul, waiting. Waiting for me, along with all the others, to tell Him what He was and was not allowed to do; and I was afraid.

I knew then God didn't need my permission to let a heathen into heaven any more than He needed my permission to create the Ring of Fire; to create a whole new universe not in seven days, but, if what the two physics teachers had said was true, in seven seconds.

Could it be Christ wasn't sent into the world so much to save us as to *let us know* we could be saved? That God understands when we don't get it right? God seemed to smile, in my dream, but gave no further reassurance, made no pronouncement of His will, no statement of what He would or wouldn't do. I was comforted by that smile and I still am.

I do not know, in any objective way, that my dream was any more than a dream. I know through faith that God was speaking, but cannot command anyone else to believe it. Yet I must offer it, not because God will refuse entry into heaven for those who don't accept the truth as it has been revealed to me, but because of the suffering and fear here on earth that it may prevent.

That was my revelation but it was not enough. People need rules, standards of behavior. If those standards aren't provided by their faith, we will seek out a faith that does provide them, even if that faith requires we sacrifice a virgin to get the crops to grow. I now believe that the most rabid devil worshiper on earth may find salvation through God's grace even if he rejects that grace here on earth, or may not. It is not my place to tell God what to do. I can guess, though.

If the Good Lord is as kind as I have come to believe He is, then we need not fear His wrath. If we need not fear His wrath, why should we even try to follow His rules—rules that we can only guess at anyway? For me the answer to that is simple. I love God and prefer not to disappoint Him any more than I can avoid.

God, after all, gave me life, and Margreth to love and be loved by. He gave me my congregation to care for. The flowers and the trees, children laughing, and a miracle when my faith had become a thing of rote rules and following instructions. Perhaps most valuable of all, He gave and continues to give me doubt. Through doubt He gave me freedom of choice. Instead of commandments carved in stone, He gave me Grantville with all its contradictions and confusions. In doing so He gave me His trust. I don't want to disappoint Him.

I do not follow God's will in fear of punishment, or even in hope of reward. I follow God's will, as I understand it, because I love God, and want to make Him happy.

The change was too sudden. For all the long months since the Ring of Fire I had been urging caution, if not outright condemning the up-timers for their belief in freedom of religion. Over my years as a pastor, I had become enough of a politician to realize that it was going to take time to change the direction I had been leading my flock. Even if I hadn't been, Margreth certainly was.

It was Margreth that I told first. She was furious with me. Her fury was, I realized, a mixture of fear for my soul and guilt, for she had been encouraging me for months to be gentler in my condemnations of Grantville and up-timer beliefs. Her motives then had been practical politics: Grantville was too powerful to fight, and too rich to ignore. I had been gradually losing support among the council and among my congregation, out of fear my sermons might damage relations between Badenburg and Grantville. Now Margreth was afraid her remonstrations were responsible for my change of heart, that in so doing she had driven me into heresy and imperiled my soul.

So first, I had to convince her through reasoned arguments. It wasn't easy, but I had an ally. Not more than five miles away God had spoken, and spoken loudly, if not clearly. At the minimum, the Ring of Fire meant we needed to reexamine our interpretation of the Bible, which said God would not do that. Obviously that was not the case. And what had the Good Lord sent us? A church or town of Lutherans, or a church or town of Catholics? Had he sent us a Buddhist monastery, a synagogue, or mosque? No, God sent us a town, a small town from the future. A town filled with simple common folk by the standards of their time and nation. But what folk? People who respected each other's right to decide for themselves what to believe and how or even whether to pray. People who, for the most part, follow God's will a bit better than we do. A kind and charitable people who feed the hungry and cure the sick, speak in a new tongue. I don't know about demons but they are a dab hand with mercenary soldiers. Should they find the need, I suspect they would do well with snakes and poison too. What they don't do is go around saying, you must believe as we do.

I persuaded her after a time. There was a comfort in this interpretation of God's will. I don't know where it came from. From the outside it must seem harsh. It offered no concrete assurance that if you did one thing or another you would gain heaven. Instead it depended on trust in God's grace.

Having persuaded Margreth I had not lost my soul, I still needed to persuade her I had not lost my mind. Telling anyone seemed, to her, a dangerous and unnecessary risk. After all, the souls of my congregation would not be endangered by leaving them where they were—comfortable in their faith in Christ, if a bit smug in the notion that followers of other faiths were condemned. But they weren't comfortable, not really. There were too many discrepancies between what they had been taught and what they could see a few miles to the east. I was not the only one who had been searching for some explanation.

A miracle without an explanation is a dangerous thing.

We worked out the politics involved between us: whom to talk to, where to keep silent, what must be done to prepare the way. First we must prepare the council and those members of the congregation whom others looked to. Individually and slowly we needed to help them to consider that God is speaking to us through the Ring of Fire and what it has brought. Help them to discover for themselves what He is saying.

The junior pastors in the congregations of St. Nicholas and St. John's were especially important. At that time, Badenburg had two main churches and each had several smaller associated ministries. Jost Duerr was the senior pastor of St. John's. We would have consulted with Pastor Duerr concerning his spiritual convictions, save for the fact that both Margreth and I were convinced he had none. Each church had the same patron: the Badenburg council. Jost had been senior to me in the St. Nicholas Church but had been passed over, mostly because he had been a little too quick to jump into council business and too quick to change sides once he did; but partly I admit, because of Margreth's family's influence.

Jost's family was more influential than mine, but not so influential as Margreth's. Jost himself was a weather vane shifting with the slightest breeze, always looking for the main chance. He was almost as fond of me as I was of him. Any mention of my new understanding that reached his ear would quickly be twisted to whatever he thought might lead to his political advantage and my detriment. No, discussion of my change in attitude must be limited to junior pastors in the two main congregations, and not all of those.

I first softened my stance against up-time corruption. My sermons were gentler, focusing on the Good Samaritan and similar passages, not on doctrine.

There were several private dinners with members of the council and the congregation. Margreth gossiped with calculating purpose, but then, she always had. There were changes in the political landscape I had failed to consider in my search for understanding. The Ring of Fire, especially the people and their knowledge, offered opportunities for the sharp-eyed, and snares for the unwary.

Increasingly Karl Schmidt carried influence. He now employed more people in his business than anyone else in Badenburg. I had known Karl for years and he was not the person I would have expected to have prospered so well. He was a plodder, and a bit tight with his money; or, at least, he had been before the Ring of Fire. Margreth explained part of the change since the Ring of Fire. Karl now had access, through the family of his fiancée and their friends, to what Ramona Higgins described as "great gobs of numbers." Karl referred to them as financial-analysis tools. Others had made investments, but none with the spectacular success of Karl's. Claus Junker, for one, had invested in a project to manufacture microwave ovens, which Karl insisted was silly. Others on the council had made better investments, but none as canny as Karl's.

Councilman Junker was going to be a problem. He had been my main support in my opposition to too-close relations with the up-timers. I had known at the time his reasons were less than fully Christian in nature. He resented their attitudes toward rank and social position, and envied their wealth. He was generally astute in business matters and publicly generous. He was also, it was safe to say, unlikely to support my changed view of Grantville. Yet I owed him my concern, and a warning if the electrical oven was to be the failure Master Schmidt was predicting. Such a warning, whether believed or not, would probably harden his attitude toward the up-timers.

The other members of the council were, to one degree or another, in favor of either closer relations or at least maintaining the status quo. So were most of the people who lived anywhere near the Ring of Fire. The up-timers meant safety and prosperity, an end to the war that had savaged this part of the world. Whatever the church might say, whatever I said, they were miracle-brought saviors. The fact that they claimed no divine authority only reinforced it. It wasn't a unanimous view but it was clearly the most commonly held one.

In spite of Margreth's objections I felt I had to at least try to warn Councilman Junker of the problems I had been told of in producing a microwave oven. He dismissed my warnings as soon as he knew the source. "Karl Schmidt," I was informed, "is an upstart crafter, with delusions of grandeur. He has engaged himself to a harlot with a bastard son. Sold his shop to a bunch of children." He held forth similarly at some length in rather boring and often inaccurate detail.

Well, at least I tried.

Meanwhile, discussions with the more junior pastors proceeded, and biblical references and conclusions ran headlong into the fact of the Ring of Fire. Margreth and I were lining up support for my heresy. I was becoming more comfortable with the term; a conversation with Uriel Abrabanel helped with that. Christians are, after all, Jewish heretics. Protestants are Catholic heretics. What's one more?

Several questions of doctrine came up in those discussions. "How long did it take God to create the universe?" I answered: "I wasn't looking but according to Margreth something less than seven seconds." Pastor Hoch gaped at me. So I continued: "The universe is now some months old and seems to be running nicely. The best estimate of the philosophers in Grantville is that the universe that we are in now is not the same as the universe of before the Ring of Fire. Certainly it's not the same as the universe that they came from. Probably we are in a new universe that took the Lord Almighty little more than the blink of an eye to create. Personally, I'm sure He could have done it faster if He had chosen to. I hope someday to meet that fellow, the one that I would have become without the Ring of Fire, and compare notes in heaven; but not, God willing, for many years."

"But wouldn't that mean we aren't in the world that Jesus came to save?"

"Do you think him so limited? We have the knowledge of his ministry, his death and resurrection to comfort us. Certainly his mercy can reach us here. What more do you need? If there is one thing the Ring of Fire made clear to me it is that God can do what he wants. He doesn't need my permission or yours or even that of the apostles. He has created a whole new universe; not just one world but worlds beyond counting. The other interpretations don't impress me. They all strive to make God less than He is, in order to make Him fit into our preconceptions. If God created Grantville and all its history in the blink of an eye, we are forced to the conclusion that God is a liar. I don't believe that God created an intricate web of lies to trap us into hell. I could be wrong. I have no more right to restrict God's actions than anyone else. But I just don't think He would do such a thing."

So it went. We discussed every aspect of theology we could think of. We tried to find meaning, and meaning we found—often contradictory and confusing but still, slowly we came to something approaching consensus, at least on the core concept. We don't tell God what to do. If our beliefs conflict with God's actions, it's our beliefs that need work, not God's actions. Second, we're going to get it wrong. If such men as wrote the Bible with God's inspiration sometimes got it wrong, certainly we would.

For these two concepts we forged strong agreement. They reflected the freedom of religion of Grantville, but in a way that touched the soul, rather than just secular law. Which was certainly God's will—

else why Grantville, instead of a town of less-fragmented beliefs?

It was mid April of 1632 when I finally gave the sermon I had been preparing since my revelation. I was unsure what reaction to expect. What I got was almost anticlimactic. It was almost as if the whole congregation sighed with relief. They didn't need to choose between God and Grantville. They didn't need to choose between God and their faith. With a little work the two could fit together. Simply acknowledge the obvious: God was all-powerful and generally kind; that He granted us freedom, and that freedom could lead us into error; that He had sent His son to us as a sign that He understood and forgave our sins. Later He sent Grantville to us to help us through a difficult time, to help us stop killing each other in His name. Not like Christ, so far above us as to be able to live a life without sin, just folks who knew a bit more than we did.

All in all, I think it has gone over fairly well. I am still the senior pastor of St. Nicholas' Church in Badenburg, with fairly solid support on the council. Badenburg is the second state in the new United States. Not everyone accepts it, of course, not even here in Badenburg. Pastor Duerr thinks me irresponsible, and insists I am endangering the souls of my congregation. That's all right. God, I am sure, understands.

Bottom-Feeders

John Zeek

Freddy Genucci found the body lying on his front lawn. Freddy was a little shaken up. Some people might find that odd, since Freddy was a funeral director and was used to dead bodies. But his normal line of work didn't involve bodies leaking on his front lawn. Besides, no one expects to see a gaping wound across a man's throat when they try to wake up what looks like a drunk.

When the call came into the Grantville police station, the desk was manned by Emil Zollner. He shouldn't have been given that much responsibility, but he was there because of Dan Frost's soft heart. Emil normally worked as a foot patrolman, but he had tripped going down the station steps and gotten a twisted ankle. Rather than have him miss a week's pay, Dan had given him desk duty.

Emil's English was not the best and Freddy was excited, so the message came across a bit garbled. In the end Emil sent two patrolmen to Freddy's house.

As he sat in the passenger seat, Jurgen Neubert watched Marvin Tipton as he drove the police car. *I have to learn to drive*, he thought.

These Americans will never believe I am a policeman if I don't. Still, it could be worse. I could be doing foot patrol.

Jurgen thought back to the time before he had heard of Grantville. He had been happy enough as a farmer, before Tilly and his army came. Still, this was a lot more interesting work. And he got to meet so many people. In the past few months, he'd met more people than he'd known in his whole life before.

Jurgen slid his hand to his belt to check, for the fifth time today, that his handgun was still in his holster. The revolver, what the Americans called a Colt Python, was one of the finest made pieces of machinery he had ever seen. Jurgen was still surprised that Chief Frost had trusted him to carry it. After checking his gun, Jurgen checked his other equipment, the "slapjack" riding in the almost-hidden pocket on his right leg, the side handle baton on its clip on the car door, and most especially the "ballpoint" pen he had been given just this morning. Tipton had explained, when he gave him the pen, that in a two-man car one man was the driver and one was the writer.

Jurgen was proud at being trusted to keep the records of their day. All in all, he thought, this was a better life than farming. A position of trust. He slipped his hand up to finger the badge that was the symbol of his office. New clothing, too, though the uniform trousers he had been issued were tighter and not as comfortable as the slops he normally wore. Most of all, it was a job worth doing, protecting the people and property of his new city.

Just then the radio squawked, "Base to car one."

Jurgen picked up the mike and answered, "Car one."

"Unknown trouble at number two Happy Hills. Contact Mr. Freddy Genucci."

"Clear base. Car one en route to Happy Hills." Jurgen saw Tipton nod his head, showing he had heard the message.

As Jurgen wrote the call on the record sheet, Tipton asked, "You have relatives out on Happy Hills don't you?"

"*Ja*, my cousin Jost and his family rent a house and farm there. My cousin Mina works for Herr Genucci. I hope nothing has happened to the Genuccis. They are nice people."

"Well, I don't like unknown trouble calls. Stay alert until we find out what's going on. I wish Emil had gotten more information." Tipton increased the speed of the cruiser.

Surely it is not another raid, Jurgen thought as he remembered the terror of the ride out to the high school with Hans driving the bus. He had emptied his revolver and forgotten how to reload, so he had relied on the shotgun someone had thrust into his hands. He checked his revolver again and looked at the shotgun mounted on the cage behind him.

When they arrived at the Genucci house, Jurgen was relieved to see Mr. Genucci standing beside the front door. Mr. Genucci was visibly upset and kept pointing to the body on the front lawn. "Look there. He was lying there when I went out to watch the sunrise this morning."

As Jurgen went to check the body, he heard Tipton ask, "Know who it is, Freddy?"

"It's Tommy Cooper. Not the old man but his son. The one everybody calls Young Tommy."

Looking at the body, Jurgen wondered why a man who appeared to be in his fifties would be called "Young Tommy." Jurgen, who had seen his share of dead bodies, was also surprised at the injuries. Young Tommy's head was almost cut off. It was nearly severed by the deep cut across his throat. Only the bones of his spine were not cut through.

"Shoot, I hate the idea of going to tell his old man someone killed him," Officer Tipton said as he walked over to stand by Jurgen. "Freddy, did you hear anything before you found the body?"

"No, Marvin, our bedroom is in the back of the house and we can't hear anything out front when we are in there. Though I thought I heard something right after I went to bed last night that sounded like a backfire from a car. You know how bad some cars are running on natural gas or alcohol. I just thought it was a car on the road."

"Don't think it was a car that killed him. Jurgen, go call the office and tell them what we have and tell them to send an ambulance. Don't use Cooper's name on the radio. No sense letting anyone with a scanner know our business. There needs to be an autopsy, though it's pretty obvious what killed him."

As Jurgen went to the car, he saw his cousins Jost Neubert and Mina Matz walking toward the Genucci house. "Jost, Mina, stay here by the car. We have a problem at the house."

While he waited by the car, Jurgen told Jost what had happened. Jost seemed to be worried. "What is the matter? Did you know Cooper?"

"*Ja*, I purchased a little tractor from him and his brother. They tried to cheat me."

While Jurgen was thinking about that, he noticed Mr. Genucci was pointing toward Jost, and Officer Tipton had his notebook out and was taking notes.

Jurgen decided he should find out everything that happened between Jost and the Coopers. So, taking out his notebook he asked, "How did they try to cheat you?"

"They sold me a little tractor. It was like the one that came with the farm I rented from Herr Moritz. I thought having two would be even more help around the farm. They said it was ready to run on alcohol like the one I have. But when Herr Genucci looked at it, he said it had to be worked on to even run, much less run on the alcohol we make. But I saw it run, they were plowing a field with it."

"How did you pay for the tractor?"

"With the silver I had when I came here. I didn't change it all to paper money. Herr Genucci threatened to take them to court and they gave me half my money back. He is helping to fix the tractor and I help him around his funeral parlor."

"Jost, when did this happen and have you seen either one of them, this one or his brother, since you got your money back?"

"I bought the tractor last week, but it was only yesterday that I got my money back. It was the brother who gave me the money. He paid me in paper money, but Herr Genucci says it is good. I haven't seen Tommy since last week. But I saw the brother, they call him G. C., early this morning. Him and his wife were walking toward their home when I went to check on the cow."

"Do you have any idea what time that was? When you went to check on the cow, I mean?"

"*Ja*, we have a clock and I checked it when I came back in. It was five-thirty when I came in, so say five o'clock when I saw G. C."

Jurgen noticed Jost was wearing a belt knife, the same knife he always wore. Jost had always been a bit of a miser when it came to money. Jurgen remembered one time in their village Jost had got in a fight over who owned a chicken.

His thoughts were interrupted when he noticed Officer Tipton waving him over. "Stay here, Jost. I have a few more questions for you and Mina."

"Well, what does your cousin say?" Tipton asked as Jurgen joined him.

Jurgen gave him a quick run-through of what Jost had told him. Tipton nodded. "Yeah, that checks with what Genucci has to say. Except he said Jost was a little more upset about the Coopers trying to cheat him." Tipton squatted to get closer to the body. "Think Jost was mad enough to do that to him?"

Jurgen was reluctant to answer. Tipton was asking him to accuse his cousin of murder, but in his mind it looked like Jost was a prime suspect. Before Tipton could press him for an answer, they were interrupted by the arrival of the ambulance, closely followed by another squad car with Chief Frost at the wheel.

Dan Frost walked up to the body. After looking around to see if anyone was in hearing distance, he said, "Boys, this is going to be a hot one. We have to solve it fast. The Coopers are in tight with the Club 250 crowd, and you know they're going to make a stink if we don't."

Tipton shook his head. "Boss, we have a suspect with a motive, but I don't think he did the killing." Jurgen's heart dropped into his boots. Tipton had to be referring to Jost.

After he had seen their notes, Frost said: "Okay, you two are in charge of the investigation, but keep me informed. If we were still up-time I'd call in the state police, but here and now we have limited resources. If you need more people, ask for them. Get Jost's knife. Dr. Nichols' people can run a comparison check to find any human blood on it."

Jurgen walked back to where Jost and Mina were standing. "Jost, we are going to need your knife for tests. If the test comes back negative, you'll get it back."

"Jurgen, I did not kill that man. I haven't even seen him since last week. Ask Mina, ask Franziska, my wife. I never left the house, except to check on the cow. And I was still in my nightshirt when I went to the barn to check the cow."

"If we check your knife, and there is no blood on it, that will prove you didn't kill him. But we are going to have to check your knife."

"But there *is* blood on it. I used it to kill a chicken yesterday." Jost untied his belt and pulled the sheathed knife from it.

Jurgen remembered the lecture Dr. Nichols had given during his police training. "Jost, they can tell the difference between the blood of a chicken and a man's blood." As Jurgen took the knife, he added, "This will prove your knife didn't kill him. If you didn't kill him you have nothing to worry about."

Watching Jost, Jurgen could see he wasn't too sure about this whole process. Well, that was easy to understand. They were all strangers here.

As they watched the body being loaded into the ambulance, Officer

Tipton joined them. When he saw the knife in Jurgen's hand, he turned to Jost. "When this is all cleared up, I'll make sure you get your knife back. Come on, Jurgen, we need to go out to the Coopers' and tell them what happened."

When the two were in the car, Jurgen had to ask, "Do you think Jost did it?"

"Nope. Oh, I bet Jost has a temper, and if you pushed him enough he could kill. But somehow it just doesn't fit. Besides, there's Tommy's pistol. Or, to be exact, there is the pistol Tommy didn't have."

"What?"

"Tommy always carried an old revolver in his hip pocket. I should know, I took it off him one time before the Ring of Fire. Dan gave it back to his dad, but Tommy had it when I saw him last week. But when I checked the body, there was no revolver. So whoever killed him probably took the revolver. In addition he still had some silver coins in his pockets. Not likely that Jost would kill him over money and not take the money."

"Strange that whoever took the revolver didn't take the money, though."

"Murder cases are always strange, you ask me. And that pistol is going to be a real lead if we find it."

"Why, Marvin? I mean, there must be lots of pistols like it in Grantville."

"Not like this one. It's an old Smith .32-20. I doubt there was another like it in Grantville. I know that even before the Ring of Fire cartridges for it were rare."

"We can talk to Herr Santee and Herr Johnson, since they are doing the most reloading, and see if anyone else has one."

Jurgen noticed that Officer Tipton gave him a surprised look. Why? Chief Frost had told Jurgen to learn about people in the town.

Finally, Tipton nodded his head. "Good idea. We'll run by Johnson's place after we talk to the Coopers and check with Santee when we head into town. By the way, when we get to the Coopers', let me do the talking. They are going to be tough to deal with. They always are. But we don't need to stir them up even more by having you talk to them."

"Why would I upset them?"

Tipton glanced at him. "G. C. and 'Old' Tommy are . . . well. Do you know the term 'rednecks'?"

"*Ja*, the Club 250 crowd." Suddenly it all made sense. The people around the Club 250 didn't like their new German neighbors.

"There you go. All the Coopers are regulars at the 250. In fact G. C.'s wife works there as a cook and waitress. Your English is very good, better than my German, but you still have an accent. That accent would be just enough to set the Coopers off. Sorry, partner, but that's how it is."

As Jurgen thought about what Tipton had said, he noticed a discoloration in the grass by the road. "Stop the car. I see something!"

Tipton brought the car to a halt and the two walked back to discover a large patch of what had to be blood in the grass beside the road. Nearby, the high grass was flattened down as if a heavy weight had been rolled over it.

"Good eyes, Jurgen, I would have missed this." Tipton pulled out a couple of paper envelopes to collect samples.

"What do you think, Marvin? Was Cooper cut here and the body moved?"

"Well, someone was cut here. We won't know if it was Tommy until we get some lab work done. I didn't think there was enough blood back in the Genucci yard."

Looking down the road, Jurgen estimated they were about two hundred yards from where the body was found. Then he noticed the bark on a nearby sapling had a large split. Walking over to it, he found what looked a lot like a bullet hole. "Hey, Marvin, look here. I think we found the sound Herr Genucci heard."

Tipton came over. "Yep, that sure looks like a fresh bullet hole to me. Want to bet when we dig out the bullet it's a .32? I'll get the saw out of the trunk and we can cut out the part of the tree with the bullet in it and take it with us."

As Tipton walked back to the car, Jurgen continued to study the ground around the blood splatter. A few feet away, he found a jacket made from the fabric the Americans called denim or blue jeans. Bending to look closer, he saw bloodstains on one of the sleeves. "Marvin, I found a jacket with blood on it."

Tipton was back now, with the saw. He squatted to look at the jacket. "Wasn't Tommy wearing a jacket?" he asked. "This might belong to whoever stabbed him."

Tipton and Jurgen both started making drawings of what they now believed was the murder site.

"Damn, I wish we still had enough film to take pictures. A camera would be better than any drawing we can make."

Jurgen had to agree. He had seen some of the almost magical pictures in the files of the police station. "Marvin, do you have the jacket in your drawing? I am going to get a bag out of the car so we can collect it as evidence."

"Got it. Hey, hold it up first. I want to see what size it is."

As Jurgen lifted the Jacket, he realized it was too small for even an average-size man and was either a woman's or a child's jacket. It was also badly torn at the shoulder of the bloodstained sleeve.

"Just like I thought. It looked a little small." Tipton hefted the saw. "Get the bag and I'll cut down the sapling. Then we can head on out to the Coopers."

When they pulled into the Coopers' driveway, Jurgen saw that the house was very run-down. Not like many of the houses in Grantville, which needed a coat of paint, but in need of major repairs. He could see that a number of the roof shingles were missing and the eaves had missing boards. In the rear of the house was what the Americans called a "mobile home," though Jurgen himself had never seen one move. Parked near the side of the house was a smaller mobile home—what the Americans usually called a "camp trailer."

A burly-looking man came out of the front door.

"That's G. C.," Tipton said. "Guess we get to talk to him first."

"What the hell you want?" Cooper demanded, as the two police-men got out of the car.

"Cooper, I need to talk with your dad."

"What about?" G. C. looked at Jurgen. "You're one of those krauts they put on the police, ain't you?"

"Cooper, you're starting to get on my nerves," Tipton said, before Jurgen could answer. "Now go get your dad before I start thinking about an obstruction-of-justice charge."

"Come on, then, follow me. His place is around back. Don't want no kraut in my house."

As Cooper led them around the house toward the mobile home, Jurgen spotted the outline of a small pistol in his right hip pocket. He also noticed that Tipton had unsnapped the safety strap on his holster.

"Hey, Dad! A couple of cops here wanting to talk to you!" G. C. yelled, as he knocked on the door. "One of them is a kraut."

"Marvin Tipton, you got a lot of nerve bringing one of those Ger-mans on my property," was the first thing the older Cooper said as he looked out through the screen door.

"Mr. Cooper, could you step outside or could we come in? What I have to say is not the sort of thing I want to yell through a screen door."

"Wait, let me get a shirt on and I'll come out."

As they waited, Jurgen looked around the yard. Next to the rear of the camp trailer he saw a very beat-up garden tractor. *That must be like the one they sold Jost,* he thought, hoping the one his cousin got was in better shape.

Old man Cooper finally came out of the mobile home. "All right, what's so important that you have to drag an old man out of bed? I'm not a well man, you know. This better be important." Jurgen could believe Cooper was not a well man. He could hear him wheezing from ten feet away.

"Mr. Cooper, G. C., this isn't easy to say, but Young Tommy was found dead this morning. It looks like someone killed him."

"What! Someone murdered my boy?" The older Cooper sat down heavily on the steps. But Jurgen noticed that G. C. didn't seem as shocked as his father.

The old man let out a couple of inarticulate gasps. Then he started yelling. "Gladys! Gladys, come here! Somebody's killed our boy!"

From the back door of the house an older woman came running, followed by a middle-aged woman.

Tipton leaned over and whispered, "Gladys and Connie Cooper. Old Tommy's wife and G. C.'s wife."

After what seemed like an hour of wailing and inarticulate muttering, the two older Coopers went into the mobile home.

"Okay, Marvin," muttered G. C., "it looks like I'm the one stuck with making arrangements. Where's my brother?"

"He's down at the medical center and you can have whoever is doing the funeral pick up the body. You don't have to go identify him. We positively identified him. Hell, I've known Tommy seems like my whole life."

"Who killed him?"

"That's what we're trying to find out, G. C. Do you know where he was last night?"

"Yeah, he was down at the Club. In fact he was supposed to walk Connie home, but he took off. I got hung up at the garage and asked him to get her."

Tipton turned to look at Cooper's wife. "That right, Connie?"

"That's right," the woman answered. Jurgen noticed that she was looking at her husband, not at Tipton as she talked. "I was working till twelve and Tommy was supposed to walk me home, but around eleven I noticed he was gone. So I called G. C. at the garage."

"And you went over and got her?" When G. C. nodded, Tipton continued. "What time was that, G. C.?"

"Oh, it was about twelve, twelve-fifteen. They were just closing when I got there. Connie was waiting outside so I didn't go in."

"If you didn't go in, I guess you don't know who was there."

"Well, I saw Wilda Bates and her daughter Marlene leaving and I saw Ape Hart walking with them, but I doubt if they saw me."

"Connie, who all was in the Club 250 last night?"

"I can't really say. I was in the kitchen most of the night. Ken, you know Ken Beasley, got a mess of venison steaks and I spent most of the night cooking instead of waiting tables. Then when I came out of the kitchen about eleven, I noticed Tommy was gone and I called G. C."

"If you're thinking someone from the Club killed him you're way off base. Forget it." G. C. glanced at Jurgen. "Using a knife sounds like a kraut to me."

"Why, G. C.? Has Tommy had any run-ins with some of our German citizens lately? We did hear something about a tractor."

"Tractor? Yeah, me and Tommy sold a tractor to that kraut that rents from Ted Moritz. Neubert is his name, I think. He wasn't happy with the deal. He even got Freddy Genucci to threaten to sue us. Is that about all you want to know? I got to make some calls. Got to find someone to do the funeral. No way I want that Genucci touching my brother."

"One last question." Tipton raised his hand to stop Cooper from walking off. "When you brought Connie home, did you notice anything as you walked by the end of Happy Hills? What would that have been, about twelve-thirty or one o'clock?"

G. C. seemed to think a bit. "No, we didn't see anything odd, and it was closer to one than twelve-thirty. If that's all, I really have to make those calls."

"Yeah, G. C. that just about does it. If we need anything else, we'll get in touch with you. Call the station if you think of anything new."

As the two policemen walked back to their car Tipton asked, "Well, what do you think?"

"Marvin, did you notice that when the wife was answering she was always looking at her husband?"

"Caught that, did you? It was almost like she was checking with him to see if her story was right. Of course the thing that made me wonder was how G. C. knew Tommy was killed with a knife. I never told him how Tommy was killed, and I doubt Freddy Genucci called him. Makes you wonder, doesn't it."

As they got to the car Jurgen looked across the top and asked, "Were you really friends with them? They seem to dislike you now."

Tipton gave a little laugh. "Yeah, Tommy and me were pretty close, but we were kids then. Our friendship ended when I put on this uniform. His choice, not mine. Sometimes that happens. You better get ready. It can happen to you. Wait and see when you have to arrest someone who's a friend."

As they started to pull out of the Coopers' drive, a school bus stopped across the end of the driveway and unloaded the younger Cooper children and the Craigs who lived on the other side of the road. As they waited for the school bus to pass, Tipton looked at his watch. "That's the two-thirty bus. Henry Johnson should be on that bus, on his way home from the middle school. We might as well follow it to the Johnson place and talk to him now."

"*Ja*, since he lives so close to the Coopers it is a good possibility he does their reloading."

When the bus stopped in front of the Johnson drive, they were proven right when they saw Henry and the four Schultz and Ekhard children get off and head up the drive.

"Henry! Henry Johnson!" Tipton yelled as they pulled into the drive. "Can we talk to you?"

They saw Johnson stop and wave to them. "Hi, Marvin. Come on up to the house. I bet I can find you and your partner something cold to drink."

As they followed Johnson up the drive, Jurgen noticed the bulge under his coat. That had to be a pistol, he thought. Thinking about it some more, he was not surprised. Johnson was one of only three male teachers at the middle school, and since the raid, people had realized the schools were major targets for the enemies of Grantville.

Soon the three were seated in the Johnson living room with glasses of iced coffee in their hands. Tipton and Jurgen had followed Johnson's lead and hung their gun belts on the hooks by the front door. Tipton sipped his coffee and then asked, "Henry, have you met my partner, Jurgen Neubert?"

"Can't say that I have." Johnson extended his hand. "Good to meet you, Officer Neubert. Now I doubt this is a social call, so what can I do for you?"

"Henry, we're trying to get a line on Young Tommy Cooper's pistol and thought he might have come to you for reloaded ammo."

Johnson chuckled. "What's Tommy done now? And, yes, I know his gun, if you're talking about the Smith .32-20 Hand Ejector."

"As far as we know Tommy didn't do anything but get himself killed. His pistol is missing and we're trying to track it down."

"We thought you might know if anyone else had a revolver in that caliber," Jurgen interjected. "And could tell us if anyone tried to buy cartridges to fit it."

"Tommy got himself killed," Johnson mused. "Can't say I'm surprised or too broken up about it. I don't have a lot of use for the whole family, frankly. Oh, I do business with them, but I keep a sharp eye on them. To answer your questions, I reloaded eighteen rounds for Young Tommy a couple of weeks ago. All the cases he had. I can do a lot when it comes to reloading, but I don't make cases for a .32-20, it's a bit of an oddball. And as far as I know there are only two other .32-20s in town, both rifles. You should check with Paul Santee, he does a lot of the rarer cartridges, but I would bet that three .32-20s are all you'll find."

"Herr Johnson, if you could see a bullet could you tell us if it was one of the ones you reloaded for Cooper?" Jurgen asked.

"You're talking about a fired bullet? Maybe, if it's not too damaged, but I loaded soft-lead round noses for Tommy. If it hit something hard it's going to have flattened out quite a bit."

"It's in a tree," Tipton said. "When we dig it out, we'll bring it out to show you."

Johnson thought a minute, "I doubt I can tell much. But you might weigh the bullet. Most .32s use a ninety- or ninety-five-grain bullet. A .32-20, on the other hand, uses a hundred-and-ten-grain bullet. I don't know if that's any help, though."

"Thank you, Herr Johnson, that might help."

"It's nothing. I am happy to help."

"No, really, Henry," Tipton said, "this really helps out. I have one more favor to ask though. Can I use your phone to call the office? I want to check and see if any word has come in on the autopsy, and I don't want to use the radio."

"Sure, it's over there by the stairs, right next to the scanner." He chuckled. "I listen in on your radio traffic myself, so I can understand why you don't want to use the radio. I'll just step out on the porch and let you have some privacy."

While Tipton made his call, Jurgen and Henry stood on the porch and talked. "Officer Neubert, how do you like living in Grantville? Must be quite a change for you."

"Ja, Herr Johnson. To you Grantville is just a small town, but compared to my village it is a city."

Henry chuckled. "Actually, I know what you mean. I worked in country schools all my life, before I moved back to Grantville, and it seemed big to me when I came home."

Just then Officer Tipton came out of the house. "Henry, we have to run, and thanks again for the information. By the way, we would appreciate it if you kept our talk under your hat."

"No problem, Marvin. As far as I'm concerned it's all on the square." Jurgen saw Johnson make a sign with his hands.

"Thanks, Henry," Tipton responded. Jurgen noticed he also made a sign.

As the two walked to the car, Jurgen asked, "Marvin, you may not want to answer this, but what was that hand sign Herr Johnson gave you?"

"No problem, Jurgen. Henry and me are both Masons. He was telling me he wouldn't tell anyone what we talked about until I said it was okay. If you're interested, I'll give you a pamphlet about it when we get back to the station."

Once they were in the car, Tipton turned to Jurgen. "Well, partner, we screwed up. They did a quick autopsy on Young Tommy and he was stabbed *twice*. We missed the wound to his chest."

"What?"

"Yep, he was stabbed in the chest. It nicked the heart, but didn't kill him until a few minutes later. He could have walked to the Genucci's place. The throat was cut after he died. Maybe an hour or two after he died."

"What now, Marvin?"

"We'll stop by the office and tell Chief Frost what we have. And I want to pick up a handi-talkie before we go to the Club 250. We'll see what Tommy was doing last night. I bet that's what got him killed, not his troubles with your cousin Jost."

After stopping the car in the parking lot of the Club 250, Tipton turned to Jurgen. "Watch your back in here. I don't think any of these yahoos are stupid enough to try anything, but you never know with mean drunks. Clip the handi-talkie to your belt and be ready to call for backup."

Jurgen picked up the little radio and clipped it on his belt. It still amazed him that he could talk into this little box and Emil could hear him back at the station. The Americans had marvelous tools.

Walking into the Club 250, Jurgen could feel every eye in the place staring at him and Tipton. No so much, he thought, because he was German, but because of the uniforms they wore. Tipton led him toward a table set near the end of the bar. At the table was seated a man who appeared to be working on records and accounts.

"Hi, Ken. We need to talk with you and some of your employees and probably some of your customers."

"Why should I want to talk to you, Marvin? Prancing in here with your pet German. Have you taught him to do any tricks yet? Bet you could teach him to fetch real easy." Jurgen noticed that Ken, whoever he was, had said that loud enough for the small crowd in the bar to hear. A number of them laughed and seemed to be inching closer.

Tipton looked around the room and said in a loud voice, "I guess I forgot to introduce Officer Neubert. He is about two seconds away from calling an ambulance for everyone we don't arrest. I'll try to hold him back, but he is determined to get some answers or put two or three of you rednecks in the medical center and the rest in jail."

Jurgen could sense the crowd studying him. Returning the stares of the people, Jurgen picked out the man he was going to hit first. Drop the biggest one in the place first and maybe the rest will back off.

"Of course, you could just answer our questions. Then all you have to deal with is me. And you all know I am just sweetness and light to talk to."

"Hell, Marvin," the big man Jurgen had picked out said with a slight laugh. "Last time I talked to you, I got thirteen stitches and two days in the county lockup. I'd rather drink." With that, he looked away and concentrated on the drink in front of him.

The rest of the customers followed the big man's lead, though Jurgen could sense they were still watching.

Tipton gave a snort of disgust and turned back to the man at the table. "Jurgen, this is Ken Beasley. He owns this outhouse. He is the person you want to question first. If he doesn't want to talk to you, we can just shut this place down for a couple of days. A health inspection will do it easily." With that, Tipton leaned against the wall behind Jurgen and seemed to be watching the few couples who had returned to the small crowded dance floor.

"Herr Beasley, we are investigating the death of Young Tommy Cooper."

"Yeah, yeah, his dad called here about an hour ago and told Fenton. Funny, Tommy gets killed by a kraut and you start harassing his friends."

"We don't know who killed him yet. It might have been a German or it might have been someone he knew from here. I am sure you want us to find the real killer. We were told Tommy was here last night. Is that right?"

"Yeah, Tommy is in every night. Last night was a Thursday so he was supposed to walk Connie home. Can't say I saw him leave with her, though. In fact I didn't see him leave at all."

"You were working the bar last night?"

"Nah, Fenton was handling drink orders. We weren't very busy after eight so I caught up on my paperwork. One thing, though— Tommy paid off the bar tab he had been running for a couple of months. Paid it in silver."

"Did you see who he was drinking with? Who he spent most of the night with?"

"Didn't you hear me? I said I was working on the books. One time early in the evening he got in a yelling match with Ape but it was nothing big. They went on drinking together afterwards."

"Who is Ape?"

Beasley pointed to the big man Jurgen had noticed earlier.

"One last question and we are done, for now. Was Tommy carrying a gun last night?"

"I guess so. Tommy was always packing. He had an old Smith and Wesson revolver he carried. He probably had it last night, but I wouldn't swear to it."

"Thank you, Herr Beasley. You have been helpful. Now, I need to talk to Fenton. Is that him working behind the bar now?"

"Yes, Fenton Mase. Hey, Fenton! Come and talk to this cop. I'll take over for you." Beasley got up from the table.

Jurgen watched Mase walk over to the table and sit across from him. Mase was an average-sized man, but walked with all the confidence of a born fighter. Jurgen thought Mase had probably been hired to keep order in the bar as much as to sell drinks. He realized that of all the customers and staff, Mase was the only completely sober one in the Club. And he also seemed to be relaxed about talking to the police.

"Herr Mase, I want to know about Tommy Cooper and what happened when he was in here last night. What can you tell me?"

"Not much. He came in about five o'clock and had dinner. I served him a couple of beers at the bar and then he started talking to Freddie Congden. They moved over to a table and started playing cards with Ape and Monkey Hart. So Brandy, she was waiting tables last night, served them the rest of the night."

"Did you see what time he left, and who he left with?"

"There you got me. I didn't see him leave. I think he was there till closing and left with Connie, but I can't swear to it. Things get busy about closing time. There's always somebody who wants one last beer. This is a beer crowd, but they drink a lot of it."

"Oh," Jurgen said, as if just remembering something. "Did you notice if Tommy had a pistol?"

Mase seemed offended. "What kind of bartender would I be if I missed that? An old Smith revolver, right hip pocket, turned so the butt was toward the middle of his back."

Jurgen realized bartenders and policemen had a lot in common when it came to watching people. "That is all I need right now. Did you say Brandy was the waitress that waited on Tommy most of the night? Is she working today?"

"Yeah, Brandy Bates, that's her, the young one." Mase pointed to the two women carrying trays of beer mugs from the bar. "The other is Marlene Bates. She and Brandy are some kind of cousins. She wasn't working last night, but was here with her mother, Wilda, and Ape. Connie was the other waitress last night."

"Are you sure? I thought Connie Cooper was the cook."

"She cooks and waits tables both. Last night Connie was in the kitchen until, oh, eight or nine at least. Then she came out and waited tables until closing. That's easy to remember. The bar always runs smoother when Connie is working. She isn't sneaking a drink all the time or getting orders mixed up like Brandy. Is that all? I need to get back to my bar before Ken screws up the beer taps again."

Jurgen waved him off after thanking him. Leaning back he asked, "Did you hear all that, Marvin? I think we need to talk to Ape and his friends next."

"We'll get around to Ape. Stick with the waitresses for now. Interesting that Connie lied to us about waiting tables last night, don't you think?" Tipton then turned and called out, "Brandy, step over here a minute, would you? Officer Neubert wants to ask you some questions."

When she came up, Tipton gestured at a chair. "Have a seat. Bet you need to get off your feet for a while anyway."

Looking across the table, Jurgen studied the young waitress. She looked to be in her early twenties, and was pretty in a rough-hewn sort of way. Her looks were spoiled by the dislike, almost hatred, he could sense in the look she gave him in return.

"Fraulein Bates, we need to know what Tommy Cooper did last night. This will help us find his killer. What can you tell us?"

"You're one of the Germans they made cops, ain't you?"

"Yes, Fraulein, I am German," Jurgen said patiently. "Now, unless you want to sit here all night, will you answer my questions? The longer we spend, the more tips you lose."

Brandy gave a little laugh. "Tips, in this crowd? You have to be joking. They wouldn't know a tip if it bit them on the ass. But I'll answer your questions. Okay, Tommy Cooper. He was in here from about five o'clock until closing. He had a steak, but complained it was too tough and was priced too high. He got drunk as a skunk, and tried to grab my butt every time I walked by. You talk about tips. Tommy left a quarter, new money, on the table. I think he was just too drunk to get all his change. I hope whoever killed him did a good job and made him suffer. There, does that make me a suspect?"

"Well, it puts you on the list, Fraulein," Jurgen said with a slight chuckle. "But I think it is a very long list. *Did* you kill him?"

"Nope, not that I'm sorry he's dead, but Fenton walked me home and I live here in town. So I never saw Tommy after we closed. Guess you'll have to keep looking."

"And keep asking questions." Jurgen continued, "After he ate what did you see?"

"Tommy played cards with Freddie Congden, Ape, and Monkey Hart for beer. He seemed to be doing most of the losing, too. At least he was doing most of the buying. After they left he sat and played solitaire. Drinking beer the whole time."

"Tommy was spending a lot of money, then?"

"Yeah, he had a lot of money. Both American dollars and German silver."

"Is that what caused the fight between him and Ape? Losing at cards, I mean."

"It wasn't really a fight. Ape and him were just yelling at each other. Call it an argument. And it was over Tommy asking Marlene to go out to his trailer with him. Wilda, Marlene's mother, and Ape live together.

When she told Tommy to keep his hands to himself, he got smart with her. Ape was just defending Wilda. At least as far as I could tell. I had other customers."

"Did you see when Tommy left if he was with anyone?"

"No, in fact I didn't see him leave at all. Last night was my night to collect beer mugs and I was back in the kitchen helping wash up."

"I guess that is about all the questions I have. Oh, did Tommy have a pistol with him?"

"I don't know. If he did, he kept it hidden. Like he kept his tips."

Tipton leaned over the table. "Here's a tip for you Brandy: get out of the bar business. You're too young to be working here. Go see Peggy Craig over at the elementary school Monday and she'll get you on working in the cafeteria. Tell her I sent you."

"Why, Officer Tipton, I didn't know you cared. I think I'll pass, though. As bad as the people here are about tipping, I doubt those snot-nosed kids are any better." With that Brandy got up from the table and flounced back to work.

"Snot-nosed kids," Tipton commented with a huff. "Three years ago she was one herself." Then in a louder voice he called, "Marlene, we're ready to talk to you now."

Watching Marlene approach, Jurgen thought, there was Brandy in a few years. Hard-bitten and world-weary.

As soon as she was seated, Marlene started talking. "I wasn't working last night. So I don't know why you want to talk to me. In fact I wouldn't be working tonight if Connie hadn't taken the evening off. What with Tommy getting killed and all. So there is not a lot I can tell you." With that she started to get up.

"Hold it, Marlene," Tipton said from his place by the wall. "Office Neubert still has a few questions for you."

Sitting back down, Marlene looked at Jurgen. "Ask away, but there is nothing I can tell you."

"We already know you were here last night, even if you weren't working. What we need is to know what Tommy Cooper was doing last night."

"Tommy was doing what he always does, getting drunk and being a nuisance. He even asked me to go home with him. Like I wanted to see his ratty old camp trailer. He got all huffy when Mom told him to shut up and called her a name. He was just being an asshole, as usual."

"This was while he was playing cards?"

"Yeah, I was sitting behind him and he kept reaching back trying to feel my leg. Ape told him to cool it after he shouted at Mom."

"What time did you see him leave? And was there anyone with him when he left?"

"Actually he was still here when we left. That was at eleven. I had to get home to see about my kids so I was checking the clock. Mom and Ape walked me home, so they left the same time I did. Monkey must have left just after we did, because he caught up with us before we got to my trailer."

"So Tommy was still here at eleven when you left?"

"That's what I said, wasn't it?"

Tipton leaned over and asked, "One last question and then you can leave. When they were playing cards, what games were they playing?"

"Euchre. Tommy and Freddie Congden against Ape and Monkey." Marlene got up and left.

"What do you think, Marvin?" Jurgen asked as he rose to stand beside Tipton.

"I think I'm getting a picture I don't like. Looks to me like Connie lied about Tommy taking off before eleven. And maybe even about not walking her home."

"*Ja*, it looks like she may be covering up for someone."

"That's what I don't like about it. As much as I dislike G. C., I can't picture him killing his own brother."

"So who do you think killed him?"

"I don't know. In fact I have less of an idea than when we started. Frustrating, isn't it? You ready to talk to the cardplayers?"

"Sure. Which one first?"

"Well, I don't see Monkey or Freddie, and since he's walking this way let's talk to Ape."

Jurgen looked up and saw the man who had been pointed out as Ape Hart heading toward them.

As Ape sat down, he waved to the other chairs at the table. "Marvin, Marvin's buddy, I guess you'll want to talk to me sometime tonight. Let's get it over with so I can get back to my friends."

Looking at Ape, Jurgen could see how he got his name. The man was huge and shaped something like the picture of a gorilla Jurgen had seen in the library. He even appeared to be as hairy, from the amount of dark hair on his arms and hands. Looking closer he saw that the hair was flecked with gray. Ape was no longer a young man. Still, he looked like he could lift a loaded wagon.

"Herr Hart, we are checking on what Tommy Cooper was doing last night. We have been told you spent some time with him. Is that true?"

"You speak pretty good, for a kraut," Ape said with a smirk. Jurgen could see Ape was enjoying insulting him to his face.

"Herr Hart, we can ask these questions here, and let you go back to your friends," Jurgen said laying his handcuffs on the table. "Or I can hook you up and take you over to the station and ask them there. Your choice."

Before Ape could answer, Tipton leaned over the table. "Remember Ape, you've been drinking all evening and Officer Neubert has about twenty years on you."

Jurgen could see Ape studying him. "Ha, I can see you'd really enjoy trying to put those cuffs on me. Wouldn't you, Neubert? Well, not tonight 'cause I got things to do. But one day we'll get it on."

"Herr Hart, you are wasting your drinking time," Jurgen said with a smile. "So tell us about your and Tommy's card game."

"Okay, Of-fi-cer Neubert." Ape stretched the name out so Jurgen could see there was no respect in the use of his title. "Me and Monkey played euchre against Freddie and Tommy for a couple of hours. We were playing for beers. I didn't buy a beer all night. Tommy can't play euchre for spit. He always orders up if he is holding a bower and an ace."

"What was the argument you had with Tommy about?"

"Wilda told him to keep his hands off of Marlene and he got a little smart with her. I told him to chill out and he acted a little frisky, but nothing came of it. It wasn't a big thing. Tommy gets like that some times. He's an asshole. Was an asshole, now, I guess."

"That didn't stop you from drinking the beer he bought though, did it?"

"Look, Tommy was spending money like he owned a bank. He said he had gotten the better of a kraut on a deal selling a tractor. He was laughing about how him and G. C. ripped the kraut off. They switched tractors on him. Then Tommy ripped off G. C. and took all the money. If I hadn't drunk his beer someone else would have."

"Did Tommy have a gun with him?"

"Yeah, he had that old Smith in his hip pocket. It caught on the chair a couple of times when he got up. If he ever tried to use it, he'd have dropped it. I told you he was drunk, didn't I?"

"When did he leave?"

"I couldn't tell you. Freddie left about ten till eleven and we played one hand of three-handed. Then Marlene had to leave at eleven, so Wilda and me walked her home. Tommy was still here when we left."

"Do you have anyone to back up your story?"

"Hey, if you think I killed him, you're way off base. Wilda, Marlene, and Monkey can all tell you where I was. In fact I waved to the mayor on my way home and he waved back. Ask him. I was on the other side of town."

"Herr Hart, I think that is all for now. We might want to talk to you later."

"Anytime, Of-fi-cer Neubert, anytime." Ape got up from the table. "I'll look forward to it."

"I wouldn't worry about Ape," Tipton said softly. "When he's sober, he's too smart to fight a cop. And when he drinking he can't fight and he knows it. That's why I wanted to wait to talk to him."

"Marvin, it looks like we have to go back and talk to the Coopers."

"Yep, I'm afraid so. Damn, sometimes I hate this job. Let's go."

Just before they arrived at the Cooper house, Tipton turned off the headlights and let the car coast to a stop. From where the car was sitting, Jurgen could see the house and the camp trailer and the edge of the mobile home. The yard and most of the house were lit by the full moon.

"I don't see any lights. Looks like no one is home, Marvin."

"We'll wait. They'll be home sometime tonight. While we're waiting, what are your thoughts on the case?"

"Marvin, you know these people and I don't, but it looks to me like they are trying to hide something."

"Yeah, they're hiding something and as usual they're doing a lousy job of it."

Just then Jurgen heard a noise from the back of the house. Looking at the mobile home, he could see two shadowy figures near an old truck parked there. Listening carefully, he could hear muffled voices. "Someone is beside the old truck."

"Yeah, let's get a little closer." Tipton flipped the switch to make sure the dome light wouldn't come on when they opened the doors. "You go right and work your way up behind them and I'll go down beside the house."

Jurgen and Tipton carefully closed the doors of the car to make no noise and separated to move toward the house. Just before closing the door Jurgen retrieved his baton, and slipped it into the ring on his belt. He should have taken that with him into the Club 250, he realized now.

As Jurgen crossed the ditch beside the road, he was keenly aware of the noise he was making. He thought he sounded like a herd of cows. But the two figures beside the truck continued what they were doing as he worked his way though the brush that bordered the yard. Soon, he was even with the mobile home and could see the figures' faces in the moonlight. It was G. C. Cooper and his wife, Connie. They were loading something in the truck.

Just then something Tipton stepped on made a slight noise near the rear of the house. Jurgen could see G. C. jump and stare toward the house. "Who's there?" G. C. called as he put his hand under the bottom of his jacket. "I've got a gun!"

"It's me, Marvin Tipton," Tipton called, "and I know you have a gun, but you better get your hand off of it. We need to talk."

Connie Cooper gave a gasp and sank to the ground leaning on the side of the truck. She sat there giving out little gasps.

"I don't have anything to say to you, Marvin. We're a little busy right now. You can come back in the morning, or better yet, stop by the garage." Jurgen could see that Cooper had drawn a pistol and was holding it beside his leg, out of Marvin's sight. Jurgen started working his way closer to the Coopers, the noise of his movements masked by their voices.

"G. C., I can't do that. I have a bloodstained jacket that I bet fits Connie, and an eye witness that saw you and her on the road walking away from where Tommy was killed. And I know Tommy walked Connie home from the Club. Now I find you loading what looks a lot like gas cans into your truck. Thinking about running away, G. C.?" The whole time Tipton was talking, he had been moving closer to G. C. Now he was less than ten feet away.

As Jurgen slipped closer, he wondered what to do. He could shoot him, but he didn't know that G. C. was the killer. Jurgen drew his baton.

G. C. brought his pistol up and pointed it at Tipton. "Marvin, stop right there or I'll shoot."

Tipton stopped moving and spoke in an almost conversational voice. "You know, G. C., the one thing I am having trouble figuring out is why you killed Tommy. It wasn't the money. He's been taking money from you and your dad for years. It sure wasn't because he was a drunk. Tommy has never spent a sober day since he could sit on a bar stool. So why did you kill him?"

Jurgen could tell that Tipton had seen him and was trying to keep Cooper from realizing there were two of them. Jurgen moved closer till he was just at the back of the truck. Three steps away, then two. A quick lunge and Jurgen brought his baton down, backed by all of his two hundred pounds of muscle and bone, on the barrel of the gun in Cooper's hand. A flash of light and a loud crack as the pistol fired into the ground. Then a quick back stroke with the baton to Cooper's chest and he was down, the pistol falling from his hand.

"Thanks, Jurgen." Tipton picked up the pistol from the ground. "I was hoping we wouldn't have to shoot him. It makes a lot of paperwork." Jurgen noticed for the first time that Tipton had his backup pistol in his left hand. Handing over the recovered pistol, Tipton told Jurgen, "Tommy's gun, keep it for evidence."

Tipton then bent over and touched G. C. on the ground, "You all right, G. C.? Roll over to your left, I want to get that pop gun you carry in your hip pocket. That's a good boy."

G. C. merely sat and gasped for breath, holding his arms close to his body as Tipton removed the small automatic from his pocket.

"I think . . . he broke my ribs," G. C. was finally able to get out.

"He could have legally put a .357 through your brain. Think about that the next time you pull a gun on a cop, you damn fool." Tipton looked to where Connie was sitting. "You got something to tell us, Connie?"

Jurgen watched as the woman pulled herself together. "G. C. didn't kill Tommy. I did."

"I sort of figured that from what I heard at the Club. You ready to tell us the whole story?"

"Yes," Connie answered with a slight sob.

As they watched G. C. being loaded into the ambulance and Connie being escorted to Chief Frost's cruiser, the two officers finally had time to talk.

"What do you think is going to happen to them, Marvin?" Jurgen waved at the taillights disappearing down the road.

"To Connie, not much. All she did was fight off a rapist. I knew Tommy had become a real lowlife, but to try to rape your brother's wife . . ." He shook his head. "That's a little much even for him."

"What about G. C.?"

"Oh, G. C. will do some time on a work crew and sleep in the jail for a while. If they had just called us when it happened . . ." Tipton's voice faded away.

"You think he was trying to make it look like Tommy was killed by someone else? Trying to cut off his head and all?"

"Let's stop talking about it." Tipton watched a wagon making its way down the road. "You see that garbage wagon, Jurgen? That's us, picking up society's trash."

An Invisible War

Danita Lee Ewing

Chapter One
June 1633

1

Beulah MacDonald eased her spare frame into the padded leather chair in Dr. James Nichols' crowded office with a carefully hidden sigh of relief. *Beulah, old girl, you're not up to those long hospital shifts anymore. A woman your age has no business on her feet twelve hours a day, most days of the week, turning patients, running a hospital, and all that.* Still, it wasn't as if there were many nurses around after the Ring of Fire. They could certainly use, oh, say a thousand fully trained registered nurses, a hundred nurse practitioners. And doctors. And pharmacists. Some physical and occupational therapists would be great, too. Enough trained people to handle everything that needed doing weren't just going to drop from the sky. Everyone had to help out where they could, including her. *No more retirement checks and social security for you, m'dear.*

"Here you go, Beulah. No cream and enough sugar to put any diabetic into a coma." James Nichols handed her a blue ceramic mug and shook his head in mock rebuke. His grin spoiled the effect a bit.

"I have to keep going somehow. I'm not diabetic you know, so a little sugar won't hurt me. At least we've got caffeine again, even if my arthritis is slowing me down some."

Beulah and James had developed a friendly sparring relationship when they were alone. When they were in public, acting in their roles as director of nursing and director of medicine, they were a little more formal but not too much. Beulah had never gone for that subservient nurse to the almighty doctor stuff in her entire forty-plus year career. She wasn't about to start at this late date even if James had been the type for that nonsense. Which he wasn't, thank God. She and James had worked together a great deal since the Ring of Fire, both in the field and here at the new Grantville hospital. Mutual respect for each other's expertise, a deep commitment to their patients, and a shared sense of humor had helped them develop a strong friendship over the last two years. Since Beulah had worked in just about every kind of nursing over the years, she had been the logical (and nearly the only) choice to be the director of nursing at the new hospital after the Ring of Fire. They needed the younger nurses for the more physical work, and the nurses older than she was were too old, too sick, or dead now.

Still, she couldn't keep up this pace forever. The willow-bark tea helped with the arthritis but it wasn't the same as her now unavailable prescriptions. Her hands wrapped stiffly around the hot mug of coffee. The heat helped the pain, as did the paraffin dips. Her definition of an old remedy was certainly changing, though. The paraffin dips had been something they did in the "old days." Without all the fancy medicines, surgeries, and other treatments from the twentieth century, a lot of people were using old folk remedies or adapting ones from the 1630s. Which caused its own set of problems. No, not problems. *Directors of nursing don't have problems, they have challenges*, she reminded herself.

They sipped coffee in comfortable silence for several minutes.

Outside James' door, she could hear the sounds of the hospital quieting down for the night. She could practically feel her tired muscles unknot as she sank deeper into the chair. Getting up again would be interesting, but James had known how sore her hips and knees were at the end of the day and had given her the most comfortable chair in the room. The thoughtfulness was as appreciated as the coffee, and typical of the man.

She wasn't sure which of them spoke first, just general things at first, chatting about the staff, the hospital, difficult cases recently. So she was somewhat sandbagged by what he slipped in next.

"You want me to what!?"

No teasing grin lit James' face now. His tone was calm but determined. "Become the dean at the College of Medicine's new health sciences department."

"I hate administration. Endless meetings. There's too much paperwork in the job I've got now. Being the dean of a brand new health sciences department will mean even more paperwork. Have you ever developed a course curriculum? Handouts, lecture notes, syllabi. Paper everywhere."

"No, I haven't developed a course. But you have," he countered smoothly.

"I taught nursing for twenty years at a community college. Part-time. What we've all been talking about this past year is a multilevel training program for everything from nurses' aides to doctorally prepared researchers. I don't have the background for that. What about you or Balthazar? Balthazar knows everyone and the local educational system. He'd be perfect."

"Even if he weren't tied up with practice and helping train our spooks, Balthazar never fully recovered from his heart attack. You may be older chronologically, but he is older physically. The rest of the medically trained up-timers are needed for more direct patient care, although we'll all probably be doing some teaching and mentoring of students—especially the hands-on aspects of instruction. More importantly, most of us have never taught so much as a CPR course. We wouldn't know how to put together lectures, handouts, or a syllabus. We're all being stretched in ways we never planned. You'll be great as the new dean."

James was good, she'd have to give him that. "What about education? Shouldn't a dean have more than a bachelor's degree? I never finished my master's degree as a midwife. Many of the faculty at Jena will have more formal education than I do."

If his snort was anything to go by, James didn't even pretend to consider that one. "You have more education than any other nurse around, up-time or down-time. You also have a great deal of experience in just about every area we need taught." James held up one hand to forestall the comment he could see forming on her lips. "Even if some of that experience is a little old, you've gotten back up to speed very quickly. Don't think I haven't seen how many times you wind up taking care of patients rather than office work. And most of your out-of-date stuff is still state of the art and then some here. Besides, some of your old-time knowledge is more within our current technology base's capabilities."

"I like taking care of patients and we're short staffed."

James pounced on that one. "Which isn't going to change unless we set up programs and start running students through them just as fast as we can. Besides, you told me you like teaching."

A distinctly mulish frown bloomed on Beulah's face. "That doesn't make me the right person for this. I'm already running the hospital."

"We needed you to set the hospital up and get it running. Things are going pretty well here now. You've got the administration side set up and running smoothly. The staff is oriented and trained. Starr Hunsaker can take over while you move on to developing the educational program. You won't exactly be alone doing it, either. We'll all help as much as we can. Getting people trained is a priority. We're staring down more years of war, not to mention smallpox, the plague, and on and on. We *have* to have people ready or we're going to lose a hell of a lot of people, Beulah." James met Beulah's dark-blue gaze in shared grief and frustration over the ones that had already been lost.

"We thought Mary Pat would be a good assistant for you," he continued. "She's already living with you, is young, smart, and energetic, and has come up through the ranks in the army. She's been a medical corpsman and LPN and is now experienced as an RN. She had good trauma experience in the army plus her experiences here. She'd really help you out creating the trauma courses. I'm sure the military will release her for detached service given how desperately they need people trained as medics, nurses, and doctors. And almost all of Mary Pat's RN training was as an up-timer. That also works in her favor." James leaned forward in his chair, elbows on his knees, hands clasped loosely together. "We need you to get the ball rolling again, Beulah. You tend to make sure the practical details of setting things up don't get missed so everything runs as smoothly as possible. You know what you're doing, have lots of experience, know how to work as part of a team and get things done. And, frankly, you'd be training Mary Pat while you're at it. You've been acting as a mentor for her for nearly the entire time since the Ring of Fire. You curb some of her enthusiasm with experience. It's a good match, one we can't afford not to take as much advantage of as possible."

Ouch, another point to James, thought Beulah. Mary Pat Flanagan had come to the wedding of Rita Sterns Simpson the day of the Ring of Fire. Her entire large family was left behind, a wound that was still raw, although she hid it fairly well from the outside world. Beulah knew how much she missed them, though.

Beulah had taken Mary Pat into her home just to give her a place to stay at first. It wasn't like Beulah's brother needed his room anymore and space was at a premium in Grantville right after the Ring of Fire. Beulah had never married. There had been a few Mr. Almost Rights over the years, but never Mr. Right. She loved kids, though, and through her work had had "her" kids strung all across the state. But Mary Pat was more like the daughter she had always wanted. They had developed more than a mentoring or landlady-and-tenant relationship. Mary Pat had almost completed her training as an RN from West Virginia University up-time. Having Mary Pat as her assistant would make the job of dean a lot more doable, as James and the others had clearly realized. Mary Pat was smart, organized, and capable.

James and company are getting way too good at this sneaky political stuff. He's hung around Mike too long.

His next sentence changed her mind.

"You'd also have help from Hayes Daniels."

"Hayes! Are you nuts!" Beulah protested, waving her mug around and wincing when her swollen knuckles hit the chair arm. The throbbing in her hand convinced her to be still but didn't change her glare. "He and I worked together on the nurses' aide/LPN course that they're teaching over at the tech center, and the combat medics course. We don't exactly have a good working relationship. And Hayes wants everything done to his standards, his way. Like we have time for that. We needed good enough to get moving, make changes as we go, and we needed those aides pronto. Mary Pat's temper matches that red hair. Mary Pat would strangle him before we were done."

Hayes was the first Silicon Valley refugee she'd ever met. He'd worked in two high-flying start-ups, working too many thirty-six-hour days figuring out how to teach the world how the Internet would change their lives. He'd finally decided that he'd had enough, and gotten out and come, of all places, to West Virginia, close to his friend Mike Sterns.

James shook his head. "I don't know that I agree with you on that entirely. The two of you got the job done and we're getting well-trained aides, medics, and LPNs now. We need to be sure we set up the best system we can from the beginning. The need right now is urgent but we won't do ourselves any favors if we cut too many corners in the name of expediency. Hayes is the only person we have who can take highly technical material and translate it into the course material we need to teach new staff, in any reasonable amount of time. We need him to help evaluate and organize the Jena material in particular. You'll be too busy setting everything else up to handle all the course materials, our teachers are busy teaching the kids, and no one else has enough of a background to even start the job."

The mulish frown was back on Beulah's face. "The faculty at Jena could do some of it."

"The faculty at Jena *will* do some of it, but they're just getting up to speed on some of our basic science material themselves. They'll be one step ahead of the students the first few years. We need someone who can do some of the higher level knowledge synthesis now. And that someone is Hayes. I doubt that any of the Jena faculty even understand some of the biology and chemistry concepts from our era."

"Look, James," Beulah said, running a hand over short curly hair, "I like Hayes, I really do. He's smart and talented and a genuinely nice guy. Hell of a cook, too, for that matter. He's also going under for the third time with everyone's projects and has been since we got here. From the stories he told us while we were doing that last course, doing what he did is like being in a combat zone. And he did it for five years, with no breaks. He got six months off, and he's right back into it. You know what that's like—you've seen it."

James looked a little uncomfortable for the first time in their conversation. "It isn't just that. How old are you now, Beulah? Early seventies? You're in good shape except for the arthritis, but that's getting worse. The odds are, you won't be around for as long as we need you. We have to get the medical knowledge out of your head and the heads of the rest of us so we can pass it on to the next generation. Hayes is the only one who can take what you know and put it in a form others can use to learn. The knowledge is too important to be lost when we lose you." His voice was little more than a whisper.

"I know that James." Her voice was almost as quiet. "Hayes isn't even half my age, but at the rate he's going, he won't make it to forty-five. Adding more projects to the man won't help any of us. I'm really worried about him. The man needs a keeper. Otherwise, we may just use him up, and there won't be anything left."

"It isn't as if there are any other alternatives we've been able to find for Hayes. Let's leave him for a later discussion, okay? Right now, you are the best person for the dean's job. Period."

"There are other issues. What about Jena? We'll need to locate the new college there. The first few years of schooling will be there except for brief intensives here. We'll be depending pretty heavily on their faculty. They don't exactly have any women deans at the university. Or faculty, either. Not to mention some of my up-time notions on any number of topics. Have any of you talked to the professors at Jena? How much flack could I expect? It may be that however qualified I am, politically, I'm not the best person. I'm not exactly known for tact and diplomacy."

Beulah saw him note the shift in her tone. She was silently conceding that she was the best-prepared person for the job but looking at the position from another angle now. She was still looking for a way out as James continued his argument.

"There have been a lot of changes at Jena. They have had a considerable amount of exposure to us and to the way women function in all aspects of life here. Some of the faculty will undoubtedly be resistant to any change, just like anywhere else. Some will be especially uncomfortable with any changes initiated by a woman. The handwriting is on the wall, though. They know that women as faculty and as deans are going to happen, as surely as the snow comes in winter. From their standpoint, having an up-time woman take the first steps would make for an easier transition. The senior faculty and other deans support it, for the most part. You and, if she agrees, Mary Pat will have to work the rest out in Jena."

Beulah sighed. She couldn't think of any other arguments against her taking the position or other questions offhand but she wasn't about to rush into a decision this important. "I wasn't expecting this. I really thought you or Balthazar would become the new dean. Let me think about it. I'm not saying yes. I'm not saying no."

"That's fine. Think about it for a bit. How much time will you need?"

"Give me a couple of days, okay?"

As they walked out into the hall, James was quiet. Beulah was running things through in her head. He could practically hear the wheels spinning. When she got her teeth into a problem, she didn't let go. The early-summer evening air was still warm, although it would turn cool again in a few hours. Her "let me think about it" was as close to an answer as he'd get. There was just enough contrariness in her nature to make pushing Beulah an exercise in futility.

As they reached the street, she turned to him with a question. "Exactly when do you plan on starting the school anyway?"

"We'd like to enroll our first class at the start of the year. Good night, Beulah." A good Marine knew when to retreat. James hurried off into the night, the sound of Beulah's creative but anatomically impossible exclamation lingering in his ears. Since he was a man of good sense, he waited until he was around the corner and out of sight before he started smiling.

2

Mary Pat came down the stairs the next morning at a brisk clip, uniform neatly pressed. Where she found the energy after three straight twelve hour shifts plus her daily morning army PT, Beulah didn't know. The kitchen at home was softly lit by early morning light, quiet and still until Mary Pat brought it to vivid life.

"Morning, Beulah. What's up? You're not dressed yet. Are you sick?" Mary Pat's concern was evident in her voice. Beulah knew that this change in routine would worry her. She was always up when Mary Pat started PT. Her arthritis meant she took a little more time to get moving in the morning than Mary Pat. When Mary Pat came back home, Beulah was always ready to go and had breakfast waiting for them both before they headed to the hospital. The familiar routine felt like having family again. She'd never seen her still dressed in her robe and nightie at 6:30 before.

"Don't worry. I'm fine. I've just got some thinking to do and if I go into the hospital, I'll get sucked into work." Beulah chuckled. "The hospital is a madhouse on a good day. Not exactly a place for reflection. I've already called and let the hospital know. I'll tell you all about it tomorrow morning on your day off." *Especially since my acceptance is contingent on you agreeing to go with me.*

Politically, it might be better to have a faculty member of the College of Medicine at Jena as her assistant. Problem was, she didn't know any of them to pick one for that kind of relationship. Her close relationship with Mary Pat could make some people feel like she was bringing her own inner circle, especially if Hayes was along. That was another potential issue. If she had her choice, Mary Pat was it, politics or no politics. *Besides, we make a good team.*

The house settled in around itself again after Mary Pat left. Not without some concern and after she had made sure Beulah had the warm paraffin dip for her hands and an extra-large mug of that nasty willow-bark tea. Heavy on the honey. Why anyone would drink tea when they could have coffee, she had no idea. Beulah smiled affectionately. Mary Pat was a good kid and Beulah loved her dearly. She had brightened any number of dark areas caused by Grantville's trip back in time. *If I hadn't had her to come home with, to talk to, and share with, I don't think I'd have made it this long. Dear Mary Pat, what is going to happen to you when I'm gone?* James' remarks about her age had hit close to home for more reasons than he might suspect. She'd have to think about that, too. Soon. But right now she had a decision to make.

She had never much liked administration. Being in a rural area or Korea meant that she'd still had to do a certain amount of it, but she'd never liked it. Being the director of nursing had too much of it, even without reams of up-time insurance paperwork. Practice and teaching were what she loved. Carrying a public-health nurse's satchel and teaching at the local community college had suited her quite well, thank you very much. Watching a student "get it" was almost as good as actually caring for a patient herself. She had the background to teach in a lot of areas, no docs hanging over her shoulder with that handmaiden crap and lots to do. Best of all had been the babies. She had even gone back to get her masters degree as a midwife in the eighties, but she'd been too old and too busy to finish it. Or so she'd thought at the time. Now, she wished she had. Maybe as a family nurse practitioner she would have the broadest possible "womb to tomb" knowledge base. *It would be nice if hindsight wasn't always so clear. Coulda, woulda, shoulda never changed anything. At least I still have all my textbooks. Those are priceless now.*

She was happy with her life overall. She had done some interesting things, helped people out here and there and had a good time.

After her stint in Korea and the army, she had stuck close to home. She'd moved back to Grantville to take care of her older brother after his stroke and then stayed on to retire from the local clinic after he died. She had done hospital work when she was younger in the little hospital over in Fairmont but she was too restless for that and had had too much of a taste for the kind of independence and responsibility a nurse could have in Korea. About the only good thing she could say about the war. No, that wasn't quite true. She had met and worked with some very special people in Korea and the experience meant she knew all too well how to handle the kinds of wounds they were seeing so much of in the midst of the Thirty Years War.

In a bizarre sort of way, here, now, she was in a place where everything she had learned and experienced came together. And she did have the skills to pass at least some of that on to the next generation, a wonderful legacy. *At least I know which end of a gun to avoid and to duck when someone yells incoming,* she thought with a flash of grim humor. Taken together with all she and James had discussed the night before, whether she liked it or not, James was right about her being the logical person for the deanship. Dammit.

3

"Okay, what's up?" Mary Pat sipped her coffee the next morning and sat back in the kitchen chair to get comfortable, trying to gauge Beulah's mood. She didn't look alarmed so much as determined and thoughtful. She had scared Mary Pat a little the day before. For a moment, Mary Pat had thought she was sick. The idea of anything happening to Beulah made her stomach tighten.

Something was going on, though. What that something might be had teased at the back of Mary Pat's mind all during her shift yesterday. Beulah taking a second day off was absolutely unheard of. Today, Mary Pat herself had a rare day off. It only happened about once a month. Between the hospital and her position in the army, she rarely had any time to herself. It was getting tiring, to say the least, even for someone as energetic as she was. She had intended to do some chores and maybe eat out at the Gardens tonight until Beulah went all mysterious on her.

"I talked to James Nichols two days ago. He and the others want me to become the new dean and get the health-care educator programs up and running here and at Jena."

"They've picked the right person for the job. Congratulations!"

"You haven't heard the rest of it yet." Beulah replied with a gotcha grin. "We want you to be my assistant."

Mary Pat didn't spew coffee all over the place but her green eyes did widen. "You could have waited until I didn't have a mouthful of coffee before you said that," she complained. "Exactly when in my spare time am I supposed to be doing this anyway? Not that I don't want to help you out, Beulah, but I just don't have any time."

"I'm sure that given the military's urgent need for doctors and nurses, they will be more than happy to have you temporarily assigned as my assistant. Your trauma skills will be invaluable. Finding a replacement for you at the hospital is going to be harder but the latest class of nurses' aides and LPNs has just graduated from the tech center at the high school. Not the same as an RN, I know, but they can take up a little of the slack so it won't be as hard. It isn't as though we'd be leaving for Jena tomorrow or anything."

"My patients—"

"I know," Beulah interrupted gently. "Neither of us wants to leave them. James and I already had a version of the same discussion. You should have seen me come up with reasons not to do this."

The tension in Mary Pat's voice didn't go unnoticed. Beulah would never say it to Mary Pat, but she was worried about the long hours and multiple commitments Mary Pat had taken on the last two years. She was an active-duty army nurse and had been deployed all over the area. That meant that although she knew a lot of people and a lot of the local area, she wasn't really close to anyone but her friends Elizabeth, Rodney, Sharon, and Beulah herself. When she was home, Mary Pat worked five or six twelve-hour shifts a week at the hospital. She was also one of the most senior officers of the tiny medical corps, which carried its own set of responsibilities and pressures. Having her with Beulah in Jena meant she would be freed up from working sixty-plus hours a week as a staff nurse and her regular military duties. Beulah knew she and Mary Pat weren't the only ones who were getting worn out. So were all the health-care types in Grantville. They were stretched way too thin and it wasn't getting any better. If anything, it was worse. Grantville's reputation as a center for healing was beginning to spread. Fortunately, right now the reputation was only local. That was going to change though, sooner rather than later. The demands on their tiny health-care system would get nothing but more intense as the war heated up and people found out that they could heal things no one else in this time could.

Beulah gave a dry, humorous recount of her conversation with James. They shared a chuckle, and a little of the tension eased from Mary Pat's shoulders. Mary Pat's sharp mind would fill in the blanks here and there. She was well aware of how strained the health-care resources were in Grantville and its military. Beulah ended her recounting with the role for Mary Pat and why she was needed for the position. *Much the same way James did it to me.*

"So you won't take the position without me as your assistant? You're perfect for it." Mary Pat was frowning a bit. "I can understand your points but I still think I could serve better here." Mary Pat reached for the coffeepot and refilled both their mugs before setting the pot back on the small kitchen table. She didn't like to see Beulah handling the heavy pot. Beulah let her think for a few minutes, enjoying the quiet and the aroma of the hot coffee.

"I don't stand a chance, do I?" she finally asked with a rueful grin. "I know that look on your face, Beulah. You've got all the bases covered and all the arguments ready. I guess we should both be getting used to being ambushed by projects like this. I could see this one coming for you but didn't see it for me." Mary Pat picked up her napkin and waved it like a flag. "Okay, I surrender. When do we get started and what do you think we need to do first?"

Beulah reached across the table and gave Mary Pat's hand a little squeeze. "That's the spirit. We need to get started now to be ready for the first class in six months. The way I see it, there are a few issues we need to start thinking about right away. Politics, personnel, and resources are the three big ones at the moment."

"One at a time then?" asked Mary Pat.

"Works for me. Have a preference for which one to tackle first?"

Mary Pat wrinkled her freckled nose and grimaced. "Let's leave the politics till last."

"Personnel and resources it is then. I don't know how much of the big picture you've been aware of and it will help me to think out loud, so I hope I don't go over too much you already know. On the personnel side, the first of the German students will be entering the nurses' aide and LPN program. We're lucky to have had the program already set up before the Ring of Fire at the high school. That has meant we haven't had to start totally from scratch, although Hayes and I had to change a few things with the curriculum given what we're facing now. Hayes will be working with us too. Garnet, Courtney, and Marcia are doing a great job in the nurses' aide and LPN program. They're all sharp and easy to work with and they have the program delivery down to a fine science. I know that ties up an RN and two LPNs but the work they are doing is too important to interrupt for direct patient care. I don't think we should change anything there. They're all ready to go with the mixed German-up-timer classes starting this summer."

"I agree about the aide and LPN program. That's been going really well. We have about sixty new aides and nearly twenty new LPNs now. We'll probably want to talk with Garnet, Courtney, and Marcia about which of their former students might be good for the new program. Some of them are so new, I don't think any of the hospital staff who have worked with them will have a very good sense of their capabilities yet. Two things, though. My German has gotten pretty good. Are we going to be teaching in German, English, or both? And what about Hayes?"

"German and English. It will depend on who is teaching what at the university and who the staff mentors are for students. Any applicants are going to have to be fairly fluent in both. Eventually, we'll probably switch entirely to German but that's a long way off. We have too many texts in English and too many people who aren't fluent in German as potential teachers and students. Some of the Germans in Jena and other areas won't be too happy about that, I imagine. English isn't known as a scholarly language in this time. Unless we're careful, it may look like we're excluding German natives from the new educational system at the same time we're using their facilities. We'll have to have some sort of English classes for some of the German students who will be coming to Jena. There's another problem with languages. Latin."

"I hadn't thought about that one." Mary Pat winced. "No one I know here speaks Latin except Father Larry. Lots of medical terms are based on it, especially anatomy and physiology terms. So we won't be starting entirely from the ground up."

"We're going to have to learn at least some Latin," Beulah replied. "Many of the textbooks used for medical information now are in Latin. Some of that information is still very relevant. How much and in which texts, I have no idea yet."

"Well, we'll be working with him over the next few months at least.

We're going to have to put together the curricula and text materials soon. We'll be focusing on the RN- and MD-level training and that will mean higher-level synthesis. Plus, I'm hoping he can help evaluate the materials they have at Jena and help us figure out priorities for copying and translation."

"Okay. You know him better than I do. I know a few of the Jena faculty. They've downsized in recent years because of the war. There aren't going to be a lot of them to help out. The botanical gardens are great though. Werner Rolfinck is probably somebody we'll want to talk to early on. He's been at Jena for several years and heads the medical faculty. He's the one who had the OR theater set up there and is very up on the latest knowledge for this time. He borrowed a copy of a couple of my textbooks a few months ago. The next time I was in Jena, I was going to pick them back up and give him some new material. I had the books copied before I lent them to him. It was lucky I was in the emergency rotation at school. I had several anatomy and physiology texts and a drug book with me that he was interested in." It was Mary Pat's turn to sigh. "I just wish the drug book had more about herbs."

"We have some more information about herbs from the gardeners in town. I was pleasantly surprised about how much medical information they had. Not to mention the medicinal herbs in various gardens. Standardization of dosages and purity are still issues. Stoner and the others are making progress on that. I just wish we had more scientific basis for some of these new medicines. Some of the herbals claim to be able to cure everything that ails a body, including the common cold." She shook her head in disgust, sending shimmers of silver light flashing around her head.

"Sorting out what they have at Jena, what we have here, and how the herbs are named and grown will take time, but once we're rolling, I think it'll be fine. We may have to take at least one of our gardeners with us to Jena. Do you think Rolfinck will be supportive of us coming to Jena and making so many changes in the program? James and Balthazar have both been sending out feelers about it and kind of paving the way. Rolfinck seems very progressive and interested in having the information but it *is* actually his school, after all. We're outsiders coming in with ideas that challenge a lot of dearly held beliefs."

Mary Pat thought about it for a minute, then shrugged one slim shoulder. "There's really no way to know until we talk with him and the other faculty members. I'd suggest talking to him first. He seems like a very reasonable guy. There are a couple of the faculty who teach what they call iatrochemistry at Jena. It's more similar to our ideas about chemistry than alchemy and that humors stuff. I can't guess how receptive those two will be since I haven't met either of them yet."

"I haven't met any of them. Haven't been to Jena either. You, at least, will be a somewhat familiar face. That should help. I'm not sure how they are going to react to some of my ideas, however progressive they may be. We're going to have to negotiate carefully. I don't want to come across as know-it-all up-timers. First, because it isn't true. Second, because that kind of attitude will cause nothing but problems. We're having a hard enough time with what we can't do. They may have a hard time with what we *can*."

"I agree. Ideas such as?"

"I've always felt that the split between nursing and medicine was artificial and caused more problems than it helped but it's the time factor that really worries me. We need people trained *now*. That doesn't even get into content issues like up-time versus down-time knowledge or some of the ethical issues we'll have to deal with. Not to mention that I see men and women having an equal role in health care."

Mary Pat grinned. "You were saying the other day that things at the hospital were starting to get too routine. A new challenge will be good for you."

"Yeah, right. Like I need any more challenges. This project will be full of them."

Mary Pat got up to look for a pen and some paper to start taking notes. "Well, we don't have to solve everything right here and now. Let's think about who we have here and who we need to put together an educational team."

Chapter Two
July, 1633

1

The four deans of the University of Jena met in Werner Rolfinck's office at the university. Werner was dean of the medical school. Next to him sat Johann Gerhard, the dean of theology. In his early fifties, Dean Gerhard was a conservative, thoughtful, and prudent man. Werner was particularly glad he was here, as Johann was known for his ability to smooth troubled waters and had studied medicine for several years in his younger days before turning to theology. He was also someone who listened to arguments, considered carefully, and then acted. Werner wasn't sure what Johann thought about the proposed merger with Grantville's medical people. He wasn't sure what he thought of it himself.

Across from Johann and Werner sat the deans of the schools of arts and law, Dietrich Wetzel and Karl Strom. Dietrich was about Werner's age and a good friend. He was a plump, cheerful sort of man who seemed to exist in a perpetual swirl of energetic chaos. Dietrich had incredible ideas. Making them happen was another story. He was usually off on the next idea before the first project was even halfway completed. Karl Strom was his exact opposite in some ways. A member of the minor aristocracy, Karl was meticulous and very cautious in his approach to life. He had a sunny smile but, most of the time, wore a sober face that he thought was more in keeping with his position. Werner wondered if he realized how young and earnest that sober face made him look. Or how like a young man dressing up in his father's clothes. Karl, only twenty-eight, was young for his position as law school dean and painfully aware of it. It could make him rather prickly on occasion.

Dietrich was all but bouncing in his chair with excitement. Werner stroked his dark, thick mustache to hide the grin trying to escape. "As I told you last time, the Americans want to start a joint . . . medical education program. If we are agreeable, they would like a formal arrangement with the school of medicine to start teaching nurses and doctors. The arrangement would be the first in a long-term partnership with us. The medical school would expand into a health sciences College with schools of medicine, nursing, pharmacy and allied health."

"From what you have told us so far, the other three schools we have now may need to be involved right away as well," Johann said thoughtfully.

Karl looked startled. "The other schools? But I thought that was further in the future?"

Werner waved a hand. "You know these Americans. They have laws for everything. They have laws for who can practice, in what area, and under what conditions. Fraulein Flanagan tells me they call it 'scope of practice' or some such. I would imagine that as we are setting up the new school, there will be some need to reconcile their laws and ours."

Karl's ruddy complexion blanched a bit. "Yes, I can see the need. Still. They do have a great many laws. I don't know anything about medical law, though, theirs or ours. I have been mostly looking at constitutional and national law. None of us in the law school have experience in the areas of medical law. We did but with so many students and faculty leaving because of the war . . ."

"You could hardly do anything about the war, Karl. We have what we have. It may be that this partnership will attract new students and we will refill the ranks of our faculty as well." Johann's calm practicality eased the anxiety from Karl's face.

"What about the arts?" Dietrich leaned toward Johann and Karl. "We've been translating a few of the books Fraulein Flanagan lent Werner. Fascinating, just fascinating! And the quality of the illustrations are amazing! We may be able to help with that, too."

"Mathematics and philosophy are other areas where we may need help, but I'm just guessing. Right now, it's too early to make many plans." Werner knew Dietrich well enough to stop that line of thought before he went to far with it. The school of arts would be in absolute turmoil if they didn't slow Dietrich down a bit. As it was, that facile brain of his would have a dozen different projects ready to start before he left the room today anyway. "I've talked to the head of the delegation they want to send next month. Frau MacDonald will be—"

"Frau? The head of their medical delegation is a woman?" Johann looked and sounded shocked.

"Yes." Werner knew he sounded a bit defensive. "I don't know about the rest of the delegation but the leader is a woman."

"I hadn't realized they had women as physicians." Even Dietrich sounded a bit shocked. Women simply weren't university-educated physicians. Nor were they barber-surgeons or apothecaries, who were seen as lesser levels of healer. Women were usually midwives or herb-wives, considered the very lowest of those caring for patients. They were necessary to care for women's mysteries but any of their other activities were not well regarded. There was simply no comparison between a physician and what amounted in their minds to an unedu-cated herb witch.

Werner gritted his teeth a bit. "She isn't a physician. She's a nurse." Which of course only made things worse.

The silence that followed was anything but comfortable for Werner. Intellectually, the deans had known that Americans didn't seem to care about a person's gender very much in terms of one's role in life. Most of the Americans they had each dealt with had been men, how-ever. That they understood. Thanks to his meetings with Mary Pat Flanagan, Werner was a little better prepared than the other three but it would be his department that would have to make this work. He wasn't entirely certain how his faculty or students would respond.

"A nurse?" Dietrich seemed nonplussed. "Nurses to teach doc-tors, to be *dean*?"

Werner hastily explained. "The nurses from the future know a great deal. They have university degrees and some have graduate degrees, including doctorates. Nurses are faculty at medical schools in the future."

"How will your faculty respond to teaching with women?" asked Johann.

"We've discussed it but more in theory than in fact. Now that we are actually faced with it and soon . . . I just don't know."

"Why aren't they sending a man for such a position?" Karl's disap-proval was all too apparent.

"I doubt it even occurred to them to be a problem. Dr. Nichols assured me that Fraulein MacDonald is the best person they have to do this. She taught for more than twenty years at one of their univer-sities." Werner carefully didn't mention that she was a midwife or that she hadn't taught doctors. It would just make things worse. "We have talked about having women as faculty this last year, even as deans.

Granted, there aren't many women with university educations in our experiences but we knew that our association with the Americans would change that."

Clearly, talking about it and actually doing it were two completely different things. Judging by the look on Johann's face, he had just thought of something unpleasant. "Will they expect us to enroll women with the men as students as well? The university's prestige may suffer if we do this. I had thought this might be a way of gaining students. Now I wonder if we will lose them."

"Women as students with the men?" asked Karl, looking rather stunned by the idea. "How do you teach women?"

"We are supposed to be one of the more forward-looking universities in all of Europe. We are part of the United States now. I have seen something of what they accomplished in the medical arena. Some of their leading scholars were women. We can build something like that here. Whatever reservations I have about merging with those of Grantville, I want to be able to treat patients as they do. And I want our students to have the very best education possible, as I am sure we all do. If that means women as deans and faculty, I am willing to at least try. I think my students and faculty will as well, but how we act, how we present this to them will be critical for shaping whether they see this as a difficult but exciting opportunity or as a lessening of the university and what we have to offer."

Werner looked each of them full in the face, his tone grim. "There are many other problems to be solved in the coming months. We must discuss at least some of those today. Ultimately, the question is whether or not we wish to join with Grantville and under what conditions."

2

It had rained the night before. As she crossed the grass in front of the hospital's front entrance, Beulah felt her shoes getting wet and soggy. At least she didn't have to wear hose anymore. She could put the socks over a chair in her office and they'd be dry before she had to be the director of nursing.

The hospital was a source of some pride in the community. The three-story building had been finished nearly a year ago despite shortages of materials and funds, and competing construction needs. The iron grillwork over the windows glistened from the rain. The hospital had been built with security in mind, given the time they were living in now, but they had still tried to make it look more comforting than fortresslike. They had tried to design a hospital that could handle casualties from battles and the epidemics every member of the health-care community feared were coming. Time would tell how successful they had been.

She had received a letter last week from Debbie Leek about building a hospital in Magdeburg using a similar design to the Leahy Medical Center, named after Dr. Leahy, a much-loved former town physician. The Leek family's story was one of the tragedies of the Ring of Fire. Jennifer Rush, Debbie's eleven-year-old cousin, had been doing very well on chemotherapy for her leukemia before the Ring of Fire. Afterward, unable to get the treatment she needed, she had lived only a matter of months. Before the family had moved to Magdeburg, Beulah had gotten to know them all well. Most of the family had been in some kind of management position pre-Ring of Fire and they saw Magdeburg as a place where their backgrounds could be put to good and profitable use. Debbie's letter indicated she was working with Mary Simpson on her educational projects with Veronica Dreeson. Long term, they wanted to found a university in Magdeburg.

That letter started Beulah thinking about something else now. Mary Simpson was working on fund-raising and other aspects of getting the girls' school up and running. The new department at Jena would need funding badly. Supplies, textbooks, tuition, living expenses, teacher salaries, the list went on and on. The cost of just one hand-painted, illustrated herbal had been stunning. They were going to need more funds. It was a certainty the current government didn't have any money to spare. In fact, most people didn't. All those deep pockets Mary Simpson was picking with such class could. . . .

"*Guten morgen*, Frau Professorin."

"*Guten morgen*, Fritz. Wait up a second." Beulah waved to the young man nearing the entrance. Friedrich Joseph Hersch, also known as Fritz, was a twenty-year-old who worked in the hospital bakery. His family were local German bakers who had relocated to Grantville shortly after the Ring of Fire. Several of them worked in the hospital bakery. Fritz was a little above average height, with sandy hair and hazel eyes. The heavy work he did as a baker had given him a strong build.

"If you have a few minutes in the next week or two, come up to my office. I'd like to talk with you about working here at the hospital taking care of patients."

Fritz seemed surprised but pleased. "I shall come to see you today at lunch. Will that be convenient, Frau Beulah?" Fritz's English was good but tended to be rather formal. He had spent a lot of time learning from English grammars as well as talking with people. Smart, kind, responsible, and motivated—excellent characteristics for what she wanted in a future graduate from Jena. As a bonus, Fritz was just plain nice.

"Perfect. I'll have some food brought in so you don't miss your lunch. Can't have a growing boy deprived of food." With a laugh and a wink, Beulah walked toward the conservatory at the center of the hospital while Fritz headed for the kitchen. The conservatory had practical as well as ornamental uses. Medicinal and ornamental plants were grown in the glass-roofed conservatory. There were cement paths and stone benches for patients, staff, and visitors to stroll or sit and rest. She had made it a habit to stop in and walk in the quiet garden for a few minutes before heading up to her office. Now, she sat on a bench sans wet shoes and deliberately set aside thoughts of all the tasks waiting for her upstairs to enjoy the fragrant stillness.

The plants had come along nicely. The aloe plant was sending out new leaves. Aloe had proven helpful in treating minor burns. It soothed the pain wonderfully and helped keep the tissue moist. The plant grew in the graveled area near the bench she was using. Nearby were Saint-John's-wort and valerian, herbs that were being used to treat depression and anxiety. There had certainly been some of both the last two years.

The garden had become something of a symbol for her. The plants meant hope for treating patients and for finding future cures for the diseases they now faced. When she lost another patient who might have been saved in the twentieth century, the hospital garden reminded her they weren't entirely helpless. They were adapting. The health-care situation was not quite so desperate as it had been when they first arrived, now that they had the hospital, its staff, and the herbal remedies. The sanitation committee was doing a great job. At the same time, the garden was not entirely benevolent. In a shady spot on the second floor was foxglove to make digitalis preparations. The plant grew four or five feet high and had lovely flowers. While good for treating congestive heart failure and some irregular heart problems, it could be deadly poison and thus was placed where curious children or adults couldn't get to it.

When she got too worried about the future, her personal faith and thinking about Mary Pat, Fritz, and the other youngsters eased her mind. Fritz would make a wonderful nurse or doctor. So would a number of others. They would have to choose the first students very carefully. Possible sources of students were likely graduates of the nurse's aide, emergency medical technician, combat medic, and licensed practical nurse programs, as well as personal recommendations from various people. Those programs all took a year or less to complete in Garnet's program at the tech center. They were running people through the programs as quickly as possible. Now that they'd opened them to German students, they'd have an even larger pool of possible applicants from which to draw.

Beulah would be recommending Fritz for the RN program. He'd need to get into the tech program at the high school as soon as possible to be ready to go to school for his degree as a registered nurse. There were several RNs she would like to see go on to the MD program at Jena. Which would leave them even shorter of RNs for a while. Some people, like Sharon Nichols, had essentially had enough on-the-job experience to be functioning as RNs. Some of the Jena students already in the medical program would undoubtedly want to be admitted. That was going to be trickier. How did you tell someone that while they were about to graduate with a medical degree, they weren't qualified to work as MDs in Grantville? A possible solution came to her. *Hm. Have to check with Mike Stearns and a few others first. Might work. Who knows, maybe I can handle this diplomacy stuff after all.* With a lighter heart, Beulah headed for her office.

3

The faces around the gleaming conference table at the medical center, or Leahy as it had come to be known, were all familiar to Beulah. She was not happy to see all of them. Mara Washaw was a thorn in her side. She was one of the small number of up-time RNs available, young but still experienced. That made her important and she knew it. Beulah had tried to be more rational about her. Mara had great experience, having worked in a large hospital as a nurse in Charleston before she married Lennon, Starr's brother. Mara and Starr were about the same age, early thirties, and both had kids. Other than that, they were very different. Mara hadn't taken it well that Starr was going to be taking Beulah's place. Frankly, Beulah was glad Mara hadn't gotten the position. Most others had stepped up to the plate after the Ring of Fire and done as much as they could for their families and community. But not everyone. Mara just sort of coasted. Since she was very bright and well educated she got away with it but she did the minimum amount necessary. She knew how bright and talented she was and didn't let others forget it. Beulah could forgive that if Mara had lived up to her potential. Or even tried to. Beulah hoped she didn't have trouble with Mara being on the committee. She didn't think Mara sitting at the opposite end of the head of the table was an accident. Beulah wished Starr was in her place but Starr wasn't at the table. She had assumed Beulah's duties this week. Which left Mara as one of the senior RNs available for the forming health care education committee.

"Morning everyone. Why don't we all get settled? We've got a lot to work on and not much time."

Garnet Szymanski, director of the high school nurses' aide, EMT, combat medic, and LPN programs, gave an exaggerated wince. "So what else is new?" A nice way to start the meeting. Grins all around. Except for Mara. *Must have been the mention of lots of work*, thought Beulah.

Beulah looked around the polished wooden table as the others got settled into their chairs. Balthazar Abrabanel sat on her left. *His* face was very welcome. *Not to mention the fact that he's far more skilled in diplomacy than I'll ever be*, Beulah thought with an inner grin. That wasn't the official reason he was here, of course. He was the first downtime physician to absorb enough up-time knowledge to become a full partner with Drs. Adams and Nichols. His knowledge of the current educational practices in Europe would be important as well. If not for his heart and the amount of time he spent training their spook squad, he was up to speed enough to be the new dean. In Beulah's opinion, he'd be a better choice for a lot of reasons, not the least of which that she and most of the others knew next to nothing about medical education in this time.

Garnet was seated next to Balthazar, wearing as usual, her beloved yellow. The woman had a bright yellow house and had driven a bright yellow car. She was fifty-three and solid in more ways than just her physical appearance. Garnet was someone you could count on. She loved teaching and it showed in the ways she interacted with her students. When Garnet was around, learning was going to be fascinating.

Her enthusiasm was catching and her two LPN assistants, Courtney and Marcia, were just as dedicated and competent. Any future nurses and docs who got run through the program at the high school would be getting a first-rate start in their careers. Licensed practical nurses took only about nine months to train now, since many of the things they could have done up-time were no longer possible. They didn't know as much as registered nurses but they knew more than nurse's aides. The program was going to have to expand again but at least the groundwork was all done and most of the kinks worked out.

Across from Garnet was Ann Turski, a health educator who had worked with Garnet before the Ring of Fire. Her time was now split between Garnet's program and helping put staff in-services together here at Leahy. She and Beulah worked well together, although Ann tended to get upset if things weren't organized to her satisfaction. The woman was an organizing machine. Disorder and chaos were the enemy. She had had quite a lot of both to combat during the last two years. When Beulah had told her about the committee and asked her to serve on it, Ann had been visibly relieved. "Finally, we'll be getting properly organized. There's been too much flying by the seat of our pants the last two years." Ann had light-blue eyes and shoulder-length dark-brown hair. When she was nervous or facing disorder, she tended to pat her hair, as if making certain that at least *her* person was still neat and tidy. Right now, she was patting her hair *and* had just smoothed her knee-length skirt. *Hmmm. Probably knows I'm about to drag her off to Jena and disrupt her routine again. At least her husband, Wells, is off on a diplomatic mission and they don't have kids to worry about.*

Next to Ann sat Raymond Little, the hospital's chief pharmacist. He was a quiet man and deliberately rather nondescript. Ray blended into the woodwork whenever possible. He knew his stuff as a pharmacist but she'd never seen him really assert himself for anything. He and Stoner worked very closely together. Beulah suspected that he loved working with the plants and in the garden. Once, she had even seen him give a plant he was cutting a tender, apologetic pat and murmur soothingly to it in his pleasant baritone. Completing the group was Mary Pat, sitting at Beulah's right hand in more than a literal sense. Hayes had been tied up with other projects and couldn't make it to the first meeting. He would be keeping track of a lot of this by minutes when he couldn't attend anyway.

Before Beulah could even get started, Mara fired the first salvo.

"This is such an exciting opportunity. I'm so glad you could be here to get us started. I'm sure that with everything going on, you're very busy."

"Yes, it is very exciting. There will be times I can't be here for meetings. Fortunately, when I can't be here, Mary Pat will sit in for me. If she isn't around, Balthazar will take over." Judging by the souring of Mara's smile, that wasn't what she had expected to hear. She'd undoubtedly thought that Balthazar would be too busy, Mary Pat deployed, and the other two easily managed, leaving her to take over and have all the glory with little of the work. Beulah had been on too many academic and public health committees to be taken in by that particular tactic, though. Normally she would have approached the leadership roles on the committee differently. Garnet was here more in a capacity as bridge between the programs to make sure they articulated well. She was already busy. Ann and Ray would be too likely to let Mara slide if they were in charge. Neither of them liked conflict and Mara in full attack mode was something to see.

"Did you all get the handouts for today's meeting? Anything in particular you'd like added to the agenda for today's meeting?" Mary Pat helped ease past the little conflict and get back to business.

"Yes, as a matter of fact there is a problem," Mara said firmly. "We have the hospital here and the most educated staff. It makes no sense to split our resources between here and Jena. It will leave us too short staffed and take too much travel time."

Beulah sternly refused to ask if Mara's concerns were really about the program or about having to work extra and not having students around to lord it over. Unfortunately, the point was a valid one, whatever the motives of the person making it. Beulah wasn't too surprised when Ann spoke up.

"I agree. We have what we need right here. The faculty and students from Jena could easily come here and we wouldn't have to leave Grantville."

"We thought about that. There are advantages to keeping it here but the advantages are outweighed by the disadvantages both in the short term and the long term. First, we need the resources and faculty at Jena. We don't have enough personnel here. We need to spend some time learning about their resources and skills, and time is short if we are going to start the first classes of new RNs and MDs in January."

Garnet nodded agreement. "At Jena," Beulah continued, "we'll have access to the botanical gardens, the faculty, and the textbooks as well as their other facilities. Space is at a premium here in Grantville for

everything from classrooms to housing. We plan on building a student dorm, a medical library, and other facilities here but right now, we
don't have the money or most of the other things we need to make
that happen. Jena has everything but the hospital and our staff. We
work with them and both of us win. The students can come here to
the hospital for intensives early in their training. We'll have had time
to get more resources in place for them here for later training when
they are ready for more clinical time. I've already sent a letter to Debbie Leek about raising funds for the health education project.

"Finally, Jena is a strong university as well as being the closest one
to us. We don't want to lose the university base for health care education. I know we've all had to do quite a bit of OJT the last few years.
We need to be proactive now and set up an educational system capable of creating the knowledge and advances we had up-time. We need
people who will be able to practice at that level as soon as possible."

Ann was nodding thoughtfully now, although she still didn't look
too happy. Balthazar took over and added some more information
about Jena and 1630s medicine. He also spoke a little about the faculty he had been corresponding with in Jena. One area smoothed over.
Beulah sighed as Mara came up with another disagreement. Time to
get things back on track.

It was going to be a very, very long meeting.

Chapter Three
August, 1633

1

Dr. Werner Rolfinck strode through the botanical gardens early
the morning of the first meeting with the representatives from
Grantville and his faculty. He bent down and pulled a weed shoot
from the row of *Matricaria recutita*. Chamomile was a useful herb for
calming the nerves, as an aide to wound healing, decreasing inflammation, and an antispasmotic. The people from Grantville had

expressed particular interest in the use of herbs and other botanical agents in healing. He didn't want the garden to look anything less than its best. Since it was July, the foliage was particularly lush.

Werner's feelings about the proposed "joint venture" with Grantville's medical personnel were mixed. So were those of the three Jena faculty members who would be sitting around the conference table with him in a few hours. Werner was thirty-four years old and had been the dean at the medical college for several years. He considered himself a forward-thinking man and made an effort to keep up with the latest information in the healing arts. He had been proud of his accomplishments and his career. He still was. Given what he had learned so far from the Grantville texts he had intently studied, he and the faculty here were on the right track in any number of areas. He was proud of the faculty, too. There may not be many of them left, but those who remained were excellent men, all dedicated healers who were devoted to their work.

None of which changed what he had read in those books and the implications of what he had read. Those things had left him frustrated, disheartened, and desperately wanting more. There was so much more to be learned, so much more that could be done for their patients. The possibilities were very exciting. He felt as though a new world was opening up and Jena was going to be a part of incredible things. *So am I so unsettled because the changes are happening at all or because they aren't happening fast enough?*

It would probably be rude to tell their guests, in the American phrase, *about damn time*. Rationally, he understood that the Americans had needed to secure their borders and that other pressing needs had kept them from addressing anything but immediate medical needs. Still, they could have shared more of their texts sooner and made medical care more of a priority. Werner began to pace through the feverfew section of the garden. Medical care could save lives just as surely as winning on a battlefield. Healing was its own kind of war. They could have been so much farther ahead of where they were now with more books and communication with Grantville's medical personnel.

Compounding his frustration was the sense of pressure he felt. So much would have to happen very quickly to be ready by January. The bits and pieces he had learned had been tantalizing but bitter. He had read the books and then seen patients in his practice that could have benefited from Grantville's level of care. But Grantville was too far away and even if they had its facilities here, he and the others didn't have the *knowledge*. That had been eating at all of them for at least a year when they began realizing what the Americans could do.

Instead, the Americans had decided to work with his school at their convenience, when they had time. He knew that wasn't really a fair way of putting it, and it certainly wasn't the frame of mind he needed for this upcoming meeting. Still, fair of not, it didn't change how he felt. He made a deliberate effort to unclench his muscles and slow his pacing. The Americans had chosen the medical college as their first real joint venture with the Jena university. It was both an honor and a burden. A lot of people would be watching how he and his faculty handled the merging. He was hardly naive enough to think the Americans didn't have their own priorities and needs but this could be a mutually beneficial partnership, a partnership among equals. He would see to it.

2

Werner tried to be subtle as he observed his new colleagues from Grantville. He had spoken with each of them at least once by radio and exchanged letters setting up the meeting today in Jena, but he also wanted to actually see them.

The leader of the delegation was an elderly woman who moved rather stiffly. He could see the arthritic changes in her hands, which the trip here and the cobblestones had probably aggravated. The sight didn't inspire much confidence. This old woman was supposed to lead the new college during a time of dramatic changes? Her evident age and ill health didn't bode well at all, even with the much younger Mary Pat Flanagan woman working as her aide. Werner was impressed with what he knew about Fraulein Flanagan and well disposed to her, given how she had gone out of her way to get texts and other materials copied and delivered to Jena. That they were in English made it rather difficult, but he had had them translated and copies made for the faculty.

Beulah MacDonald, as the elderly woman was named, eased stiffly into the hard wooden chair at the long table and smiled reassuringly up at Fraulein Flanagan. Werner could hardly miss the concern or the affection between them. Then Frau MacDonald turned to look at Werner and the others on the opposite side of the table. The smile changed but it was her eyes that Werner studied. Those navy blue eyes held humor, understanding, and shrewdness. There was an air of experience and competence about her. He wasn't quite sure how to describe it. He would watch and see how this played out.

Coming into the room behind MacDonald and Flanagan were a man and woman. Werner had gotten better about judging ages of Americans. They both looked around ten years older than Mary Pat Flanagan, give or take a few years. The man was of an intimidating size. What Werner suspected were permanent dark circles lay under his eyes. This would be Hayes Daniels, the only man in the group. The last woman to enter the room sat in her chair and carefully arranged pen and paper in front of her. Process of elimination meant this was Ann Turski. Werner still wasn't exactly clear what a health educator was and how that was different from a faculty member. Still, they each gave the impression of confidence and I-know-what-I'm-about he was coming to associate with some of the Americans he had met.

That attitude wasn't always justified, in his opinion. But . . . *At least they all speak decent German. That will make things a little easier,* Werner thought as the Americans introduced themselves. Now it was his turn to make introductions.

"At my far right is Conrad Herbers. He teaches iatrochemistry and theories of medicine." Conrad, whom they all called Kunz, gave a small seated bow, his expression polite but a bit cautious.

"Next to him is Wilhelm Hofacker, who teaches iatrochemistry and assists me in the botanical gardens."

"I am Willi, please. I shall be happy to give you a tour of the gardens later if you would like." Willi's English was accented but very understandable. He'd spent some time talking to other Americans before the meeting. The two iatrochemists were remarkably similar in more than appearance. Both were blond, forty-ish family men who were interested in what Grantville had to offer but wary of what it might mean for them both personally and professionally.

"On my left is Phillip Ackermann. *Doktor* Ackermann teaches anatomy and runs the operating theater." Ackermann had just turned fifty. His thinning blond hair was going gray. Werner noticed that although he was over twenty years her junior, Beulah had fewer lines on her face than Phillip. More than about any of the others, Werner was concerned about how Phillip would handle the coming changes. Werner was considered somewhat radical himself and he was younger than the more conservative Phillip. Phillip hadn't said much about his thoughts or feelings on the merger. He was facing the coming changes toward the end of his career, not the beginning. Phillip was terse at the best of times. Now he just gave a stiff inclination of his head in their guests' general direction.

"It is a pleasure to meet others from Grantville at last. We have had so little contact with other healers from Grantville in the last two years." A hint of hostility was present in the polite tenor voice, and it was that hostility Beulah responded to.

"It is a pleasure for us as well. If there had been any way we could have made things happen on our end more quickly so we could meet you sooner, we would have. As it is, we finally feel that we have enough to offer to entice your faculty into a long-term partnership."

That comment wasn't what any of them expected. Willi blinked several times and Kunz raised his eyebrows.

"What you have to offer us?" Kunz asked. "Surely, with all you know, the concern should be whether we have enough to offer you?"

No stranger to negotiations himself, a well-briefed Hayes stepped in. Hayes always did his homework. "On the contrary. You have a great deal to offer us. Books with useful knowledge, buildings to hold classes in, the operating theater, and, of course, your faculty."

"I've seen your facilities, especially the gardens," added Mary Pat. "They're impressive. We brought a few people from Grantville who are gardeners to help us figure out names of plants since we probably won't call them all the same things you do. You know far more about herbal remedies than we do. You know the local artisans who can make medical equipment and have your own practices here in town. Now, we can offer you our knowledge and the hospital in Grantville as a training site."

"We've been pretty disorganized while we were trying to get everything up and running. There wasn't time to plan anything properly before the Ring of Fire," Ann added with a wry grin.

No, Werner thought, *definitely not the way I thought they'd approach us.*

"You're already set up and fully functional here," Beulah said. "We've spent two years trying to get ourselves organized and dealing with various crises to get to the point where we could approach you. We do have things to offer. I think you'll agree that those things are important. But this merger won't be easy. This is important to us. We don't want to mess up this venture or any future ones."

Even though he had spoken with them over the radio, Werner

wouldn't have predicted this. It was better than he had hoped for and the room's atmosphere was warmed by more than the summer sunlight.

Beulah smiled gently. "There is another bonus to working together. You have students who are much further along in their training than those we have in Grantville."

All four of the Jena representatives became very intent. They had been prepared to fight for their students and defend their students' caliber but it looked like that might not be necessary.

"We will be counting on them almost as heavily as on you. I know that the students will need to learn what we have to teach in addition to what you have already taught them," Beulah continued delicately, "but they are still much better trained in any number of areas than the students we would bring from Grantville. Few of our potential students have studied anatomy or performed surgery, for example. The most many of them have ever dissected is a frog in high school biology. One of the things we'd like to ask is whether or not you think your students would be willing to be teaching assistants for the incoming students. We're trying to put together funding for the positions now. We hope to be able to offer room and board, clinical at the hospital in Grantville, and access to our textbooks and equipment sooner. In exchange, in addition to acting as teachers' assistants, we'd want a commitment from anyone we offered the positions to stay in the area, one year for each year of study under the joint system. Naturally, we wouldn't restrict them just to Grantville. We don't think we can come up with enough funding for a stipend but we'll try."

"I think the students will be happy with that plan, if we can make it work," Werner said. "We had been concerned about our students and how they would fit in. None of us is under any illusions that we or the students could just go to Grantville and practice. That has not been an easy thing for any of us to admit. Do you see a similar role for the faculty?"

Again, it was Beulah who spoke. "Not exactly. We do think that there will be things you will need to learn and learn quickly. Part of the reason we wanted to come here is to get to know you and your backgrounds more personally. You are all experienced faculty. You don't need to learn how to teach any more than I do." She gave a little shrug. "There may be a few teaching strategies you'll need to adapt because of different material but you know how to deliver a lecture or teach students in a clinical setting already. There will also probably be some differences in styles that we will need to work on but I think that would be the case anyway. And, it wouldn't necessarily be *you* adapting to *our* style all the time, either. We're hoping that you will be the ones doing most if not all the teaching of material like chemistry and anatomy, at least at first."

"That's part of what I'm doing here," said Hayes. "I'd like to work with each of you on course materials, what you have here, what we have, and how they can be combined to get the material to the students in the best way."

"You'll probably not be too far ahead of the students sometimes in terms of learning some of the new material," Ann said. "It won't all be new to you, though, and it will get you ready to learn the practice stuff at the same time."

"What about our learning about your kind of practice? We are already physicians. If you expect us to teach more than the basic courses, we must know more about your kind of practice." Phillip's tone was very firm but without hostility.

"I had hoped to arrange time in Grantville for all of us before we began in January." Judging by the looks the Grantville team exchanged, Werner didn't think they had considered that. "We've studied all you have lent us but the material is complex and has not been given to us in any systematic way." Werner held up a hand. "This is not a complaint. It is just a fact. We would be able to learn more material more quickly if we spent some time with all your material, resources, and medical people in Grantville. We would also be able to see how you practice."

Mary Pat chuckled. "We'd been thinking the same thing but from the other direction. How much time would you want to spend in Grantville? Maybe we could split our time between the two places. Hayes will have to be going back to use his desktop computer for this anyway. We could spend some time here and then all go to Grantville together."

Werner thought a few moments. "Two months would be good. We would need time to see what was there and then decide what to focus on to bring copies of material back with us."

"We would need some time to make other arrangements as well." Kunz sounded a little hesitant. "Willi and I have wives and children."

"If you would like to bring them along, I would be happy to start making arrangements for housing," Ann volunteered. "It might work out even better if we can make arrangements with medical personnel for places for you to stay."

"What about bringing some of the students?" asked Phillip.

Beulah cleared her throat. "I think we should take a week or so and decide who should be approached about the teaching-assistant positions. That way, if we stay here a month, the students still have several weeks to prepare for the trip. And we'll all be back here by November to get ready for the students. Does that sound reasonable?"

Nods all around. "Now, how many children do you each have and how old are they?" asked Ann.

3

"*Guten morgen, Doktor* Rolfinck."

Werner looked up from his contemplation of the rather wilted looking mugwort. He'd have to speak with the gardeners about watering the plants more frequently. Mugwort was a versatile sort of herb in medicine. He used it regularly.

"*Guten morgen, Frau Professorin* MacDonald."

"I see you like to walk in a garden early in the morning as well. This is so lovely. Very nice layout, too. I try to stop for a bit at Leahy's garden each morning as I start my day. Some days, it is the only calm or quiet I get. Mugwort, isn't it? Stoner, our best herbal expert, has been talking about how useful it is, but I don't know much about it."

"I am pleased you like the garden. Feel free to walk here whenever you wish. I use mugwort primarily for pain, as a diuretic, an emetic, or laxative. I've also used it for headaches, insomnia, and as an appetite stimulant." Heartened by her admiration of the botanical garden he had created, Werner probed a bit. "From what you and the others said yesterday, I gather you are quite busy in Grantville."

"Fortunately, I've been too busy to tell myself I'm too old for all this very often." Her eyes were distant and grave. "We had casualties within the first hour and not even a clinic in town, much less a hospital. There were several pharmacies so we had a small supply of our usual medicines, but most of those were set aside for those who already needed them. They didn't last long. The pharmacies up-time also had some other supplies, bandages, and such. We nationalized those supplies right away but most of them didn't last long either. At first, we turned the high school into a makeshift hospital. There were only about ten doctors in town, some of them retired. All told, we had fewer than two hundred people with any medical training at all. Some, like me, were retired. Some have died. We did have the aide and LPN vocational technology program at the high school, thank God. We've been able to train some new people but not many and not at the higher levels. It's been a real scramble to get organized and get the hospital built. Everyone was just trying to get themselves and their families through each day at first. We had some things to work with but we didn't even know what materials, personnel, equipment, or problems we had initially. Fortunately, we had an architect and Mayor Dreeson put together a sanitation committee within the first week to oversee the public health needs. We've done the best we could but . . ." Beulah broke off with a grimace, eyes still distant.

Werner remained quiet and after a bit she continued. "Add to that the rapidly expanding population as refugees flooded in, most of whom didn't have a lot more than the clothes on their backs and maybe a few items of furniture or tools and a little food. The resources we had, in terms of supplies and building materials, were very limited when you think of the need. Then there were the deaths. There have been so many people we had the knowledge to treat but couldn't. Instead, we had to watch them suffer, sometimes die. Too often, there was little or nothing we could do about it, however hard we worked. I'll warn you now, that has left a mark on us all to some degree. Even with the most advanced materials, the best-trained staff, there were still plenty we couldn't have saved anyway. We know that. None of us are miracle workers. I hope you and the others aren't expecting us to be."

"It still hurts to lose a patient, whatever the circumstances. I knew things had been difficult, but I hadn't realized how difficult. I am sorry." Werner could certainly understand what it was to be spread so thin. The university had gotten much smaller with the war. Everyone was taking on a variety of roles. His feelings about the lack of materials from Grantville diminished. In its place was the realization that none of them had gone to Grantville's aid. When Grantville had first appeared, no one had known what was happening or what to think or do about them. Later, he had thought the Grantvillers could handle things themselves and that they were so advanced, he and his colleagues wouldn't have been of any use. Now, he wondered if that had been true. *How can they be so cheerful then, so optimistic? The situation there may be worse than I thought. What does that mean for us?*

"We don't expect you to be miracle workers. From our view though, the things you can accomplish do seem miraculous. Thank you for explaining. We did not understand why you didn't approach us sooner. Truthfully, we resented it. I understand a bit more now about why you are here and why now. To be frank, the meeting yesterday went far better than I had hoped."

"I'm also pleased by how the meeting went yesterday. We still have a great many details to take care of but I think we can do it. At least as we started getting down to some of the details in the afternoon, we weren't having major disagreements."

"It is, as you Americans say, early days yet. I hope we can work out any problems. Tell me, Frau MacDonald, do you think all your people in Grantville will be as open to working with us and our students?"

Beulah paused a moment before answering. "Most of them will, just as I hope is the case here." Hearing the questioning tone in her voice, he nodded but kept silent. She provided him with what she called "thumbnail sketches" of some of those he would be meeting soon. He would have to remember the phrase. He looked forward to meeting Ray and Stoner to talk about plants, and Balthazar, who was from his own time but was being treated as a valued member of the team by the Grantvillers. Werner had a great many questions for Balthazar Abrabanel. The respect in her voice when she spoke of him was obvious. Less obvious were her reservations about Mara. It wasn't anything she said, so much as what she didn't say that piqued his interest. The contrast with the way she spoke of Starr and Garnet was what made her reservations so evident. Werner could appreciate both the gesture of trust she showed by providing the information about her staff, and the discretion. When she spoke of Fritz and her hopes that he would be in the first class, Werner fit that in with the rest of what he had seen and heard the last few months. *They really do want to make this a partnership.*

"I have no doubt you'll want to share some of what we have talked about this morning with your faculty. That's fine. I would also like to arrange time to talk with you privately about some things as my counterpart. There are undoubtedly things that we wouldn't even consider because we aren't originally from this time or issues we should discuss between us before talking with the others. I hope you will share any concerns or problems you see."

"An excellent idea. Since we both enjoy the garden, perhaps we could meet here early each morning to talk."

"I'll look forward to it. And please, call me Beulah."

4

"Everyone ready to go?" Ann looked around the common room of the Black Bear Inn in northern Jena to make sure the others had everything they needed for the Jena tour. Werner and Phillip arrived to be their tour guides as she finished speaking. Willi and Kunz had classes this morning and couldn't come. Since there would be six of them and the streets were rather narrow, that was probably just as well.

"All set here." Mary Pat was carrying what Beulah would have called a visit bag in her public health days. Instead of the brown leather bag Beulah had carried, Mary Pat had turned her WVU book backpack into a mobile emergency kit. The kits had been standardized and accompanied all the teams that left Grantville with a medical type. Other kits had been made up for those without trained medical personnel along, given the skills needed to use some of the equipment.

As they stepped into the street, Ann couldn't help but appreciate the lack of odor. Jena's town fathers planned on developing indoor plumbing but right now, emptying chamber pots wherever was still the order of the day. Jena did have one crucial advantage however. At night, the city flushed the streets from a water reservoir so the city was actually much cleaner than most. What having raw sewage flushed downstream did to others was another issue. They were all concerned about what the level of sanitation meant for public health. Now wasn't the time to say anything about that, though, and the Grantville team followed Werner and Phillip through the streets with their colorful red-roofed buildings to the local clinic. They were only a short distance from the clinic when they were hailed.

"*Herr Doktor!* Ah, *und Herr Doktor* Ackermann." The rather breathless student looked relieved to see Werner and Phillip but barely glanced at the others. From what Beulah gathered between pants, a young printer had been working, suddenly became short of breath, and collapsed. His fellow workers had brought him to the clinic. Werner and Phillip headed for the clinic at a rapid walk. Mary Pat and Beulah exchanged a glance. *Someone this short of breath and they weren't running?*

*   *   *

The clinic was on the first floor of a building indistinguishable to Mary Pat from its neighbors. Inside, the clinic was an open area divided into several sections. One section looked like storage, another a procedure area, and the third had cots set up. About half the cots had patients in them, including one near the door with the breathless young man. *Tall, thin, Caucasian, young male, severe shortness of breath, supraclavicular retractions, touch cyanotic. Don't see any jugular venous distention or tracheal deviation.* Mary Pat could see Beulah making her own assessment as automatically while Werner and Phillip bent over to examine him.

"What happened to him before this started?" Mary Pat asked a nearby man in a printer's apron similar to the young man's.

"Veit just coughed and suddenly there was terrible pain in his chest and he couldn't breathe."

"He hadn't been injured or feeling ill before this?" she asked.

"No." The man turned away to watch the doctors, clearly thinking that Mary Pat was asking questions that were none of her business. It wasn't the first time she had seen that attitude and wouldn't be the last, no doubt. She had seen it during her deployments in Somalia and Yugoslavia but not to the degree she had seen it traveling around 1630s Germany. Right now, she didn't have time to pander to their delicate sensibilities about women and health care.

"Spontaneous pneumothorax?" Beulah's pronouncement caught the attention of Werner and Phillip. Mary Pat was already swinging her backpack around and unzipping it. She nodded and handed Beulah the stethoscope, then reached back into the bag. "I need to listen to see if air is still moving properly in his lungs. Sit him up, please."

No one moved despite the clear command in Beulah's voice. "We will treat him, Frau MacDonald." Phillip's voice held enough dismissive know-your-place to make Mary Pat flush angrily. She hadn't had too much exposure to that attitude in her previous life. Beulah glanced quickly at her, then back to Phillip.

"In just a minute, I can tell you if this is what I think it is. I need to use this to listen to his chest. If I'm right, we only have a few minutes to act before he is in very serious trouble."

"You do not consider this serious?" Werner's tone was disbelieving.

"Serious headed for critical and possibly life threatening. If there is nothing you're going to do for him in the next couple of minutes, what have you got to lose by letting us try to help him?" To someone who knew her as well as Mary Pat did, it was obvious it took everything Beulah had not to physically push them out of the way and to keep her voice level. The patient would soon be losing consciousness. There was no time for this. Beulah obviously thought so too.

"Hayes? About a thirty-degree angle. Please take care not to compress his chest."

Hayes didn't waste time with questions. He just moved behind the gasping young man and propped him up. Given his size and the element of surprise, the others moved out of his way quickly. Ann started clearing out the ward to give them more room, moving people out of the way. She knew what a spontaneous pneumothorax was, even if she wasn't a clinician and couldn't treat it. There were still people hovering in the doorway but now there was a good-sized circle of empty space around the cot. From the looks on Werner and Phillip's faces, however this turned out with the patient, it wouldn't be good. She took note of the confusion, anger, curiosity, and resentment there. She hoped things went well for the patient but the timing probably couldn't have been worse. *Hi, we've been here less than twenty-four hours to set up a partnership with you and we shove you aside to treat the first of your patients we see.* There didn't seem to be a good resolution from a political standpoint. If they couldn't save the patient after this, it would be even worse. If they did, it was rubbing salt in a very tender wound but at least the patient would be alive.

Beulah looked up at Mary Pat. "Pneumo, big one. Left lung is almost entirely down. Got a flutter valve in there? Lay him back down please, Hayes, and prop up his feet."

Mary Pat handed her an alcohol-based cleaning agent in a squirt bottle, and gauze. "Yeah, there are only a few left. I'll insert it." Mary Pat went after his shirt with a pair of industrial-sized scissors. They were great for cutting through clothes. The young man was losing consciousness now and they were out of time. She wished she had even a few liters of oxygen by cannula to make this a little better.

"Hurry, trachea beginning to shift." While Mary Pat cut the shirt away, Beulah was already wiping the skin under the shirt with the alcohol. Ideally they'd let it dry but this would have to do. Mary Pat had the small package containing the flutter valve and a few other pieces of equipment in hand.

"Wait, what are you doing?" demanded Werner.

"I'll explain later. For now, get out of the light," snapped Beulah.

Mary Pat hooked up the syringe to the end of the one-way valve and pulled the 16-gauge needle cap off the other end. She'd splashed alcohol over her hands. She didn't take time to put on gloves, just hoped she didn't hit a vessel. Second intercostal space, midclavicular line. She'd done this before and her movements were rapid and crisp. No fumbling. The needle slid right in and Mary Pat pushed a little further, feeling for it—*ah, got it*—and ignoring the gasps and chatter of the onlookers. The one-way flutter valve allowed air and fluid to escape but not to go back into the patient. As the air began to rush out of the pleural space through the valve, it made a honking sound, further startling the onlookers. Werner and Phillip were demanding to know what was going on. There was more to do so she and Beulah ignored them for the time being. Beulah had the suture ready to go and stitched the valve in place while Mary Pat reached for dressings, scissors, and tape. They needed to get this secure. The valves were almost gone, since they needed plastic materials to make them. Plastic Grantville couldn't produce anymore. The flutter valves were just a stopgap with a big pneumo anyway. There were a few minutes of onlooker chaos but Ann had them in hand.

"His breathing is easing. Hayes, put this pillow under his feet. His pressure is probably somewhere in the basement." Beulah reached for the stethoscope again, listened. "Breath sounds are improving, respiratory rate a little better, too. Nice work you, guys."

Werner was tight-lipped. "Does this mean you will finally explain what you have done to our patient?" Phillip looked too angry to even talk without yelling.

"Given the signs and symptoms we saw and the brief history Mary Pat got, we realized we were probably dealing with a medical emergency called a spontaneous pneumothorax. Young, thin white males are at particular risk for this. What happens is that a part of the lung is weak and bursts. Instead of air going in and out when he breathes, it gets trapped in the pleural lining between the lung and the chest wall. Each breath, more air goes in than comes out. The air builds up in the pleural space and begins pressing on the lung. The lung cannot properly expand anymore. If enough air gets into the space, the lung will start to press on the heart. A sign of that was the tracheal shift I mentioned. The air has to be removed right away so that the lung can reexpand and heal. We used a small piece of equipment called a flutter valve that will help with that." Beulah kept the explanation simple but Mary Pat could tell that some of it still went over their heads.

Beulah glanced back at their patient. His breathing was more regular and he was beginning to pink up nicely. Mary Pat took a turn explaining the procedure and how the valve worked. When she got into chest tubes and x-rays, Beulah stopped her. It wouldn't do any good to make the local doctors look more ignorant in front of their townfolk. *Besides,* she though uneasily, *I don't think they're getting this. Is it that they are too angry to think or something else?*

Mary Pat frowned and turned to Beulah. "He needs a chest tube. You can't just drop a lung like that and expect a flutter valve to fix it. An x-ray will tell us how bad it is."

"Agreed. We may not be able to hook him up to wall suction but at least in Grantville, they can put in a chest tube and hook him up to a waterseal system."

Phillip had had enough of them using words that he couldn't understand. Even if they were speaking German for most of it. There was nothing he or Werner could have done for the man but watch him die. They didn't even know what had happened to him. These women had known at a glance. Phillip didn't even understand what had happened in just a few minutes. The two women had done something in front of their students and townfolk that seemed incredible. The speed and skill with which they had acted was impressive. More confused than he had ever been in his entire life, he turned around and walked out, not waiting to see what those women, who weren't even doctors, would do next.

5

"I had thought you would be getting some sleep but *Leutnant* Flanagan said you had come here."

Werner's voice brought Beulah out of her thoughts. The stone bench she had been waiting on was not exactly comfortable but at least it had a nice view of the garden. She noted the change from *Fraulein* to *Leutnant* when he referred to Mary Pat with a sinking heart. "We had agreed to meet here in the mornings. Did our patient get off to Grantville all right?"

"Our patient? Interesting choice of words, but yes, Veit and *Leutnant* Flanagan just left. I would have thought you would be getting some sleep."

"It will take them most of the day to get to Grantville. They'll have to go slowly, even with the new suspension on the coach." She smiled softly. "As for sleep, talking with you is far more important. It's been a while since I've sat up all night with a patient. Not that I could have done much else for him if anything had gone wrong. The supplies and equipment are in Grantville. So are the people who can fix it if the lung doesn't reexpand. As for Veit being our joint patient, yes, he is." The testiness she heard in her own voice was enough to make Beulah wince. Every joint she had hurt and she had to face the fact that what had started so promisingly in Jena was rapidly falling apart. Add that to her fears about their patient's outcome and a sleepless night, and she wasn't at her most tactful. That was still no excuse for taking her feelings out of Werner.

"Look, I'm sorry. I shouldn't have snapped at you, now or yesterday. Not exactly professional behavior on my part. Let's be clear on a few things here. I'm not sorry that a man who would have died is still breathing. I *am* sorry for the way things happened. There were two choices, treat him or stay silent. I knew you didn't have the resources we did to treat him. If I had stayed silent, he could have very well died. How would you be feeling about this if I had and later, you found out we could have treated him but didn't for the sake of political expediency? What else could I have done?"

Werner was quiet a moment, weighing what she said. His innate fairness was warring with his anger and humiliation. How much of the humiliation he felt was because Veit had been saved by two women who weren't even physicians? What would he have done in her place? Given the stakes, would he have held one life as highly as she clearly did? What else could she have done, indeed? He spent a few minutes trying to get his thoughts together, to say what he had to say without making things worse.

"I can understand why you did what you did and I am very glad Veit did not die. That doesn't change the facts. You brushed us aside to treat one of our people. As though we were nothing, knew nothing. We are not used to being treated in such a fashion, especially by women. Don't you understand? That you were right, that we could do nothing while you could save him just makes it harder for us to bear. Phillip and I have spent our entire lives caring for our patients, studying, teaching, and trying to give the best care we could. You gave us a graphic demonstration of how little we know, how limited is our skill. And you did it in front of our students and townfolk. I know things happened quickly, but what happened couldn't have been more poorly timed or more painful to us. How can we have any confidence that we have anything to offer you? That we aren't nothing next to you?"

"Please, Werner, sit down with me."

While he sat stiffly at the opposite end of the bench, it was her turn to struggle to find words. "If any of us thought you were nothing or that you had nothing to offer, we wouldn't be here. What you have to offer hasn't changed since our first meeting. The last thing any of us wanted is to make you feel that way. I've thought about it all night but I don't know what to do to try to make this better."

"Show us what you did and why," Werner demanded promptly. "If we can understand it, then it won't seem so mysterious or out of reach."

Beulah smiled hugely. "That I can do. Can we have both students and faculty present?"

"Yes, I think we should. I'll set it up for tomorrow so you have a chance to sleep and I can take care of some other things today."

"Would Phillip be one of those things? Is he all right?"

"He is struggling with this. I hope he will be calmer by tomorrow. Get some rest now, Beulah. I will send a message to you tonight about the class." He didn't want her to ask about the other things he needed to address today. He was on his way to a meeting with the other deans. News spreads quickly in a small town. He had a feeling there would be more than just medical-school faculty and students at the lecture Beulah would give tomorrow. He thought about warning her but dismissed the idea. She and the others needed to understand just how serious what had happened was to his people. Part of him also wanted to know how she would handle such a surprise. *It was not very Christian of him*, Werner thought, as he watched her leave the garden.

Chapter Four
September, 1633

1

Mary Pat flopped back onto the bed in their room at the inn with a loud moan. "The roads are awful. I should have just found a horse."

"I can sympathize, but you got Veit to Grantville safely and he's doing well. I'm sure your sacrifice of more road time was worth it." Beulah's cheer sounded a little forced to Mary Pat. She sat up and looked across the room to where Beulah sat.

"Okay, what's wrong? Start at the top and fill me in. I've only been gone a few days. How much worse could things have gotten?"

"Just about everything has gotten worse, actually. It's become pretty clear that we managed to offend the entire university in a matter of minutes. Werner and I talked the morning you left. Werner suggested a lecture to the faculty and students to explain what had happened and what we did and why." Beulah's tone was discouraged.

"Sounds like a good idea. What happened?"

"First, a lot more than just the med students and faculty showed up. The other three deans and some of the other faculty and students were there as well. I've given lectures for years. Never given one like this. They kept interrupting with questions. That usually isn't a problem for me. Tells me the students are still awake and paying attention. This time, though, the questions were a problem for a couple of reasons. It was pretty clear that they don't have a lot of basic concepts. I had Ann there to draw some of this out, you know how good at sketching she is, but I thought we were going to be dealing with a few dozen people, not nearly two hundred, so the drawings didn't help as much as I'd hoped. They had to be passed hand to hand and by that time, I'd gone onto other points. Points they also didn't understand sometimes. I'd have killed for an overhead projector or even a large blackboard and some colored chalk. The gist is that it is pretty clear that a lot of the basic principles we are counting on them to teach, they just don't have."

"From talking to Balthazar, I had thought things were further ahead than that."

"Well, they aren't. I wish I had talked to him in more depth about this. It was also pretty clear they shouldn't have sent me. Everyone from the students to the deans were ridiculing things I had to say. One of the law school faculty even got up and walked out, saying he saw no point in listening to anything a woman had to say about science. I think some of the others would have walked out too, but then they'd have missed their chance to laugh at Ann and me."

"What, they laughed at you?" Mary Pat was off the bed and pacing angrily now.

"Oh, yeah. I had to slap 'em down a bit, which didn't go over well either. Their ideas of science don't have anything to do with the experimental method, trust me. They are more about authoritative sources and since they don't believe a woman can be an authoritative source of anything scholarly . . ." Beulah paused. "To be fair, there weren't that many who were in need of a serious attitude adjustment. The ones from the law school were the worst. All that training in rhetoric certainly made things interesting. I was about to strangle them. Their dean didn't have any control over them at all. I'm not sure he even wanted to have any control; he seemed very much on his dignity, if you know what I mean. The arts dean, Wetzel, at least made an attempt to rein in his students. Werner's students and faculty just looked grim and angry and resentful. They had enough of a background to get at least some of what we were talking about, but that just seemed to have made it worse. It has made them more aware of what they don't know, not less. They don't understand 'vacuum' and why negative pressure is necessary for the lungs to work properly. Nor do they have a very thorough knowledge of the circulatory system, much less what happens to the cardiovascular system during a shock state. Trying to explain why it was a medical emergency and why we had to act that quickly didn't quite get through. I had to keep going over things that a high school student would have known and backing up to explain basic science."

"I was afraid of this. I spent some time in the library the last few days. It doesn't have very much but I got enough to get a sense that they may know less than I thought they did. I can't blame them for being upset about it but they still shouldn't have treated you that way."

"That isn't all. Poor Hayes has had quite a time of it the last few days. I think he's about frustrated enough to give up and go home. Faculty are suddenly too busy to meet with him and Ann. Since we demonstrated that we know things they don't, the faculty and students don't want to give us their books. They want ours. I had read some things in teaching theory about the received view of knowledge, where the greatest authority had the knowledge and therefore 'truth.' They may hate the fact that this knowledge came through women and that it doesn't agree with their worldview, but in a way that just makes them more determined to get their hands on our books. They all want to go to Grantville and raid the library. Immediately, if not sooner. Since Hayes is the only male, they think he has the authority to just hand them the books and can't understand why he is letting women stand in their way. They also don't understand why he wants to spend time looking at their material. Right now, I'm not sure either. Hayes is ready to pack it up and go back to all the other projects he has in Grantville. He's even muttering about walking the distance if there isn't a way to get back sooner."

Mary Pat gave a low whistle. "Wow. How's Ann doing?"

"The schedule we had has been effectively destroyed already. We've been lecturing and dealing with upset people instead of finding out what we need to know to move forward. Ann hates disrupted schedules. They aren't letting us anywhere near their patients at the moment. She and Hayes haven't been able to do anything to evaluate the material they came to look at, either. Ann is an experienced educator. She is none too happy with how the lectures are going and how we're being treated. Neither am I. The urge to snarl at them is getting pretty intense. That wouldn't exactly help."

"So where do you think we should go from here?"

"Good question. I hate to say it but maybe Mara was right. We should have just started our own med school from scratch."

2

A discreet consultation with the proprietor of the Black Bear a few days later had led to Beulah reserving the best private room at a local restaurant. The room looked nice and she had paid for a good dinner. *Maybe I should have ordered more booze. Question is, for them or me? At least the white wine is really good. I have a feeling we'll be drinking quite a bit of it tonight.*

The idea was to get away from the university environment and the other deans and faculty to talk about the future of the joint med school in a more relaxed environment. After the last week, Beulah wasn't too sure there was a future. She'd known it would be hard to pull this off but she hadn't realized it would be this bad. To make matters more interesting, Veit was due to come back from Grantville in a few more days, a week at the outside. Human nature being what it was, she was absolutely sure he would be talking about what he saw there, maybe even exaggerating a bit. At this juncture, she couldn't see that making things anything but worse. The Jenaites were convinced by now that Grantvillers were out to steal their herbal knowledge while depriving Jena of the up-time knowledge they craved. Rumors were flying all over town. Jena's mayor had hinted about the political consequences of Jena not being treated as an equal just this morning, for Pete's sake. She'd given Mike and James a heads-up the day Mary Pat had come back, but things had deteriorated since then.

James had told her yesterday that in the last few days the deans had already contacted him over the radio. And Mike. And Balthazar. When they found out a woman was running the hospital, they had just plain had a fit. James, Mike, and Balthazar had all told them the same thing: *We're sorry to hear that but Beulah and her team have our full confidence. We're sure this can be worked out.* So much for their end run around the women.

Wish I had a Tums right now, the way my stomach is churning. This mint tea just isn't getting it.

Predictably enough, Ann was the first to arrive. She was positively twitching. Beulah hadn't ever seen her do that much smoothing and hair checking before. Her eyes had darkened with her agitation until they were almost as dark a blue as Beulah's. As far as Ann was concerned, this trip was an unqualified disaster and she wished she had stayed in Grantville. She wanted to go home. So did Hayes. Neither of them had been shy about telling Beulah that.

Phillip seemed solidly in the you-are-withholding-information camp. He wanted the information and he wanted it now. Werner was still trying to work with them but he didn't seem to really trust them. Kunz and Willi weren't talking much, so Beulah wasn't sure where they stood. They had both somehow managed to be too busy to do much more than say hello in the halls in passing. Mary Pat had sarcastically begun calling them Tweedledee and Tweedledum. Beulah had put a quick end to that but she couldn't change what Mary Pat actually thought. Mary Pat deeply resented the treatment they were getting. While Hayes thought they had better things to do and Ann just wanted to go home, Mary Pat was ready to get in their faces and demand respect. Beulah had done that in her younger days. It usually didn't work but Mary Pat was too pissed off to listen to any words of wisdom on the subject. If it was only herself she perceived as being attacked, she would have restrained herself. Beulah knew that part of what had pushed her over the edge was the way she saw Beulah being treated.

Beulah firmly quashed the Tweedledee and Tweedledum thought that flickered through her head when Kunz and Willi walked into the room together, both garbed in sober dark-brown clothing. Mary Pat followed hard on their heels and gave Beulah a speaking look. Beulah gave her a tiny frown, *None of that Tweedle stuff now*. After the good-evenings were said all around, Hayes walked in and then Werner and Phillip. More good-evenings. Then silence.

"Please everyone, have a seat. Supper should be here soon. I hope everyone likes fish. Felix, could you start serving, please?"

Felix was a thin sixteen-year-old who would be their waiter tonight. He was apprenticed to the tavern keeper and had only recently started serving in the parlor. Beulah had arrived early while he was finishing setting up the steam table for supper. Supper looked good. There was salad to go with the fish, some wonderful smelling bread, cheese, and fresh fruit. She had taken a few minutes to chat with him and set him at ease. He seemed pretty nervous. He'd been surprised when she'd apologized for being so early and volunteered to leave if she was in his way. While Felix deftly slid plates in front of the diners and poured the wine, Beulah struggled to find small talk that would help ease the tension a bit, without any success that she could see. She was trying to pass the time until Felix left before they could get started talking about the school. When he took a position near the steam table, she realized he wouldn't be leaving. *So much for privacy. Might as well get this over with.*

"I need to ask you straight out. Is there any future for a joint med school with Jena and Grantville? Or have things gone too badly to repair before we could even really get started?"

Werner took a sip of wine to give himself a moment to think. "I don't know. I had wondered if you called this meeting to tell us you were leaving. There certainly seems some sentiment for that among your party."

"I realize things haven't gone as any of us thought it would. I want this to work and so do the rest of us. More than that, I think both Jena and Grantville *need* this to work. Perhaps what you are hearing is frustration and disappointment. I'd like to talk about what can get in the way of being successful at this and how we can remove barriers so that we can build something to benefit us all."

"Pretty words, *Frau Professorin,* but that is not the message your actions give," Phillip said. "You say you wish to be colleagues. You say we can contribute to a partnership. You say many fine things but you don't bring your books to share with us, you ask to see ours. You don't treat us with respect. You don't talk to us as equals."

"And you do?" That was too much for Mary Pat. "I've seen nothing but a lousy attitude since I got back. Okay, so we did something you couldn't do. So we did it in public. What else could we have done? You've been choosing to ignore everything we've said and done or put the worst possible spin on it. Respect, my ass. *You* are the ones who haven't treated *us* with respect. Respect is earned, buddy. You think that walking out on a teacher in the middle of a lecture, being rude, and laughing at her entitles you to respect? I've got a news flash for you. It doesn't. You've taken one incident and blown everything out of proportion. We didn't mean any disrespect to you and I think deep down you know it. This just gives you an excuse to quit so you won't have to face things you don't want to see. And take the easy way out by blaming it all on us."

"That is untrue," snapped Kunz. "We have acted in good faith. We welcomed you to our town and you repay us by shaming us, withholding your knowledge, and taking over. That is not a partnership."

"Let me address those points one by one. I think they're important," Beulah said. *It should also keep our resident hotheads' mouths shut while they cool down a bit. At least Werner has a hothead on his side to deal with, too.* "We do see you as colleagues. We wouldn't want to shame you any more than we like you treating us disrespectfully. Actions are important. I hope you will have seen from our actions that what you thought was shaming was actually simply an attempt to save a young man's life. We truly did not intend to shame you."

Ann spoke up next. "We didn't think to bring the books because we didn't know what you had or what you knew. It took quite a while before Dr. Abrabanel was ready to practice in Grantville and he hadn't been trained at your university or even in this country. That was part of the reason for the trip here. As for not sharing our knowledge, it isn't that simple. The things we have to show you can't just be learned by opening up a book and studying the text. If you do that, it will just be more confusing. There have been almost four hundred years of advances in medical care between now and our time. If all we did was give you the books, it would be like giving a beginning student the texts to study for their last set of exams. We need to figure out what you know and what you don't and then put the information together for you and help you integrate it into your practices."

"It doesn't help when you won't even let us look at your books so we can actually figure out what we have to work with here," growled Hayes.

"That is the attitude I am talking about," snapped Phillip. "You helping us, not us helping each other."

Hayes snorted. "You haven't given us a chance! We brought two gardeners along to learn about the botanical gardens and how you use them. You could be showing us something we need to know. Instead, I get nothing but the runaround from everybody I talk to. No one will let any of us anywhere near your precious books. We have to know what we are dealing with before we can make any plans."

"We didn't believe that our books had anything to offer you. We have seen the books *Leutnant* Flanagan shared with us. We have seen something of what you can do. Where do we and our students fit in to that? It will not be, as Beulah said that first day, a matter of us learning a certain amount and then being ready to teach it to our students. Ann is right. It is more complicated than that." Werner looked at each of his faculty in turn. "I don't know if we are ready to merge our schools. Yet we have no real choice. How can we live with ourselves if we don't learn what they have to offer? Are we so proud then? So angry? What is that next to those we might help, the lives we might save?"

Beulah said slowly, "It sounds as though you've been concerned about this since before we even got here. And we haven't been concerned enough about it."

Willi looked up from shredding a piece of bread. Beulah didn't think he'd taken a bite of food yet. "It is not easy to see what is in those books. How do I take care of my patients now? There is so much more to know."

"The books . . . I thought I was helping by giving you the copies of the books. Instead I just made it worse. I'm sorry. I only meant to help."

"You did help, Mary Pat." Werner used her first name deliberately. "Without that, we might not have realized there was such a problem until much later. Perhaps we were ready to make certain assumptions given any excuse."

"Which brings us to the start of this conversation," said Willi. "Does the joint venture have a future? For myself, I too wish to learn what you have to teach."

"This won't work at all unless we are all for it. Does everyone agree that we want the merger to work?" Beulah asked. There were nods around the table. "Okay. We have some issues here already to address. How about starting tonight by identifying what we think the problem areas are and then we all take a few days to come up with possible ways to solve them before we meet again?"

"An excellent suggestion. We could all use some time to think and for tempers to cool." Werner glanced around the table. "Let us each take turns bringing up one issue until we have covered all our concerns."

Ann reached into her suitcase-sized purse for the paper and pen she carried everywhere with her. "I'll take notes so we don't miss anything at our next meeting."

3

They had all had to send for or buy warmer clothes before they got back from Jena as the weather had changed considerably over the last two months. The trip back had been cool, rainy, and generally uncomfortable. Beulah wanted nothing more than her bed and some willow-bark tea. They had been able to distill the active ingredient for the equivalent of aspirin from the birch bark into a pill form, since it worked better in pill form than the willow bark, but she usually drank the tea. The heat from the mug was a double benefit for her hands.

She had sent James, Balthazar, and Starr a long letter a few days ago catching them up so she didn't have to meet with anyone tonight. Tomorrow was slated as a settle-in day, so she was planning to take things easy. The group from Jena wanted to get started right away. Beulah thought they needed at least a day or two to get accustomed to Grantville. She hoped the trip had taken some of the starch out of them. It certainly had taken the starch out of her. It had also given her more time than she needed to think on the last few months and what lay ahead. The changing leaves on the trip back had just seemed to emphasize the running-out-of-time message playing in her head.

Veit's arrival in Jena a week after the supper meeting had had several consequences. As she had feared, he'd spread his view of Grantville's medical capabilities far and wide. Beulah and the others had been approached by Jena natives for all sorts of medical needs. Most of them, they couldn't meet. Some of those could be fixed in Grantville. When they had explained that they didn't have the equipment they needed, a considerable number had shown up at the Grantville hospital. It hadn't been a flood exactly, but it had strained resources and personnel, who were already stretched thin. The doctors in Jena saw their patients look to Grantville, not them, for help. It was a double-edged sword. Some of those who went to Grantville were helped. They had brought back stories of relieved pain or even cures over the last two months. Others weren't helped and no one in Jena had enough of a background to understand exactly why one particular patient could be helped but not another.

She and Mary Pat had had to do a lot of explaining. The Jenaites just wanted answers while she and Mary Pat wanted to put things in a larger context. So the answers the Jenaites got didn't really make sense to them, because they didn't always want to listen to the underlying reasons and what nurses called critical thinking that went into the processes of assessment, diagnosis, treatment, and evaluation.

They hadn't been too eager to share their medicines when Beulah and Mary Pat ran out, either. The doctors had seen that Mary Pat and Beulah could help with some things in Jena without sending the patients to Grantville. It had kept the wounds from the episode with Veit fresh in everyone's mind.

Beulah and Mary Pat had hoped to establish a better relationship between themselves and the doctors and students at Jena. There had been a little progress but the things that helped them make progress sometimes hurt rather than helped.

That was true for more than the med school and the town. The rest of the university was watching all that happened very closely. So closely, in fact, that they had sent along several university delegates. The dean of theology was one, as were representatives from the law and arts schools. She was grateful the other two deans hadn't come. The arts school dean made her dizzy, hopping from topic to topic and the law school dean had a permanent scowl etched on his face. Beulah thought their goals were to find out as much as they could about the knowledge in their areas that might be affected by Grantville know-how before they were confronted with it more directly. She had to admire their being proactive and wanting to learn. She just wished they were coming after the med school delegation left. The Grantville library wasn't too well organized yet and there wasn't a lot of space for people to go looking around. The other schools would also be watching how the med school faculty and students were treated. That put the med school faculty and staff under a microscope instead of letting them just deal with the Grantville people. Beulah felt for them. It wasn't an easy position to be in.

Werner and his entire faculty had come, which was what they had planned at the beginning, more or less. The entire student body had also come. Since there were only about thirty students, and as Werner pointed out, the students couldn't do much with the faculty gone, that had made sense. Given the extra time, they had even found space for everyone. But more people trekking to Grantville meant more time was needed to get everything organized. Which had put them further behind schedule. Ann had been a godsend, although the frequent changes in plans as one more person (and usually his family) just had to be added had kind of gotten to her. At least it had given all the Jenaites time to work on their English. One of the few nice surprises on the trip to Jena was that all the med school faculty and some of the students had been practicing English for some months before they got there, so they actually spoke it pretty well.

Beulah stared at all the horses, carts, and wagons disgorging people and baggage into the cold night air. *We looked like an old-time wagon train headed west,* she thought tiredly. It was a toss-up whether she was going to brave the crowd of people or just wait till everything settled down. Mary Pat had met up with Rodney and his girlfriend, Pris, then headed to the hospital to drop off her emergency bag for restocking and to check in with the army officer on duty. Beulah hoped to already be asleep in her own bed by the time Mary Pat got home. Rodney had told Beulah someone was coming to help with her bags, but he hadn't been sure who was coming.

The Grantvillers who were taking in some of the Jenaites were moving among them, trying to figure out whom they were supposed to meet and take home. The smarter ones were holding signs, but in the gaslight and the confusion, it wasn't easy to make out what was written on the signs. The ones going to the town's only hotel were in a group and those people had ridden up together so they and their bags could be rounded up all at once. It still took time and was noisy. Fritz was standing right beside her before she heard him call her name.

"Frau MacDonald, are you all right?" he asked in concern.

"I'm just tired, Fritz. It was a long trip."

"I asked to come carry your bags home for you tonight. I thought you would have many and it is some distance to your home. I shall find your bags and help you get home with them if you would like."

"That would be wonderful. I wasn't sure how I was going to get my things out of this mob."

Fritz dove into the crowd and found the bags with Beulah's name on them. "I also wanted to thank you for recommending me to the nurses' aide courses. I am enjoying my new work very much." He set off with Beulah toward her home. They walked quietly for a while, Beulah letting her thoughts settle and Fritz apparently gathering his nerve.

"I have heard that the classes in Jena will start in a few months, that you and the others will be picking the first students soon."

"The reason I wanted you to get started in the nurse's aide courses so quickly is because I wanted to see how you did and if you liked the work. I hope to be able to recommend you for the first class. I don't know what the outcome will be and I can't promise anything. But I think you'd make a fine nurse or doctor, Fritz."

"Thank you, Frau MacDonald. I would like that. I had heard that things did not go smoothly in Jena. I was afraid that there would be no school or that there would be no chance for me there."

"We're working it out but it hasn't been easy. We have some of what we need pulled together. All of us want this merger to work out." She wished she could give him the reassurance he was looking for but this was the best she could do. They were farther behind than she liked. "Thanks for carrying the bags for me. You saved me a major hassle. I'll see you again soon."

4

"Come in, James." Beulah stepped back to let him in the kitchen door the next morning. He had his hands full with breakfast. "Thanks for bringing breakfast. We didn't have time to shop last night and the cupboards are pretty bare."

"I see Mary Pat has your favorite beverage at the ready." James nodded a good-morning to Mary Pat, who was starting to pour mugs of coffee. She'd been ready to go off to work but Beulah had insisted she take the day to catch up on what was happening in Grantville. At least it got her to rest a bit. She was wound too tightly, and had been for too long, especially the last few months. This wasn't exactly time off but it was the best Beulah could do.

Mary Pat glanced up and gave a casual wave. "Morning, James. Thanks for breakfast."

"Fritz came by and walked me home last night. He mentioned some talk in town about the med school merger. What have you heard?" Beulah asked.

"Jeez, Beulah, let a man put down breakfast and get a cup of coffee first. See if I bring you breakfast again." To Beulah, his smile had a bit of an edge to it. *Stalling*.

"All right, all right. I'll quit pushing."

"For now, anyway," Mary Pat laughed, while she helped him off-load breakfast. "Let's get some food before she gets going again. Once she's had a cup of coffee, we're in trouble."

"How was the trip home, Buelah?"

"Cold, wet, bumpy, and long. Okay. Get it over with." In response to his questioning look, Beulah explained. "You're giving me your clinician look. Assessing my movement, general appearance, yada, yada. I'm a seventy-three-year-old woman who is tired, sore, and aggravated. Otherwise, I'm fine."

He turned to Mary Pat. "She always this grouchy in the mornings?"

"Just lately. It's been a pretty rough few months." Mary Pat seemed to take his comment more seriously than he had intended. Now it was her turn to get the clinician look. Beulah didn't think he liked what he saw.

"I gathered that from the letters you both sent back. You sketched out the broad picture. How about you fill me in some more? We have a few days before all of us are officially supposed to get together, but in a town this small, we may run into each other sooner. I'll pass whatever you think is important on to Starr and Balthazar later today. Then you two can get some well-deserved rest."

"I'll leave you two to it. I think I'll go get some groceries. Rodney can fill me in on how things are going in town and points beyond." Mary Pat grabbed a slice of heavy dark bread and headed for the door, carefully avoiding his stare. "Thanks for breakfast. See you in a bit."

James turned slowly back to Beulah. "You want to tell me what just happened?"

"I think she thought it was confession time. Irish Catholic, you know. Very good at the guilt thing."

"Ah. Not exactly enlightening. I take it she felt she had something to confess? From that look, you feeling the need for confession, too?"

"I'm a Methodist, remember? No confession, but I do have a few things to catch you up on. Mary Pat first, because it's all of a piece really." Beulah took a fortifying sip of coffee. She'd been good and had the medicinal tea first but it didn't seem to work quite as well of late except to help turn her stomach into a vat of acid. And the tea didn't even taste like coffee. "I'm old enough to remember how women were treated in nursing and medicine even comparatively recently where we're from."

He nodded in understanding. "So am I. Mary Pat isn't. I take it she took issue with their attitudes."

"Yeah. She thought showing them the error of their ways would be enough, that once they saw the evidence that she was every bit as good, if not better, than they were in the healing arts, they'd get it and that would be that. Sometimes that strategy actually works, but it isn't without its drawbacks and it usually takes more than two months. The thing is, Mary Pat knew that. She knew better but it was like she couldn't stop doing it. She was going to *make* them see. Whatever was going through her mind, I don't think it was just about Jena or the merger."

She sighed. "Part of the problem is that I agree with her about most of it. For all I've tried to be politically correct and culturally tolerant, we've come from a time that has been through history that has disproven or otherwise challenged some of this time period's views that were driving us nuts. Especially their views about women. I'm not a feminazi but I won't be less than I am just because it threatens notions I find ridiculous anyway."

"We are all products of our time and culture, just as they are of theirs. Being aware of that is fine. So is trying not to come across as arrogant know-it-alls. That doesn't mean we're all going to agree with their views. We can't even agree about plenty of things among ourselves."

"She saw me as not being very supportive when I tried to talk to her about modifying her approach or about being sensitive to their side of things. She was frustrated with them for not listening to reason and not seeing what, in her opinion, was right in front of their faces. She got madder. They got their backs up even more. Vicious cycle. I didn't exactly help matters. I know you sent me along as the mature member of our little party, but I certainly had my own moments."

"I'm almost afraid to ask. What moments?"

She slumped a little in her chair. "They quoted Galen to me one too many times and they did it at the same time that they were pulling a nicely subtle 'you're a woman, we don't expect you to be able to comprehend this' crap. Galen was just plain wrong about a lot of things and I, ah, took exception. I brought up the fact that in ancient Greece, most of the healing deities were women. I brought up Hygeia and Panacea and pointed out that their precious Galen spoke highly of women physicians like Margereta, who was an army surgeon, or Origenia, a physician, and even extolled the virtues of some of her treatments."

James started snickering.

"I'm glad you find it so amusing," she said quellingly. "They didn't. These are very devout men, James. I respect that. I may not park my butt in a pew each and every week, but I take my beliefs pretty seriously. I'd talked to Balthazar a bit but evidently not enough. With a daughter like Rebecca, his viewpoint isn't exactly typical, although he does know what those attitudes are.

"If I'd asked the right questions and paid more attention to what is going on right here in Grantville, I might have been better prepared for this. I haven't spent a lot of time with our new German citizens, certainly not enough to realize how deeply their attitude toward women in general and women as healers in particular goes. They truly don't believe women can learn this sort of material, much less teach it. Their beliefs aren't just about academics or medical practice. They're founded in beliefs about the basis of their society and the roles of men and women in their daily lives.

"I'm afraid that by sending women as the medical delegates, we made a serious error. We've been here two years; I should have been more aware of the culture here but I've been somewhat isolated by working in the hospital so much and mainly with other Grantville professionals. Most of the Germans I've met have been as patients, family of patients, or casually in town and on 'my' turf."

"I kind of expected something like this," James told her. "I had the advantage of talking with some of the people here, including Balthazar, who were born in this time. It's been enlightening. Whether or not it was a mistake to send a mostly female delegation or not remains to be seen. It's certainly got the issue out in the open. What did Machiavelli say about a leader figuring out all the cruelties necessary and getting them out of the way all at once?"

"Medicine by Machiavelli now, is it? You're really hanging out with the wrong crowd, James." She shook her head in mock rebuke, clearly grateful for his support and for him lightening the mood a bit. "I don't know what the long term consequences will be. We have to face them but right now, we need to get through the short term without making things worse."

"I agree. After we realized what some of the problems were, we had a group of up-timer and down-timer health care people get together to brainstorm solutions and try to identify any other trip-wires we might face. We've been giving in-services based on their recommendations to all the staff. The members of our ad-hoc committee have also been trying to prep the rest of the town."

"And how are they taking it?"

"It varies. Some are unsurprised by the attitudes and just plan to work around it or think that it doesn't really affect us here in Grantville. That's rather shortsighted, given that the USE is lots bigger than just Grantville. Others have a milder version of Mary Pat's reaction. There are a few people who have been problems."

"Let me guess. Mara and her little band of twits," Beulah said acidly.

"Um hum. She's been quietly stirring up some of the staff, exaggerating the cultural and academic differences in our positions and goals. Most people know enough to ignore her but she's smart enough and good enough that she is making headway. Everyone here is a bit tense. On the upside, some of the tension is that most of us want this to work and want to get off on a good foot with our guests. Most of our people will be on their best behavior."

"Thanks, that is good news. So, Machiavelli-in-training, is that why we don't have an official meeting for another few days?"

"We're going to show them around a little first. We thought that might make a number of points without having to rub anybody's nose in it. Then, when we get to the official meet and greet and the hospital tour, two days from now, things might have loosened up a bit. Each of the host families or some other designated tour guide will be showing them around town tomorrow. Today is a rest, unpack, and get-to-know-your-hosts day."

"Sounds good. Fill me in on any of your other plans and then tell me the story with Rebecca and her group. Have you heard anything from Julie and Andrew yet? Are Melissa and the others okay? From what little we've heard in Jena, it sounds like things are heating up."

5

Mary Pat slid the groceries onto the kitchen counter early that afternoon. Diving for the nearest exit this morning meant that she hadn't taken either the cloth bags she used or Beulah's little two-wheeled pulley cart to the store. *No "paper or plastic" at the grocery in 1633.* She'd stopped by Rodney's place to borrow his bags rather than come back and face Beulah and James. Cowardly retreat wasn't her style, but this morning she'd just had it.

Things hadn't gotten any better when she went to Rodney and Pris' place. Last night in the dark, she hadn't noticed the engagement ring that Pris was wearing. Rodney was like her little brother. She certainly didn't think of him in any romantic way but she had felt a stab of something like hurt or grief when she'd seen the ring. She knew they were getting serious and had sort of seen this coming. She also knew from experience with two of her brothers that things would change now. Rodney would, quite naturally, be changing his priorities to his wife and eventual children. That had to come first. She understood and even applauded that.

She had admired the ring and congratulated both of them. She'd even managed to smile and joke. Inside, though, it was different. Normally, she'd have talked to Sharon or Elizabeth but Sharon was deployed with one of the mobile units who were trying to help out Gustavus Adolphus, and Elizabeth was doing railroad stuff somewhere. And Beulah. . . .

Things were pretty strained between the two of them at the moment. Mary Pat *knew* Beulah didn't approve of the attitude of the Jenaites toward women or nurses. She also knew that Beulah had to play diplomat, a role she wasn't too comfortable with. Beulah had talked to her about trust building and potential and need and different cultures. Beulah was a public health nurse. Beulah knew how to do that kind of stuff. Mary Pat however, was more on the trauma end of things. "Grab 'em and go" was closer to her reality. *And my own impulsiveness and temper didn't exactly help out either.*

Mary Pat reached into the bag for the cheese and eggs. She still needed to stop by the bakery but the bread James had left would do for today. One of the nice things about being in the seventeenth century was that the bread wasn't that store-bought yuck she'd grown up with. This bread had some real taste to it.

Rationally, she knew Beulah had been trying to teach and comfort her under circumstances that were a strain for Beulah as well. Emotionally, she felt betrayed. She trusted Beulah, counted on her. The incremental approach Beulah had taken didn't suit Mary Pat's nature at all. Beulah had tried to laugh it off as one of the benefits of age. Well, Mary Pat was thirty-one, not exactly a kid. Rodney was nearly ten years younger than she was and he was getting married. Before she knew it, he'd have kids and . . .

The hanky was lace-trimmed. Beulah had tatted before arthritis had ended her hobby and now she was handing Mary Pat one of the few remaining hankies she'd made. Mary Pat had been so deep in thought she hadn't heard her come in, much less realized she herself was crying. "Thanks, Beulah," she said stiffly. "I don't know what's wrong with me. I'm not the crying sort."

The floodgates suddenly opened and she was babbling, a jumbled collection of two years of grief and stress and confusion. Rodney and Pris. Sharon and Hans. Jena. Marriage and kids. No connections. Work and how tired she was. Missing her family. Aunt Heather and her brothers and Mom and Dad and the rest of the Flanagan clan. On and on and on. Beulah just listened and handed her another hanky.

"I'm glad you're crying. About time. You've been carrying a lot of things around with you for a long time and not letting any of us in. When we came through the Ring of Fire, no one handed you a cape and tights or put a 'Super Mary Pat' on your chest, my dear." She'd been trying to sort out what Mary Pat was really saying while she listened.

"Things are changing, but you aren't alone. Rodney and Pris, Sharon and Hans just expanded your family. When the kids come along, you'll be Auntie Mary Pat. Yes, your relationships will change but that's life. Right now, you're looking at what you've lost instead of what you've gained."

The next area was more sensitive and Beulah wished for some of Rebecca Stearns' subtlety. "As for marriage and a family of your own, you're going to have to stop hiding in work and being deployed all over the place. I've seen you turn down several offers for dates during the last two years using that as an excuse. What are you really afraid of, loving someone that deeply and then losing them the way you did your up-time family?"

Mary Pat bolted. Beulah had anticipated her maneuver and reached over to grab her wrist. Mary Pat was younger and stronger and could have broken the grip and left, but the pain on Beulah's face wasn't just from arthritis. There was such understanding, such shared grief there that all Mary Pat could do was lean against the cabinet and cry. Beulah reached out and took her in her arms, hugging her fiercely, knowing Mary Pat wouldn't have accepted that comfort earlier. *I should have brought a hanky for myself, too. Is this what mothers feel when their children are hurting so badly? This need to do anything to take the pain away, the intense empathy with their pain?*

"I'm sorry," Mary Pat said dully, looking spent and hollow. "I gave you nothing but trouble in Jena and now I'm whining like a baby because my life's a mess and it's my own fault."

Beulah loosened her grip and leaned back, pretending shock. "You mean you were the one responsible for the Ring of Fire? You were the one who shaped the attitudes of the early modern era? I'd have never guessed. Shame on you."

To her own surprise, Mary Pat gave a watery laugh, a little shaky but still a laugh. "Cut that out."

"You were more help than you know in Jena. I had quite a bit of time to think the last couple of days. They needed to see that we wouldn't take their attitudes lying down. I was so worried about being culturally sensitive and not putting my foot in my mouth that I didn't put forward much about *our* culture and beliefs. You did and in a way they couldn't miss. That may not be the disaster you're making it out to be. These are not stupid people and we're all motivated to make the project work. It'll take time and effort but we'll get it done. You aren't the only one trying to make it happen. I'm sorry that I was so selfish in asking you to be part of this. I thought it would help you get a break."

She let go of Mary Pat and motioned toward the kitchen table. That was where the two of them always sat and talked. She wished she could promise her that she would always be there for her. Reality was different. Beulah was not getting any younger in a time with a lousy life expectancy.

"I never had kids myself but I've still had a great life. I wouldn't change any of it—including the Ring of Fire, oddly enough. Without that, I'd never have met you. I'd have just been another retiree with too much time on her hands. I'd never have met so many interesting people or grown as much. I didn't think an old dog could still learn so many new tricks. I know things have been a little tense with us lately but I wanted you to know that I love you as though you were my own daughter. I'm not your mother but you still have someone who loves you that way. You have more connections than you know here. It's time to start reaching out a bit, letting your heart heal. You do have a future here. You can shape that future. It's up to you but you won't be alone while you're doing it."

Chapter Five
September 1633

1

Gary Lambert literally tripped over his own feet. The man coming toward him early that morning was Johann Gerhard. Gary had known he would be coming with the Jena delegation, but he hadn't thought to run into him the very first morning. Yet there he was. The peaked eyebrows, the balding head with its ring of shoulder-length wavy hair, just like it was in the copies of Grandpa's books. Johann Gerhard was one of the most respected Lutheran theologians of his day. Gary had a copy of an 1871 edition of one of his books and had picked up a CD of some others just before the Ring of Fire. The books were still highly regarded and had been pretty much in continuous print after he wrote them.

Since Gary was the business manager at the hospital, he'd been hoping for a chance to talk with Pastor Gerhard. Gary preferred things low-key and was not comfortable being the center of attention for any reason. When he'd thought about it, the falling-flat-on-his-face part had not been included in meeting the pastor. Or should he call him Dean Gerhard?

"Here, young man. Are you all right?" Johann caught the young man under the elbow to steady him.

"You're the Pastor Gerhard," Gary blurted and then blushed as he juggled an armload of papers. "I'm sorry, sir. Of course you know who you are. I didn't mean . . . it's just that I've just read your work since I was a kid. Your picture is in several of my books. That's how I recognized you. I've been rereading some of it when I have any spare time since the Ring of Fire. I wanted to thank you. It's been a great comfort to me," he finished with a little more dignity.

"Thank you. I have only been wandering through your fair town for an hour. With what I have already seen, I am not sure of much at the moment. It comforts me to know that some of what I believe now still holds true. May I introduce my companions? Jakob Arnold is one of the faculty in the College of Law, and Christoph Burkholtz is one of my students."

"An honor to meet all of you. I'm Gary Lambert. I work at the hospital as a business manager. I was hoping to meet the pastor and ask him to autograph a copy of one of his books for me." Gary just managed to not point out that today was to be a day of rest and that they weren't supposed to be out wandering around alone yet. Evidently, these three had set out on their own first thing in the morning. It wasn't like they were being kept prisoners or anything, but he wasn't sure what he should do about this, if anything.

When he paused, apparently speechless, Johann spoke. "Perhaps we could talk a moment more unless you have to be off somewhere else? I'm sure Jakob and Christoph can look about some more on their own." Jakob and Christoph shook hands with Gary and said their goodbyes.

"You work at the hospital then? That is fortuitous. I have been looking forward to touring both Grantville and the hospital, but I understand the hospital tour is not planned until tomorrow."

"Yes, sir. I usually have breakfast in the cafeteria but I had to stop by the printer this morning first. These are some drafts I'm working on for the new hospital in Magdeburg. I could show you around a little if you'd like, buy you breakfast," Gary volunteered hesitantly. After reading so much that he had written, he realized the pastor just didn't seem like a stranger. Still, he didn't want to derail the plan. "I'm not anybody special there and I don't know the medical stuff, but I could still show you around some of the other areas. Later, you'd see more."

"That would be most kind of you. I would like that."

A large, bright-yellow vehicle rumbled by, filled with children. Gary waved casually to them and headed up the street toward the hospital. Johann's gaze lingered on the children, some in American garb, some in the garb he was familiar with, all chattering or waving or bent over their studies for some last-minute cramming. *To be as accepting as a child. I could use some of that right now.* He turned and set off with Gary, a little uneasy about what he might see, but curious. He needed more information, wanted to get more of a sense of the people here in their own environment. Gary seemed like a nice tour guide. He pointed out some places he thought Johann might find interesting. The town was clearly busy and thriving, if a bit chaotic.

Fortunately, the rain held off until they got inside the hospital. He hadn't been tempted to linger, knowing that he would be seeing more tomorrow. As it was, he simply admired the fact that, according to Gary, the hospital had gone up a year or so after their arrival. He noted the pride with which Gary spoke of the hospital and what had been accomplished.

"Of course, you'll be hearing more about the other plans tomorrow. There is a plan to build a hospital in Magdeburg soon. This building and the record system I set up will be prototypes. Do you think Jena will build one, too?"

"I don't think our thoughts had gotten that far." Johann sat in a large open room that Gary took him to. There were tables and chairs grouped around an area with food already prepared by the kitchen staff.

"Sure you wouldn't like something to eat as well?" Gary asked.

"Thank you, but the ale will be sufficient. I've already eaten with Christoph and Jakob before we left this morning." Johann took the opportunity to look around and observe the people in this "cafeteria" while Gary went to get food and drink. A German family had pushed two tables together to accommodate their numbers and were talking softly a short distance away. Men and women in various groupings were scattered through the cafeteria. They wore loose-fitting blue shirts and pants and soft-soled shoes. Whitish jackets covered them to just above the knee, and an array of books and implements he couldn't identify protruded from ample pockets. There seemed to be some sort of name placard on their left breast but he couldn't read them from where he sat without staring. Some were speaking English and some German. Their mien wasn't any different in their way than that of plowmen eating a meal on the edge of a field.

"Here's your ale." Gary slid his breakfast tray into place across from Johann and set the beer in front of him. "I can take you around as soon as we finish."

2

Johann Gerhard wouldn't have thought he'd be at the hospital this morning discussing Lutheran dogma and answering Gary's questions about the various schisms in Lutheranism when he got up this morning. Gary had put up the tray, waved to some of the people in the cafeteria, and begun the tour. They had started with the second floor, which seemed to hold office and meeting rooms as well as storage and some medical rooms. There were some areas that Gary called exam and clinic rooms. Johann was surprised to see the chapel that was located on the second floor. It was small but he could tell it was carefully tended. The third floor held more office space, a largely empty but sizable medical reference library, and a few rooms for staff to stay in if they had to sleep over during bad weather or times of short staffing. Most of the rooms for patients were on the first floor. The operating theater that was on the first floor was two stories tall so that students could observe the surgery from the second floor.

He had been impressed with the spaciousness and craftsmanship of the hospital. All those they had met on the tour had greeted them cordially as they went about their tasks. If someone they met had a moment, Johann was introduced. Otherwise, they just walked around and observed, with Gary pointing out a few features as they strolled.

The first floor of the hospital, where most of the patients were cared for, proved a different experience for Johann. What struck him most were the things Gary didn't point out. In this corner of the surgical ward a doctor and nurse spoke in hushed tones about a patient. He noticed that there was mutual respect but no subservience in the way they spoke. On the medical ward, he saw a nurse showing the doctor a chemical analysis of some kind. From what he could catch at a distance, the nurse was clearly knowledgeable and even discussing courses of treatment. Those images were repeated throughout the hospital. Gary pointed out the technology to a degree, or architectural details. He showed Johann the glassed-in conservatory and introduced him to people. But he didn't even seem to notice the way the staff all worked together.

As he said good-bye to Gary at the hospital entrance, Johann had a lot to think about. He needed to speak to the others in the Jena delegation about what he had seen as well. First, he was going for another stroll through Grantville.

Chapter Six
October, 1633

1

Ten days after returning to Grantville from Jena, Beulah ran her hand through her hair for the second time in the last half hour and looked around the conference table on the third floor of Leahy. She suspected the tangled curls were sticking up and gave her the appearance of an aggrieved rooster. *This is what I hated most about academia. Curriculum meetings. Wrangling about nothing much as though the fate of the world depended on it. The things that actually are important get lost in all the noise.*

"It sounds like there are some areas we agree on and some that will need further work. I'd like to summarize the areas of agreement before we adjourn this afternoon and then set some priorities for discussion tomorrow. Is everyone agreed?"

Nods around the table. She had been careful to instruct those from the Grantville curriculum group to scatter themselves in with those from Jena. She didn't want these meetings looking like opposing forces gathering to negotiate a peace treaty. The group from Jena had spent more time looking around Grantville than they'd planned, but Beulah thought it time well spent. Nothing like an up-close-and-personal look to make them a little more willing to consider other points of view, and she'd been agreeably surprised by the things they did have in common.

"At the baccalaureate level, points in agreement are length of time to degree completion, a rigorous examination for licensure to practice after graduation, a defined scope of practice for the new nurses, and some of the course content. Given the amount of science education that will be needed, it is more likely to take four years rather than three to complete the baccalaureate curricula, although with year-round courses and intensive clinicals, we may be able to cut it to three years."

Mary Pat looked around at the group. "I've been asked as a representative of the military side to stress the need for medical personnel to be trained as quickly as possible. Next year, we will probably be facing more conflicts and more injuries. We're also concerned about the possible spread of diseases."

"Ann, please make a note of Mary Pat's concern in the minutes." Beulah glanced at the representatives from Jena. "I realize that it is a somewhat less pressing concern from your end, but the military is going to be using some of our students and graduates as soon as they can get them. I don't know if any of the current students are particularly interested in military medicine. But, later, I'd like to talk about a few interested students doing a residency in trauma and military medicine with some of our military staff, Mary Pat for one."

Phillip spoke up. "There are several students that I think might be interested. Werner and I can talk to them if you would like. The ones I am thinking of are particularly interested in surgery techniques such as the one you demonstrated at Jena on Viet." His smile was small but genuine. Beulah was glad to see it. Phillip looked to have relaxed somewhat in the last few weeks. He wasn't quite as confrontational. She'd been dreading that attitude in these meetings but it hadn't materialized.

"That would be very helpful. Thank you. If everyone is agreeable, I think that after the curricula are agreed on, we can put together an examination with a smaller subgroup of this committee and the staff at Leahy. For now, I think it is enough to just acknowledge the licensure issue and then move on to more pressing matters. May I see a show of hands?" Every hand rose. Beulah nodded to Ann, who was taking meeting minutes. She jotted the vote down. "Where we seem to be having problems is in three areas. First, grandfathering in students and professionals from Grantville and Jena. Second, content, and third, faculty."

"There is an additional concern, Beulah," Werner corrected. "There is a difference between a trade school or guild education and a university education. What you have been proposing sounds too close to a trade school for our comfort."

"Perhaps we can discuss that when we speak about content and faculty responsibilities," suggested Johann. "After the last few days of meetings, I have a feeling Beulah has an idea about how to deal with the grandfathering issue."

"I do in general. It's some of the specifics that concern me. I think that both Grantville and Jena people who want to practice at the baccalaureate level should take the exam, even those who are already nurses here."

"Wait a minute! That's illegal!" Mara was outraged. "You can't take away our licenses! We're already nurses and should just be grandfathered in. Those from Jena can take the exam and the new students from here can take it after they graduate."

Thanks, Mara. That went over like the proverbial lead balloon with the crowd from Jena. At least the rest of our group is waiting to hear me explain before passing judgment.

"Normally, I'd agree with that and I am concerned about the precedent that could be set. The legal types will undoubtedly get involved but I think we should at least consider it for several reasons. First, we are making entry into practice at the baccalaureate level. Not all the up-time nurses have that level of training, particularly the public health content we need so badly. There are also new content and new ways of doing things that we have developed in the last two years. I believe it is important to start out clean. I don't want there to be any doubt about our nurses' qualifications by future graduates or anyone else."

Mara's mouth shut with a faint but audible click. Beulah had known that would hit home and had prepared her arguments carefully. The Jenaites might not understand it, but she had no doubt that the up-timers would. The highly contentious debate within nursing about entry into practice education and licensure had raged for nearly a century in the U.S., flaring up every decade or two in ways that were not always very helpful. A classic example, Beulah had often thought, of circling the wagons and shooting inward.

Registered nurses or RNs could come from any one of three educational backgrounds but all took the same licensing exam. Hospital-based diploma schools were three years with minimal coursework and an emphasis on on-the-job training at a particular hospital.

Those schools were largely closed in the U.S. up-time. The second group was taught in junior colleges. Although in theory it took only two years of courses to complete the degree and be eligible to sit the RN exam, Beulah had rarely seen anyone get through the program in only two years. The third group was those who attended four-year universities and obtained baccalaureate degrees. Those students had public health, teaching, and administrative content as well as greater depth in other areas.

Mara was as aware of all that as any other up-timer would be. Since a license wasn't something that could legally be taken away by changing the law, nurses with different preparations would have to be grandfathered in to RN status. Grandfathering the current crop of nurses in would always leave that kernel of doubt about their knowledge and competence. Since the legal authority that had granted those licenses, namely the state of West Virginia, didn't really exist anymore, the legal types could probably make a case for not needing the grandfathering fairly easily, but she really didn't want to get into that at all. Beulah hadn't mentioned the fact that it would go down well with the Jenaites to have everyone sit the same exam for licensure. She would if she had to, but Mara made no further comments beyond a quietly murmured, "I hadn't thought of that." The group from Jena clearly noted her response but made no comments. Beulah appreciated their tact.

"I think we should all think about that for a few days and then revisit it after we talk more about content and faculty roles. The content difficulty seems to be between what we up-timers would call liberal arts and professional education. As I understand from what's been said, grammar, literature, rhetoric, and logic are the basis for the trivium and start in what we'd call grade school. Literature includes Latin and Greek classics, and basic mathematics is part of logic. At the baccalaureate level are more of what up-timers would call liberal arts. Courses like physics, which we are all agreed should be in the curricula, are taught as part of astronomy. We up-timers find the placement of physics in astronomy a little odd. I don't know how helpful it will be to have a nurse or physician study astronomy and physics related to astronomy rather than physiology, but at least we agree that we need physics. Engineering, which we are conflicted about including, is taught under mathematics and so on as part of the quadrivium. Masters' level education is for teaching at Latin secondary schools in the arts, and doctoral education is what we'd call a professional doctorate, such as a doctor of medicine or a doctorate of jurisprudence. The current doctoral level doesn't really have any liberal arts content at all. Professionals without a doctorate can get a license to practice in a particular area after they earn a baccalaureate. Professional schools such as law or medicine need a doctorate to teach. There is not a research doctorate like the doctorate of philosophy we're used to. Have I got it right so far?" Nods again from the Jena group.

"Your contention is that without the liberal-arts courses such as astronomy, the students will be getting essentially a trade-school education, not a university degree. Without those courses, you can't say they are graduates from Jena. Our contention is that some of those courses need to be shaped more toward practical need for the medical or nursing profession and be heavier on the sciences at the expense of some of the courses you regard as essential. We don't believe, at least initially, that there is time for courses like drama right now. We need nurses and doctors who can practice. To you, they aren't able to be fully functional without the liberal arts courses."

"You have captured it succinctly," Johann agreed. "We cannot call what we are creating here a university education without those courses. Any graduates of the program would be unable to be employed or to continue their education anywhere else. It would also bring us into conflict with the guilds and make our students appear more like barber surgeons than university graduates. The courses must be included in the curricula."

Whatever else Johann would have said was interrupted when a very pale Starr came into the conference room. "Can I talk with you a minute, Beulah?" Starr was wearing what Beulah thought of as "nurse face." It was the kind of neutral, calm look that nurses used to avoid alarming patients or their families when things were going seriously wrong. Beulah felt her own face automatically assuming the same mask as she excused herself and stepped into the hallway with Starr. Once in the hallway, Starr's mask cracked and her soft brown eyes began to fill with tears.

"Oh, Beulah. There's been a battle at Wismar. Hans, Larry, and Eddie have been killed in action!"

The shock of it made everything sway sickeningly in front of her for a few moments. Isolated, fragmented images and incomplete thoughts went spinning through her mind. Sharon and Hans at dinner. Larry coming into the high school infirmary banged up from something after the Ring of Fire. So many people were going to mourn the loss of those boys. They'd achieved legendary status in the Battle of the Crapper and with all they had done since. Aside from his notorious driving, Hans was well loved here, too.

"Where are Sharon and James? Veronica Richter and the others? Do they know?"

"They're being told. Sharon was there in Wismar. James is here and I'm not sure about Frau Richter. I wanted to tell you before I made a general announcement over the PA."

"That was the right thing to do." Beulah heard her own voice from a distance, making suggestions and giving instructions, slow tears falling down her cheeks. *Oh, God. How will I tell Mary Pat?*

2

"May I join you, Beulah? If it won't disturb you," Werner asked quietly. At her nod, Werner sat on a bench next to her in Leahy's conservatory. "This is a lovely spot. I can see why you start your mornings here. Especially lately."

"It's been especially comforting this last week. The memorial service yesterday was pretty intense. We're going to miss them. At least Mary Pat got to go to Magdeburg to be with Sharon for a while. Given the unrest there, having a trauma nurse on the spot might not be a bad thing. She'll be back in another week or two if things settle down there. I hear she and Phillip had organized a trauma rotation for a couple of the students."

Werner gracefully accepted the change in topic. She clearly didn't want to talk too much about what had happened. He understood taking refuge in work. While he hated to push at a time like this, the needs and responsibilities that had brought him to Grantville still existed. "So I am given to understand. Phillip and the students are very excited about it. We have spent a considerable amount of time in the library reading basic texts and sharing the texts we brought with us with Hayes and Stoner. I have had some very interesting conversations with Stoner. When he can be spared from his work here, and before he leaves for Italy, I should very much like to have him visit me in Jena and look over our gardens there."

"I'm sure he'd be happy to see them. You've done a great job with them."

"Thank you. As we have been reading in the library, the complexity of public health measures that are taken to prevent the spread of illness are of particular interest, especially as it will be spring soon. I was wondering if it would be possible to have a lecture given to the students and faculty on public health and the prevention of communicable diseases? I understand you have some expertise in this area."

If she was at all unhappy or angry about being in essence asked to give a lecture to the group from Jena after what happened last time, Werner saw no sign of it. Then again, she was an experienced faculty member. The circumstances were different and one incident out of a long career wasn't going to stop her. He doubted much of anything would stop this woman once she set her mind to something, and he both needed and wanted to have a better relationship with her and the other medical personnel in Grantville. But particularly with her. She was very highly regarded and involved in some way in every aspect of medical care here. It was Beulah who was the liaison with the program at the high school, who had been the director of nursing, who consulted with the sanitation committee, and on and on. While they had been here less than a month, her central role in the small medical community was clear. He and the other faculty would make sure the students stayed in line this time.

Not that he thought it would be really necessary. Kunz had had a severe talking-to for some of the more rigid students. Being left behind with Grantville's treasures before them had weighed more heavily than some of the views currently being shaken. He rather thought Kunz had been surprised to find himself as an advocate for Beulah and the Grantvillers, however reluctant he had been. Werner thought that the students had responded very well to the lead the faculty had taken. They had all had their eyes opened to another way of practicing, a highly effective way at that. He didn't know what they would take from the Grantville way of doing things in the long run. But, in the short run, all of them were very curious and being very observant. And polite about it, too.

"Makes sense. I'd be happy to give the lecture myself if you'd like. I'd want to pull some materials so they have a few of the basic science concepts down before I gave the lecture. We could set it for say, two weeks from today?"

"I was hoping you would agree to do it. Two weeks from today then."

3

Beulah paused in the ER exam room door that evening to watch Ernst, one of the Jena students, with Fritz as his assistant, stitch up a small shin laceration. The patient was an up-time youngster of about eight, whose mother was watching carefully. Beulah didn't see any extra anxiety because a down-timer was working on her son. Fritz was translating Ernst's comments when he needed help with English. Nice bedside manner, reassuring and calm. A little gentle teasing to set the little one and his mom at ease and distract him. She noticed with a tiny smile that he was being very, very careful of his sterile technique.

Beulah slipped away unseen by the group in the small room. She didn't want them to feel she wasn't confident in them. The scene heartened her. This was what they were working toward. The child would have had to wait until James or one of the RNs was free to do the suturing otherwise. He'd have been in pain and the normal inflammatory response to injury would have made the wound more difficult to close. Since James was in surgery and the only RN available to cover the ER was with another patient, that wait might have been an hour or more.

They would make this work. It had taken no time at all for Phillip and two of his students to start spending every spare moment in the ER. Phillip the adrenaline junkie. Who'd have thought it?

Chapter Seven
October, 1633

1

"What happened?" Phillip asked as he hurried into Leahy's emergency room. Two of his students, Ernst and Heinrich, trailed closely after him as he more or less trotted beside Mary Pat. She'd grabbed them out of the grand rounds they'd been having on the surgery ward. Phillip, Ernst, and Heinrich were doing a trauma and surgery mini-rotation. They spent every spare minute they could in the ER.

Beulah had instituted grand rounds as a teaching tool. The rounds gave them a chance to review cases with Beulah, who did hands-on teaching and explanations of actual patient conditions and their treatments for small groups of students. Much as Phillip and the other two students appreciated the floor time, they'd fallen in love with trauma, and any opportunity to get in on something that got Mary Pat moving that quickly was to be pounced on with speed. Beulah had waved them on with a "Catch up in a few minutes. Go on."

"Just got a call from the ambulance. We've got a couple of casualties coming in; they're about ten minutes out now. I left Mara prepping before I came to get you and grabbed some supplies from the OR on the way. The report the EMTs called in is that there was an accident at one of the farms. The loft in a barn gave way and the two men getting hay for the cows went down with it. One of the men is in pretty good shape. Bumps, bruises, stable vital signs. He's got a possible concussion but also has a scalp laceration that's bleeding even through the pressure dressing."

As they arrived in the ER, she directed them to the side-by-side exam rooms where Mara was prepping IV fluids and setting out linen bandages. Mara worked quite a bit in the ER because she got calmer and calmer the more desperate the situation. She was sharp as the proverbial tack to boot. Mary Pat appreciated her abilities, but the fact that Mara's thick drawl also got slower during a crisis drove her nuts sometimes. Mara looked up at them and waved Ernst over to a cabinet. "Great. Our master of the suture is here. Going to put all the suture practice you've had to use today, Ernst. Can you get your stuff ready?"

As Ernst headed over to the supply cabinet, Phillip and Heinrich looked at Mary Pat, who continued her report. "The one we're most concerned about, Harmon Manning, wasn't so lucky. Evidently, he fell directly onto the concrete floor rather than the hay, and some equipment stored in the loft fell on his chest. Looks like he's got crushing chest injuries as well as a broken arm and collarbone. May have some spinal-cord injuries. They're bringing them all in on backboards just in case. Mara, any new info?"

"Vitals are going downhill on Manning. Carotid pulse is palpable, rhythm sinus tach with a rate of one-sixty, up from one-forties." Seeming to remember who else was in the room, she glanced up and then went on. "They don't have much time with someone that far out and that seriously injured. So they don't spend a lot of time on blood-pressure taking. Instead, as a general rule of thumb if you have a carotid pulse, you have a systolic—ah, that's the top number on the blood pressure—of at least sixty. Sixty is the minimum amount necessary for the brain to be perfused, although it isn't optimal. Sinus tachycardia means that the heart rhythm is regular but too fast."

"Can you two start setting up the splints and chest-tube trays?" Mary Pat headed for the oxygen cylinder set up near the wall. They didn't have oxygen piped through the walls the way an up-time hospital would have, but at least they could make it and refill the cylinders from the nursing home. With the curtains open between the ER "rooms," they could all talk freely. The rooms were large so they could handle lots of people and equipment if needed. Phillip, Heinrich, and Ernst had spent a fair amount of time here and they'd been shown where things were located and some of the basics during the last few weeks. "A pulse at the femoral artery should indicate a pressure of at least seventy, radial at the wrist at least eighty. That they're looking at a carotid pulse and that his heart rate is that rapid is a probable indication of being in shock. The shock could be from hypovolemia, that is, too much blood loss, or from cardiogenic shock from injury to the heart. That is, that the heart has been hurt too badly to function well."

Mara laid out toweling and said, "Okay, everybody, get scrubbed up. They should be here any minute. The last report indicated that his respiratory status was bad. Supraclavicular retractions, respiratory rate is almost forty, and he's cyanotic. They've been able to cut away his clothes in the ambulance to get a better look at him. They've got a flail segment. Sounds like a big one."

Phillip looked from one to the other. "And the significance of that is . . . ?"

Mary Pat looked back at them and scrubbed her hands harder. "With a flail segment, a contiguous group of ribs are broken. The person can't breathe normally because the rib cage doesn't move in a unified fashion. When the person breathes in, the flail segment sinks instead of expanding and vice versa. There isn't enough negative pressure to fill the lungs with air sufficiently if the segment is big enough. That means we're probably dealing with a pneumothorax, maybe a hemopneumothorax, which is blood as well as air building up in the chest cavity."

"Ah, like Viet."

"Worse than Viet this time, I think. Heinrich, I'd like you to handle the ambu bagging please. You'll be monitoring his respiratory status. You've done it before. You may be at it a while this time."

James came in through the double swinging doors from the OR. He pulled off the surgical gown he was wearing, dumped it in a linen bag, and began scrubbing his hands. While Mara briefed him quickly, Mary Pat looked around to make sure that everything was ready and got a final report from the ambulance crew. Their patient sounded unstable as all hell. Mary Pat felt the adrenaline pumping through her system, sharpening her mind and slowing everything down with an odd crystalline clarity. They were lucky to have this much prep time but every minute that their critical patient was in the field was a minute too long. Beulah came in and caught the report while she joined James at the sink to scrub.

"Beulah," James began, "I'd like you and Heinrich to take the possible concussion. Evaluate him and get him patched up as much as you can. Give a shout if you think he's got an intracranical bleed cooking in there or anything else you think I ought to look at. The rest of us will work on the patient with the flail segment."

Two things happened as James finished speaking. The outer doors opened with the ambulance crew bringing in the stretcher with their critical patient while the LPN and nurse's aide stationed outside to wait for the ambulance helped get the second patient out. Another aide came rushing in carrying two glass bottles of blood from the blood bank. Mara had ordered them as Mary Pat had gone out earlier.

From the looks of Harmon Manning, they were going to need both of them, and then some.

2

Phillip didn't like the way the man looked as the EMTs wheeled him in. There wasn't a great deal of bleeding apparent, but the man's skin was a grayish blue color he'd recently learned to call cyanotic. Each rapid breath was a labored, pain-filled gasp. Phillip knew what death looked like and this was death before him. He exchanged glances with Ernst and Heinrich, who both looked grave but still optimistic. Phillip, who had seen far more death than they, wasn't so confident. They had seen amazing things in Grantville these last weeks, true.

Ernst and Beulah headed for the second patient while Mary Pat, Mara, and one of the EMTs helped move him over onto the ER gurney, since it was wider. Phillip managed the IV and oxygen tubing as James leaned over to expose his chest, stethoscope in hand. Phillip had been reading about "breath sounds" and he'd been able to actually hear an asthmatic child's wheeze just that morning on rounds. He didn't think James would be happy with whatever breath sounds he heard out of this patient.

He could hear Beulah talking with the second patient, hear his slurred speech and concern about his friend. Beulah was talking quietly with him behind the drawn curtain and reassuring him that his friend was being treated. Phillip had moved a tray of instruments and gotten out of the way as the others settled Harmon and began the examination. Mara's face was the only one he had a good view of, and something in her face made him edge closer to the gurney, trying to see what had occasioned that sad, compassionate look.

As he got closer, he could see the look on James' face as well. James was very carefully touching—ah, palpating, the word was palpating—their patient's chest. Phillip frowned. He thought that normally, one listened to the chest first in an assessment. That was what the book had said. He remembered the passage clearly. As James lightly touched his chest on the right front side, Phillip could hear a crackling kind of sound.

"What is that noise? His ribs?"

"Crepitus," answered Mary Pat. "That means that the ribs have probably punctured the lung, and air is being forced into the skin by the building pressure. See how the area is swollen, too? James is trying to get a sense of how big the flail is. An x-ray would tell us more but the patient doesn't have that kind of time."

"About twelve by sixteen centimeters," James reported grimly. He turned to Chester, the EMT. "Is the family on the way?"

"Won't be here for at least an hour."

Phillip felt it again, just as he had with Viet all those months ago. It was clear that Mara, Mary Pat, and Chester knew what to make of James' question. He didn't, and neither did Heinrich, who was carefully using the ambu bag to help the patient breathe. Beulah stepped softly to Phillip's side. He could hear the LPN working with Ernst as they stitched up the bleeding laceration on the patient in the next bay.

"Want me to get some morphine?" she asked quietly.

James looked up at her and nodded. "Yeah. Let's make him as comfortable as we can."

Phillip walked with Beulah to the medicine cabinet at the nurse's station in the center of the room. "He is not going to live, is he?"

"No. The flail is too large and the bones are pulverized under his skin. I watched as Mary Pat took his blood pressure. I could tell she didn't get a very good pulse and when I saw the mercury pulse the first time in the glass, it was only around fifty. His heart rate is becoming not just rapid, but erratic. We'd rush him into surgery at this point if we could, giving him more blood and IV fluids to keep his pressure up as much as possible. We'd also put in at least one chest tube and so on. But we don't have any ventilators. Ventilators are machines that can breathe for the patient when the patient can't manage. With a flail chest, we'd need to do that so the bones could knit together while the machine breathed for him. We can't splint the ribs when they're broken that badly because we could drive a piece of bone into his lung. Plus, unlike limbs, which can be immobilized by casts or splints to heal, the ribs will move multiple times each minute with every breath. It would take too much strength for him to do that himself for a few weeks. With a small flail, we'd give it a try but this is just too large. The other injuries he has might kill him as well but if we can't keep him breathing, it's a moot point."

She finished drawing the morphine into a syringe and headed back to the patient. "All we can do is make him comfortable. We don't have a vent to breathe for him for weeks after the surgery. We also don't have any of the substance that could help glue the bones together. Even though we know he won't make it, we could try to keep him alive until his family gets here so they could say good-bye." She handed the syringe to Mara. "There's ten milligrams in the syringe. I thought you could space it out as needed."

She turned back to Phillip and motioned him back from the bed. "We can't use the supplies to buy him an extra hour and give them a chance to say goodbye. We only have so many chest tubes. That blood was scheduled to be used this afternoon in surgery. We don't have all the resources we once did. Even then, we never had endless resources anywhere I worked. Which means making tough choices sometimes."

Everyone who remained was oddly hushed, their movements and aspect subdued, Phillip thought. They continued to do small tasks for their patient and to clear away material, used or not. There was an air of sadness and frustration in his Grantville colleagues. He was familiar with the feeling of losing a patient. How much more difficult must it be to lose one that you might have saved, that you had the knowledge to save.

3

"For God's sake, Mary Pat, did you have to come armed?" Beulah hissed the aside as she looked out into the lecture room on the third floor of Leahy. They were using the future medical library for a lecture on the history of public health and infection control for the Jena students. A lecture Beulah was giving. Damned if she was going to let anyone else face them after her experience last time in Jena.

Mary Pat tenderly patted the Berretta 9mm pistol her oldest brother had given her and tried very hard to look innocent. Beulah didn't think she looked at all repentant and the sparkle in those green eyes was far from innocent. "I'm on duty. So of course I'm in my basic dress uniform and carrying a sidearm. Do you really think I'd shoot one of these med students for getting out of line?"

"*I* don't think you'd do it but they might. This is serious overkill here. Not that I don't appreciate the sentiment but even I'm more subtle than that." She looked at Mary Pat out of the corner of her eye. "That smile would reassure me and our audience a little more if it had fewer teeth in it."

"I'm on duty. I wouldn't go around shooting unarmed civilians for no good reason." She pursed her lips thoughtfully. "Like say, oh, disorderly conduct."

"We have cops to handle that. I don't buy the 'just happened to turn up here of all places while on duty' line, Lieutenant."

"Didn't think you would but it got your mind off the lecture, didn't it? I'll be on my way, Officer Flanagan, always at your service."

Beulah laughed and shook her head at her. She was so relieved to see Mary Pat teasing again, she'd forgive her just about anything. "Brat. Okay, okay, it worked. Besides, I think they've already got your point. The lecture's about to start—now scoot. You're scaring my students."

Besides, she thought, *I've got to be in the right mood to pull this off.* These were not stupid people. In fact, some of those in that room, like Werner, had first-rate minds. They also wouldn't be strangers to some of the political maneuvering she was about to try. Ah, well. Misdirection and cooptation were tried and true strategies. She just had to make sure she approached it properly so that she gave them an "invisible war" that they would be fascinated enough by not to look too closely to see what other invisible war they might be fighting. *And to think I've given James such a hard time of late. Maybe I should start hanging around Mike and Balthazar more often myself.*

4

"Good morning. For those of you I haven't already met, I'm Beulah MacDonald. Today, I'll be giving a lecture introducing some of the developments in public health as we use it in Grantville. The readings I assigned should have provided you a basis for understanding terms and concepts I'll be using. I know you've all had to learn a lot of information about statistics quickly."

In fact, that had nearly led to an interdisciplinary wrangle. There was only one basic statistics book at the high school. She knew that the students would need that content to understand simple concepts in public health, particularly in epidemiology. The medical students and faculty from Jena had set up a roster to share the book and essentially taken over the high school library for the duration. Those not studying the statistics book had been studying other material until it was their turn. Copies were being made as quickly as possible when the book wasn't actively in use. Basic statistics had lots of applications.

One of the Jena delegates was a high-ranking math faculty member. Seeing clear evidence that the math part of the university quadrivium would be needed by future nurses and doctors, he wanted the book for the math faculty and students. He was genuinely interested in the concepts and quite ready to stake a claim to the text. The school librarian had found him some other texts on probability theory to hold him off for a time, but just who had the priority need for the text had been a bit sticky for a moment. The librarian was both amused and appalled. She was thrilled to have people wanting to get to a textbook but the arguing over it was a different matter. Beulah gathered that the argument had gotten quite heated. That was perhaps the most blatant conflict over up-timer books among the Jenaites but not the only one. It made Beulah a little uneasy. There were more faculty and students coming from Jena. This was getting out of control. Each group had some reason attached (not always peripherally) to why they needed access to information or books or specialists to help get the new health-sciences program up and running. They seemed to have started an avalanche. Or a train wreck.

She had had the Grantville high school math teachers tutoring the students in the evenings, whenever one had a break between classes and at lunch so the group from Jena had at least a little information about statistics. Math students had joined the med school group. Fortunately, there were only a few math students here. So far at least. She'd also given them quite a bit to read in terms of foundations of public health. According to James, the med students and faculty had spent a late night at the Gardens with their notes cramming before this morning's lecture. She hoped they weren't too hungover.

"The public health situation has been frightening and in some ways shocking to us. Public health measures for us have been so interwoven into our lives that we no longer noticed many of them. We took for granted that our water would be safe to drink, our air clean to breathe, and that our food wouldn't make us sick. Children are taught the basics of hand washing when they are toilet trained. No one has to specify that the reason for washing your hands after going to the bathroom is to avoid spreading certain diseases. It's part of the knowledge we absorb as small children, unquestioned and just there. It's considered rude to sneeze or cough without covering one's mouth and nose. The reason isn't openly stated, that the person who sneezes or coughs without covering their mouth and nose could spread airborne diseases to other people. It's automatic, part of everyday life. Then, suddenly, we've found ourselves fighting an invisible war, a war we thought largely won, against communicable diseases. That is, diseases like measles and smallpox that can be spread among a population. Many of those diseases were controlled or eradicated in our time. Vaccination had been around for several centuries. School children were required to be vaccinated before entering school. Before the measles vaccine was developed in 1963, there were millions of cases every year in the U.S. By the time children were six, more than half had had the measles and ninety percent had the measles by the time they were fifteen. After the vaccination programs began, the number of cases dropped by ninety-eight percent. What was once a common disease became rare. While many of the public health supports that we took for granted are gone now, much of the knowledge remains and we are putting those supports back into place just as quickly as we can. I'd like to talk with you today about how public health developed, how we got to where we were, and where we are moving toward in the future. As you learn about these measures, you could become soldiers in an invisible war against diseases that have been the scourge of humankind from time immemorial.

"Public health efforts focus on measures that prevent illness or injury, track disease outbreaks, and promote life and maximum functionality in groups of people. I'd like to talk with you today about historic developments in public health history and how those have led to changes in public health practice. I'll be focusing on three areas primarily: epidemiology, public health measures, and vaccination. Obviously, this will be a brief introduction to what can be a very complex subject.

"Epidemiology is a cornerstone of public health. Epidemiology gives us a way to study how factors that affect health and illness are distributed in a given community or population. Epidemiology is really a form of research and uses many of the same methods as research. The epidemiologist collects a variety of data from many sources in order to identify at-risk populations and to prevent or ameliorate the spread of disease and illness and promote health."

So far no one looked lost. She turned on the computer she'd borrowed from Hayes and pulled up the first slide. "Hippocrates was the first known epidemiologist. In fact, Hippocrates was far more accurate in his perceptions about public health and the spread of communicable diseases than about his medical treatments. He developed a number of principles of epidemiology that are still important. Hippocrates gave very accurate descriptions of diseases in his practice. He also wrote about natural factors such as water supplies that are important to consider in public health. He stressed that clinicians should be observant and should consider lifestyle factors such as activity in treating illnesses. He noticed that certain diseases occurred at certain places or times of year. We'll talk more about some of these things as class progresses today."

Beulah paused for a sip of water and let the students catch up a bit on their notes. She hoped that hearing a familiar name and that he had contributed relevant, accurate information to public health would reassure her audience that all they knew didn't have to be relearned. Some but not all of it had later been proven inaccurate. Hayes had found copies of Hippocrates' *Epidemics I* and *Epidemics II* that were being translated. She planned to use some of it in the developing curriculum. Not only was some of it still relevant, but use of some "classics" added legitimacy to the things they were teaching. She was acutely aware that in the long term, there was more involved here than just the university at Jena. She also wanted to make the point that they all stood as it were, "on the shoulders of giants." Knowledge had been created, lost, accepted, ignored, and tested in various ways, moving forward in fits and starts. Such was the nature of scientific advances.

"Did you all have a chance to attend the sanitation committee meetings?"

Most of those present nodded. James had commented that there hadn't been so many people at the committee meeting last week for over a year. *We take the risk of infection too lightly. We're too used to antibiotics and clean streets and an immunized population. So we don't pay attention to them. Despite all the preparation we've been trying to do, most of our people still have, at most, an intellectual understanding of an epidemic. Even the oldest of us, who ought to remember our younger years, aren't immune to that attitude.* She shared the fears of James and the others. It was only a matter of time until they were hit here in Grantville. How bad it would be depended in part on how prepared their neighbors were. *There's never enough time to get everything done. There are too few of us, spread too thin. We should be having programs like this all over the USE. At least this is being videotaped. I've got to talk with James and the others on the sanitation committee about spreading this information out. We need to put together a basic primer and recommendations for prompt action.*

She'd given lectures like this so many times that part of her had gone on autopilot while she talked about how to identify potential problems or disease outbreaks. The classic example she'd given was John Snow's work identifying the cholera epidemic in 1850s London. The initial outbreak in the early 1830s had caused at least sixty thousand deaths in Great Britain. Snow's investigations of the 1849 and 1854 epidemics had occurred years after the first outbreak. She saw the way the students' attention sharpened when she pointed out that the epidemiological approach he'd taken to identify geographic clusters of outbreaks had helped identify the water source as a culprit before the cholera germ was identified. She emphasized his use of epidemiological data such as mortality rates, too. He'd spotted the crucial fact that, among other things, the source of drinking water had changed but the population had stayed the same. Those with the better water source were twenty times less likely to die from cholera. He'd done door-to-door validation of water source to get an accurate rate, a typical public health approach to collecting data. The result was that they were able to take appropriate public health measures and control the contaminated drinking water sources. She thought that the students leaning forward a bit in their chairs got the point that you needed knowledge, not just technology, to address these problems. Public health and spreading knowledge were two types of invisible war. They weren't fought in the open but the effects could be profound and even more lasting. Kunz and Willi were both nodding thoughtfully in separate parts of the room. Kunz had a particularly intense look on his face. *And if they thought that example was pointed, wait till I bring up Florence Nightingale.*

With an effort she pulled herself back to the matter at hand and went on to talk about the work of Koch and Pasteur in discovering microorganisms and how to set criteria to determine the role of the microorganism in a given outbreak. "In order to transmit an infectious disease, you need three things: a vulnerable host, an agent, and an environment that can result in an infection. I'd like to take each one at a time. Host factors may be things that can be changed or things that indicate the public health professional should pay particular attention to that group in certain situations."

Beulah moved onto a discussion of passive and active immunity and immunization. Active immunity to a particular disease was acquired through immunization or a previous infection with the microorganism that caused the disease. Passive immunity was a bit more difficult to explain. Maternal antibodies and gamma-globulin prophylaxis weren't as easy to understand but she thought they were getting it. She noted another student perk up when she talked about the idea of herd immunity. If at least eighty percent of a community was vaccinated, it was more difficult for communicable diseases to find a vulnerable host. The example she used was of the development of smallpox vaccine using cowpox by Jenner. She was careful to point out how long some form of vaccination had actually been around and what Jenner had done that was different and why what he did was so effective. The drops in death rate were impressive statistics.

From there, it was a fairly easy step to talk about personal hygiene and cleanliness before she moved onto the agent of disease part of the lecture. "Are you all familiar with childbed fever? During the 1840s, many women died of childbed fever. Often, the child became ill and died as well. A doctor named Semmelweis conducted a classic epidemiological study of what caused the fevers. He noticed that in the two clinics he was director of, one had higher rates of death than the other. The mothers were ill during the birth or up to thirty-six hours later and then quickly died in the clinic with the high mortality rates. He observed that the problem seemed to start during the examination of the mother during dilation." She went on to discuss the data he'd collected and analyzed and the controlled experiments he'd conducted to try to determine the cause of the deaths.

"He realized that the deaths were caused when the medical students came to the hospital from the death house after performing autopsies and conducted pelvic examinations on the laboring mothers. The doctors' hands carried germs from the dead bodies to the mothers because they didn't wash their hands. The traditional Hippocratic view of disease was still held and, initially, his findings weren't accepted. He was successful, however, in instituting hand washing by every nurse or doctor entering the ward. At first, he thought it would be enough just when entering the ward. Later he realized that it was necessary to wash between each examination. Something as simple as consistent hand washing dropped the mortality rate by ninety percent in just six years. I know you've seen how often we wash our hands in the hospital and clinics here. It is a very simple but very effective way to stop the spread of infection. It's quick, cheap, and anyone can learn to do it.

"The presence of infectious agents is another concern I'd like to touch on. One of your handouts gave common infectious agents, which we also call pathogens, that are found on or in the body and that are found in the USE."

One of the students waved his hand.

"Yes?"

"Excuse me, *Frau Professorin*, but if these pathogens are in and on the body and all around us, why aren't we all sick all the time?"

Beulah beamed at him. "An excellent question, Mr . . . ?"

"Georg Holtz." His voice sounded a little more confident.

"Well, Mr. Holtz, you've raised a very important issue about pathogens. That has to do with part of the agent, namely the vector, as well as how strong the pathogen is. The vector is the way the pathogen gets to the person in a way to do harm. The vector may be biological, such as a person or animal that has the disease, or it can be mechanical. A mechanical vector can be something like a contaminated surgical instrument or piece of clothing." She very carefully didn't notice them stiffening. She remembered how she and all the students she'd met had reacted when they came face to face with some of this. As she recalled, she hadn't been the only one who'd suddenly wanted a shower with lots of hot water and soap. A truly evil thought encroached. *Well, it's all for the greater good. It certainly made an impression on other students and it's fairly easy to do. The lab is going to love this one.*

"As a matter of fact, if you're interested, I'll talk to the lab folks for you. They can show you how to culture some of those organisms we live with all the time on our hair, skin, clothing, and so on. Most of the time, we call those organisms benign. Even benign microorganisms can be nasty under the right circumstances. Let me give you an example you've probably seen in practice. A person with a wound has an open area that the germs that normally are on your skin, such as the staphylococcal class, can get into. If the person had an intact skin, the microorganism couldn't get into them to cause an infection. The host was vulnerable, the microbe was there, and it had a way to get in."

She finished what she had to say about agents of disease and went on to control measures such as quarantines. The students seemed surprised that the practice of quarantines had begun in the fourteenth century and that she still considered it a relevant measure of infection control.

When she talked about the role of disasters such as floods or war in creating conditions that promoted the spread of disease, she saw that they were fitting what she was saying into their own experiences. War as a topic led her to Florence Nightingale and the Crimean war.

She talked about how Florence had used epidemiology and statistics as well as astute political and other lobbying to improve conditions and reduce mortality and morbidity of the soldiers and later, of people in England. Making the point that when she'd arrived in 1854 in the Crimea, she'd immediately worked to improve the conditions for the ill soldiers by organizing measures such as kitchens, laundries, and a central supply department. The end result was that in ten days, the death rate dropped from thirty-eight percent to two percent. Mentioning that she was a nurse near the end didn't hurt either. Beulah fully intended to discuss Clara Barton, the U.S. Civil War, and the founding of the Red Cross later in her lecture.

"The methods Nightingale and others have used rely on incidence, prevalence, and relative risk ratios." She went to the board and put the formulas up with discussions of each, how it was calculated, and what it meant. That naturally led her to a brief mention of statistics such as infant mortality that gave important clues to a population's health.

"But that is really beyond the scope of our talk today. I'd like to talk some more about modes of transmission of disease and then we'll talk about ways to break that chain of environment, agent, and host determinates leading to infection. Biological modes of transmission are physical contact such as spitting or touching, sexual contact such as intercourse, and airborne contact such as dust or droplet nuclei. Those modes of transmission are direct or airborne. Indirect transmission results from mechanical transmission. Books, coins, toilets, soiled dressings, food, and many other things can be a reservoir for an infectious agent. For the last hour today, I'd like to talk about ways to interrupt the transmission vector, to strengthen potential hosts, and to reduce risks from the environment."

During the next hour, she covered everything from adequate sewage disposal to hand washing. The work of Joseph Lister and the use of antiseptic techniques and carbolic acid solution fit in here. She also brought up Thomas Syndenham, who was only nine years old at the present time. She made an effort not to stress too much that he used observation and other techniques to diagnose different diseases and avoided Galen's approaches. Syndenham's work classifying fevers in London during the 1660s and 1670s and how he treated the different classifications went against the Hippocratic and Galenic approaches. For which he took considerable flak. His treatments were effective, however, even if he hadn't understood what was causing the fevers. She did make a point of talking about the criticism and threats he endured. He persevered despite that and influenced an up-and-coming generation of physicians with his use of empirical techniques.

She gave them additional resources to read on all the areas she'd introduced and hoped it would be enough to get them started. Hopefully, they'd take the ideas back to Jena. "If any of you have specific areas of interest in public health, please see me. I'll try to set up an experience for you so that you can learn more in a clinical setting, and I can probably point you to more references. Thank you for your attention today. Do you have any other questions before we adjourn?"

5

"May we join you, *Frau Professorin*?" Georg sounded a little hesitant but eager.

"The Leahy garden is always better for company. Please, Georg, Kunz, have a seat."

"We wanted to thank you for showing us around the lab and setting up the culturing experience after the lecture yesterday." Kunz sat next to her on a bench and grinned at her. "We really enjoyed it. Georg and I are very interested in aspects of public health and would like to talk with you more about books to study and a clinical experience in public health."

"With you, if we can," Georg blurted and then blushed right up to his straw-olored hair. "I'm particularly interested in microbiology."

"While I am interested in the methods of disease surveillance you spoke of," said Kunz. "We were on our way to check on the microbial growth but when we saw you here, we thought we'd take the opportunity to ask."

The smile she gave them both was slightly blinding. "I'd love to. I'll make up a list of materials for you. I can even lend you my personal texts, if you'd like, in some cases. Most of them have been copied already. I'll check and see what's at the printers right now."

"You're all certainly keeping the printers in Jena busy." Kunz grinned back at her. She couldn't help but contrast that with the attitude a few months ago, and took heart.

"Please excuse me, *Frau Professorin*, but in the lab, they said that there would be growth within a day. I'd like to go check the petri dishes before things get too busy there."

"Have fun. Kunz and I will set up a time to meet and talk some more."

She and Kunz grinned after the tall young man as he dove for the door.

6

"What are you doing here?"

Georg nodded politely. "I am one of the medical students from Jena. My name is Geo—"

"I know you're one of the Jena students. I asked what you're doing here in the lab?"

Georg straightened to his full height. "I have permission to be here. I was checking the growth of the cultures we took yesterday."

Mara stared at the young man standing a few feet away. She couldn't believe he was arguing with her this way. *Little know-nothing.* "There won't really be anything to see if you just took the cultures yesterday. I don't know why anyone is letting you do cultures in here, anyway. It's a waste of our resources to be using materials that way."

"*Frau Professorin* MacDonald didn't think so. She called it a good learning experience. I and the other students found it most interesting."

"We only have so many supplies. They should be used for patients or for our students." Mara heard the belligerence in her tone but didn't care. She was sick of everyone trying to make them happy. She'd already figured out she wasn't going to be one of those asked to be in the MD program at Jena. She should be. God knew she'd earned it and she was certainly smart enough. She'd even volunteered for the education committee. It was all going to be people's pets who got in, especially Beulah's pets. She'd heard someone talking with Mary Pat in the hall yesterday, asking if she was going to apply to the MD program. The other nurse thought Mary Pat would be great. Mary Pat had laughed and said she wasn't interested, she liked nursing too much. Hearing one of Beulah's pets dismiss what she herself wanted had just frosted the cake. *She* should be in that program. *She* should be getting special attention. But no. Beulah was sponsoring Fritz and now it looked like she was going to have one of the Jena students, too.

"I am one of the students," Georg replied in evident confusion.

That was more than she needed to hear. All thoughts of running a pregnancy test before her shift started and anyone else was around went flying out of her head. The injustice of it, the slights were more than her temper could stand. "Well, you are sort of a student. Not that any of you'll be worth much for a long time. We'll have to spend a lot of time and effort just getting you up to speed on things any junior-high student would know. *Some people* may think you'll be useful teaching assistants but I'm not one of them. We'd be much better off starting from scratch with our own people."

Georg's attempt to interrupt went unheeded. "You're nothing but a bunch of parasites. You'll take and take but you sure won't give much back. You don't know enough. Your ideas about everything are from the dark ages. There's no way you'll be able to catch up on hundreds of years of knowledge in a few years, much less a matter of weeks."

"How dare you say such a thing!" Georg's voice was rising toward a yell and echoed oddly in the lab. "We are *not* parasites. The others would not be spending so much time with us if they didn't think we could learn. More than that, we are not some sort of ignorant fools who . . ."

Even Mara knew she'd gone too far. With an effort that left tears in her eyes, she stopped herself from saying any more. She spun away from him and slammed out of the lab.

7

"Hi, Kunz, Georg. Are you all right, Georg?" Beulah asked in concern. Georg and Kunz had just come into the conservatory as she was about to leave, and looked upset.

"Fraulein Beulah. No, I do not think I am but I will be fine."

Beulah tried again. She thought she had an idea of what was wrong. Young people had tender egos about such things, sometimes, so she proceeded rather obliquely. "Did you just come from the lab?"

"Yes. I had permission to be there." His tone was both defensive and angry. He looked pale. "I was just checking the samples."

"An excellent idea. Did somebody say you couldn't be in the lab or look at the samples?"

"Not exactly."

"What did happen? Exactly." Beulah noticed that Kunz was getting red blotches in his face and clenching his fists. Something was really off here.

"I can handle it."

"I have no doubt of that but since I was the one who suggested the lab experiment, I feel a little responsible. Humor me, okay? What happened?"

"One of the nurses felt that I should not be in the lab."

Kunz jumped in. "She did far more than just tell him that he shouldn't be in the lab. She also felt that our presence was a waste of time and told him that in the rudest way. There is no excuse for such behavior."

Beulah was adding one and one and coming up with . . . Mara. She had a pretty good idea what Mara had been doing in the lab since she was the one who'd told Mara to have a pregnancy test. Beulah had seen lots and lots of pregnant women in her career and Mara definitely had the look. She'd like to be able to blame Mara's behavior on hormones, but the hormones had probably just made her less subtle in her attack methods. "Let me guess. About this tall?" She help up her hand to around five feet and a bit. "Strawberry blonde, big blue eyes, tanned, looks harmless?"

At Georg's nod she gritted her teeth and said one word. "Mara." This certainly put her in an interesting position. Starr and Mara were sisters-in-law. She needed to go to Starr about the behavior of one of her staff. It was going be awkward for Starr but she would handle it. In the meantime, Beulah got damage control duty. Lovely. "Help me up, please, Georg. We'll all get something from the cafeteria and then go to my office to talk. I'm upset at Mara, not at you. I just want a little privacy."

Georg and Kunz were largely silent after that except for an offer by Georg to carry her coffee mug. She hated being glad of that offer. The cold weather wasn't doing her joints any good and she'd had to cut back on the willow bark tea. The tea and stress was turning her stomach sour and she was starting to get bruises at the slightest touch. She'd been able to hide them with long-sleeved sweaters or shirts and since she almost never wore dresses, no one had noticed the bruises. Delayed blood-clotting times was one of the side effects of the tea. So, less tea. Which didn't leave her much for the pain unless she wanted her mental state interfered with by some of Stoner's crops of marijuana or poppy. She couldn't afford that right now. A break in the tea would give her body a chance to recover. It would be weeks, though, before her clotting times were close to normal again. She was also trying more stress management techniques. So far, so good. Except for the pain.

Beulah nodded toward the small table in her office. She used it for meetings sometimes or when she needed to spread her work out. She didn't want to be sitting behind the desk with Georg in front of it like an errant schoolboy. The walk had helped her calm down a little and given her some space to think. "Can you tell me what happened, please?"

By the time Georg had finished the description of what had just happened downstairs, Beulah was ready to do Mara a mischief in a dark alley. Kunz would probably help by holding Mara still for it. The description rang too true to some of the things she'd seen Mara do, but she'd never gone this far over the line before. She'd been tripping over little bits of poison strewn by Mara and a few others over the last month. This was the last straw. *I don't care if it is her hormones, we do not need this kind of crap.* Specifically, she didn't need to be doing more damage control right now. Now, how did she avoid undermining one of the few senior nurses they had but support Georg while one of the Jena faculty was watching and not looking at all friendly? She had no doubt that this would spread among the Jenaites at the speed only good gossip can obtain. Einstein should have made gossip an exception to the travel at the speed of light stuff.

"What do you intend to do about this woman?" demanded Kunz.

"I'll speak with Starr first. Mara is one of her staff. Second, I'll speak with Mara personally. I know I'm not the DON anymore but Georg is one of our students and that should give me a say in how this is handled. It won't happen again if I have anything to say about it. I'm really sorry, Georg. If Mara had pulled anything like this in an up-time hospital, she'd have been out the door so fast she'd have left skid marks on the linoleum." Beulah sighed. "As it is, because we don't have enough staff, we can't do what I'd like, which is fire her. Between Starr and me, we'll come up with something . . . suitable. One thing for sure. This won't happen again to you or any of the other students. If you or any of the other students get so much as one whiff of attitude from anyone, come right to me."

Just wait till I get my hands on little Miss Twit. Maybe I'd better watch some WWF reruns first.

8

Beulah peeked into Garnet's hospital room. Garnet was sitting up in bed, awake. Beulah didn't like the way she looked or was breathing at all. *This is what happened when people pushed themselves this hard for so long.* She'd just got the call after Kunz and Georg left her office. Garnet had just been admitted to the medical ward. She hadn't been able to get to see Garnet for another few hours, which was probably just as well. She had other things to take care of, including meeting with Starr, finding the treat she'd brought, and that didn't even touch what she had to get through before today had started going downhill. The meeting with Mara at the end of the shift today was just going to finish up a lousy day with a lousy mess. Garnet, however, didn't need to know or see any of that. She needed to get well.

"Come on in. I'm not contagious. It's just pneumonia."

"There isn't any 'just' to pneumonia anymore and you know it." Beulah came in and set the small package she was carrying on Garnet's nightstand. Bringing flowers to someone with pneumonia was out, so she had brought some of the lemon candy Garnet loved. It would help soothe her throat, too.

"I shouldn't even be in here. I can lie around in bed at home."

Beulah settled herself in a chair by Garnet's bed and said pleasantly, "You even try to get out of that bed and I'll personally put you in four-point leathers and abscond with the key."

"We don't have leather restraints here."

"There are plenty of people around here who could make up a set real quick. Besides, it'd do wonders for my reputation."

Garnet gave a choking laugh that started a coughing fit. Beulah helped her sit up and handed her a handkerchief. She poured Garnet a glass of water when the fit was over.

"Don't make me laugh, okay?"

"Sorry. I'll be sober as a judge. Promise. I'm just glad Stoner's got some more antibiotics on hand. I've seen your micro report. What we've got will cover you, so you should be able to go home within a few days and be back at a limited work schedule in a few weeks."

"We've got classes going. I have to teach—"

"Class material that you aren't teaching will either be taught by someone else if we can find them, or not get taught till you're better. The students won't mind a break, especially before the holidays. We'll think of something, maybe more clinical time. They can always use more of that. You just concentrate on getting better, okay?"

"Okay. But I could probably . . ." She broke off at Beulah's frown and firm head shake. "I thought it was just the flu."

"That's been going around. I've been working with our outbreak tracking team all week. Looks like the flu is all it is and we've got it pretty well contained so far. I don't think we're looking at a major outbreak. Flu isn't anything to mess with, though. I'm going to be showing Kunz and some of the others how the tracking team works later and how we're responding to this. It should be a good small-scale object lesson." She switched the conversation briefly to the interest Georg and Kunz had shown in public health and then left after making sure Garnet had plenty of handkerchiefs and cold water. She didn't want to tire her out.

As she left, she was mentally trying to rearrange the teaching schedule. She needed to talk with Courtney or Marcia as soon as she could get in touch with them. There was going to have to be some shuffling but they'd work it out. The sooner Garnet had a definite solution, the sooner she'd be able to relax a little and focus on getting well again. Beulah would stop by again as soon as she had things worked out with the other teachers at the vo-tech program. The EMT and LPN courses would be most affected. She'd have to contact Starr again today and talk about what that would do to staffing projections, especially with some of the staff being pulled as students at Jena in two months. *Starr is going to start running when she sees me coming after today.*

9

"Please come in and sit down, Mara." Beulah kept her voice even and pleasant with an effort. This was a professional conversation. She wasn't going to stoop to name calling, ranting, or even incivility. Well, probably not.

"I wasn't exactly surprised to get a summons to your office at the end of the day. Don't you think using your authority to protect one of your pets is stretching it a bit? Especially since you aren't the DON anymore. Starr is."

Mara had evidently decided she didn't have much to lose and that there wasn't much Beulah could do about what had happened. *Wrong move, Mara. The best defense isn't always a good offense.* "I'm not talking to you as the DON. I'm talking to you as the dean of the health sciences school and the chair of the health education committee. Of which, at the moment, you are a member." A brief pause to let that sink in; then, "I'm here to talk about your unprofessional behavior and the fallout from it. Mr. Holtz told me what you said to him in the lab this morning."

Mara crossed her arms over her chest and glared at Beulah. "And is what I said so wrong? Okay, calling them parasites went a little far but the truth is that they are parasites. They don't have what we need to do this and by the time they get it, we could have trained our own people to the level we need. We give; they take. That's parasitism."

"And how many of our own people could we train, Mara? How many of us are there available for health care? How many of us have any significant time to teach the math and science that we need taught or the—"

"But they don't have what we need taught, so why do we want them teaching any of it? They don't understand the scientific method. They don't understand being skeptical and observing and testing what they see. For them, knowledge flows from the authority. They've just figured out that we're now the authority. You want that attitude passed on to students? And that doesn't even get into content. They don't know the basics of virtually anything."

"You're exaggerating. Just the experience of having to look at what has changed historically, how and why, is already leading them to question their knowledge and how it was generated. They've made a lot of progress and we've got a plan in place to move them forward. The seeds of the scientific method are already present. Autopsies and other ways of observational learning are already going on and have been for a while. See one, do one, teach one has worked for a long time. We still use it in our time. They do have content we need and some of their knowledge is valid. They do have skills we need. Yes, some of what they know will have to be unlearned. Yes, they'll have to make changes in their worldview. But they're smart and motivated and I think they can do it."

"In two more months?" sneered Mara. "Yeah, right. Meanwhile, we'll be splitting our resources and wasting our time on them. Just splitting the campus so that some of us are here and some in Jena is a waste of time and resources we don't have. You aren't the only one who knows what we're facing. I tried to tell you this months ago, but you wouldn't listen. If I said it, it had to be wrong, didn't it?"

Beulah took a firm grip on her slipping temper. "Have you ever heard the old saying about putting all your eggs in one basket? Right now, all our eggs are in Grantville's basket. What happens if we have one nasty epidemic wipe out most of our medical staff? You and I both know that in epidemics and plagues, the healer death rate is sky high. If we have some of our people and knowledge in Jena, they may be far enough away to have some of it survive. Not to mention that the time issue is really a wash. Yes, splitting the campus takes more time but it also means that we can have students, the students you don't think know anything, teaching basic anatomy lab and skills like how to dissect, how to suture. We don't have the people or the time to do everything that needs doing."

"Most of our people may lack those skills but they've still got more basic science knowledge and they've got the mentality, the worldview that the Jenaites don't." Mara leaned forward, fists clenched on Beulah's desk. "Why won't you see that?"

"I do see it," Beulah returned angrily. "I just don't see it as an insurmountable barrier. These are smart people and they've very motivated. They can get it and they will."

"As fast as we need it? Have you thought about the fact that your little jaunt to Jena has already meant the word about our medical care is spreading even faster? Most people will think it's a fairy story and dismiss it, but not everyone, and not for long. We can't take care of our own people and now you're spreading this around. We've got more people coming in. What if one of us gets sick? They can't take care of us but we can take care of them. You can damn well bet that if my kids or husband are ill, I'm not going to want the medicine or care my family needs going to someone else. And I'm not the only one who feels this way."

"The only way to change that is to train more people and make more resources. Does that mean there will be a bottleneck, for a while? Yes. Does that mean that we're vulnerable right now and will be for a while? I know that better than you ever will. That means we have to look beyond ourselves for both teachers and students. There. Are. Not. Enough. Up-timers. Why won't *you* see that? Or is it just that you don't want to hear anything *I* have to say? You talk about content but do you know how to judge the potency of herbs from a particular place? And how to grow and collect and administer them safely and effectively? They do. They may not know all the whys and wherefores but together we can figure that part out. That's just one example. We can help each other and that's symbiosis not parasitism." Forget professionalism. She'd had enough of Mara and her attitude.

"So what are we supposed to do? All turn into little Jenaites? You've been in those meetings. They're still trying to hang onto the quadrivium and the trivium even when it doesn't make sense. We need people who can think and practice nursing and medicine. We don't need nurses and doctors who can debate how many angels dance on the head of a pin because they've had years of theology as part of their basic education. That's bull and you know it. But you won't call them on it. They're fighting for things that aren't what we need, things that don't matter. That doesn't sound to me like they're getting it at all. They have their definition of knowledge and what makes a university and *it isn't anything like ours and never will be."*

The truth of some of what she was saying stung Beulah. *But she's skewing things, twisting them. How much of it does she really believe and how much is to fight me?* Beulah suddenly felt exhausted. Rage had given her a temporary burst of energy but she couldn't sustain it. "They're trying to hang onto what they, and others here, believe a university education to be. It's difficult but we're working it out." Even to Beulah's ears, that sounded pretty lame. She was getting so mad that she couldn't think too clearly. This meeting had gone way far afield. Maybe Mara's strategy hadn't been so off target after all. "Debating what is going on with Jena isn't the reason you're here. I'm relieving you of your position on the education committee. Unless I see changes in your behavior, you won't act as preceptor for any students, whether from here or from Jena. Starr will talk with you about your behavior as a staff nurse tomorrow. Dismissed."

10

After Mara left, Beulah stood shaking in her office. She hadn't been this mad in a long time. Or this scared. Mara's comments went round and round in her head. They argued for a very different course of action. But there were other voices, too. The voices of the dead and of those who would die if they didn't succeed. She had worked in poor areas of West Virginia. She had a pretty realistic idea of what could happen if they didn't get modern public health and other methods in place. The specter of epidemic was real but not as visible as the other threat, war. She'd seen so many die in Korea. Now, war was taking children from her town, people she knew. And it was going to get worse, not better. At least for a time.

No. They'd chosen the best path. None of the choices were without risk. Certainly none were ideal. Mara was just being spiteful. Even as she tried to rationalize it, Beulah knew she couldn't just dismiss all that Mara had said.

The pain hit suddenly. Something with lots of dull teeth was trying to gnaw through her stomach from front to back. A cold sweat broke out on her skin as she lurched for the bathroom just down the hall. A few very unpleasant minutes later, she looked down into the toilet bowl. Blood.

There wasn't that much really. Probably only a few ounces. And it didn't look that bright a red. If the bleed was arterial, she'd be in a world of trouble already. She got shakily to her feet after flushing the toilet, thankful that most people were gone from the second floor for the day. The blood wasn't a big surprise, given her symptoms. After washing her face and rinsing her mouth, she wobbled down the hall to her office, sank down into a chair, and reviewed the 1633-available options for a bleeding ulcer.

She'd already changed her diet, although she'd have to add more greens and liver to up her iron intake and correct for the blood loss. She could start a baking soda slurry to help reduce the acid. Not too much; she didn't need metabolic alkalosis on top of everything else. Instead of cutting the willow bark dosage, she'd have to stop it entirely. She didn't have anything else for the pain. She wasn't going to try to deal with these problems stoned. She'd just have to tough it out.

They didn't have the equipment to do a scope and see what was down there and then cauterize any bleeders. Surgery for something that might not be so bad, just to see what was there, was too risky in this time. If it came to that, the surgery would be both exploratory and repair work. There wasn't time for surgery. Things were at a crucial juncture with the Jena project. They were already behind where they needed to be, and events like this morning didn't help.

She'd have to hide this from Mary Pat, which wouldn't be that hard as busy as they both were. She could tell her that she had had her tea before Mary Pat left on her run each morning. There would even be a hot teakettle there. Getting the variety of calendula and licorice she needed wouldn't be hard. Ray wouldn't ask what she needed it for. He'd just assume she was helping out with a patient or working with the Jena students. The calendula would help with the bleeding as well as the healing. She could possibly use some sucralfate but that was expensive and time-consuming to make. They didn't have much in stock and she couldn't get that without rousing some suspicions. If she had to, she'd get some but that would mean going to James. She'd set a little more time aside for the stress reduction exercises. Just a few minutes here and there could make a difference. The exercises would also help with the pain.

There were options. She'd take them. There wasn't any point in adding to anyone else's worry, especially Mary Pat so soon after the death of Hans and Larry. There really wasn't anything else anyone could do, either. She'd make the changes, take the meds and monitor her condition. If things got much worse, she'd talk to James.

Chapter Eight
November, 1633

1

The stress didn't abate over the next two weeks. If anything, it was getting worse. The meetings with the Jenaites weren't going as well as Beulah had hoped. Mara's words came back to nibble at her more often than she'd have liked. Garnet was back on light duty starting today. If Garnet had gotten ill just a week earlier, there wouldn't have been any antibiotics to treat her pneumonia. They'd sent them all to the siege areas. She might have survived the pneumonia but the odds were much worse without antibiotics. Garnet wasn't just a colleague. She was a friend. She knew her so well. Garnet the gun nut who loved to debate for hours on caliber and range and anything else gun or hunting related.

Garnet who was positively phobic when it came to spiders and who loved the color yellow. They'd already lost so many people they couldn't treat. Beulah firmly believed in the moral stand they were taking and the pragmatic logic that also went with it. But there were consequences. Always consequences.

They were still arguing with the Jena faculty about things like astronomy, for Pete's sake. Great, you've got an observatory. We're happy for you. What does being able to find Venus have to do with diagnosing and treating a patient? Beulah's patience wasn't endless and they were running out of time. It wasn't just the January start date she was thinking about. It was almost Thanksgiving. The Jenaites would be leaving the first part of December and they still hadn't been able to iron out some basics in the curriculum. Every time she thought they'd gotten ahead there was another stumbling block. She also wanted to get some more knowledge squeezed out of them. Just yesterday, Werner came up with a botanical treatment none of them had heard of for a patient that they'd been trying to treat without success for weeks.

She was able to hide the bleeding for those two weeks, even from Mary Pat although she was beginning to watch Beulah pretty closely. At first, the measures Beulah tried seemed to be helping enough. The bleeding stopped for a while but the pain was worsening over the last few days. She was debating whether or not to see James in the morning when the decision was taken out of her hands that night.

2

"Beulah?" Mary Pat shrugged out of her coat and shook the raindrops off as she stood by the front door. She put the coat onto the coatrack and headed for the kitchen. Dinner preparations were partway made and the light was on, but no Beulah. Mary Pat had stepped out of the kitchen and headed down the short hall to the stairs when she heard the sound of vomiting. The flu was going around but it was more respiratory this year than GI.

She quickly headed up the stairs and opened the door, calling Beulah's name. What she saw wasn't what she expected. She had caught a whiff of the blood as she approached the door but it hadn't had time to register. Beulah had almost made it to the toilet before she was sick. Despite all Mary Pat's experience, the sight of Beulah half-lying amid reddish black blood, deathly pale and shaking, hit her hard. For a heart-beat, then another, she couldn't move, couldn't think. Then training kicked in and her nursing skills came flooding back. She touched Beulah gently on the shoulder, then the neck, doing an at-a-glance assessment. The feebleness of Beulah's pulse, her pallor, and the moisture on her skin worried Mary Pat. Beulah was going into shock.

"I'm here. I'm going to call an ambulance and be right back." She didn't remember later whether her feet even touched the steps on the way down the stairs. The phone was in her hand and she cursed under her breath. Why couldn't Beulah have a touch-tone phone instead of the slow black rotary phone? The second it took after dialing 9 in 911 would have been all the time she needed to punch in 911.

"EMS, Walter Allen. What is the nature of your emergency?"

"Walt, it's Mary Pat. I just got home and Beulah's throwing up a lot of blood." She gave him a concise assessment, not that there'd been time to gather more information. She didn't hear anything from upstairs. Had Beulah passed out?

"Chester and I are on our way. Be there in a few minutes. I'll notify the ER staff on the way. They'll gear up for her."

Mary Pat was relieved that Walt and Chester were on duty. Both were experienced EMTs in their fifties. "I'll have the door open for you." She hung up and rushed back up the stairs, praying all the way. *Please, please God, help her.* And, more selfishly, *Don't take her from me yet.*

3

James sat on the edge of her hospital bed and glared at her. "Don't think we aren't going to have a long talk about you hiding this the last few weeks just as soon as you're up to it."

"Mary Pat . . ."

"I'll see she's taken care of. Right now she looks like hell. I'm going to send her home with something to help her sleep."

"She won't take it."

"Then I'll come up with another plan. You're going to rest if I have to hog-tie you to that bed. I heard about you threatening Garnet with leathers. I'll have a pair made up for you."

"Haven't worn leather in years. Don't have the body for it anymore."

As comebacks went, it was a little weak, but James' lips twitched just a little. She couldn't be that bad if she could still come up with a joke.

"We'll see about that. You can bet that everyone who walks into this room is going to be on your case if you overdo. And we all know you well enough to watch you like a hawk. In the meantime, I'm giving you four milligrams of morphine. It'll help with the pain and let you get some sleep."

He stayed with her for a few minutes waiting for the medicine to take effect and then got up. He had an idea of how to handle this before he faced the crowd outside. And he had no doubt there would be a crowd, even this late.

Mary Pat was at the desk talking with the nurse who'd be caring for Beulah tonight. James' gaze lit on Fritz and he relaxed a little. "Fritz, come over here a minute."

A very concerned Fritz walked out of the group of others hovering near the door. Hospital staff and EMTs, off duty or not, a couple of Jenaites even. Word had spread fast even though it was after ten at night. Garnet was there, too. He'd have to see she got back to bed as well. *Dammit, didn't anybody know how to get some rest around here?*

"I'd like you to special Beulah tonight. It'll let Mary Pat get some rest and her bearings. Then she can help me deal with Beulah tomorrow. Can you do it?"

"Of course. I was planning to study for another few hours anyway. Now that Fraulein Garnet is back, we are catching up on our studies for the LPN courses. I was off tomorrow anyway. Just let me get my books." As Mary Pat approached, the crowd moved in a little closer. Fritz patted her on the shoulder a little awkwardly before moving off. "She's going to be well soon. She is very strong and we'll take good care of her."

"How is she?" asked Mary Pat anxiously.

"Sleeping. I gave her some MS for the pain. I've got a couple of patients I'm keeping a close eye on, so I'll stay here tonight. Fritz was going to be up studying anyway, so I've asked him to sit with her." Anticipating her protest, James continued firmly, "I'd like you to go home and get some sleep tonight, Mary Pat. You get some rest so you can help me sit on her tomorrow."

"I'd rather stay. Not that I don't appreciate Fritz being willing to stay."

"I just gave her four of morphine. She's out like a light. She needs the rest and so do you. When she wakes up tomorrow morning, we're going to have a stubborn patient on our hands." James looked past her to see Hayes coming down the hall with Gary and a stack of papers. Hayes lived not that far from Beulah and Mary Pat. "Hi, Gary, Hayes. Hayes, could I ask a favor? If you're leaving, could you walk Mary Pat home? We just admitted Beulah and Mary Pat's a little shaky."

"Wait a minute. I haven't even said I'm leaving. Besides, Hayes, I don't want to bother you."

"No bother. Beulah going to be okay?"

"Bleeding ulcer." Mary Pat steadied her voice with an obvious effort. "If she gets some rest and with treatment she should be okay. James is hoping not to have to operate. She's getting blood and pain meds and she's stable right now. I found her when I got home."

"We'll call you if anything changes with her. I promise. Please get some rest. You know she's going to want to get out of that bed tomorrow and take on the world again."

"I'll be glad to walk you home," said Hayes. "Sorry to hear about Beulah. I'll come in for a visit tomorrow if she's up to it." He nodded to James. "Please tell her I told her to get some rest and hope she gets better soon. Let's go, Mary Pat. I'll see you tomorrow, Gary. 'Night, everybody."

His tone may have been a little abrupt but he looked at Mary Pat with concern and crooked an elbow in an old-fashioned gesture that brought a brief, wan smile to her face. "How about I make you something to eat? I'm a great cook and I need to eat anyway."

4

An hour later, Mary Pat was sitting on the couch in the 1633 equivalent of comfy sweats. The scent of old blood still lingered and it was too cold out to open up the house to air it out. She shivered anyway. *Beulah's blood.* She'd cleaned up the mess in the bathroom and was now staring at the phone. It was stupid to be staring at an inanimate object this way. She'd kept finding excuses to come stare at it while she was cleaning. And changing her clothes, too. Which was also stupid. It wasn't like she could will Beulah to get better and the phone not to ring. Hayes' knock on the door came as a relief.

"Hi. Look, I really appreciate you going to so much trouble."

"No trouble. Always nicer to eat with company, especially yours.

Where do you want me to set it down? Hope you like pasta. I've got a standing arrangement with Senior Nasi to have some of the special flour I need and good olive oil brought up with the coffee. Took some doing but it's worth it to have the right ingredients. And pasta dough doesn't take long to whip up. I put up some really great sauce before we went to Jena this summer. I can't wait till we get some tomatoes going but a white sauce will do for now. I've made up the tortellinis so if we can get some water boiling, we'll be ready in a few minutes. There's salad, dressing, and bread, and some wine to go with it."

"This way to the kitchen, master chef. That sounds perfect and very impressive. Especially the wine. A glass of that would be very welcome right now."

Dinner and the cleanup afterward were surprisingly pleasant. The phone didn't ring and Hayes kindly didn't say anything about how many times she stared at it. He just kept up a light conversation to help distract her. Partway through the second glass of wine, sometime before 1 A.M., she fell asleep curled up in a corner of the couch. She didn't stir when Hayes covered her with the brightly colored crocheted afghan from the back of the couch, then opened the work he'd brought with him. He'd be there for her. Just in case the phone did ring.

5

It was a conspiracy and they were all in on it. Two days after she'd been admitted, Beulah was convinced of it. The old saying about even paranoids having enemies had a corollary. Your friends can make you paranoid in the first place. It wasn't that she didn't appreciate the attention. She was touched. Really.

"But if I don't get out of this room soon, Mary Pat, I'm going to scream."

"You've been out of this room. Hanna caught you trying to sneak up to your office last night. At this rate, we're going to have to post guards outside your door to keep you in this room. I know a couple of Marines who'd love to volunteer."

"I just wanted to look at a little paperwork."

Mary Pat grinned. "Now I know it's bad. You're eager to do paperwork. And you're still not getting out of this room. I know all the arguments about what you have to do and how much you have to get done. That still won't get you out of here any faster. The only thing that is going to get you out of here is no more signs of bleeding and no more pain. That won't be for a few days. Deal with it."

She reached into her satchel and pulled out a stack of letters. "These are from home over the last few days. I'm not letting you at anything official that comes into the hospital. I'll be back later tonight. Hayes is bringing over something special for you for supper. He's been consulting medical books and me about what you can have to eat."

"Anything is better than just sitting here. And I'll be sure and tell Hayes thanks when he brings supper. One of the great mysteries of the universe is how otherwise normal food becomes the dreaded hospital food the moment it clears the hospital doors. The phenomena wouldn't dare affect anything Hayes fixes."

6

Much as she hated to admit they were right, having some time to rest and think was precious. She really needed it. She'd had a couple of days to do nothing but think about the current situation with Jena and the need for more modern medical education. The ideas simmering in her brain would mean changing their approach pretty radically.

If Mary Pat had known what was in those letters, she'd have kept them away from Beulah at all costs. She probably thought they were ordinary correspondence since they came to the house. There were two letters that concerned Beulah. The first letter was from a man named Johannes Schultes, or Scultetus in the Latinate version of his name. She'd known about him uptime because of his work in obstetrics. The Scultetus bandage was still in use. His publications were famous and sometimes infamous, as was the case for his book illustrating a Caesarean section surgery, then rarely performed. He was writing to her from Ulm.

She'd had some letters from physicians, mainly over the last year or so. Usually they were asking for specific advice and often wanted to correspond with James or one of the other doctors rather than with her. A few had been willing and able to come to Grantville but they hadn't been willing to do what Balthazar or the Jena faculty had done, learn or relearn what they thought they already knew. This letter was different. Schultes was brilliant, comparatively local, and his letter reeked of desperately want to learn, ego checked at city limits. She'd hoped that they'd have the courses at least sketched out before outside physicians started coming to them. By now, she shouldn't be surprised that as usual, they were a step behind the need. It had been that way ever since the Ring of Fire.

Looking at the second letter, she thought, *Make that a step behind in multiple directions.* The letter from Debbie Leek contained a not so simple request. Magdeburg was growing at an incredible rate. There was a great need for a more modern medical system. Debbie wanted to be sure that the hospital that they wanted to add had the ability to use or add on up-timer medical technology. That made perfect sense to Beulah. Part of the letter was asking questions about which technology could be incorporated into the new hospital now and which would have to wait another five to ten years for their tech base to get to that point. Beulah could ask some of the people here and have them pull the information together for Debbie.

The second part of the letter was about the need for trained personnel to work in the hospital. Which would be built in the next eighteen months or so. The first part was easy enough to answer. The second, far more problematic. Quite understandably, the Jenaites were already making polite noises about upgrading their facilities in Jena. It would benefit them and the students. Which was true. So they'd need even more staff. There had to be a better way of doing this project.

Beulah swung her feet over the side of the bed and used the rail to help pull herself up. She was still pretty woozy even with all the blood and IV fluids she'd been given. She still had an IV line but was otherwise unencumbered. Poking around in the bedside stand yielded not a scrap of paper or even the stub of a pencil. Mary Pat had been thorough but Beulah wasn't ready to give up yet. It was an hour before the aides would be bringing lunch trays. Most of the staff would be busy in patient rooms right about now. If she could just sneak out to the nurses' station, she could find pen and paper and get started on the list for Debbie. She had another idea, too. The fight with Mara may have had something good come out of it. They weren't just putting all their personnel eggs in one basket, they had all their tech eggs in one basket as well at Leahy. Maybe it was time to change that, although that could lead to one heck of a wrangle. She'd have to think a lot about that and sound out a few people before she brought it up.

She stuffed her feet into her slippers and slid quietly out of bed. There was no dignity in these hospital gowns, or in a woman her age skulking about. But if they caught her, she'd be back in bed with nothing to do but count ceiling tiles. At least the IV pole rolled well. The hospital's floors didn't have carpeting.

She'd made it a few feet past her door when she heard the sound of a fretting child coming from a few doors down. Kid sounded congested. From crying or something else? She changed direction and headed down the hall toward the sound. She almost made it.

"Ahem."

Beulah wasn't sure if the polite throat clearing was from Dean Johann Gerhardt or from Dean Werner Rolfinck. Judging by the folded arms and the frown on Werner's face, it had probably been Johann. Either way, she was busted. Again.

"I'm going to have to sign up for some special-ops training in order to learn proper sneaking technique. I was just going for a little walk when I heard the crying."

"I'll check on the child. Johann, if you'd escort the *Professorin* back to her room, please?"

"Thanks, both of you. By way of the nurses' station, if you don't mind. I was just thinking about you two and needed some pen and paper to jot a few things down."

"I'll get the pen and paper after I see you to your room." Johann gestured courteously but firmly toward her room.

7

"Beulah, you have got to be nuts!" Mary Pat snapped, hands gripping the arms of the kitchen chair she'd brought into Beulah's living room for this informal meeting.

Beulah looked from Mary Pat to James. He and Johann were in the room's two armchairs. Werner shared the worn, floral-pattern couch with her. Mary Pat wasn't through holding forth on Beulah's temporary insanity by a long shot.

"You just got out of hospital a few days ago. Now you want to move to Jena?" Her attention was caught as James stood up and retrieved a leather wallet from his back pocket. He pulled a Yankee dollar from it and handed it across to Beulah. "What's going on?"

"I do so admire a man who pays his gambling debts promptly," Beulah graciously acknowledged James before turning back to a confused Mary Pat. "James bet you would wait to hear what I had to say before you freaked about me going to Jena."

Werner chuckled. "And what would he have won if she hadn't, ah, freaked?"

"My top secret family christmas ham recipe."

"You must have been sure I'd freak if you were willing to bet that. Okay, you two have gotten my attention. Unveil the great plan." Mary Pat sat back in her chair.

"I've spent the last week with nothing to do, really, but think. I've thought about what we're trying to do and the things that have happened in the last six months. It was pretty clear that we were going to have to make some changes in our plans. I'm not proposing going to Jena for another few weeks. I really can use the rest and it will give me time to figure out what I want to take with me."

Johann nodded. "It would also give me time to catch up with my students in Jena, and for Werner and the others to catch up with their patients."

"Yes and no," Beulah replied. "I'd like Phillip and half the students to remain here in Grantville. Or maybe go back to Jena for a few weeks and then be here the first of the year. I don't know what other plans they have. Phillip, Ernst, and Heinrich are working on trauma and surgery. Mary Pat, you're our trauma and military medical expert. You're the one who can best prepare them for that. They can even accompany you on deployments to see battlefield conditions and our MASH system if you can get clearance for it. They can also keep learning more surgical techniques from James. Phillip and all the students here can have intensive clinicals and class time for, say, three months."

"And the rest of us?" Werner asked.

"You, Willi, Kunz, and I will start work on the curriculum in Jena. I can also do more teaching of public health content to those like Kunz and Georg who are interested. We can still have grand rounds in the clinic in Jena. We can also coordinate with the other deans and faculty about some of the courses we'll need from them."

"I still don't like the idea of you being the one to go. If you had any problems, you'd be pretty far from Leahy." Mary Pat looked uneasy but Beulah could tell she was thinking now, not just reacting protectively.

"That's part of the reason I'm not proposing leaving right away.

I'll be here for several weeks and I'll rest up." Seeing the varying degrees of open skepticism on the faces off the other four, she decided to change the topic. "I know it isn't what we'd planned but if we delay opening the revised programs, I think the downside is offset by a couple of things. For one, we all get some of the pressure taken off. We also get more time to prepare and we'll be more ready if we have the curriculum set up and the faculty and med students have a chance to get more up to speed."

"If we switch the students and faculty between here and Jena say, the end of March, that would give us the summer to polish up the curriculum," Werner said thoughtfully.

"We should be able to take in more students than we'd originally planned." Beulah said. "That should help offset the delay. I'm also concerned that right now, all of our medical personnel are pretty much here in Grantville. Granted, we have a few elsewhere but not many."

James followed her train of thought immediately. "We aren't at risk of too many battles in the near future here in Grantville but if there is an epidemic, we could be in trouble."

There was silence except for the crackling of the fire for a few moments while everyone thought about the implications of the changes she was proposing. Beulah looked contentedly at the fire. She loved a nice fire on a cold, snowy day like today.

"There's another thing I've been thinking about. We have a very diverse student body, to use the up-time phrase." Beulah took a sip of her coffee, savoring the taste. Although it was very weak, this was the first cup they'd let her have. All her protestations that coffee could be considered a clear liquid too had gotten her precisely nowhere in the hospital. "Let me give you a couple of examples. Fritz is literate and by the time the classes start, he'll have completed the LPN training and have a little experience at that level. His formal education before coming to Grantville was fairly minimal, though, because his family needed him in the bakery."

"Ah. The reverse will be an issue as well for the up-timers," Johann chimed in. "While they have stronger math and science backgrounds than any of us, they will need preparation for our type of university education."

Mary Pat nodded. "We've also got a wide array of experience and education for those who'll be going into the MD and RN programs, not just the fact that some will be up-timers and some down-timers."

Werner nodded as well. "For the medical students and faculty, most of us will need fairly standardized content. We all need to know similar basics. For the incoming students it will be different. If we can get them better prepared now, on—what is the phrase—a more even playing field, then things should go more smoothly and the students will be better able to learn."

"I think this is the best idea I've had in a long time. This will solve a lot of problems. Granted, it isn't what we'd originally planned but this way, we'll be able to enroll a lot more students in the fall and be able to teach them better, too."

Chapter Nine
Early January, 1634

"Here, let me get that." Mary Pat took the sweater from Beulah's hands and folded it herself. "Are you sure this is a good idea? You've only been out of the hospital for a month now. Why don't you sit down a minute?"

Beulah obediently sat on the edge of her bed. Mary Pat was still not too sure about Beulah moving to Jena for months on end away from Leahy and James' eagle eye. And hers, of course. If sitting on the bed for a few minutes and letting her help pack eased her mind a bit, Beulah was willing to let her do it.

Mary Pat made one final, rather weak attempt at a protest. "I still don't think you should be the one to go. I could go instead. Or maybe Balthazar could go. It's slow season for spies, isn't it?"

"Actually, I think it's heavy duty plotting season for spies. I'll be counting on you, Balthazar, Starr, and James to get the ones staying here ready, including your three trauma junkies."

Mary Pat reached into Beulah's closet for another sweater to fold and pack. The bright yellow thing was a going-away gift from Garnet. Beulah had no idea where she'd found thread dyed that vivid a shade to knit the sweater and matching mittens. Much less the time.

"I have to admit, I was pretty surprise by Dean Gerhardt's idea about the high school classes. I wouldn't have thought they'd have gone for something like that," Mary Pat said.

It had been Johann's suggestion that selected faculty and students from the other schools plus half the med school students and Phillip take the basic science and math classes at the high school with the high school students. Beulah hadn't been too sure about shifting their problem onto the already busy high school teachers but they'd kept it down enough that there were only three or four more students in each class. Some of them were taking junior high classes too. They were still hitting the books at night in some adult education-style classes. Between that and the clinical time, there was barely time for the Jenaites to sleep but it didn't seem to faze them a bit.

They'd figured out who would be enrolled for MD or RN school in the fall and were designing specific plans for each of them to help them prepare. All the texts were going to be translated into English or German. Skipping the Latin had been a compromise for the Jenaites. In exchange, the students would be getting enough astronomy to squeak through any discussion with outsiders but most of the physics would be health related.

"Johann's a very practical sort. I'm looking forward to staying with him and his family in Jena."

"I'd rather you were staying with Werner, Willi, or Kunz."

"So they can keep a better eye on me? Don't worry. I'd imagine there isn't anyone in Jena by now who doesn't have watch Beulah duty. I probably won't even be able to lift a textbook off a shelf by myself." Beulah carefully didn't share her suspicion that Johann might have an ulterior motive for having her stay with them. After all, it had also been Johann who had suggested that Gary Lambert come show them all how to set up a medical records system for the clinic and model public health department. Johann had taken a strong liking to Gary. The fact that he had an unattached daughter about Gary's age had nothing to do with it. Yeah, right.

"I'll be seeing Werner, Kunz, and Willi almost every day while we work on the curricula and the public health project. I have no doubt that between the three of them and the students, they'll hover just as much as even you could want."

The public health project had come out of her discussions with Werner, Kunz, Georg, and Balthazar. They were going to have people from Magdeburg and other towns come as well to see them set up a more modern public health system in Jena. Jena would be the model for other places in the USE, which pleased the Jenaites enormously. In addition to helping disseminate infection control and sanitation methods, it would be teaching the students. She'd spoken to the mayor of Jena last week. He was thrilled with the idea. It was going a long way to repair some of the damage done by the last visit. He was also happy to be getting most of the town's medical community back at last. The town should be seeing an influx of more university students soon, which didn't hurt a bit either. Jena's economic picture was continuing to improve, and the mayor and town fathers were happy campers again.

"I'd like you to do a couple of other things while I'm gone." At Mary Pat's curious look and nod, she went on. "Keep an eye on Fritz for me. He loves what he's doing and is too apt to study and work without sleeping or eating. With all the pressure he's feeling as the first member of his family to go to university and being one of the downtimers admitted to the RN program, he may go a little overboard."

"Ah. In other words, make sure he doesn't follow in his role model's footsteps and wind up collapsed and rushed to the hospital."

"You're never going to let me live that down, are you? But, yes, that's basically it. Also, I want you to keep an eye on Hayes. I've asked him to drop by with the occasional meal using the excuse that I don't want you to be lonely with me gone."

"You're worried about him, too."

"He isn't looking too good. I hate to go behind his back like this but if he thinks he's helping you out, he may actually slow down a bit and take better care of himself."

"Gotcha. It certainly won't be hard to put up with the man's cooking. He's got a real gift there. I'll be happy to look out for both of them for you."

The sad part, Beulah thought, was that she didn't feel one bit guilty for playing matchmaker. Mary Pat needed a nice, reliable, smart guy. Hayes fit the bill beautifully. Besides, Mary Pat was, at best, a mediocre cook. At least they wouldn't starve if they got together.

"There's still a lot to do to get ready for fall, but I think we're going to be able, not just to pull something together, but to do it really well. I think that's everything I need. Let's get these bags downstairs. I can't wait to get started." A recharged Beulah reached for the smallest bag, already wondering what she'd find in Jena this time.

FACT

A Quick and Dirty Treatise on Historical Fencing

Enrico M. Toro

> *"Et l'oggetto di questa scienza altro non è che il riparare et il ferire ... le quali non potrà alcuno sapere se prima non havrà la cognitione dè tempi e delle misure ..."*
>
> [... and the goal of this science is nothing else but to parry and to wound ... Things nobody can perform unless they are aware of times and measures ...]
> —Nicoletto Giganti, 1606

A Short History

It's easy today to have a very distorted view of what fencing was at the time of the Ring of Fire. Real fencing is not Errol Flynn or the Three Musketeers. Hollywood swashbuckling movies set in the early modern era feature unrealistic flamboyant fencing. The only other fencing moderns see is lightning-fast Olympic fencing. Both of these are far different from the fencing taught in the 1630s in hundreds of academies throughout Europe.

The slow rate of fire and the poor accuracy of firearms made fencing the most common form of self-defense. And as any form of self-defense it was quick, lethal, and, most of the time, brutal.

Dueling and the use of the sword are as old as human civilization. During the period from the end of the Middle Ages until the Ring of Fire, the art of sword fighting changed radically. Those changes set the foundations of fencing as we know it now. This article will focus on Europe during that period.

In the fourteenth and fifteenth centuries, the use of plate mail transformed fencing into something very technical. The first known treatise was written in 1295, in Germany. This manuscript, called I33, codifies a form of combat with sword and buckler. During this time fencers developed the thrust with a long sword. Its purpose was to find openings in a foe's armor. This attack became a well-known technique amongst fighters. The use of the two-handed sword, with a complex system based on many different guards, began a codification of the techniques used, the birth of the first styles and what is considered the first form of true fencing. General military sword fighting was still based mostly on strength. Cutting blows, as opposed to the thrusts and lunges, were still used in combination with grappling techniques to knock down an adversary who was well protected by plate armor.

A radical change happened once the invention and the development of firearms greatly reduced the effectiveness of armor. Because firearms began to appear on the battlefield during the sixteenth century, the use of a complete plate armor was limited mostly to heavy cavalry in tournaments and in battle. After 1490, duels were fought mainly afoot and with much lighter weaponry.

The rise of the thrust, and the decline of the cutting stroke in fencing, began a demand for different swords. Sword making answered this call for lighter weapons, and swords became longer, thinner, and more suitable for lunges. The broadsword became a sidesword easy to carry all the time. Typical Renaissance sword fighting required the use of sword and a small target shield or sword and dagger. Even the use of a target shield faded during the sixteenth century, giving way to fighting with sword and dagger. This last style is considered more effective, as a dagger can be used as a defense, and it can become a terrible offensive weapon in close combat.

Another innovation of this period was the growing use of the sword alone. This was permitted by the development of fencing techniques that favored the use of the blade both for defense and offense. In the second half of the sixteenth century, numerous fencing treatises were printed and the number of wards (ten or sixteen) dropped to the four standard wards based on the different hand positions. The wards (or guards) are the basic fighting stances from which any attack and defense develop. The *Pallas Armata*, a fencing treatise of 1639, describes the different wards:

> There are but four guards according to the four ways thou canst turn thy hand, viz. Prime, Secunde, Tertz, and Quarte.
>
> The Prime is when thou holdest thy Rapier in such a manner that the outside side of thy hand doth look towards thy left side out, and the inside of thy hand look towards thy right side out. This is subdivided into a straight Prime, when thy point looketh straight forwards, and into a hanging Prime, when thy point doth look towards the ground.
>
> The Secunde is, when thou holdest thy Rapier in such a sort that the outside of thy hand looketh upwards, and the inside of thy hand towards the ground. This is likewise subdivided into a straight Secunde when thy point looketh straight forwards; into a handing Secunde, when thy point looketh downwards towards the ground, and finally into the middle Secunde, when thou holdest thy Rapier with a Secunde and a bowed arm, so that the point of thy Rapier looks sheer out towards thy left side.
>
> The Tertz is when thou dost hold thy Rapier in such fashion that the outside of thy hand looks towards thy right side out, and the inside of thy hand towards thy left side out.
>
> This again is subdivided into the High Tertz when thou holdest thy point upwards yet with bended arm, so that thy hilt equalize thy Right breast in height; into a Middle Tertz, when thou holdest thy weapon with a bent arm that the point looks straight out forwards, so that the Hilt in height equalize thy waist: And lastly into a Low Tertz, when thou holdest thy weapon with a straight arm downwards, so that thy Hilt be equal to thy knee in height, or a little below.
>
> The Quarte is when thou holdest thy Rapier in such a manner with a bended arm, that the outside of thy hand look down towards the ground, but the inside upwards. This is likewise subdivided into a straight Quarte when thou holdest thy Rapier with a Quarte and let the point sink down.

*　　　　*　　　　*

All the writing about fencing in this period (mostly in Italian) was abundantly detailed and showed a very quick evolution of the art of combat.

Italian-style fencing was practiced throughout Europe, in courts and salles, the private gyms where fencing was taught. At the end of the sixteenth century the sword assumed a shape that would last for another fifty years. It was enriched by a basket hilt to better protect the sword wielder's hand, and it was longer and thinner than a side-sword. Englishmen called it a rapier. The end of the century also brought the birth of the disengagement technique that would be thoroughly developed in its many variants during the following century. The most used of these disengagements is the *cavazione* or trade, the maneuver that permits one to exchange or switch sides on the opponent's sword, without making contact with it.

It is the seventeenth century that sees the birth of national styles and a more clear-cut division between dueling styles and military styles.

This development can be attributed to several factors: the growing influence of the printing press, the beginnings of a modern mentality that brought the rise of centralized nation-states, the birth of "modern" scientific methods (many books have amazing anatomic and geometric details), the rise of the middle class with the consequent increase in students of the "gentlemanly arts of combat," and the need for a more codified method of teaching.

Dueling swords became lighter, fencing became faster, and the combination of thrusts and parries more complicated. Furthermore, the seventeenth century saw the introduction of two new kinds of blades: the small sword, a thrusting-only sword, thinner and shorter than a normal rapier, and the saber.

The saber, a curved sword with one cutting edge, began to be used in Western Europe but became widespread only during the eighteenth century. The small sword was developed in France at the time when a distinct French school of fencing was also coming into being. The small sword's lightness permitted a faster style that influenced greatly the future classical fencing and modern fencing and began a path that brought the introduction of the foil in the nineteenth century.

The second half of the century saw the transition from fencing in single to double time. In "single time," the swordsman's main goal is to provoke an attack and counter into the opponent's offense while blocking the path of the incoming blade with one's own. In "double time," an incoming attack is first parried with the sword blade and then followed up with a fast counterattack (riposte). Fencing in double time wasn't unknown before, but it was neglected as the fencer's movements required were too fast to be performed with a rapier. The favorite technique was instead the time thrust—a thrust along a line that opposes the attack and permits the swordsman to parry and to hit simultaneously.

While dueling fencing based its movements on agility and reflexes, military fencing maintained the use of power moves and larger movements. The use of a dagger as a defensive weapon disappeared. One century later it would be taught only by Neapolitan academies.

A Seventeenth-Century Swordsman's Training

The seventeenth century was a period of great sword masters, of experimentation, and of development of the art of combat. Ridolfo Capoferro, Marco Docciolini, Salvatore Fabris, Nicoletto Giganti, Francesco Alfieri, Bondi di Mazo, Morsicato Pallavicini, Don Luis Pacheco de Narvaez, and Girard Thibault were some of the great masters of the time. It was the time of the Italian and Spanish styles that used predominantly thrusts, but didn't neglect cutting blows especially in defensive actions.

The training was rigorous and focused on self-preservation in an actual combative situation. The goal was to enable a fencer to survive a combat on any terrain.

The styles taught were strict, essential, and conservative as with any things where human life is at stake. Fencing in Italian is *scherma*, a word that means "barrier, shelter." The main tactic is closing with the enemy, finding his blade, and using touches, disengagements, and counterdisengagements to create an opening in his defenses.

The thrusts were aimed with precision at vital organs or at the limbs to incapacitate the adversary. The sword was held with delicacy (the Italian school called this method *a straccio bagnato*, the wet-towel way) so that it is possible to control the sword in the most subtle way and use a vast array of techniques.

The main difference between the Italian and the Spanish school is that the Italian style was more energetic, more animated, more of a linear style prone to the attack, rich of lunges (long thrusts). The

Spanish style was more defensive, cool, and deliberate. It used circular footwork movements waiting for the opportunity to strike the enemy. The second style is more dancelike and has a single flat-footed stance and only two basic positions compared to the multitude of the Italian style. The stress on defense permitted the Spanish swordsmen to use just the rapier, whereas the Italians still used a dagger. A typical Spanish swordsman would keep his body straight upright and use fast circular paces with arm and rapier held straight, menacing the face or body of his enemy.

From the end of the sixteenth century, the rapier had become the predominant civilian sword. These swords were custom-crafted for each swordsman. They were very long and still quite heavy (around two and a half pounds) compared to today's swords. Their ideal length was twice the length of the fencer's arm. The blade was divided into two parts: the strong and the weak. The first goes from the hilt to half blade and is used mostly to parry; the second, from half blade to the tip and is used to hit. As to military swords, the seventeenth century saw the growth of the use of sabers and of the *schiavona*. This two-edged sword combined the full hand protection of a deep-basket hilt made up of a number of connecting iron bars, and a very efficient blade that allowed both cut and thrust. The schiavona won a wide popularity in several European armies. Fitted with a long blade, it became the favorite sword of the heavy cavalry.

If you are taught the Italian style, the use of a dagger as a defensive weapon is recommended. The main functions of a dagger are to parry, hit, and trap the enemy's blade. There are two types of fencing daggers. They usually both have a straight, pointed, double-edged blade between fifteen and twenty inches long. The first type is a simple cross-hilted design, usually with slightly drooping or forked quillons (the two arms, straight or bent, that are the sides of the hilt), creating an acute angle with the blade itself. This is to entrap and break the enemy sword by a simple twist of the wrist once its attack has been parried. It also has an additional side ring called an *anneau*, whose purpose is to protect the knuckles. The second form of fencing dagger is called a shell-guard dagger or main gauche. This weapon's hilt is formed by long straight quillons and a shell protecting the whole hand.

Almost no academy taught the use of the sword alone. Much time was dedicated to fencing with daggers in close combat. The name for dagger and knife fighting was *scherma corta*: short fencing. In the seventeenth century, short fencing reached extraordinary levels of complexity, and the training was performed with the dagger alone or with other tools (cloak and dagger, dagger and hat, dagger and pistol, dagger and cane).

Multiple techniques of offense and defense with the dagger were developed and taught. Because of the brutality of knife fighting, it wasn't uncommon for the duelers to fight with knife alone, especially when the duel was to the death. These are the words of Salvatore Fabris, fencing teacher in Padua:

"There are moments, where there is neither time nor the occasion to use a rapier, and it's important for a gentleman to never neglect his skills with the use of a dagger."

When not busy studying fencing with rapier or dagger, a good swordsman would be studying other forms of codified combat. These included the use of spear and pike and the use of batons and walking canes as self-defense weapons. There were, of course, moments when none of these weapons were available, so a good swordsman had to learn hand-to-hand combat. European unarmed forms are not so different from modern martial arts. A treatise written in Florence at the beginning of the century states in its introduction: "my system teaches both the use of fists and kicks and the use of limb locks and torsions depending on the occasions and the intentions of the enemy."

In conclusion we may say that a seventeenth-century swordsman had to be good at fencing both in a melee and during a duel as well as a ruthless fighter ready to defend himself from assaults when simply walking on a lane. He would have to know how to use all the weapons at his disposal: his own hands, daggers, one or two sticks as tall as a man or as long as an arm or as short as a dagger; rapiers, sabers, spears, halberds. In a few words he was a tough nut to crack.

Links

The Internet is full of interesting pages about the Western martial arts. I selected a few of them for whoever is interested in studying the topic in more depth.

www.schooleofdefence.co.uk
This is an extremely interesting site, full of pictures and a very detailed description of a ten second duel in twenty-five sequences.

members.lycos.co.uk/rapier/contents.htm
Another interesting site. It contains "La scherma" of Francesco Alfieri (1640) with description of the techniques, plates and some pictures.

www.thehaca.com/Manuals/pallas.htm
This is another treatise, one of the best English texts on differences between Renaissance sword and rapier.

www.kismeta.com/diGrasse/index.htm
Another treatise of the period.

www.thehaca.com/terms3.htm

www.classicalfencing.com/glossary.shtml
These pages contain a dictionary of words used commonly in historical fencing.

jan.ucc.nau.edu/~wew/fencing/masters.html
A brief description of the masters of the sixteenth and seventeeth centuries.

www.kismeta.com/diGrasse/index.htm
A useful page with links to many fencing resources.

www.ahfi.org
Follow the link to the articles. It contains numerous interesting information.

www.classicalfencing.com/articles.shtml
Another list of useful articles.

www.martinez-destreza.com/articles/spanish1.htm
The Spanish school, a complete description.

www.deltin.it/swords6.htm

Pictures of sixteenth- and seventeenth-century swords, complete with description, by one of the most renown Italian sword smiths.

So You Want To Do
Telecommunications in 1633?

Rick Boatright

(Note: illustrations referred to in the story can be
accessed at www.baen.com/library)

Introduction

David Freer's story, "Lineman for the Country" in the *Ring of Fire*
anthology, described the beginnings of wired telecommunications in
the 1632 universe and the founding of AT&L. Like any good story,
much of the technology was mentioned, but not described in detail.
This article seeks to fill in the gaps in that story, and to provide a glimpse
into the development of nonradio telecommunications in the USE.
This article will not attempt to go into the details of the history of
various types of telecom. Please see the references at the end for such
history.

Basics of Telecommunications

You have used a telegraph. You don't know that, but it's true. Have you ever stood inside your house and flicked the lights on and off to signal to someone in the driveway? Have you ever pressed a doorbell and had a bell inside the house go *ding*? You, my friend, have used a telegraph! At its base, a telegraph is nothing more than a doorbell. Press a button here, and something makes a sound "over there." The very first telegraph, made by the famous American scientist Joseph Henry, used a switch and an electromagnet to move an iron bar and ring a bell.

I just can't write an article about the telegraph without a physics lesson. How does that doorbell ring? The answer took the work of half a century by scientists on two continents. Electricity running through a wire produces a magnetic field. (And vice versa, but let's stay focused here.) If you take a flashlight battery, and hook a long piece of wire to it running up and down, a magnetic compass brought near the wire is deflected from north. Sadly, the compass wiggles slowly and only a little, even if you use a lot of electricity. It certainly won't ring a bell. What did Henry do? He took the wire, covered it with silk so that it did not short out against itself, and wrapped it round and round a horseshoe. As the electricity wrapped around in a circle over and over and over, each bit of wire added its bit of magnetism, and together they did what one small length of wire could not do. More wire allowed more loops and generated more magnetism.

By making up a "code," we can send complex messages using this system. The simplest code is just to count letters. You can do this with a doorbell. One ding indicates a step along the alphabet. So, the message "abc" would be sent *ding, ding-ding, ding-ding-ding.*

This simple code is very inconvenient. Sending a "Z" requires pressing the doorbell button twenty-six times. Samuel Morse and others came up with a number of clever ways to make the process shorter. The most important was making the system make a sound both when you *press* the doorbell button *and* when you let it go. Ding-*dong*, or more accurately for Morse's sounder: click-*clack*. This lets you distinguish long and short presses, and you can make a much better code. (Morse code for "Z" is "— . .")

There are several variants on "Morse" code. Two of them are known to be used in Grantville: "international" Morse used by the ham radio operators, and "railroad" Morse used by the operators for AT&L. The two codes are slightly different, but many operators are comfortable in either.

Telegraph Details

So, we have a wire, we have a doorbell button, we have the new weird doorbell that goes click-*clack*, we have a code . . . *Done!* Not hardly. What else do we need to make a commercial telegraph operation?

First, we need wire. Modern telephone and electrical wire is copper, but copper wire alone is weak, and requires too many telegraph poles. The transcontinental telegraph in the US used No. 8 iron wire at 375 pounds per mile. Sometime after the Civil War, the telegraph companies switched to copper-clad iron wire, then to multistranded copper over a steel weight-bearing core. No one in seventeenth-century Europe will be making that anytime soon. It's iron for us.

The problem is, iron wire placed up on poles in the air rusts; No. 8 iron wire hung out by itself alone in typical North American weather rusts through in a year. The solution in the 1860s and for the USE is to "galvanize" the wire, that is, to coat it with zinc. For every mile of wire, we will need ten pounds of zinc.

This raises another problem. We can't just lay the wire on the ground. We need poles. Iron wire needs the support of twenty-two poles per mile. That's a theoretical number, incidentally. In practice, allowing for the effects of terrain, you have to figure that 40 miles needs approximately 1,000 poles and 135 miles needs 3,500 poles.

The use of fewer poles results in the wire sagging, and if multiple wires are strung from each pole it becomes possible for the wires to touch when swaying in the wind. Live trees make poor telegraph poles for several reasons. They grow, and the wires get pulled, they have leaves and other branches that can short out the wires, and they have sap running through them that acts as a conductor, helping "earth" the signal. Additionally, frequently there's no strong tree where you want one. It's far better to have poles made from dead trees that don't have sap, don't grow, and lack branches. Don't lose count. We need twenty-two per mile.

There is another complication. You can't just hang the wire from the pole itself. We need insulators. Wire simply stapled to the pole will work over very short distances (a few miles) when the pole is utterly dry, and the weather is fair. However, the least hint of dew, or moisture or rain, and the wire is "earthed" or shorted to ground. No signal can get through when the water running down the pole carries the electricity into the ground. Insulators prevent the electricity in the wire from reaching the ground.

This photo shows a Hemingray 16 insulator. In service it would be supporting a galvanized iron wire held on by a loop and wrap of galvanized wire. This is the "standard" installation of a glass or porcelain insulator. Note the design of the insulator. There is a groove near the top, which supports the wire, and then there is a *very* long path down the outside of the insulator, around a "petticoat" or "skirt," and then back up *inside* the insulator before it finally touches wood. Glass insulators get their surfaces dirty. Soot from town fires or passing trains is particularly conductive. Insulators crack and water settles into the cracks, and so on. With this skirted-cup design there is a long path for any electricity to reach the wood, and in all but the hardest storms, the inside of the insulator is dry and provides a poor path for electricity. Conductive dust and soot wash off glass insulators easily in the rain. The most common modern insulators are porcelain. Porcelain attracts water less than glass, but it is harder to make, and must be vitrified entirely through. Glazed ceramic insulators absorb water if the glaze cracks in the least bit and then fail as insulators.

Good insulators are critical to telegraph (and telephone) operation. Without insulators, maximum signal distances are a few miles and only that in good weather. Fortunately, making insulators is not all that difficult. Even "threaded" insulators which "screw" on to the support rod that holds them can be made by apprentice glassmakers with little training. A few samples should suffice to allow any glass shop to make adequate insulators. The Hemingray 16 shown here is a good example of an advanced design that is simple to cast. It incorporates advanced features such as internal threads, "drip points," and a fluted skirt lip.

At this point, someone usually asks, "Why do we need insulators like that at all? Why not just use insulated wire?" Of course, today we do. If you look at modern telephone lines in most places, the insulators are disappearing as the bare wires are replaced with Teflon and other plastic-coated lines held off their poles with plastic spacers. I hope that I do not need to go into why Grantville will not be making Teflon-coated wire or fiberglass for several years.

Second, we need batteries. Wait, it's not second anymore is it? Oh well, fourth then. We need batteries. Yes, of course, as long as our main telegraph office is in Grantville, we can power the telegraph from the power lines. But even in the twenty-first century, that's not really done. Up-time telephones are run from batteries that are charged from the power lines. Down-time, unless you're in Grantville, you don't have power lines to charge your batteries from, and you must use "primary" batteries that, like the batteries you buy at the drugstore, make electricity due to their chemistry, rather than being charged. The typical main-line telegraph office needs one-hundred to two-hundred gallon-jar batteries.

The most common battery used by telegraph companies prior to the mass electrification of the U.S. was one or another variation on the Daniell cell sometimes called a Crowfoot or gravity cell. It had two advantages. It could be refreshed without complication, and it did not have a drop in voltage as it was used up. The "dry" cells—be they traditional carbon cells or NiCads—that you buy at the store put out less and less voltage as they age. Daniell cells give constant voltage if they are operating at all, and were therefore called "constant" cells by many telegraphers. The open circuit voltage was about 1.02V. It is no accident that the cell voltage is close to 1.0V, since the Daniell cell was the original standard of voltage.

To make a gravity battery a zinc electrode (Crowfoot zinc) is hung near the top of a glass jar. A copper electrode (battery copper) is placed in the bottom surrounded by blue vitriol (copper sulfate or "bluestone"). The jar is filled with water and a little sulfuric acid. The electrical action of the cell quickly forms zinc and copper-sulfate solutions that remain practically separate because the copper-sulfate solution is much heavier, hence the term "gravity" battery. Battery oil or heavy mineral oil is poured over the top to prevent evaporation. This battery has an excellent capacity. An average main-line cell will use eight pounds of vitriol, two pounds of zinc and a pound of copper per year. Copper fingers plate out on the zinc, and must be knocked off nightly with a bent rod.

Each main-line station, then, will have 120 cells and use 250 pounds of zinc, 125 pounds of copper, 1200 pounds of copper sulfate (blue vitriol), 60 gallons of mineral oil, and 60 gallons of sulfuric acid each year. We will need a main-line station approximately every 30 miles at first. Eventually, we should be able to run 300 miles on a main line without a relay, but perfecting that kind of technology will take time.

While we're at it, clearly our telegraph operator is not going to be staring at a compass wiggling back and forth. They aren't going to be pressing a doorbell button either. What other things do we need for a telegraph office?

First, there is a sounder. This is a bar, arranged over an electromagnet that wiggles up and down as the electricity of the telegraph goes on and off. As it goes down it makes a distinctive click, and as it comes back up, it makes a distinctive clack. Thus, every key-up and key-down at the sending end produces a *click-clack* at the receiving end. Note the adjustable points that allow the sounder to be adjusted for differing line conditions relating to weather, and the condition of the battery at the sending end.

Next is a relay. Relays allow a fading signal reaching one station to be refreshed and sent on to the next station with full vigor. The relay looks a lot like a sounder turned on its side. The magnetic coils have many more turns of wire, and produce a very strong magnetic field for very little electricity. As the relay goes back and forth it acts as a switch for the next piece of the telegraph line.

Then a telegraph key. The pressing of the key makes and breaks the circuit, removing the need to manually touch and untouch the wires. It is a lot easier on your arm than pressing a doorbell button. Note the side-arm switch on the key that allows the circuit to be closed when the key is not in use. Since stations act as relays when they are not sending, and since the same wire is used for sending and receiving, it is important to remember to short your key when you are not using it.

Next are switches used to take the line in and out of service, and to control if the station is set up as a sending and receiving station, or as a relay.

Finally we have a combination main-line instrument. This is a key coupled to a very sensitive sounder used to directly send and receive on the main line itself without a local relay.

You will notice that most of those instruments (except the key and the switch) feature tightly wound coils of wire. You remember that Joseph Henry figured out that you need to wind coils in order to get a strong magnetic field to make clicks, or to make relays close. Prior to a Beldon Wire company employee's invention of flexible enamel in 1909, there were only two solutions, wrap each layer carefully, placing a thread between each coil of wire and its neighbor and a layer of paper between each layer of the coil, and "silk-covered wire." Silk-covered wire was the hottest thing in the wire biz until well into the twentieth century. The problem is, we don't have a machine to wrap No.30 thin magnet wire with silk. Further, the Grantvillers need hundreds of feet of No.30 wire for each sounder and relay. Making the wire itself is simple enough. German artisans were making wire for centuries before Grantville appeared, but wrapping the wire in silk thread will be tricky, and will require a long process of experimentation. Expect orders through Venice for substantial amounts of silk thread. In the meantime, coils will be laid up by interwinding thread, layering with oiled paper and lacquer (exactly the same way that the generator coils at Hoover dam were made in the 1930s).

How much of these supplies does the USE need? Consider the simplest network that the USE would want to set up as soon as possible. Grantville to Jena. Grantville to Saalfeld. Grantville to Rudolstadt. It is silly to consider going to the work to put up poles and maintain them, and make insulators and so on for a single wire that might be broken or otherwise fail. I presume we will put four wires on a cross bar on each pole. The distances needed are about 39 kilometers, 10 kilometers, and 15 kilometers. Call it forty miles. So, we need a thousand telephone poles, thirty tons of No.8 iron wire, a half ton of zinc for galvanizing wire, four thousand insulators, five thousand gallons of creosote or coal tar to paint poles with, a thousand cross bars, four thousand lathe-turned insulator spindles (wooden dowels) to screw the insulators onto. Three main-line stations need four-hundred battery jars, a ton of zinc crowfeet, two-hundred-fifty pounds of copper crowfeet, one-hundred gallons of sulfuric acid, a ton of blue vitriol, and the various sorts of telegraph equipment for each station.

What about the next logical line to Magdeburg? The ground path distance following modern rail lines is 225 kilometers or 135 miles. With allowances for local conditions and losses this line will require thirty-five hundred poles, a hundred tons of iron wire, fourteen thousand insulators and dowels, thirty-five hundred cross beams, two tons of zinc, twenty thousand gallons of creosote, and four more main-line relay stations. AT&L will need some serious investment.

Prior to the appearance of Grantville, annual European iron production was around 17,000 tons a year, and production in "the

Upper Palatinate" (the part of Europe comparable to where Grantville showed up) was in the neighborhood of 2,200 tons per year. Zinc production was, of course, zero.

Venice is a thousand kilometers away. A four-plex telegraph line to Venice would consume half the annual production of iron of the area around the USE. Clearly, no such expansion of the telegraph can rely on only down-time extant metals production.

Fortunately, iron production can be scaled rapidly. Consider the following chart of the growth of steel production in the U.S. in the post-Civil War era:

Steel Production in Tons

Date	Crucible	Bessemer/ Open Hearth	Cementation/ Blister Steel	Total
1863				9,044
1873	34,786	174,153	13,713	22,652
1883	80,455	1,788,305	5,599	1,874,359
1893	71,247	4,298,358	3,143	4,372,748

"Crucible Steel: The Growth of Technology" by K. C. Barraclough

The reality is, of course, that telegraph use of iron disappears as a blip in the curve resulting from the introduction of railroads. Forty-pound main-line rail uses more than a hundred tons of iron per mile. The demand for a third of a ton of wire per mile to run alongside the railroad is scarcely noticeable. Between 1830 and 1861 more than thirty thousand miles of railroad were built in the United States. The authors and tech team of the 1632 series project European iron and steel production to jump one hundred fold over the first ten years after the ROF.

Why the excursion into metallurgy then? The team working on background to the 163x series refers to this as the "Tools to make tools" problem.

- We know how to make a telegraph.
- We know how to make wire for a telegraph.
- We know how to make iron to make wire for a telegraph.
- We know how to make a blast furnace to make iron to make

wire for a telegraph.
- We know how to make a Bessemer converter to make steel from the pig iron from the blast furnace to make iron to make wire for a telegraph.
- We know how to make an air pump to pump air into furnaces and converters to make iron to make wire for a telegraph.
- We know how to make a steam engine to power the air pumps to feed the converters and furnaces to make iron to make wire for a telegraph.
- We know how to make boilers to make the steam for the steam engine
- We know how to make the rolling mill to roll the iron plate to make the boiler
- We know how to make the lathe to turn the rolls to make the rolling mill . . .

However, making each of these things takes time. Furthermore, this is not the only chain of need. For example:

- Finding the fire clay so that you can
  - grind the raw materials
  - to make the raw brick
  - to place into the kiln which you must make
  - to make the fire bricks
  - to line the blast furnace takes time . . .

The telegraph has many such chains of need. Zinc, tool steel for machinists, bluestone, sulfuric acid, magnet coils, brass for keys and sounders, springs, insulators, poles, creosote, and battery jars each have their own chains, or in some cases webs of need. Thus the phrase, "Tools to make tools to make tools . . ."

Assuming you have no better use for the up-time resources, we could extend Grantville's telephone system into Rudolstadt, and run a single line to Jena or Suhl using up-time wire. The first long-distance circuits will be run using salvaged wire that originally led out of the Ring of Fire to places that no longer exist. Many miles of insulated up-time hard copper wire can be salvaged from dead-ended lines.

Depending on your funding, you can build a handful of other telegraph lines using wire made from iron bought in Nuremberg or elsewhere in Europe. You can also produce a spider's web of government telephones in Prague. (See Eric Flint's story in *Ring of Fire*, "The Wallenstein Gambit.")

Beyond that, landline telecommunications will have to participate in, or wait for, the expansion of iron production in Europe that will follow the demand for rail and wire and telegraphs and telephones. This is why all the discussion in the various 1632 books to date about long-distance telecommunications rely on radio. Up-time radios are a limited resource, but they are more available than the wire to build a telecom network across Europe.

Telephones in 1632

What then of Prague? Why did Wallenstein go to the trouble of building Europe's second telephone exchange? Only Eric can be sure. The tools-to-make-tools discussion allows us to understand why the owners of AT&L said, "Yes!" to a project that was a major distraction from setting up the European telegraph network. They needed the money.

We can't do much to help understand the "why" of the telephone network in Prague, but we can pursue the "what." What was done, and how was it accomplished?

A telephone exchange has three major advantages, and a host of disadvantages over a set of telegraphs. The advantages are simple enough:

- Anyone can learn to use a telephone in about one minute.
- Telephones send messages as fast as one may talk.
- Using a telephone exchange, any telephone instrument can be attached to any other.

Telegraphs require trained operators, they are "line" instruments, one attached to the next to the next, you can't "dial" a telegraph, and they are comparatively slow. Average commercial operators transmit twenty to forty words per minute. Try speaking one word every two seconds, and see how slow it feels.

But these advantages come at a substantial cost. Telephone exchanges are complex, as are telephone instruments.

Consider a two-telephone circuit. A set of batteries provides current in a loop. The action of sound waves acts on a diaphragm that compresses carbon granules and creates electric waves that mirror the sound waves. This causes the receiver at the other end to be magnetized in a waving manner, which attracts and repels the diaphragm that vibrates air so that you can hear the sounds at the other end.

Note, however, that *both* receivers are in the circuit, and *both* microphones are in the circuit. In early telephones, much of the power was wasted in producing sound at the receiver of the person speaking. To avoid this requires a bit of electronics called an anti-side tone circuit. How those work is beyond the scope of this discussion but they are the reason you don't hear yourself when you talk on the phone.

There is, of course another problem. You don't want to sit all day with the phone pressed to your ear just in case someone might speak to you. (Unless you're a party-line snoop but that, too, is a subject for another day.) We need a way to signal that someone wants to talk. So, our phone just became more complex. What we need is a classic three-box crank wall phone like you have seen in movies and television. This phone has five important elements. The transmitter (the part you talk into), the receiver (the part you hold to your ear), the ringer (that claps the bells), the magneto (the part that you crank that signals the folks at the other end and rings *their* bell) and the local battery, which is a Daniell-cell battery in the slope topped box at the bottom of the phone.

When the phone is "on hook" or hung up, the magneto and ringer are connected to the line and the battery is disconnected. If you crank the magneto, 100V signals are sent to the central office. If the central office cranks *their* magneto, 100V signals are sent to this phone, and the bell rings.

The magneto consists of three horseshoe magnets with a finely wound coil of wire (more of that silk-covered wire) inside, with a gear arrangement to cause the magneto to turn twenty times for each turn of the crank outside the box. The ringer has two coils (more silk) that alternately push and pull the bell clapper as the AC ringer current pulses through the phone.

Silk importers are going to be doing a bang-up business, huh? Why silk? Because it's thin, allowing the wires to be placed very close to each other, and because prior to the invention of rayon, silk was the only monofilament thread. Silk thread is not "spun" from bundles of short fibers. It is a single long fiber produced by a silkworm and uncoiled from a cocoon. The silk thread does not have any holes in it. It isn't "lumpy" at a microscopic level. It is smooth and covers the wire evenly. Cotton, or linen, or hemp thread can be used to cover wire, but the coils are more loosely spaced, and occasional shorts occur where the lumps in the thread line up and open a gap in the insulation.

One of the tools to make tools Grantvillers and their allies desperately need to invent is a machine to wrap silk thread around thin copper wire, or a chemist needs to reconstruct how to make flexible enamel.

We now have a telephone, and the mechanism to ring a bell at need. But there is still an element missing. One or even two telephones does not a phone system make. It is necessary to wire up many phones together. However, it would be bad if all phones' bells rang anytime any phones' bell rang. Further, it would not work. The ringing impulse would be wasted. We need a way to connect together *just* the phones of interest. Hello, central! One of the things AT&L had to reinvent for the installation in Prague was the central office exchange cordboard. You've seen these. Operators sit in front of a big panel with lots and lots of sockets, and reach up and plug cords into them. People of the right age can think of Ernestine on *Laugh-In*. Each socket on the board is connected to a phone line going out into the world. Each socket in the board has a small metal flag above it that is usually black.

The process of operating the board is not complex. To pick up an incoming call, the operator hears her bell ring, and notes which signal flag has fallen (and turned red) in the socket array. She plugs into that socket, resets the flag, and talks with the caller on her handset. Once she is told who the caller wishes to be connected to, she rings out to the target caller.

To ring a customer, an operator inserts a plug from the right-hand bank into a customer's socket, and spins the crank, ringing the customer's phone. Pulling the switch in front of the plug toward the operator connects the operator's handset so that she can talk with the person who answers. ("Is this the party to whom I am speaking?") When she has an answer, she flips her switch forward, connecting the pair of plugs. When the callers hang up, the flag on the socket falls again, and the operator knows to unplug them. On a typical small town-board, up to nine simultaneous calls can be wired. A typical small-town board would also support three "long distance" trunks to connect to *other* exchanges elsewhere. (It is universally the case, even today, that no phone system can support more than a small fraction of its phones having a call at the same time.) A small-town board supported 150 lines. A single line can have up to eight phones attached to it. This saves metal, but is inconvenient for the subscribers since anyone can snoop on their neighbors' calls on the "party" line. Calls for different houses on a party line are distinguished by a different pattern of ringing. (My grandmother's house was long-short-short.)

Fortunately, once we have built phones, the plug board requires nothing but down-time craftsmanship and patience. No inventions or tools are particularly needed excepting, of course, insulated wire (more silk).

Each plug has wires running to it, each socket has a "flag" that is dropped by a pin retracting when ringer voltage is applied, so there has to be a coil of (silk-covered) wire behind the flag to pull the pin on each socket. Then, each plug has to have a (probably wooden) insulating handle, and a cord of braided copper wires (two of them) covered individually with—you guessed it—silk, and then covered together with a fabric tube to keep them from binding. The switches are simple brass levers and contacts. Oh, more zinc. Oh well.

This magneto exchange is "local." The telephones have a limited range of a few dozen miles. "Long distance" telephones require balanced lines, impedance matching, and amplifiers, all of which are beyond the capacity of the USE's engineers for the short-term future. For the time being, communication between cities will have to be handed over to Morse-code operators, be they radio or wire-line operators.

For the short term, that is the state of telecommunications in the USE and the 1632 series. There will be a few "local" telephone exchanges, in Grantville, in Magdeburg, and Prague. There will be "long lines" telegraph between cities as the money becomes available and as the pressure of the railroads increases steel production, and there will be radio.

I hope this brief introduction to telecommunications helps with an understanding of the difficulties and opportunities facing AT&L, and other telecom developers in the world after the Ring of Fire.

References:

Old Telephones: How to Repair and Rebuild Them by Jeffrey Race
Cambridge Electronics Laboratories
20 Chester Street

Somerville, MA 02144 USA
Telephone +1 617 629-2805
Telefax +1 617 623-1882
camblab@attglobal.net
www.camblab.com

www.insulators.com/books/mpet/
The best source for information on telegraphic practice prior to 1900 is probably Pope, from whose work the drawings above come.

www.civilwarhome.com/telegraph.htm
Excellent site detailing telegraphy during the American Civil War.

www.unitedstatesmilitarytelegraph.org
and another.

www.privateline.com/TelephoneHistory/History1.htm
A good general history of telecommunications.

www.si.edu/archives//ihd/jhp/index.htm
I can't believe you don't know the story of Joseph Henry, but just in case . . . (Yes, this has two slashes in the middle.)

www.insulators.com
More than you ever wanted to know about insulators.

www.woodstelephonepioneers.org/museum/
An excellent phone museum.

www.privateline.com/TelephoneHistory5/History5.htm
The last central-office magneto hand-crank phone system in the U.S. to go dial.

Mente et Malleo: Practical Mineralogy and Minerals Exploration in 1632

Laura Runkle

One of the advantages that the people of Grantville have in the novels *1632* and *1633* is their technology. With their tools, the people of Grantville can turn out cannon, rifles, and steam engines. With their chemical knowledge, they can create antibiotics, aspirin, and DDT. With their electronics, they can create diplomatic and broadcast radios. Everything's a piece of cake, right?

Need for Strategic Minerals

Everything is very far from a piece of cake. After making many cannon, the cutting edges of their machine tools will be worn out. There is no Hi-Speed™ tool steel in the 1630s. It wasn't even invented until the late 1890s. In order to keep a cutting edge, the people of Grantville need some form of tool steel. Early tool steels contained iron, tungsten, and a small amount of carbon. Better tool steels also contain chromium and vanadium, and even more tungsten. Tungsten, chromium, and vanadium weren't known in the 1630s. The people of Grantville have no easy way of purchasing them.

Things get worse. In order to make pharmaceuticals, the people of Grantville need stainless steel, or glass-lined vessels. To make stainless steel, they will need chromium, nickel, and perhaps vanadium. Nickel wasn't known in the 1630s. (Yes, nickel ore was known. So were the ores for zinc and tungsten. The metals weren't known. More about those later.) For the proper glass, they will need borates. Borates were imported from Turkey and Italy.

There are many strategic minerals for Grantville that are necessary to gear down up-timer technology. Grantville has not brought the idea of strategic minerals to the seventeenth century, however. Already people are making a fortune in the creation of war-related brass and bronze. Gunpowder production was a booming industry.

The table below shows some of the resource needs to gear down Grantville's technology.

Technology	Materials Needed	Known in 1631	New	Known source in existing mines or friendly areas as of October 1632
tool steel	iron, tungsten, nickel, chromium, molybdenum, manganese, magnesium, vanadium refractory materials, crucible clays, coal	iron, some refractory materials, some crucible clays	Tungsten, nickel, chromium, vanadium, molybdenum, manganese, magnesium	iron, tungsten, nickel, chromium, manganese, magnesium, coal
galvanized steel	iron, zinc, refractory materials, coal	iron, zinc from Asia, coal	European zinc	All
Babbitted bearings	zinc, copper, antimony, tin, lead	copper, tin, antimony, lead, zinc from Asia	European zinc	All
Aluminum and aluminum alloys (many uses)	bauxite, cryolite	Neither	bauxite, cryolite	cryolite and the best bauxite are not in friendly territory
radio	muscovite, tungsten, copper, zinc, thorium, borates for glass, coal	copper, borates, zinc from Asia	muscovite, tungsten, thorium, European zinc	All
stainless steel	iron, chromium, nickel, vanadium, cobalt, coal, dolomite, limstone, quartzite	iron, coal, limestone, dolomite, quartzite	nickel, chromium, vanadium, cobalt	All

Even though this is a complex problem, the answer seems simple. Get out a CD-ROM atlas of the world, and search for needed minerals in or near Germany. If there isn't a CD-ROM atlas, look up mining sources for each of these metals. Then find maps of the places in a paper atlas, and start mining the material.

The problem comes down to three things: the politics of mining, the economics of mining, and the technical parts of geological surveying. Each of these will be covered in a section of this article.

There aren't enough up-timers to send out on the search. Only a few up-timers could be trained and sent out on surveys. No up-timers have all the needed skills. The last part of this article will deal with the role of the up-timers as they work with down-timers to obtain strategic minerals.

The Politics of Mining

It's important to remember that Grantville didn't appear in a vacuum. Germany had been mined for a very long time by 1632. Political structures, bureaucracies, and economies had already been built around mining. Some important resources aren't in friendly areas right now. Cryolite is found only in Greenland, a province of Denmark, which is at war with Grantville. A middling good ore of bauxite is at Vogelsberg, within striking distance of Duke Bernhard. It's very hard to start a mine in a war zone. But even outside of a war zone, there are problems with just walking up and digging.

Mining law is complex stuff. Seventeenth-century European mining laws differ from up-timer mining law. The most important variations in Germany were not from place to place, but from product to product. The up-timers don't just have to deal with a different set of rules—they need to remember variations on these rules for different products and different areas.

In Germany, the status of mineral ownership depended heavily on the sort of the mineral. The emperors gave rights, which were often theoretical, to sovereigns of all sort (rulers, abbeys, towns, and so on) in the Middle Ages. But these rights didn't include all minerals. Only silver, gold, lead, copper, tin, and salt followed the strict rules.

Other mineral resources (iron, coal, hard rock, sand, clay, etc.) usually belonged to the landowner. Usually. In some parts of Germany sovereigns claimed ownership for all minerals. These claims were only partly successful in the first half of the seventeenth century. However (mining law is complex), iron was sometimes treated as a valued metal if it was high-quality hard ore that was mined, rather than quarried.

In general, permission was needed to prospect for minerals. More permission was needed for mining, and for using nearby wood and water. Permission for prospecting came from the landowner. The permission for mining valued minerals came from the ruler and/or the mining administration of the area. Base minerals were mostly considered the landowner's property, and could be mined without much trouble from a mining administration.

In practice, if the prospector or mine operator showed that they had enough money and people to carry out the mining in an orderly fashion, permission was almost always granted. A mine was a source of free royalties to the ruler of the territory. The landlord usually got one or more shares, and these shares sometimes had some special privileges. Claim sizes were pretty standard, but there was some variation by the resource.

The way mine ventures were organized is beyond the scope of this paper. They weren't organized in the same manner as shipping companies, although shares were bought and sold. The thing to remember is that share owners also had to pay ongoing operating expenses if the mine was not able to make a profit. Think of owning a share in one of these ventures as a game of financial chicken.

Mine operators needed to pay out shares and royalties. Royalties were paid out with money or with a portion of the ore. If royalties were paid with ore, every tenth or so standardized basket of ore was set aside for the ruler. Shares were usually paid out to owners on a quarterly basis with money. Miners were sometimes the owners of shares or part shares, and sometimes the employees of the mine operator, or both. Owners paid for work that needed to be done on the mine, even if the mine had not brought in a profit. Even though rulers received royalties, they did not pay mine expenses, unless they acted as mine operators as well, or were shareholders.

Timber for supports, smelting, and machinery had to be purchased from the local holders of wood rights. In many places, part of the mining profits were set aside for the support of churches and charities. Unless the church or charity was acting as the mine operator, it did not need to pay expenses.

Mine claims had to be worked. In some cases, mining claims were leases for three to ten years. In most cases, they were perpetual leases, as long as mining lasted. If mining ceased for a period of time, the mine claim was forfeit. That was usually not a problem. (As long as two or more miners were working, the mine would be working legally and could not be forfeit.) If the district mine administrator requested that a mine improve its drainage or ventilation, and some effort was not made for improvement, the mine operator was fined. In some places, the mine was forfeit, and could be mined by another operator. In practice, if a mine was taking money out of the pockets of the mine operator, rather than making profits, the owners had to subsidize the mine.

Rules existed for mines. By 1632, there had already been several notable mining disasters. Usually the resulting rules did not involve the safety of individual miners, but rather the safety of the whole mine—drainage, ventilation, and the placement of tunnels and shafts.

There were environmental laws for the users of wood rights and for smelters. Mostly these laws involved the harvest of trees and the use of water. Water rights were even more complicated in heavily mined districts. Deforestation was a risk near the larger mines and an ever-present danger near the smelting ovens. Before the up-timers go in and try to create a mining bureaucracy, they need to remember that bureaucracies and mining consortiums already exist under the aegis of each local ruler.

Even with those rules, mining was a hard, dirty, and very dangerous job. It still is today. There are very few civilian jobs with a greater risk to health and life than underground mining. Even the best drainage and ventilation of the time was not always good enough. Because the miners used open flames (candles or oil lamps with reflectors), pockets of methane gas sometimes caused explosions. Other times, they just suffocated the miners. In the lead and silver mines, arsenic poisoning was sometimes a risk.

The Knappschaft, or miners' guild, was different from many other guilds in the seventeenth century. All miners, not just the master miners, belonged to the Knappschaft. There were miners' strikes, and mining law was changed to accommodate some demands of the miners. The Knappschaft also paid for the construction of a chapel for before-shift prayer outside most mines, and paid for charities for the members and families. The Knappschaft was *not* a modern miners' union, but the reactions of down-timer miners to the UMWA will be filtered through their experience with their local Knappschaft.

Mining Economics

A mine is a hole in the ground that sucks up money. The world is full of abandoned mines that someone once felt worth starting. The greatest reason that mines are abandoned is that they don't pay enough to cover expenses.

The mines in the twentieth-century CD-ROMs and atlases are mines that are profitable using twentieth-century techniques for mining, ore dressing, and smelting. With a few notable exceptions, the mines in the oldest encyclopedias in the Ring of Fire were mines that were profitable using nineteenth-century techniques and transportation. Many of these mines could not be profitable with seventeenth-century mining, milling, and transportation. They might not be profitable after high explosives have been developed, and sometimes even after steam engines are available. Someone will need to survey the areas around known sources of the strategic materials to see if it is feasible to mine them.

Factors beyond the ore are important for mining profit. An ore body would have to be unbelievably good if all of the other factors were bad. These factors include ventilation and drainage, energy for ore dressing and smelting, refractory material for smelting, and transportation at several different stages of the process.

The difference between prospecting and mineral surveying is that prospecting only takes the ore body into account. Mineral surveying takes all of the factors for the mine into account. Down-timers already knew this. The silver ore near Joachimsthal was so good that it was profitably mined, even with lots of disadvantages. Some of the ores in the Harz mountains were not so rich, and wood and water were much bigger considerations.

The ore body itself is an important part of any equation. What mineral is being searched for? How close is the ore body to the surface? If it is not directly at the surface, what type of overburden exists? Would a strip or open mine work? Would a (very expensive) underground mine be needed?

Every mine needs ventilation and drainage. Open quarries and strip mines have built-in ventilation, but they still need to be drained. Underground mines often need long ventilation shafts and drainage tunnels, which are very time consuming and costly to create. Water- and wind-powered drainage and ventilation pumps are less expensive to operate than animal- or human-powered pumps, but they depend on the location of the mine, and on the weather. Water- and wind-powered pumps need cooperative weather and climate.

Ore dressing separates the ore from unwanted minerals and rocks. It can be done with hammers, mills, washing, cradles, or other methods. Smelting melts and purifies the ore. Energy for ore dressing and smelting is a must, and it needs to be convenient to the mine, unless the ore is extremely rich. In the seventeenth century, ore dressing was most often done with a combination of water-powered hammer mills, water mills, hand mills with hard-rock millstones, and vigorous washing. Smelting was done with hard coal, charcoal, peat, or wood. In a drought, such as Europe had in the summer of 2003, water power would not be available for many mining tasks. Ore dressing, ore transportation, and drainage pumping would need to be done by gravity, animal power, or human power. All of these are more expensive than water power.

The heat needed to melt many ores and refine them can be quite high. Any smelter needs to be lined with stuff that can take this heat. This heat-tolerant lining is called refractory material or lining. The type of refractory material for smelting can be important. Steel made with one refractory lining is different from steel made with another refractory lining, for instance. Because refractory materials are just a special type of building material, they need to be easily quarried and transported. A convenient means of getting refractory material to the smelter is important.

In the twenty-first century, it's hard to imagine how difficult and expensive transportation was in the seventeenth century. Today, Europe has an excellent network of roads, canals, and railroads, created at great cost over the last few hundred years. These are set up to handle vast amounts of freight, and the shipping cost does not add large amounts to the cost of goods.

Transportation in the seventeenth century was horrible. There's a reason large cities were either on seaports or on rivers that could be navigated with barges. Many of the roads in Germany were muddy or rocky. The distance that a wagon could travel was limited by the strength of the animals pulling it. The transportation costs for wood and peat usually doubled the cost for townspeople not too far from the source. For some goods, customs duties and taxes alone doubled the price. Rocks are heavy, and so even more expensive to ship.

The most economical mines had either gravity-based transportation or river-based transportation close to the mine. Some mines in the Harz and the Erzgebirge already had very well-organized networks of horse carts. They also used water power to lift the ore and rocks out of the mine. Other mines used animals, children, women, or miners (in order of increasing expense) to pull rock to the surface. (In many iron mines, which in most cases didn't fall under the "normal" mining laws, women did much of the work.)

The ideal mine, then, was one easily mined near the surface; close to a plentiful source of water for moving ore, ventilation, drainage, and ore dressing; with plentiful fuel for smelting; with an inexpensive source of nearby transportation; and close to the final market for the smelted material. Any mine that didn't have these would be worked harder for a smaller profit.

Geologic Surveying

Let's say that you have a known location of a mineral in friendly territory, that you want to mine it, and that you have a market with a guaranteed price, so that the economic aspect of the mining will be covered. Now it will be simple to get the mine started, right? Not so fast.

Although a mineral location is known in a book or on a map with a scale of 1:2,000,000, that doesn't mean that the mineral will be seen or recognized on the ground. A geologic survey team would need to find the spots for mining the mineral, and find the materials needed to transport the mineral to the market. The current maps also don't show if the mine is a surface mine or an underground mine. Drilling is very expensive, especially if you are not sure that you are drilling in the right place.

Most mineral field guides and rockhound magazines give driving directions to collection locations. They don't show when the mine or quarry was first worked, or even when the road was built. Even when the locations are mines and quarries that existed in the seventeenth century, there is no knowing whether the given mineral formation has been reached yet.

So surveying and prospecting need to be done, and there aren't enough up-timers to do it. Can the up-timers contribute anything? Certainly!

Although the down-timers have lots of experience in surveying a mine site for the economic and political factors, there are some techniques that up-timers know that would be very useful. Up-timers are aware of the chemistry of minerals and the environments in which the rocks formed. Up-timers also use fossils to date rocks over a large area. They know topographic mapping, and geologic mapping. Up-timers have tools for measurement, surveying, and mathematics that can be duplicated. They have worked out simpler methods of determining positions. Up-timers could offer training and tools to the down-timers.

Although the down-timers have lots of experience with minerals, rocks, and mining, they don't have systematic knowledge of minerals. That requires up-timer chemistry. It's no accident that chemistry and mineralogy developed hand in hand. The up-timers know the desired minerals. They could teach down-time prospectors and surveyors how to work with properties such as streak color, hardness, specific gravity, cleavage, and luster. The down-timers know of many of these properties, but not for the new ores.

Down-timers know how to look at the direction of a vein of mineral, and figure the trend and shape of the vein. Up-timers have had much more time to study how rocks are formed. Some geologists study the formation of rocks, figure how the layers of rocks fit together, and where desired resources might be likely to be found. (It would be wrong to say that down-timers don't know this. It's just that this area of exploration has grown by leaps and bounds over the past couple of centuries.) There wouldn't be time for up-timers to teach down-timers dedicated semester-long classes, but up-timer texts could be reproduced.

Up-timers know how to use fossils to determine the age of rocks over a large distance. This is very useful, since similar resources are often found in similar environments.

Topographic mapping and geologic surveying don't exist in the seventeenth century, although accurate surveying on a small to medium scale certainly does. Topographic lines, which connect areas of equal height, give an accurate picture of the lay of the land, all to scale. Geologic surveying throws in the information about the layers of rock in the area. When a geologic map is placed on a topographic map, and information about current mining operations is placed on the map, the result can be an accurate picture of good places to look for desired minerals.

Accurate surveying to scale needs good instruments. The towns of Augsburg and Nuremberg had many makers of fine instruments, including telescopes, and several types of surveying tools, including early theodolites. The surveyors of the time did not have alidades, mountain transits, nor pocket transits like the Brunton compass. (Geologic surveyors in the United States preferred alidades to theodolites, because they were much sturdier and less expensive than theodolites. Civil surveyors might still use theodolites instead.) The instrument makers would have been able to make them, but at a high price. Every instrument out of Nuremberg and Augsburg was a work of art and craft, produced one at a time. Each instrument took a craftsman from several weeks to several months.

The instrument makers did not have access to a circular divider. A circular divider makes it possible to put consistent small regular divisions (such as degrees and minutes) onto a circle. (The inventor of the circular divider shared in the longitude prize given out by the British admiralty, because it allowed the mass production of very accurate surveying and measuring tools.) One of the machine shops should be able to turn out a circular divider, given a short time to create it. From there, accurate surveying tools would be able to be produced much more quickly than the master craftsmen can make them.

Up-timers could also help with mathematical methods of surveying. In the early seventeenth century, there was not a truly accurate measurement for a degree of longitude or a degree of latitude. (In 1637, this and many instructions on more accurate navigation and surveying were due to have been published.) The slide rule had only just been invented, and it wasn't the slide rule we know today.

Eventually, up-timers could even help with mine safety and techniques. The first safety helmets would be made out of hard leather and have oil lamps attached. In time, when kilns and arcs capable of the work came online, calcium carbide and acetylene could be used. The safety helmet might not take long to introduce. Steam-powered ventilation and drainage pumps will take much longer to introduce. The first down-time steam engines will be produced from hand-mined materials, and will be very expensive. It will take a long time until engines and motors are cheap enough for every mine. Cement-lined shafts for areas of wet or loose ground will also take a while to introduce.

There is one mining introduction from up-time that will not always help safety. Underground mining by hand is a slow and tedious business. Underground mining with explosives is much faster, but it is more dangerous. The explosions can loosen rock and make a mine less stable. The up-timers and down-timers will need to work together on handling explosives, and on safety with explosives. In some places, however, the miners set fires underground to crumble the rock, and make it easier to mine. Explosives would be less ghastly to work with than these underground fires.

There's one category of help I haven't mentioned yet. It will probably be the most important, in the short run. Some of the desired minerals (the ores for tungsten, zinc, and nickel, for example) were already known, but were considered junk minerals.

The cheapest route to many mineral resources is to prospect the rubble and slag heaps of existing mines and smelters for desired minerals. Gold is one mineral that can be obtained from slag heaps; another is silver. Down-timers had plenty of experience separating gold and silver from other ores. They did not have experience using cyanide or electrolysis. In order to check slag heaps for desired resources, some method other than straight mineral surveying would need to be used.

Until 1635, Grantville will have a working X-ray spectrometer that will be able to do a nondestructive assay on any samples of slag sent back to it. The X-ray spectrometer is part of the quality and safety equipment at the power plant, and so cannot leave Grantville. After 1635, the spectrometer will not work well enough to give good results, so there is some urgency to the task of getting samples sent from every existing slag heap and rubble pile.

Two types of destructive analysis will take the place of the X-ray spectrometer, eventually. Blowpipe analysis involves holding a piece of stuff in a flame, and blowing a stream of air at it to heat up the flame and the sample. When it's done in a dark room, subtle and unsubtle color changes show what elements are present. The use of a prism, a flame, or an electric arc and a dark room will also reinvent the field of destructive spectroscopy.

Finding Strategic Minerals—Cooperation Between Up-timers and Down-timers

Why can't the up-timers just go prospecting? There aren't enough of them, and very few have enough geologic knowledge to do a survey, rather than just prospecting. Grantville is very lucky, as it is a mining town. They have an experienced, German-speaking mining engineer and mine surveyor, two teachers with bachelor's degrees in geology, a quality engineer at the power plant with training in the X-ray spectrometer, a civil engineer and surveyor, a few chemistry and math teachers, and several rockhounds. Most towns with thirty-five hundred people just don't have that many people with some experience in geology or surveying.

However, there just aren't enough up-timers. The experienced ones have inescapable responsibilities in or near Grantville. The best they can do is to train others, make tools, and print books.

A Modest Proposal

How would the up-timers teach down-timers about the advances in mineralogy, mining, geolog,y and geologic surveying in a systematic fashion and in a short time? How would they make known the advances in instruments, and train down-timers in their use in short order? The simplest way would be through a field camp for down-timer miners, surveyors, and underground surveyors. Up-timer high-school graduates with a strong background in science and math could also be trained.

Of the first students taking this field course for ten weeks, fewer than half of the experienced miners, engineers, surveyors, and very good high-school graduates would complete it successfully. Learning straight surveying is tough enough. (It's more than a ten-week job.) Good geological surveyors require four skill sets beyond straight surveying. They need to identify the rocks. They need to recognize fossils to help correlate rocks over long distances. They need to picture things in three dimensions, including the boundaries of the layers of rock. Successful students will also need to be people who can work underground without mental problems—even now, it's hard to predict who will be able to work long periods underground.

Today, geology students do much of their learning during field trips. The mother of them all is field camp, an opportunity for them to spend a summer mapping rocks. During field camp, students check their knowledge of several different types of terrain, different types of mapping, and different types of rocks. An extended field camp with a classroom session in the beginning would be the best method for getting the new up-timer information out.

Today, with modern transportation, field camps can range over several hundred miles. In the 1632 universe, any field camp would be limited to within thirty to forty miles of Grantville, for all practical purposes. Fortunately, thanks to the location of the Ring of Fire, there are enough different terrains and rocks to provide a meaningful field camp.

Who would be the students at any field camp? If the first field camp were held in the summer of 1631, the students would be recent female graduates from the high school who were good in math and science. Students would also be engineers, miners, and even some underground surveyors from the mercenary troops and from nearby areas.

In order for the students to work with geared-down surveying techniques, they would need good instruments. Someone would need to make enough instruments for the students to use for field camp, and for successful graduates to purchase after camp. The only way enough instruments could be made would be if an instrument maker were in town. Between the machine shops and the town optician, there is an instrument-making shop in town. However, this would take a lot of time. Fortunately, the optician is married to a geologist turned teacher, so he could be persuaded to spend time on this project. There is a machine shop at the school that might be able to do some of the work over the first summer of 1631.

In order for the mapping to be useful on a large scale, the students would need to be able to locate themselves in time and space. With the help of the alidades, a watch with known slip, and an ephemeris, the students would be able to locate themselves. An ephemeris is a list that gives the rising and setting times for the sun, the moon, the planets, and some bright stars for a given time and place.

The students might be able to locate the geologic time of rocks they were mapping with the help of fossils. Textbooks and fossil field guides have many of the more common, worldwide fossils that help geologists to date layers of rock.

Inside the Ring of Fire, the students would need to learn to use slide rules and refresh themselves on trigonometry, in order to do the necessary calculations for accurate mapping. The first type of mapping they would learn would be topographic mapping. Then they would work on geologic mapping.

Ron Koch, the mining engineer, might be able to spare as many as four mornings to work with the students on mapping the coal mine, allowing them to work and map in the mine on those afternoons.

Any good field camp provides opportunity to work on sedimentary, igneous, and metamorphic rocks. The West Virginian rocks that came through the Ring of Fire are sedimentary. Near Saalfeld (less than ten miles from the Ring of Fire) are some interesting metamorphic quartzites and schists near the Kamsdorf mine, and the Jeramiah's Gluck mine (Feengrotten). If there's time, the students might venture as far as Suhl, about forty miles to the east, to see igneous granites, rhyolites, and andesites, as well the copper mines of nearby Goldlauter.

The only hope for having all the crucial skills in a survey team would be for the team to divide up the tasks. A successful team might consist of an experienced surveyor, an experienced miner, a rodman, and a person dedicated to calculations.

The bad news is that there wouldn't be enough time to teach everything; this would be a crash course. Any survey teams that go out after camp would be serving out apprenticeships in the field. Transportation would be mules or horses—only the down-time surveyors would be used to working with them. Down-time miners and up-time girls (with a couple of exceptions) would have had little experience with horses. Two or three up-time girls may have ridden horses, but would not have used packhorses or pack mules.

The good news is that any field camp near the Ring of Fire would have a wonderful advantage—the Ring of Fire itself. Since it was cut to a molecular level, the Ring of Fire field camp would have the unparalleled advantage of many fresh cliff faces. These cliffs would give an underground glimpse of the geology of both sides of the Ring of Fire. Geologists drool over fresh cliff faces. The Ring of Fire has many fresh cliff faces, of varied height. Instant cross sections! It would be very easy to get across several concepts, just by using the Ring of Fire as a teaching tool.

Money and Politics—The Elephant Under the Rug

A field camp such as this is expensive. The cost for teachers, transportation, food, and instruments and gear can be quite high. The town might be able to pay for the first summer's field camp and instruments with good will and high hopes, but any subsequent field camps would need to be attended by paying students. If any students were sponsored, someone other than the taxpayers would need to pick up the tab.

Equipping the surveyors with good instruments of their own (rather than instruments made for the field camp) would also be very expensive. Any instrument sales would need to be paid for by the purchaser—Grantville could not afford to give them away.

No field camp can operate without the permission and cooperation of the existing landowners and mining administration. Fortunately, Duke Johann Philip of Saxe-Altenburg, the landowner and ruler for the mines around Saalfeld, is a forward looking man. He might well be willing to allow a field camp to work on his lands, if he could get the benefit of the best of the final maps and reports. He would certainly be encouraged by the idea of greater mining revenues.

After field camp, the successful students would need to get jobs. Topographic mappers would certainly be in demand by the military—several might even reenter the military. Whether or not others get employment would depend on the various mining administrations and rulers; builders of streets, dams, and canals; as well as the owners of iron and coal mines. Some, such as Gustavus Adolphus, might even pay for students to attend field camp, and assign them to difficult problems immediately on graduation. (That would be how Gustavus Adolphus would have people prospecting for chromite in 1633.) Other areas might show no interest whatsoever in people with this new training.

That's where correspondence would come in. Word-of-mouth advertising was even more important in the seventeenth century than it is today. If employers were happy with the results from their new surveyors, then they would be sure to let others know.

Letters would be important for another reason. Even if all the people who completed field camp in the first two years were offered jobs or went into business for themselves, there still wouldn't be enough people to get samples back from all the slag heaps and rubble piles. The word would need to get out to all mine operators. Only a down-timer who is good at several types of correspondence could do this.

That type of correspondence would really be the start of a formal geologic survey. The government of either the USE or of the Grantville-administered area might want to pick up the tab for a modest geologic survey, but it could not afford to pay for a full survey, complete with many teams.

Grantville would need to take advantage of people who already make public opinion as far as science goes. Geology would need to come into fashion. This isn't far-fetched. In our timeline, geology was a very fashionable science in the first part of the nineteenth century. Correspondence from happy mine administrators, rulers, and land-lords to their many acquaintances would be the best possible advertisement for Grantville-trained surveyors. Whether this word would work fast enough to get samples to Grantville before the spectrometer could no longer be used is an open question.

Conclusion

The actual mining and marketing of strategic resources will be carried out mostly by down-timers. One exception might be any mines near Saalfeld. Another would be any easily found petroleum, because of the drilling equipment within the Ring of Fire.

Up-timers can train down-timers in new techniques, and in some cases can be part of down-timer-led teams for geologic and topographic surveying.

Many up-time technologies to make mining more efficient and safe will take a long time to be widespread. Safe lighting and high explosives will spread before engines for drainage and ventilation.

The effort to obtain strategic minerals has the potential to be a strong way to bring together the up-timers and down-timers in economic, educational, and political cooperation.

The fastest way to desired minerals is to survey and work existing mines and slag heaps.

Any eventual formal geologic survey would need a down-timer with superb organizational and political skills as its director. Up-timers will be part of the technical team, but none would immediately have the necessary skills to enable work to be done in multiple jurisdictions.

Acknowledgments

The 1632 Chem Team. Dr. Manfred Gross and Dr. Virginia Easley DeMarce for assistance with the legal and social structure of mining in the seventeenth century. My son Samuel helped me to make this clearer. All errors are my own.

Further Reading

www.wvgs.wvnet.edu/www/allabout/allabout.htm
A Brief History of the WV Geologic Survey

pubs.usgs.gov/circ/c1050/index.htm
A Brief History of the US Geologic Survey
Pay special attention to the political and scientific skills needed by any successful Geologic Survey Director.

region.tu-clausthal.de/obwm/trip.html
A Trip Through Our Mine: The Upper Harz Mining Museum:
An excellent description in English of some of the mining processes used in the Upper Harz mining district. Note the drainage tunnel that took 120 years (with grants of respite) to build, the use of artificial lakes to run the water wheels, and the amount of hard rock tunnel one miner could carve in one year with only iron tools.

Agricola, Georgius. *De Re Metallica*, Hoover, H. C. and Hoover, L. H., Translators. Dover, 1950. New York.
Much of my information on mining, geology, and mineral knowledge in seventeenth-century Germany comes from the miner's bible of the time, Georgius Agricola's *De Re Metallica*. Herbert and Lou Henry Hoover published a brilliantly annotated translation of *De Re Metallica* in 1912. Mrs. Hoover was an excellent Latinist, and had a degree in geology from Stanford. Mr. Hoover was a mining engineer. Both of them had an interest in metal-

lurgy, as well. All later translations into other languages, even German, owe much to the Hoover translation.

De Re Metallica was published in 1556, less than a year after Agricola's death. He had finished the manuscript in 1550, but the elaborate and wonderful woodcuts took a long time to prepare. Even though the novel *1632* takes place eighty years after *De Re Metallica* was published, mining and refining had not changed greatly in that time.

Geologic map of West Virginia
www.wvgs.wvnet.edu/www/geology/geolgeom.htm

Geologic map of Germany
www.grosskurth.de/GK%20Deutschland.htm

Poster "Tag des Geotops 2003" (2.7 Mb)
www.tag-des-geotops.de/pdf/poster.pdf

General economic geologic map of Thuringia
www.tlug-jena.de/contentfrs/fach_09/60_00101_01_a01.html#sm11
These give no detail, but a general idea of what the geology will be in the area. The poster has the best resolution, but is a large file.

Lord, John, *Capital and Steam Power*. Web reprint in the University of Rochester's Library of Steam
www.history.rochester.edu/steam/lord/
A very good review of just how expensive steam engines were during their introduction. Steam will not be this expensive, but it will still be very dear at first. Steam will take a long time to be fully introduced.

The Maps of Mike Barthelemy's 1632 Research Site
homepage.mac.com/msb/163x/maps/
Mike Barthelemy's topographic map of the Ring of Fire in Thuringia and Gorg Huff's three-dimensional rendering give a good introduction to reading a topographic map. They also show just where the open cliffs would be located.

USGS Minerals and Mining Yearbook 1998
minerals.usgs.gov/minerals/pubs/commodity/myb/

The 1998 version would be the latest version sure to be in the mine office. Many mines do not have a copy of this book, but many do. Quentin Underwood is the kind of manager who would buy a copy every year.

Utrecht's opposition to the Münster peace process
www.lwl.org/westfaelischer-friede/wfe-t/wfe-dok.htm

Note the description of mineral profits made during the Thirty Years War.

The Secret Book of Zink

Andrew Clark

[We present to you for the first time translated into English, the remarkable and exciting news from Doctor Erasmus Faustus, as originally printed in the Fraenkische Wochenzeitung.*]*

By vows to God and from pious reflection, this humble man offers to mankind the secret story of the princely metal of Zink which can now be told. The Lord has revealed this hidden weapon in the fight of life force against its enemies. In prophetic words, I will utter things hidden from the foundation of the world. The Americans know of these things, and to us they speak freely, for they are persuaded that none of these things are to be hidden from us. These things are not done in a corner.

Practitioners of the Work of Alchemy have long known Venus' copper marries well with the crackling thunderbolt of Jupiter's tin to yield Bronze. Paracelsus warned in dark words of the danger in confusing Bronze with Brass and now we know the source of this confusion. Hear now how Zink differs from Tin, for it works through unsung power instead and its marriage to the Cyprian metal brings forth Brass, easily as shiny as Bronze, but allowing the timbre of the copper to sing felicitously. Zink loses not its masculinity with such deference much as charity is the more pious with anonymity.

We have long been allied with this prince, despite its shy, yea reclusive, nature. We have long known the Red Lotion of Calamine as discovered in ancient times by the Egyptians, applied to soothe irritations of the skin. We have seen the application of the oil of vitriol to Calamine yields white vitriol and know how this agent toils against the powers of destruction and rot. So it may now be told that Zink is the vital essence and fused earth in Calamine ore. Thus it is we take another step of Ascension, growing our knowledge and ourselves. Although Zink yearns to stay humble and hidden, its strength is not diluted with revelation.

The distillation of Zink is done thusly. First the Calamine ore must be roasted to remove volatile antagonists. Second, the resulting calx is charged with Charcoal in a crucible pierced by a pipe. The crucible must be sealed tightly by lid and placed in a furnace. The Zink vapor is collected after it travels through the pipe and condensed into liquid Zink and which may thusly be cooled to solid.

To preserve its secretive nature and remain hidden, Zink fights its enemies in the air. The outermost layer sacrifices itself to form a dull armor, not the brilliant silver as when first the Zink be cast. This armor is of humble and reclusive nature, desiring not to attract attention unto itself, but it now lies in our arsenal. We may gather this armor and allow the remaining Zink to form a new shell. Collecting the twisting scrapings, called by the Americans "Zink Oxide," we shall follow Alchemical convention and name them "Flowers of Zink."

A lotion is to be made of Flowers of Zink thusly. Prepare with parts Comfrey, Lavender, Sage, and Thyme using Olive oil to make a wonderful treatment for any inflammation of the skin, including rashes, irritation from cloth, bed sores, wrinkles and burns from exposure of sensitive skin to the sun and elements, prolonged excitement of baby's skin including cradle cap or milk crust, and relief of rashes associated with many feminine discomforts.

Just as papermakers have applied white vitriol to prevent spoilage of their sizing, the princely Zink prevents other spoilage as well. It is a powerful assistant to the iatrochemist in allowing the life force in humans to fight its enemies. Hear now another fearsome weapon the American doctors use and that we might as well, butter of Zink. We may apply spirit of salt, or "Hydrochloric Acid" as the Americans say, to Zink to produce a white waxy and oily substance and also known as Zink chloride. The American alchemical symbol for this is "$ZnCl_2$." Small applications of butter of Zink are used by Americans to remove warts and fight many other diseases of the skin that sink deeper than a mere redness. Be warned that it is caustic and will eagerly eat away at more than just warts.

Just as it fights life's enemies, Zink can do the same for the king of metals, iron. Application of Zink to iron will "Galvanize" it, allowing it to fight its enemy, rust. When iron is dipped in molten Zink, the Zink coats iron and the outermost layer of metal again sacrifices itself to make an armor to protect the rest which may be applied to most any iron product we wish to. One such application is dipping iron wire. We may use it in applications where more strength for weight is needed than can be provided by copper wire or hemp rope.

Zink is also used in construction of "elektrode buttercups" which can store the potential of elektricitate. A jar of glass shall contain a star of copper fingers mounted on the bottom. A buttercup of Zink is hung near the top. The jar may then be half filled with blue vitriol to which some water and vitriolic acid is added until the fluid reaches the buttercup. This device is called an "Earth Power Cell," obviously a harness for the fluid power found in the fight between the dark powers of the earth and the life force of thunder and lightning.

So has that which was hidden been revealed. Here ends the Secret Book of Zink.

AFTERWORD

Eric Flint

I should take the time here, I think, to explain to interested readers where the *Gazette* fits into the 1632 series as a whole, and where other projects in the series stand at the moment.

First, a number of readers have asked me when *1634: The Baltic War* will be coming out. That's the direct sequel to *1633*, which came out three and a half years ago, in August of 2002. Not surprisingly, many fans of the series have been waiting for it with increasing impatience. Some—though not many, I don't think—have even been irritated by the appearance of other 1632 titles in the interim, such as *1634: The Galileo Affair*.

Let me start with the good news, which is that Dave Weber and I will be starting the novel very soon. For the rest, I sympathize with the impatience of readers who've been waiting for it, but I also need to explain the logic of the delay. Yes, there is a logic, it's not simply because either I or Dave Weber forgot about it. The problem, in a nutshell, is that both Dave and I are writers with a lot of work on our hands and a number of other commitments. That means that getting our schedules to match up well enough for the months it takes to do a collaborative novel is ... not easy. Since we completed *1633*, we've had only two windows of opportunity that were long enough to do the trick. The first, in 2003, got taken up with writing *Crown of Slaves*, a novel that Dave felt was important to the development of his very popular Honor Harrington series. And the second, which was supposed to have been last year, wound up never materializing at all because of a variety of factors.

So it goes. In the meantime, I saw no reason to tie up the other lines of the story that began with *1632* and have kept them chugging along. One of the most important of those lines—call them "side" lines, if you will, but that's really a misnomer—is the one I began with Andrew Dennis in *1634: The Galileo Affair*. Three sequels are planned to *Galileo*, the first of which Andrew and I now have well underway.

I said that thinking of *The Galileo Affair* and its sequels as a sideline was a misnomer. In fact, it's nothing of the sort. True, it began as a separate adventure that was, in a sense, a spin-off from *1632* and *1633*. But, as will soon enough become obvious, the ramifications of those events in Italy will have a greater and greater impact on the events taking place in Europe as a whole—indeed, the entire world. My problem, at the moment, is that I can't prove it to you without revealing the plots of several books that haven't been published yet. Just . . . take my word for it, please. Trying to determine what's an "important" story and what isn't, in this alternate universe, is a lot trickier than it looks at first glance.

Which is the way I intended things, from the moment I decided to turn *1632* from the stand-alone novel it was originally written to be into a series. Whatever else, I am *not* going to produce a formulaic series, in which one book succeeds another by simply rehashing the same basic material. The world has more than enough of such series, I think.

There's a second consideration involved, also, which has to do with the way I see this entire story in the first place—and did from the beginning. *1632* was written as much as an American novel as a science fiction or alternate history novel. More precisely, as a novel that fits within that loosely defined literary category known as Americana. In particular, it was written from a desire on my part to make a relatively ordinary American small town the collective protagonist of the story. And then, as the story unfolded, to keep the focus as much as possible on what you might call the level of the common man and woman—understanding that, as the story unfolded, more and more seventeenth-century Europeans would become an integral part of that collective protagonist.

I didn't do that from some preconceived notions of what constitutes the "right" way to tell a story. I have no objections at all to grand epics. In fact, I just completed one myself: *The Dance of Time*, the sixth and last volume in the Belisarius series, which by happy coincidence is being published at the very same time as the volume you hold in your hand. (Yes, that's a shameless plug.)

I'm quite proud of the Belisarius series, as is my coauthor David Drake. Yet, you would be hard-pressed to find too many common men and women in that massive six-volume story. The main characters run almost entirely to emperors, empresses, kings, queens—existing or in the making—and generals and other top commanders. Even the occasional commoner is typically someone like the cataphract Valentinian, who is also universally recognized as one of the greatest swordsmen in the known world.

Grand epics of that sort are a perfectly valid form of fiction and I enjoyed writing the Belisarius series. But the *1632* series is a very different kind of story. One that certainly has its share of great historical figures—it's enough to mention that Gustavus Adolphus and Cardinal Richelieu are both major characters in it—but always, ultimately, has a different focus.

So, the novels and anthologies that have been or will be produced in the series have a variegated character. Some, like *1633*, will center on the "big" issues and the actions of the "big people." Others, like *1634: The Galileo Affair*, will start small and grow . . . very big. The same description could be applied to the immediate sequel to *1634: The Baltic War*, which is *1634: The Bavarian Crisis*, which I coauthored with Virginia DeMarce. (I should mention, by the way, that we've finished the first draft of *The Bavarian Crisis*, so fans of the series don't have to worry about another long delay. That book will be coming out soon after *The Baltic War*.)

There's yet another level of storytelling in the series, however, and those are stories that start on the ground level and more or less remain there throughout. I was especially concerned to produce stories like this, because the 1632 series is ultimately a story about a great political, religious, social, and economic revolution in Europe begun by the Ring of Fire—and I think people generally have screwy ideas about what revolutions are and how they work. That's especially true in science fiction, where revolutions have typically been depicted as the product of magical hand waving by a handful of big-shot heroes. They decree, and therefore it is done.

Oh, what a laugh. In the real world, no social phenomenon is as turbulent, complex, contradictory, and downright *messy* as great revolutions are. The only thing that compares to them are great wars, and wars have the advantage of being (usually) somewhat better organized and under tighter control from the top. Of course, even making the distinction is artificial, since most great revolutions include wars as part of them, foreign as well as civil—and, on the flip side, there has never been a great war in history that didn't revolutionize many things beyond military tactics and hardware.

As much as anything else, I want to capture that reality in this series. One of the ways I'll be doing that is by producing—as both the editor and one of the major writers—at least two somewhat unusual anthologies. The first of these is entitled *1634: The Ram Rebellion,* and will be published May 2006. The second, which serves partly as a companion volume and partly as a sequel, is entitled *1635: The Torturer of Fulda,* and will probably be published about a year later.

These two volumes are anthologies, in the sense that they are comprised of separate stories written by different authors. But, unlike most anthologies, the stories are directly connected to each other—not necessarily in a linear fashion—and, taken as a whole, constitute what amounts to quasi-novels. What both of them deal with is an issue that was initiated at the end of *1632,* and then mentioned in *1633* and *1634: The Galileo Affair*—usually in passing, although most of Chapter 21 of *The Galileo Affair* is devoted to it.

The issue is this: At the end of *1632,* in the course of the negotiations between Mike Stearns and Gustavus Adolphus that end with the creation of the Confederated Principalities of Europe, the king of Sweden hands over the large and poorly defined region of Germany known as Franconia to the American-dominated little United States (which consists of a portion of Thuringia) to govern and administer. To put it a different way, a big region of a nation is disposed of in exactly one paragraph of the book:

> Quentin nodded. "Yeah. And if I'm following the latest twist and turn in the debate, Mike just got half of Franconia added along with the rest of Thuringia. I think he's shooting for all of it, too." For a moment, his eyes grew a bit dreamy. "Be one hell of an expansion in the market, that's for sure. Every business in the U.S. will start growing by leaps and bounds. The railroads alone—" He broke off, scratching his chin worriedly. "Still—"

How sweet it would be . . . to just leave it at that. The President proposes, the king disposes, and everyone does what they're told and lives happily ever after.

Not hardly. What *The Ram Rebellion* and *The Torturer of Fulda* deal with is the messy reality of what really happened after. The story—stories, rather—of how a small number of Americans sent to Franconia fared in that mission. And, just as much, the related and intersecting stories of the Germans who allied with them, or conspired against them, or set their own course—or, often enough, did all three at one time or another.

And so, finally, we come back to the question I posed at the beginning of this afterword: Where does the *Grantville Gazette* fit in all this?

That's not an easy question to answer. In the nature of things, being a magazine, the *Gazette* tends to go wherever the best writers contributing to it decide to take it. As editor, I can direct that process to a degree, but I don't really try to control it.

More accurately, I don't *want* to control it. We started the *Gazette* because Jim Baen and I thought it would be, if nothing else, an interesting experiment in commercial publishing. Which it has been, on its own terms. But with experience, I've learned that the *Gazette* serves the series as a continual wellspring. It's a constant source of new ideas, new viewpoints, and new angles on old viewpoints. And, as often as not, the seeds sown in the magazine wind up growing in very unexpected directions, and can produce some very large and luxuriant narratives.

It's perhaps enough to say that *1634: The Ram Rebellion*, which will be coming out soon, began as a series of whimsical in-jokes concerning a scruffy sheep that appeared in one story. Before the issue of the magazine that story was planned for could come out, those little whimsies had produced a crop of other stories, all of them related in one way or another, and often in very odd ways. What, after all, could be the connection between a belligerent ram, an American farmer trying to expand his acreage, a ballet, a peasant rebellion, and a dungeon?

Those of you interested can find out in three months. But remember: it all started in this magazine.

Eric Flint
April 2005

Images

Note from Editor:

There are various images, mostly portraits from the time, that illustrate different aspects of the 1632 universe. In the first issue of the *Grantville Gazette,* I included those with the volume itself. Since that created downloading problems for some people, however, I've separated all the images and they will be maintained and expanded on their own schedule.

If you're interested, you can look at the images and my accompanying commentary at no extra cost. They are set up in the Baen Free Library. You can find them as follows:

1) Go to <u>www.baen.com</u>.
2) Select "Free Library" from the blue menu at the top.
3) Once in the Library, select "The Authors" from the yellow menu on the left.
4) Once in "The Authors," select "Eric Flint."
5) Then select "Images from the Grantville Gazette."

Submissions to the Magazine

If anyone is interested in submitting stories or articles for future issues of the *Grantville Gazette,* you are welcome to do so. But you must follow a certain procedure:

1) All stories and articles must first be posted in a conference in Baen's Bar set aside for the purpose, called "1632 Slush." Do *not* send them to me directly, because I won't read them.

It's good idea to submit a sketch of your story to the conference first, since people there will likely spot any major problems that you overlooked. That can wind up saving you a lot of wasted work.

2) Your story/article will then be subjected to discussion and commentary by participants in the 1632 discussion. In essence, it will get chewed on by what amounts to a very large, virtual writers' group.

You do *not* need to wait until you've finished the story to start posting it in "1632 Slush." In fact, it's a good idea not to wait, because you will often find that problems can be spotted early in the game, before you've put all the work into completing the piece.

3) While this is happening, the assistant editor of the *Grantville Gazette*—Paula Goodlett—will be keeping an eye on the discussion. She will alert me whenever a story or article seems to be gaining general approval from the participants in the discussion.

4) At that point—and *only* at that point—do I take a look at a story or article.

I insist that people follow this procedure for two reasons:

First, as I said, I'm very busy and I just don't have time to read everything submitted until I have some reason to think it's gotten past a certain preliminary screening.

Secondly, and even more importantly, the setting and "established canon" in this series is quite extensive by now. If anyone tries to write a story without first taking the time to become familiar with the setting, they will almost invariably write something that—even if it's otherwise well written—I simply can't accept.

In short, the procedure outlined above will save *you* a lot of wasted time and effort also.

One point in particular: I have gotten extremely hard-nosed about the way in which people use American characters in their stories (so-called "up-timers"). That's because I began discovering that my small and realistically portrayed coal-mining town of thirty-five hundred people was being willy-nilly transformed into a "town" with a population of something like twenty thousand people—half of whom were Navy SEALs who just happened to be in town at the Ring of Fire, half of whom were rocket scientists (ibid), half of whom were brain surgeons (ibid), half of whom had a personal library the size of the Library of Congress, half of whom . . .

Not to mention the F-16s that "just happened" to be flying through the area, the army convoys (ibid), the trains full of vital industrial supplies (ibid), the FBI agents in hot pursuit of master criminals (ibid), the . . .

NOT A CHANCE. If you want to use an up-time character, you *must* use one of the "authorized" characters. Those are the characters created by Virginia DeMarce using genealogical software and embodied in what is called "the grid."

You can obtain the current edition of the grid at: www.1632.org .

Look on the menu to the right for the item titled "Virginia's Up-timer Grid." While you're at it, I recommend you read at least the two following items in the menu, "Dead Horses" and "The Many Halves of Grantville." That might save you some wasted effort.

The "Dead Horses" section goes over the many issues that have been thoroughly thrashed out in the discussion in Baen's Bar in the "1632 Tech Manual" conference that has been going on for six years now. I should stress that it is not impossible that someone new to the discussion might resurrect one of these dead horses and bring it to life. That has happened in the past, although not often. But you should still look at this to see what's considered a dead horse in the first place, and why.

Yes, you *might* have a new angle on, for instance, the use of ultralights or lighter-than-air craft. But, frankly, it's not likely. And you for sure and certain won't if you don't take the time to examine what has already been discussed at great length.

"The Many Halves of Grantville" is a short and, um, rather sarcastic essay by me. It's worth reading for two reasons. First, hopefully, you may be amused by it. Secondly, it will give you a good sense of the things to avoid if you decide to write a story for the magazine.

You will be paid for any story or factual article that is published. The rates that I can afford for the magazine at the moment fall into the category of "semipro." I hope to be able to raise those rates in the future to make them fall clearly within professional rates, but . . . That will obviously depend on whether the magazine starts selling enough copies to generate the needed income. In the meantime, the rates and terms that I can offer are posted below in the standard letter of agreement accepted by all the contributors to the magazine.

In the event that Baen Books decides to issue a volume of the magazine in a paper edition, as they have now done for the first two volumes, you will be paid additional money for your story or article which brings the total advance up to professional rates. In addition, you will be entitled to a pro rata share of the authors' royalties, based on the length of your piece.

Standard letter of agreement

Below are the terms for the purchase of a story or factual article (hereafter "the work") to be included in an issue of the online magazine *Grantville Gazette,* edited by Eric Flint and published by Baen Books.

Payment will be sent upon acceptance of the work at the following rates:

1) a rate of 2.5 cents per word for any story or article up to 15,000 words;

2) a rate of 2 cents a word for any story or article after 15,000 words but before 30,000 words;

3) a rate of 1.5 cents a word for any story or article after 30,000 words.

The rates are cumulative, not retroactive to the beginning of the story or article. (E.g., a story 40,000 words long would earn the higher rates for the first 30,000 words.) Word counts will be rounded to the nearest hundred and calculated by Word for Windows XP.

In the event a story has a payment that exceeds $200, the money will be paid in two installments: half on acceptance, and the remaining half two months after publication of the story.

You agree to sell exclusive first world rights for the story, including exclusive first electronic rights for five years following publication, and subsequent nonexclusive world rights. Should Baen Books select your story for a paper edition, you will not receive a second advance but will be paid whatever the differential might be between what you originally received and the advance for different length stories established for the paper edition. You will also be entitled to a proportionate share of any royalties earned by the authors of a paper edition. If the work is reissued in a paper edition, then the standard reversion rights as stipulated in the Baen contract would supercede the reversion rights contained here.

Eric Flint retains the rights to the 1632 universe setting, as well as the characters in it, so you will need to obtain his permission if you wish to publish the story or use the setting and characters through anyone other than Baen Books even after the rights have reverted to you. You, the author, will retain copyright and all other rights except as listed above. Baen will copyright the story on first publication.

You warrant and represent that you have the right to grant the rights above; that these rights are free and clear; that your story will not violate any copyright or any other right of a third party, nor be contrary to law. You agree to indemnify Baen for any loss, damage, or expense arising out of any claim inconsistent with any of the above warranties and representations.

Grantville Gazette II

An electronic magazine of stories and fact articles based on Eric Flint's 1632 "Ring of Fire" universe

Volumes 1 through 6 are already available, in electronic format, with Volumes 7 and 8 on the way. Volume 1 and 2 are also available in paper editions, with Volume 3 in preparation.

In Volumes 3 and 4, Gorg Huff and Paula Goodlett continue the adventures of their teenage tycoons-in-the-making, and two stories depict the early days of some American military units after the Ring of Fire. In other stories, Grantville becomes a magnet drawing Europe's most ambitious young musicians and a woman terrorized by the notorious Hungarian countess Bartholdy finds peace and sanctuary in Grantville.

These volumes also contain factual articles exploring such topics as the mechanization of agriculture in the 17th century, the logic behind the adoption of the Struve-Reardon Gun as the basic weapon of the USE's infantry, the development of an oil industry, and differing views on the prospects of creating a machine gun using the resources and technology available after the Ring of Fire.

Later volumes of the *Gazette* continue with the same sort of enjoyable stories and interesting factual articles.

The *Grantville Gazette* can be purchased electronically through Baen Books' Webscriptions service at www.baen.com. (Then select Webscriptions.) Volume 1 is in the Baen Free Library (www.baen.com/library) and can be obtained electronically at no cost. All other volumes of the *Gazette* can be purchased as single copies for $6, or you can purchase them as part of a $15 three-volume packages: Volumes 2-4 and 5-7, with more packages on the way.